SEA OF
AKERI

KINGDOM OF
VENDA

★ SANCTUM

TERR

EUX

GREAT RIVER

FALWORTH ★

KINGDOM OF
DALBRECK

REUX
LAU

CRUVAS

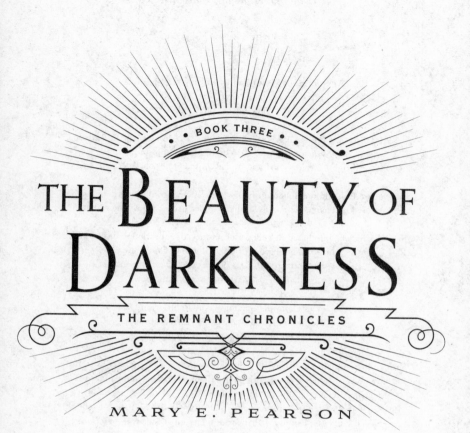

BOOK THREE

THE BEAUTY OF DARKNESS

THE REMNANT CHRONICLES

MARY E. PEARSON

SQUARE FISH

Henry Holt and Company

NEW YORK

For Rosemary Stimola,

who makes dreams come true

SQUARE FISH

An imprint of Macmillan Publishing Group, LLC
175 Fifth Avenue, New York, NY 10010
fiercereads.com

Our books may be purchased in bulk for promotional, educational, or business use.
Please contact your local bookseller or the Macmillan Corporate and Premium
Sales Department at (800) 221-7945 ext. 5442 or by e-mail at
MacmillanSpecialMarkets@macmillan.com.

Library of Congress Cataloging-in-Publication Data
Names: Pearson, Mary (Mary E.), author.
Title: The beauty of darkness / Mary E. Pearson.
Description: | New York : Henry Holt and Company, 2016. |
Series: The remnant chronicles ; 3 | Summary: Princess Lia and her love, Rafe,
have escaped Venda and the path before them is winding and dangerous.
Identifiers: LCCN 2015049900 (print) | LCCN 2016019792 (ebook) |
ISBN 978-1-250-11531-7 (paperback)   ISBN 978-1-62779-652-1 (ebook)
Subjects: | CYAC: Fantasy. | Princesses—Fiction. | Survival—Fiction. |
Love—Fiction. | BISAC: JUVENILE FICTION / Fantasy & Magic. |
JUVENILE FICTION / Love & Romance.
Classification: LCC PZ7.P32316 Be 2016 (print) | LCC PZ7.P32316 (ebook) |
DDC [Fic]—dc23
LC record available at https://lccn.loc.gov/2015049900

Originally published in the United States by Henry Holt and Company
First Square Fish edition, 2017
Book designed by Anna Booth
Square Fish logo designed by Filomena Tuosto

11   13   15   17   19   20   18   16   14   12

AR: 5.4 / LEXILE: HL760L

Journey's end. The promise. The hope.

A place of staying.

But it is still not in sight and the night is cold.

> *Come out of the darkness, girl.*
>
> *Come out where I can see you.*
>
> *I have something for you.*

I hold her back, shaking my head.

Her heart flutters beneath my hand.

He promises rest. He promises food.

And she is both tired and hungry.

> *Come out.*

But she knows his tricks and stays at my side.

The darkness is all we have to keep us safe.

—*The Last Testaments of Gaudrel*

CHAPTER ONE

DARKNESS WAS A BEAUTIFUL THING. THE KISS OF A SHADOW. A caress as soft as moonlight. It had always been my refuge, my place of escape, whether I was sneaking onto a rooftop lit only by the stars or down a midnight alley to be with my brothers. Darkness was my ally. It made me forget the world I was in and invited me to dream of another.

I sank deeper, searching for its comfort. Sweet murmurs stirred me. Only a sliver of golden moon shone in the liquid dark, floating, rocking, always moving, always out of my reach. Its shifting light illuminated a meadow. My spirits lifted. I saw Walther dancing with Greta. Just beyond them, Aster twirled to music I couldn't quite hear, and her long hair flowed past her shoulders. Was it the Festival of Deliverance already? Aster called out to me, *Don't tarry now, Miz.* Deep colors swirled; a sprinkling of stars turned purple; the edges of the moon dissolved like wet sugar into black sky; the darkness deepened. Warm. Welcoming. Soft.

Except for the jostle.

The rhythmic shake came again and again. Demanding.

Stay.

The voice that wouldn't let go. Cold and bright and sharp.

Hold on.

A broad hard chest, frosty breaths when my eyes rolled open, a voice that kept pulling the blanket away, pain bearing down, so numbing I couldn't breathe. The terrible brightness flashing, stabbing, and finally ebbing when I could take no more.

Darkness again. Inviting me to stay. No breaths. No anything.

When I was halfway between one world and another, a moment of clarity broke through.

This is what it was to die.

LIA!

The comfort of darkness was stripped away again. The gentle warmth turned unbearably hot. More voices came. Harsh. Shouts. Deep. Too many voices.

The Sanctum. I was back in the Sanctum. Soldiers, governors . . . the Komizar.

My skin was on fire, burning, stinging, wet with heat.

Lia, open your eyes. Now.

Commands.

They had found me.

"*Lia!*"

My eyes flew open. The room spun with fire and shadows, flesh and faces. Surrounded. I tried to pull back, but searing pain wrenched my breath away. My vision fluttered.

"Lia, don't move."

And then a flurry of voices. *She's come to. Hold her down. Don't let her get up.*

I forced a shallow breath into my lungs, and my eyes focused. I surveyed the faces staring down at me. Governor Obraun and his guard. It wasn't a dream. They had captured me. And then a hand gently turned my head.

Rafe.

He knelt by my side.

I looked back at the others, remembering. Governor Obraun and his guard had fought on our side. They helped us escape. Why? Beside them were Jeb and Tavish.

"Governor," I whispered, too weak to say more.

"Sven, Your Highness," he said, dropping to one knee. "Please call me Sven."

The name was familiar. I'd heard it in frantic blurred moments. Rafe had called him Sven. I looked around, trying to get my bearings. I lay on the ground on a bedroll. Piles of heavy blankets that smelled of horses were on top of me. Saddle blankets.

I tried to rise up on one arm, and pain tore through me again. I fell back, the room spinning.

We have to get the barbs out.

She's too weak.

She's burning with fever. She's only going to get weaker.

The wounds have to be cleaned and stitched.

I've never stitched a girl before.

Flesh is flesh.

I listened to them argue, and then I remembered. Malich had shot me. An arrow in my thigh, and one in my back. The last I remembered I was on a riverbank and Rafe was scooping me into his arms, his lips cool against mine. How long ago was that? Where were we now?

She's strong enough. Do it, Tavish.

Rafe cupped my face and leaned close. "Lia, the barbs are deep. We'll have to cut the wounds to get them out."

I nodded.

His eyes glistened. "You can't move. I'll have to hold you down."

"It's all right," I whispered. "I'm strong. Like you said." I heard the weakness of my voice contradicting my words.

Sven winced. "I wish I had some red-eye for you, girl." He handed Rafe something. "Put this in her mouth to bite down on." I knew what it was for—so I wouldn't scream. Was the enemy near?

Rafe put a leather sheath in my mouth. Cool air streamed onto my bare leg as Tavish folded back the blanket to expose my thigh, and I realized that I had little on beneath the blankets. A chemise, if that. They must have removed my sodden dress.

Tavish mumbled an apology to me but wasted no time. Rafe pinned down my arms, and someone else pressed down on my legs. The knife cut into my thigh. My chest shuddered. Moans escaped through my clenched teeth. My body recoiled against my will, and Rafe pressed harder. "Look at me, Lia. Keep your eyes on me. It'll be over soon."

I locked onto his eyes, the blue blazing. His gaze held me like fire. Sweat dripped down his brow. The knife probed, and I lost focus. Gurgled noises jumped from my throat.

Look at me, Lia.

Digging. Cutting.

"Got it!" Tavish finally shouted.

My breath came in gulps. Jeb wiped my face with a cool cloth.

Good job, Princess, from whom I didn't know.

The stitching was easy compared to the cutting and probing. I counted each time the needle went in. Fourteen times.

"Now for the back," Tavish said. "That one will be a little harder."

I WOKE TO RAFE SLEEPING BESIDE ME. HIS ARM RESTED heavily across my stomach. I couldn't remember much about Tavish working on my back except him telling me the arrow was embedded in my rib and that probably saved my life. I had felt the cut, the probe, and then pain so bright I couldn't see anymore. Finally, as if from a hundred miles away, Rafe had whispered in my ear, *It's out.*

A small fire burned in a ring of rocks not far from me. It illuminated one nearby wall, but the rest of our shelter remained in shadows. It was a large cave of some sort. I heard the whicker of horses. They were in here with us. On the other side of the fire ring I saw Jeb, Tavish, and Orrin asleep on their bedrolls, and just to my left, sitting back against the cave wall, Governor Obraun—*Sven*.

It hit me fully for the first time. These were Rafe's four men, the four I'd had no confidence in—governor, guard, patty clapper, and raft builder. I didn't know where we were, but against all odds they had somehow gotten us across the river. All of us alive. Except for—

My head ached, trying to sort it all out. Our freedom came at a high cost to others. Who had died and who had survived the bloodbath?

I tried to ease Rafe's arm from my stomach so I could sit up, but even that small movement sent blinding jolts through my back. Sven sat upright, alerted by my movement and whispered, "Don't try to get up, Your Highness. It's too soon."

I nodded, measuring my breaths until the pain receded.

"Your rib is most likely cracked by the impact of the arrow. You may have cracked more bones in the river. Rest."

"Where are we?" I asked.

"A little hideaway I tucked into many years ago. I was thankful I could still find it."

"How long have I been out?"

"Two days. It's a miracle you're alive."

I remembered sinking in the river. Thrashing, then being spit up, a quick gust of air filling my lungs and then being pulled under again. And again. My hands clutched at boulders, logs, everything slipping from my grasp, and then there was the fuzzy recollection of Rafe leaning over me. I turned my head toward Sven. "Rafe found me on the bank."

"He carried you for twelve miles before we found him. This is the first sleep he's had."

I looked at Rafe, his face gaunt and bruised. He had a gash over his left brow. The river had taken its toll on him too. Sven explained how he, Jeb, Orrin, and Tavish had maneuvered the raft to the planned destination. They'd left their own horses and a half dozen Vendan ones they had taken in battle in a makeshift paddock, but many had escaped. They rounded up what they could, gathered the supplies and saddles they had stashed in nearby ruins, and began backtracking, searching the banks and forest for us. They finally spotted some tracks and followed them. Once they found us, they rode through the night to this shelter.

"If you were able to find our tracks, then—"

"Not to worry, Your Highness. Listen." He cocked his head to the side.

A heavy whine vibrated through the cavern.

"A blizzard," he said. "There will be no tracks to follow."

Whether the storm was a blessing or hindrance, I wasn't sure—it would prevent us from traveling too. I remembered my aunt Bernette telling me and my brothers about the great white storms of her homeland that blocked out sky and earth and left snow piled so high that she and her sisters could venture outside only from the second floor of their fortress. Dogs with webbed feet had pulled their sleds across the snow.

"But they will try to follow," I said. "Eventually."

He nodded.

I had killed the Komizar. Griz had lifted my hand to the clans who were the backbone of Venda. He had declared me queen and Komizar in a single breath. The clans had cheered. Only producing my dead body would prove a successor's claim to rule. I imagined that successor to be Malich. I tried not to think about what had happened to Kaden. I couldn't allow my mind to drift there, but still, his face loomed before me, and his last expression of hurt and betrayal. Had Malich struck him down? Or one of his other countrymen? He had fought against them for me. Ultimately, he chose me over the Komizar. Was it the sight of a child's body in the snow that had finally pushed him over the edge? It was what had pushed me.

I had killed the Komizar. It had been easy. I'd had no hesitation, no remorse. Would my mother think of me as little more than an animal? I'd felt nothing as I plunged the knife into him. Nothing when I plunged it in again, except for the slight tug of flesh and gut. Nothing when I killed three more Vendans after that. Or was it five? Their shocked faces blended together in a distant rush.

But none of it had come soon enough to save Aster.

Now it was her face that loomed, an image I couldn't bear.

Sven held a cup of broth to my lips, claiming I needed nutrition, but I already felt darkness closing in again, and I gratefully let it overtake me.

CHAPTER TWO

I WOKE TO THE SOUND OF SILENCE. THE HOWL OF THE STORM was gone.

My brow was sticky, and strands of hair were plastered across my forehead. I hoped dampness was a sign the fever was breaking. And then I heard strained whispers. I carefully slivered my eyes open, peering from beneath my lashes. There was soft light filtering through the cave, and I saw them huddled close together. What secrets were they keeping now?

Tavish was shaking his head. "The storm's over, and they'll be on the move. We need to go."

"She's too weak to ride," Rafe said in a low voice. "Besides, the bridge is damaged. They can't get across. We have time."

"True," Sven said, "but there's the lower river. They'll cross there."

"That was a good week's ride for us from the Sanctum," Jeb countered.

Rafe took a sip from a steaming mug. "And now with the snow, it will be twice that."

"Which will also slow us down," Tavish reminded him.

Orrin rocked on his heels. "Hang me, they probably think we're all dead. I would. No one could ever make it across that demon river."

Rafe rubbed the back of his neck, then shook his head. "Except that we did. And if they don't find a single body floating anywhere downriver, they'll know."

"But even once they cross, they'll have no idea where we are," Jeb said. "We could have exited anywhere. That's hundreds of miles to search with no tracks to follow."

"No tracks *yet*," Tavish warned.

Sven turned and walked over to the fire. I closed my eyes and heard him pouring something from the kettle into his tin cup, then sensed him standing over me. Did he know I was awake? I kept my eyes closed until I heard him walk back to the others.

Their discussions continued as they weighed their options, Rafe arguing in favor of waiting until I was stronger. Was he risking himself and the others because of me?

I mumbled as if I was just waking "Good morning. Rafe, can you help me up?" They all turned and watched me expectantly.

Rafe came over and knelt by my side. He pressed his hand to my forehead. "You're still hot. It's too soon—"

"I'm feeling better. I just—" He continued to resist, holding my shoulders down.

"I have to pee, Rafe," I said firmly. That stopped him. He looked sheepishly over his shoulder at the others. Sven shrugged as if he didn't know how to advise him.

"I'm afraid to even think of the indignities I may have suffered these past days," I said. "But I'm awake now, and I will relieve myself in private."

Rafe nodded and carefully helped me up. I did my best not to grimace. It was a long, awkward, painful process to get to my feet, and putting the slightest amount of weight on my now-stitched thigh sent fiery shocks through my leg and up my groin. I leaned heavily on Rafe for support. My head spun with dizziness, and I felt beads of moisture spring to my upper lip, but I knew they were all watching, gauging my strength. I forced a smile. "There now, that's better." I clutched the blanket around me for modesty's sake, because all I had on were my underclothes.

"Your dress is dry now," Rafe said. "I can help you put it back on."

I stared at the wedding dress spread out on a rock, the crimson dyes of many fabrics bleeding into the others. Its weight had pulled me under in the river and nearly killed me. All I could see when I looked at it was the Komizar. I felt his hands running down my arms, once again claiming me as his own.

I knew they sensed my reluctance to put it back on, but there was nothing else to wear. We had all narrowly escaped with just the clothes on our backs.

"I have an extra pair of trousers in my saddlebag," Jeb said.

Orrin gawked at him in disbelief. "Extra trousers?"

Sven rolled his eyes. "Of course you do."

"We can cut away the bottom of the dress so the rest can serve as a shirt," Tavish said.

They seemed eager to busy themselves with something that would distract them from my more personal task at hand, and began to move away.

"Wait," I said, and they paused mid-stride. "Thank you. Rafe told me you were the best of Dalbreck's soldiers. Now I know that he didn't overestimate your abilities." I turned to Sven. "And I'm sorry I threatened to feed your face to the hogs."

Sven smiled. "All in a day's work, Your Highness," he said, and then he bowed.

I SAT BETWEEN RAFE'S LEGS AND LEANED BACK AGAINST HIS chest. His arms circled around me, and a blanket covered us both. We huddled near the mouth of the cave looking out at a mountain range, watching the sun dip between its peaks. It wasn't a beautiful sunset. The sky was hazy and gray, and a dismal shroud of clouds hung over the mountains, but it was the direction of home.

I was weaker than I thought, and my few solitary steps down another arm of the cave to my requested private moment had me collapsing against a wall for support. I took care of my business, but then had to call Rafe to help me walk back. He had scooped me into his arms as if I weighed nothing and carried me here when I asked to see where we were. All I saw for miles was a white canvas, a landscape transformed by a single night of snow.

My throat swelled when the last glimpse of sun disappeared. Now I had nothing else to focus on, and other images crept in behind my eyes. I saw my own face. How could I possibly see my own terrified expression? But I did, as though I watched from some high vantage point, maybe from the vantage point of a god who could have intervened. Every footstep replayed in my head, trying to see what I could have done—or should have done differently.

"It's not your fault, Lia," Rafe said, as if he were able to see Aster's image in my thoughts. "Sven was standing on an upper walk and saw what happened. There's nothing you could have done."

My chest jumped, and I stifled a sob in my throat. I hadn't had a chance to mourn her death. There'd been only a few cries of disbelief before I had stabbed the Komizar and everything tumbled out of control.

Rafe's hand laced with mine beneath the blanket. "Do you want to talk about it?" he whispered against my cheek.

I didn't know how. Too many feelings crowded my mind. Guilt, rage, and even relief; complete, utter relief to be alive; for Rafe and his men to be alive; thankful to be here in Rafe's arms. A second chance. The better ending that Rafe had promised. But in just the next breath, a drowning wave of guilt overwhelmed me for those very same feelings. How could I feel relief when Aster was dead?

Then rage at the Komizar would bubble up again. *He's dead. I killed him.* And I wished with every beat of my heart that I could kill him all over again.

"My mind flies in circles, Rafe," I said. "Like a bird trapped in the rafters. There seems to be no way to turn, no window to fly through. No way to make this right in my head. What if I had—"

"What were you to do? Stay in Venda? Marry the Komizar? Be his mouthpiece? Tell Aster his lies until she was as corrupted as the rest of them? *If* you lived that long. Aster worked in the Sanctum. She was always a step from danger long before you ever got there."

I remembered Aster telling me *nothing's safe around here*. That was why she knew all the secret tunnels so well. There was always a quick exit at hand. Except this time, because she was watching out for me instead of herself.

Dammit, I should have known!

I should have known she wouldn't listen. I told her to go home, but telling her wasn't enough. Aster yearned to be a part of everything. She wanted to please so very badly. Whether it was proudly presenting me with my polished boots, ducking low to retrieve a discarded book in the caverns, guiding me through tunnels, or hiding my knife in a chamber pot, she always wanted to help. *I can whistle loud.* It was her plea to stay. Aster was eager for any kind of—

Chance. *She had only wanted a chance.* A way out, a greater story than the one that had been written for her, just like I had wanted. *Tell my bapa I tried, Miz.* A chance to control her own destiny. But for her, escape was impossible.

"She brought me the key, Rafe. She went into the Komizar's room and took it. If I hadn't asked her—"

"Lia, you're not the only one questioning your decisions. For miles I walked with you half dead in my arms. And with every step, I wondered what I could have done differently. I asked myself a hundred times why I ignored your note. Everything might have been different if I'd just taken two minutes to answer you. I finally had to push it out of my head. If we spend too much time reliving the past, it gets us nowhere."

I laid my head back against his chest. "That's where I am, Rafe. Nowhere."

He reached up, his knuckle gently tracing the line of my jaw. "Lia, when we lose a battle, we have to regroup and move forward again. Choose an alternate path if necessary. But if we dwell on every action we've taken, it will cripple us, and soon we'll take no action at all."

"Those sound like a soldier's words," I said.

"They are. That's what I am, Lia. A soldier."

And a prince. One who was surely wanted by the Council now as much as the princess who stabbed the Komizar.

I could only hope the bloodbath had eliminated the worst of the lot. It had certainly taken the best.

CHAPTER THREE

RAFE

I KISSED HER AND LAID HER DOWN CAREFULLY ON THE BED of blankets. She'd fallen asleep in my arms, mid-sentence, still insisting she could walk back in on her own. I covered her and went outside to where Orrin was roasting tonight's dinner.

Nurse the rage, Lia, I had told her. *Use it.* Because I knew the guilt would destroy her, and I couldn't bear for her to suffer any more than she already had.

Orrin had built the fire under a rocky overhang to diffuse the smoke. Just in case. But the skies were thick with gray and mist. Even if there was someone searching the horizon, smoke would be impossible to see. The others warmed themselves by the coals while Orrin turned the spit.

"How is she?" Sven asked.

"Weak. Hurting."

"But she put on a good show of it," Tavish said.

None of them had been fooled by her smile, me least of all. Every part of my own body was beaten and bruised by the river, knuckles cracked, muscles strained—and I hadn't been pierced by two arrows on top of it all. She'd lost a lot of blood. Little wonder her head swam when she stood.

Orrin nodded approvingly at the roasted badger that was turning a dark golden brown. "This'll fix her up. A good meal and—"

"It's not just her body that's hurting," I said. "Aster's death weighs on her. She's second-guessing every step she made."

Sven rubbed his hands over the fire. "That's what a good soldier does. Analyzes past moves and then—"

"I know, Sven. I know!" I snapped. "Regroups and moves forward. You've told me a thousand times. But she's not a soldier."

Sven returned his hands to his pockets. The others eyed me cautiously.

"Not a soldier like us, maybe," Jeb said, "but a soldier just the same."

I shot him an icy stare. I didn't want to hear about her being a soldier. I was tired of her being in danger and didn't want to invite more. "I'm going to go check on the horses," I said and left.

"Good idea," Sven called after me.

They knew the horses didn't need checking. We'd found a stand of bitter pea for them to graze on and they were securely tethered.

A soldier just the same.

There was far more that I looked back on during my twelve-mile walk than just my failure to answer her note. I also saw Griz, over and over again, lifting her hand and declaring her queen and Komizar. I saw the alarm in her face and remembered my own rage surging. The barbarians of Venda were trying to sink their claws in deeper, and they'd already done enough damage.

She was not their queen or Komizar, and she was not a soldier.

The sooner I could get her safely to Dalbreck, the better.

CHAPTER FOUR

ONE BY ONE, THEY DROPPED TO A KNEE, OFFERING FORMAL introductions. Though they had all already seen me half naked and held me down in the most familiar ways while I was stitched, perhaps this was the first time they thought I might actually live long enough to remember any of it.

Colonel Sven Haverstrom of the Dalbreck Royal Guard, Assigned Steward of Crown Prince Jaxon. The others laughed at that title. They were free with their jest and jabs, even with an officer who outranked them, but Sven gave it back as good as he got it.

Officer Jeb McCance, Falworth Special Forces.

Officer Tavish Baird, Tactician, Fourth Battalion.

Officer Orrin del Aransas, Falworth First Archer Assault Unit.

I bit the corner of my lip hesitantly and raised my brows. "And I can trust those are your real names and occupations this time?"

They eyed me uncertainly for a moment, then laughed, realizing I was jesting along with them.

"Yes," Sven said, "but I wouldn't trust that fellow you're leaning on. Claims he's a prince, even though he's nothing but a—"

"That's enough," Rafe said. "Let's not wear the princess out with your mindless yammering."

I smiled, appreciating their levity, but I sensed a certain unease behind it, an effort to mask the grimness of our situation.

"Food's ready," Orrin announced. Rafe helped me sit down against a makeshift backrest made of saddles and blankets. In the process of sitting, I bent my leg and a fiery jolt shot through it as if I was being pierced with an arrow all over again. I bit back a groan.

"How are the back and the leg?" Tavish asked.

"Better," I answered once I caught my breath. "I guess you need to add skilled Field Surgeon to your list of titles."

Orrin watched me eat as if every bite I took measured his cooking skills. Besides the roasted meat, he had also made a soup from the carcass and some turnips. Apparently Jeb wasn't the only one who had stowed some luxuries in his saddlebag. The conversation centered around the food and other game that they had spotted for future meals—deer, possum, and beaver. Gentle topics. Not at all like their plotting this morning that they had tried to keep from my ears.

I finished my meal and turned the conversation to a more pressing topic. "So, it sounds like we have a week's lead," I said.

They paused from their eating and glanced at one another, quickly assessing how much had been said this morning and what I might have overheard.

Rafe wiped the corner of his mouth with the side of his hand. "Two weeks' lead with the heavy snowfall."

Sven cleared his throat. "That's right. Two weeks, Your—"

"Lia," I said. "No more formalities. We're well beyond that by now, aren't we?"

They all looked at Rafe, deferring to him, and he nodded. I had almost forgotten he was their sovereign. Their prince. He outranked them all, including Sven.

Sven confirmed with a single nod. "Very well. Lia."

"At least two weeks," Orrin agreed. "Whatever Rafe put in the gears of the bridge did the job."

"Lia gave it to me," Rafe told him.

They looked at me, surprised, perhaps wondering if I had conjured some sort of Morrighese magic. I told them about the scholars in the caverns below the Sanctum who were unlocking the secrets of the Ancients and had devised the powerful clear liquid I gave to Rafe. I also described the Komizar's hidden army city and the things I'd witnessed—including the charging brezalots that carried the packs that exploded like a firestorm. "The Komizar was planning to march on Morrighan first and then the rest of the kingdoms. He wanted them all."

Sven shrugged and marginally confirmed my story, saying the

Komizar talked up the power of the army that the governors and their provinces were financing. "But at least half the governors were skeptical. They thought he was inflating the numbers and their capabilities to get greater tithes out of them."

"Did you see the city?" I asked. "He wasn't overstating his claim."

"I didn't, but the other governors who had still weren't won over."

"They probably only wanted him to sweeten their own stakes. I know what I saw. There's no doubt that with the army and weapons he was amassing, Venda could easily quash Morrighan—and Dalbreck too."

Orrin snorted. "No one can beat Dalbreck's army."

I looked at Orrin pointedly. "And yet Morrighan has done so many times in our rocky past. Or do you not study history in Dalbreck?"

Orrin glanced at me awkwardly, then back down at the tin of soup in his hands.

"That was a long time ago, Lia," Rafe intervened. "Long before my father's reign—and *your* father's. A lot has changed."

His low opinion of my father's rule didn't escape me, and strangely, it made a defensive spark ignite within me. But it was true. I had no idea what Dalbreck's army was like now, but in the past several years, the Morrighese army had shrunk. Now I wondered if that was by the Chancellor's design—to make us an easier target—except I wasn't sure that as overseer of the treasury, he alone could make that happen, not even with the Royal

Scholar's help. Was it possible that more in the cabinet conspired with him?

Rafe reached out and rested his hand on my knee, perhaps perceiving the harshness of his comment. "It doesn't matter," he said. "If such an army does exist, without the Komizar's calculating ambition, it will fall into disarray. Malich doesn't possess the wit to lead an army, much less keep the loyalties of the Council. He may be dead already."

The thought of Malich's arrogant head rolling across the Sanctum floor warmed me—my only regret being that I wasn't the one who had sent it rolling. But who else might step into the powerful shoes of the Komizar? What about Chievdar Tyrick? Governor Yanos? Or maybe Trahern of the Rahtan? They were certainly the most nasty and driven of those left on the Council, but I was sure none possessed the cunning or finesse to secure the loyalty of the entire Council, much less follow through with the Komizar's staggering ambitions. But with so much at stake, was that an assumption that any kingdom could afford to make? Morrighan needed to be warned of the possible threat and be prepared for it.

"Two weeks easily," Jeb said, trying to return to the more positive subject of our ample lead time. He tore off another piece of the badger meat. "The Sanctum was in chaos when we left, and with more grabs for power, they may not set out for the lower river at once."

"They will." Sven eyed Rafe with cool gray eyes. "The question is not how soon but how many will they send? It's not just her they'll be after. You'll be a highly sought prize too. The crown prince of Dalbreck has not only stolen away with something they value but has no doubt greatly injured their pride with his deception."

"It was the Komizar's pride," Rafe corrected him, "and he's dead."

"Maybe."

I looked at Sven, incredulous, and my heart squeezed to a cold knot. "There's no maybe about it. I stabbed him twice and twisted the blade. His guts were in pieces."

"Did you see him die?" Sven asked.

See him?

I paused, taking my time to compose a reasoned answer. "He was on the ground, choking on his last breaths," I said. "If he didn't bleed to death, the poison released into his gut finished him off. It's a painful way to die. Sometimes slow, but effective."

Wary glances were cast between them.

"No, I haven't stabbed someone in the gut before," I explained. "But I have three brothers who are soldiers, and they've held nothing back from me. There's no chance the Komizar survived his injuries."

Sven took a long, slow sip from his mug. "You were shot in the back with an arrow and fell into a raging icy river. Not good odds, and yet here you are. When we left the terrace . . . the Komizar was gone."

"That means nothing," I said, hearing the panic rise in my voice. "Ulrix or a guard could have carried his body off. He's *dead.*"

Rafe set down his cup, the spoon clattering against the side. "She's right, Sven. I saw Ulrix drag the body through the portal myself. I know a corpse when I see one. There's no question, the Komizar is dead."

There was a strained silent moment between them, then Sven quietly acquiesced, dipping his chin in acknowledgment.

I hadn't realized I was leaning forward, and I lay back against the mound of blankets Rafe had made for me, weak with exhaustion, my back damp.

Rafe reached out and felt my forehead. "You're running a fever again."

"It's only the fire and warm soup," I said.

"Whatever it is, you need to rest."

I didn't argue. I thanked Orrin for the supper, and Rafe helped me over to my bedroll. The last few steps drained me, and I was barely able to keep my eyes open as Rafe helped me get settled. It was the most conversation and activity that I'd had in days.

He leaned over me, wiping strands of damp hair from my face, and kissed my forehead. He started to stand, but I stopped him, wondering what else he had seen.

"You're sure you saw him dead?"

He nodded. "Yes. Don't worry. You killed him, Lia. Rest now."

"What about the others, Rafe? Do you think they survived? Governor Faiwell, Griz, Kaden?

His jaw clenched at the mention of Kaden's name. He was slow to answer. "No," he finally said. "I don't think they made it. You saw the soldiers swarming in as we left. Kaden and the others had nowhere to flee. There was Malich too. The last time I saw Kaden, he was engaged in combat with him. If Malich made it down to the river, you can guess what happened to Kaden."

The ache of what he didn't say swelled in me—Kaden was no longer an obstacle for Malich.

"He got what he deserved," Rafe said quietly.

"But he helped us fight so we could escape."

"No. He was fighting to save your life, and for that I'm grateful, but he wasn't trying to help you escape. He had no idea we even had a way to escape."

I knew he was right. For their own reasons, both Kaden and Griz wanted to keep me in Venda. Helping me leave wasn't their motive for raising swords against their brethren.

"He was one of them, Lia. He died the way he lived."

I closed my eyes, exhaustion already making my lids too heavy to keep open. My lips burned with heat, and my mumbled words stung on them. "That's the irony. He wasn't one of them. He was Morrighese. Noble born. He only turned to Venda because his own kind had betrayed him. Just like I did."

"What did you say?"

Just like I did.

I heard Rafe walk away and then there was more whispering, but this time I couldn't discern what they were saying. Their muffled words wove with the darkness into a silky black fog.

I STARTLED AWAKE AND LOOKED AROUND, TRYING TO remember what had roused me. A dream? But I could recall nothing. Rafe slept next to me, his arm protectively around my waist as if someone might whisk me away. Jeb sat back against a large rock, his drawn sword at his side. It was his watch, but his eyes were closed. If we had a two-week lead, why did they feel the need for a watch? Of course there were wild animals to consider that might like this nice roomy cave to take refuge in. Orrin had mentioned seeing panther tracks.

Jeb must have just stoked the fire, because it blazed with heat, and yet a chill tiptoed over my shoulders. The flames flickered with a breeze, and the shadows grew darker.

Don't tarry, Miz.

My head throbbed with the sound of Aster's voice, and I wondered if it would forever haunt me. I rose up on one arm and sipped from a canteen. Rafe sensed my movement, and his arm pulled tighter, his body edging closer. I found comfort in his small tug. It felt as if he would never let anything come between us again.

Sven was snoring, and Orrin lay on his side with his mouth wide open, a thin line of drool trickling from the corner. Tavish was curled in a ball, his blanket pulled over his head, only a rope of his thick black hair peeking out from beneath it. All of them peaceful, getting the rest they very much deserved, their bodies healing from their wounds too.

I had started to ease back onto my bedroll when the chill hit me again, stronger this time. It pressed on my chest, making it harder to breathe. The shadows grew darker, and dread snaked through me like a viper waiting to strike. I waited. Knowing. Fearing. Something was—

Don't tarry Miz, don't tarry, or they will all die.

I sat upright, gasping for breath.

"Can't sleep?" Jeb asked.

I stared at him, my eyes prickling with fear.

Jeb yawned. "Sun won't be up for another hour or so," he said. "Try to get some more rest."

"We need to go," I said. *"Now."*

Jeb motioned to quiet me. "Shhh. The others are sleeping. We don't need to—"

"Everyone up!" I yelled. "Now! We're leaving!"

CHAPTER FIVE

KADEN

FIND HER. DON'T COME BACK WITHOUT HER. ALIVE OR dead, I don't care. Kill them all. But bring her back.

There wasn't much else to occupy my thoughts but what may have very well been the Komizar's last words. He needed her head as evidence. A way to quell the unrest once and for all. The random slaughter of cheering clans in the square hadn't been enough for him.

I looked back at the perilous footbridge we had just led our horses over. "I'll do it," I told Griz, grabbing his ax from him. He started to protest but knew it was no use. He couldn't lift his left arm without paling. What would have taken him a dozen swings when he wasn't injured took me more than twice that, but finally the stakes toppled free and the chains jangled into the water below. I stowed the ax and helped Griz back onto his horse. The trail ahead was thick with snow, and we had no tracks to follow. All we had to go on was a hunch of Griz's and a faded memory.

I pulled my cloak tight against the cold. Conniving, all of them. I should have known Governor Obraun was part of her plotting. He gave in too easily during our Council negotiations because he knew he would never have to follow through with giving tithes at all. And the prince. *Damned liars, he was the prince.* My fingers were stiff in my gloves as they gripped the reins. It all added up now. Every detail added up, all the way back to the beginning in Terravin. He was a trained soldier just as I had suspected—probably with the very best training Dalbreck could offer. When Griz confessed to having known his identity all along, I wanted to kill him for his treachery. In turn, he reminded me of my own treasonous ways. I couldn't argue with him. I had betrayed my oath months ago when I hadn't slit her throat as she slept in her cottage.

Bring her back.

The Komizar would see her dead one way or another for what she had done. For what they had all done. But his preference was to get her back alive—and then make her suffer publicly in the worst possible way for her betrayal.

Find her.

And with my last Vendan breath, that was just what I would do.

The winds bore down, the heavens raged,
and the wilderness tested the Remnant
until the last of the darkness spilled into the earth,
and Morrighan charged the Holy Guardians
with telling the stories, for though the devastation
was behind them, it should not be forgotten,
because their hearts still beat with the blood of their forbears.

—*Morrighan Book of Holy Text, Vol. II*

CHAPTER SIX

RAFE

WE STARTLED AWAKE, ALARMED BY HER SHOUTING, JUMPING to our feet, drawing swords, looking for imminent danger.

Jeb was saying it was a false alarm, that there was nothing wrong, but Lia had somehow gotten to her feet on her own, her eyes wild, telling us we had to leave. A relieved breath hissed between my teeth and I lowered my sword. She'd only had a nightmare. I stepped toward her. "Lia, it was just a bad dream. Let me help you lie back down."

She hobbled backward, determined, sweat glistening on her face, and her arm stretched out to keep me at a distance. "No! Get ready. We leave this morning."

"Look at you," I said. "You're tottering like a drunk. You can't ride."

"I can and I will."

"What's your hurry, Your Highness?" Sven asked.

She looked from me to my men. Their feet were firmly planted. They weren't going anywhere based on her wild-eyed demands. Had she spiked another fever?

Her expression sobered. "Please, Rafe, you have to trust me on this."

That was when I knew what she was saying. She was speaking of the gift, but I still hesitated. I had little knowledge of it and less understanding. Which could I trust more: my experience and training as a soldier or a gift that even she couldn't fully explain to me?

"What did you see?" I asked.

"It's not what I saw but what I heard—Aster's voice telling me not to tarry."

"Didn't she say that to you a dozen times?"

"At least," she answered, but her stance remained determined.

All this rush over *don't tarry*?

Ever since I had gathered her into my arms on that riverbank, I had been looking over my shoulder for danger. I knew it was there. But I had to weigh that uncertainty against the benefits of healing too.

I looked away, trying to think. I wasn't sure if I was making the right decision or not, but I turned back to my men. "Pack up."

CHAPTER SEVEN

PAULINE

THE CITY WAS DRAPED IN BLACK, EXCEPT FOR THE WIDOWS. They wore the white silk mourning scarves that only a few months ago I had worn. The past days had been a nightmare, both for Civica and for me. Morrighan had not only lost a whole platoon of young soldiers, including the crown prince, but also its First Daughter, Princess Arabella, now branded the most vile of traitors and responsible for her own brother's death. In taverns some of the gossip grew ugly, claiming the worst of the news wasn't publicly announced—that Lia herself had plunged the sword into Walther's chest.

The king had taken ill. Everyone whispered that he was sick at heart. Walther was his pride, but Lia—as much as they had butted heads, as much as she exasperated him—everyone always said she was more her father's daughter than her mother's. Her betrayal laid him low.

And what had she done to me?

I still hadn't confronted Mikael. Instead, in these last several days, I'd dredged up every one of my conversations with him, sifting through them word for word, as if they were pebbles and I was searching for one stone that shone with truth.

Of course, Pauline, as soon as my final patrol is over, we'll settle in Terravin. Wherever your home is, my heart is already there.

But, Mikael, if by some chance I should have to leave before you return, you'll know where to find me. You'll come?

Always, my love. Nothing could keep me from you. Let's go now, one last time before my platoon leaves.

And then he kissed the knuckles of my hand one at a time and led me into the abandoned caretaker's cottage at the edge of the millpond. He always said the right words, did the right things, so steady in his gaze I believed he looked into my soul. Even now my chest burned with the memory of his kiss. I still wanted him. I wanted his words to be true. *I have his baby growing in my belly.*

But I couldn't deny there had always been worry behind those weeks in Terravin when I had waited for him to come. I had thought it was worry for his safety, worry that he'd been hurt on patrol, but now I wondered if my worry was of another kind. One I wouldn't even admit to myself.

Somehow Lia had known. It had to have been Walther who had told her terrible things about Mikael, what he had thought was the truth. And yet she'd had so little faith in me and in Mikael that she wouldn't tell me. *Walther could have been wrong.*

Then why hadn't Mikael come for me in Terravin? Why wasn't I going to him now? What kept me from revealing my presence to him and watching relief flood his eyes? I knitted more furiously.

"Planning for a baby with two heads?"

I pulled on the yarn, ripping out my stray stitches, and looked up at Gwyneth. She was dressed for the public service. It was time for us to go, and I welcomed a walk through the city to the abbey graveyard. The king and queen wouldn't be there—the king was too ill, and the queen would stay by his side—but Bryn and Regan would attend. They had fallen silent, and I'd feared that they too had turned on their sister, but Bryn finally sent us a note. They wanted to talk. Though the rest of Morrighan may have turned against Lia, the brothers still had a shred of belief in their sister, and Bryn had other news he wanted to share—news he said wasn't safe to put in a note.

I tucked my knitting away, and as we walked out the door, I wondered if it would ever again be safe for Lia to return home.

CHAPTER EIGHT

AS THEY SADDLED THE HORSES AND PACKED SUPPLIES, THEY conferred among themselves about the best route to take. The choices were to ride south, where the climb over the diminishing mountain range would be easier, or head due west for a pass through the range that was steeper and more difficult, but faster.

"We'll go west," I said.

Tavish stiffened and stopped loading his horse. He'd been pushing for riding south before we crossed the range. He stared at Rafe, refusing to look my way. "We aren't familiar with that pass, and with the deep snow, it will be more dangerous to cross."

Rafe strapped my saddlebag to the horse I would ride and rechecked the cinch as he answered. "But it does shave off some miles to the nearest outpost, plus it has the advantage of dumping us into the Valley of Giants, where there's plenty of ruins for shelter—and hiding places."

"You're assuming we'll need to hide," Tavish countered. "Aren't you the one who said we had a two-week lead?"

Everyone paused, including Rafe. Tavish's tone held unmistakable challenge. It was clear that he had no regard for the gift, and I realized it was possible that none of them did.

"We're regrouping, Tavish," Rafe said with finality. "We have new information."

Regrouping. I could almost see the word blazing in Tavish's head. Still avoiding my gaze, he nodded. "West it is."

We rode in twos, wearing makeshift cloaks that they'd made from the Vendan saddle blankets to protect us from the cold. Sven and Tavish led, with Jeb and Orrin and the extra horse following behind us. I felt Rafe watching me, as if I might topple from the saddle. In truth, when I first sat on the horse, I thought my thigh was splitting open. The initial pain had subsided but was replaced with a burning ache. I hardly needed the cloak, because with every hoof fall, another bead of sweat formed on my brow. Whenever the horse stumbled on the snow-covered terrain, I clenched my teeth to mask the pain because the words *don't tarry, or they will all die* haunted my thoughts. I didn't want anything, including a painful moan, to slow us down.

"Keep riding," Rafe told me. "I'll be right back." He turned his horse around and called for Sven to fall back into his place.

Sven stopped, waiting for my horse to catch up to his. "How are you holding up?" he asked.

I didn't want to admit that my back and leg screamed with pain. "Well enough. I'm in far better shape than I was before Tavish removed the arrows."

"Good to hear. It's a long way yet to the safety of the outpost."

Tavish rode ahead, never glancing back. I watched him navigate the terrain, every step uncertain in snow that swallowed our horses' legs up to their fetlocks.

"He wasn't happy about our sudden departure," I said.

"Perhaps just the circumstances of it," Sven answered. "Tavish is a well-regarded tactician in his unit. Yesterday he had argued for a quick departure."

"And Rafe said no."

"But one word from you . . ." The way Sven left the sentence hanging in the air made me wonder if he questioned Rafe's decision too.

"It wasn't just any word. It wasn't my opinion. It was something else."

"Yes, I know. But Tavish doesn't believe in magic either."

Magic?

I stared at Sven until he felt my gaze and turned my way. "Then we have something in common. Neither do I."

Rafe signaled for everyone to stop and caught up to us with Orrin by his side. He said he'd looked the horses over and that Orrin's horse had longer, sloping pasterns, a looser back, and smoother gait. "You'll trade. It will give you an easier ride."

I was grateful for the switch and especially grateful it wasn't

Tavish who'd had to trade with me. I had already bruised his ego. I didn't want to bruise his backside too.

The next several hours went by in considerably more comfort. Rafe knew his horses—and riders. He still watched me out of the corner of his eye.

Once he was sure I was more comfortable, he rode ahead to speak with Tavish. He knew his men too, and I was sure Tavish's terse remark this morning hadn't been forgotten. Sven fell back with me again, and we watched them riding together. Tavish actually threw his head back once and laughed. His long black ropes of hair dangled down his back. Sven told me that Rafe and Tavish had been close friends since they were pledges and often got into mischief together. Around the palace and city, one was rarely seen without the other. It made me think of my brothers and the troubles we would stir, and a dull pang swelled within me. My last vision in Sanctum Hall had showed me that the news of Walther's death had reached Civica. Had the Komizar's lies of my betrayal reached there already too? Did I even have a home to return to anymore? It was likely that the only kingdom that didn't have a price on my head now was Dalbreck.

We stopped well before sunset when we came upon a shelter on the leeward side of a mountain that would give us some protection from the weather. I was grateful for making camp early because I was well and truly spent. It angered me that I couldn't force the weakness away by sheer will. It was a new and humbling feeling for me, having to rely on someone for the smallest of favors. It made me think of Aster and so many others who had walked this fragile line their entire lives, trading on favor and mercy. True power was always just beyond their reach, held in the tight grip of a few.

I insisted on hobbling inside on my own, then looked over tonight's lodging while Rafe left to gather firewood. Once the horses were taken care of, Tavish said he'd go help Rafe gather firewood. "We're going to need a lot."

It was obvious the comment was directed at me, but I ignored it and began to untie my bedroll.

"Better move as far to the back as you can, Princess," he added. "This cave is shallow and won't be as warm as the last one."

I spun to face him. "I'm well aware of that, Tavish. But at least we'll all be *alive*."

I heard the scuff of boots behind me, the others turning at the remark, then silence. The air was taut with expectation.

Tavish immediately backed down. "I meant nothing by it."

"Of course you did." I took a step closer. "You have strengths, Tavish, that I greatly admire. Your skills helped save Rafe's and my lives, for which I'll always be indebted to you. But there are other kinds of strengths too. Quiet, gentle ones that are just as valuable, even if you don't entirely understand them."

"Then help him understand."

I turned toward the mouth of the cave. Rafe had returned with a load of firewood in his arms.

He set it down and walked over with the rest of us. "Help us all to understand."

They waited for me to say something. I braced myself for that familiar feeling of failure that always came with the mention of the gift, but instead, a new feeling settled over me, a feeling that was firm and solid. For the first time in my life, I didn't feel something shrink back within me. The shame that had plagued me in the Morrighese court had vanished. I wasn't compelled to offer apologies for what they couldn't—or refused to—grasp. That was their burden to bear, not mine.

I hobbled over to Rafe's sword, sheathed in its scabbard on the cave floor. I drew it out in a swift motion and held it high. "This is your strength, Rafe. Tell me, is it is loud or quiet?"

He looked at me, confused. "It is a sword, Lia."

"It's loud," Jeb offered. "In battle, at least. And deadly."

Sven reached out and gently pressed the tip downward out of his face range. "A quiet warning too, when hanging at your side."

"It's well-honed metal," Tavish added pragmatically.

"Which one is it?" I demanded. "Metal? Loud? Quiet? Deadly? A warning? Even you can't decide."

"A sword can be many things, but—"

"You define a sword by terms and a world that is familiar to you in all the ways you can see, feel, and touch, but what if there was a world that spoke in other ways? What if there was another way of seeing, hearing, and feeling? Haven't you ever sensed something deep inside? Saw a glimpse of it play out behind your eyes? Heard a voice somewhere in your head? Even if you weren't sure, this knowing made your heart beat a little faster? Now increase that tenfold. Maybe some of us know more deeply than others."

"See without eyes? Hear without ears? You're talking magic." Tavish made no effort to keep the cynicism from his tone.

Strangely, it reminded me of myself the first time I spoke with Dihara. I thought about what she had said to me: *What is magic but what we don't yet understand?* I shook my head. "No. Not magic," I answered. "It's something deep inside, as much a part of us as our blood and skin. It was how the Ancients survived. When they'd lost everything else, they had to return to this language of knowing buried deep within them in order to survive. Some were stronger in this knowing than others, and they helped others survive."

The skepticism remained etched in Tavish's eyes. "It was only a few words you heard, and you were half asleep," he said. "Are you certain it wasn't just the wind?"

"Are you any more certain of your own skills and gifts? Do you know with certainty how your carefully laid plans will play out? Does Orrin always know exactly how straight or far his arrow will fly? When any of you swing a sword, do you know with complete confidence that you'll bring down your enemy? No, I'm not always certain about the gift, but I am certain about everything I heard this morning. It wasn't *just the wind*, as you call it."

Rafe stepped closer, a scowl darkening his face. "Just what did you hear this morning, Lia? Everything."

His gaze chilled me. He knew I'd held back.

"Don't tarry," I answered, which they had already heard me say. I cleared my throat and added, "Or they will all die."

There was a tight moment of silence. Glances were exchanged between Tavish, Sven, and Orrin. They still believed in their long lead. I knew it was a reasonable conclusion. The bridge was heavily damaged. Kaden himself had told me the only other way across the river was far to the south. But I trusted what I'd heard too.

"I don't expect you to believe everything I've said right this minute. Even though Rafe told me you were the best soldiers of Dalbreck, I didn't believe you'd make it alive to the Sanctum, much less be able to help us get away. But you proved me wrong. Sometimes all it takes is a single ounce of trust for more to grow. Maybe that can be a starting point for us."

Tavish chewed on his lip and finally nodded. A shaky truce.

Rafe dusted off bits of leaves and dirt on his sleeves as if trying to dispel the tension in the air. "We're out of harm's way now. That's what matters," he said. "And headed for home—if we don't starve first. Let's get dinner going." They all gladly followed Rafe's lead, occupying themselves with the business of making camp—something solid that they could all understand.

OVER THE NEXT FEW DAYS, I CAME TO KNOW MY RESCUERS better. I often had the opportunity to ride beside one of them when Rafe veered off to a higher lookout or scouted a blind trail ahead—which happened with great frequency. He claimed he was only checking for ragtag Vendan patrols that might still be out here. I suspected he was simply itchy in his saddle. After all the weeks he'd had to hold back and forcibly restrain himself in the Sanctum, he was finally free, and it seemed his long-pent-up energy needed release. If I'd thought his smile was disarming before, now it undid me. When he came back from a vigorous ride, his face flushed with heat, his hair tossed with the wind, and an easy smile lighting his face, I longed for us to be off the trail and somewhere private.

I often found Sven watching Rafe with what I thought was a father's pride. One day I had asked how long he had been Rafe's assigned steward. He said Rafe had come from a wet nurse to his care—give or take a few years.

"That's a long time. You raised up a fine soldier."

"More than a soldier. A future king."

Yes, the pride had been unmistakable. "And yet you let him traipse across the Cam Lanteux after me?"

Sven had snorted. "I didn't *let* him. In fact, I tried to talk him out of it, but there was no stopping him. He had lost a treasure that he was determined to get back."

In spite of the crisp air, rivers of warmth had spread through my chest. "Yet at considerable risk to all of you. I'm sorry about your face."

"This little thing?" he said motioning to his cheek. "Pfft. Nothing. And as these young rogues have pointed out numerous times, it's probably an improvement, not to mention it adds to my credentials. Wait until the new cadets see it. Maybe it will even spark some clemency in the king."

"He'll be angry that you didn't stop Rafe?"

"It's my job to keep the heir apparent out of danger. Instead I practically escorted him right to it."

"Why would you do that?"

"As I told you, his decision was made." He paused as if contemplating the why himself and sighed. "And it was time."

Talking with Sven, one thing quickly became apparent—he was not at all like the arrogant blowhard Governor Obraun, whom he had pretended to be. Instead of constantly wagging his tongue, he chose his words carefully. Those days in the Sanctum, he'd been as good at deception as Rafe had been, but then, he had been Rafe's mentor for many years. His long, silent pauses made me wonder what he was thinking.

Orrin, on the other hand, reminded me of Aster. Once he began talking, he was hard to stop.

Jeb was the most solicitous of the group. It was as if he had adopted me as one of his sisters. I learned why the others teased him about the extra trousers he had stashed away. They revealed that he was quite the dandy back at the palace, always dressed in the latest fashions. His mother was head seamstress of the queen's court.

"When your trunks arrived in Dalbreck, it caused quite a stir," he told me. "Everyone was feverish with curiosity about what was inside."

I had almost forgotten that my clothing and other personal belongings had been sent ahead in anticipation of my arrival in Dalbreck. "What did they do with them? Use them for a bonfire? I wouldn't blame them if they did."

He laughed. "No, they wanted a good look before they did that," he teased. "But opening the trunks did become a coveted secret event everyone wished to attend. It was left to the seamstresses, but my sisters and even the queen gathered round as my mother opened a trunk on the pretense of hanging up your gowns in case circumstances should change."

I couldn't hold back a snort. "What circumstance? That my running away had only been a mere misunderstanding? That I had accidentally shown up at the wrong abbey?"

Jeb grinned. "My mother said they were expecting something quite different from what they saw. She said your gowns were beautiful and elegant, but so . . ." He searched for the right word. "Simple."

I stifled a laugh. By Morrighese standards, they were lavish. My mother had gone to great lengths to have a new fancier wardrobe made for me because the Dalbretch were known for their sartorial delights, but I had refused most of the embellishments and had insisted on taking along my everyday dresses too.

"My mother was actually pleased," Jeb said. "She felt it showed respect, that you weren't aiming to outshine all the other ladies in court. Of course, she immediately said she could make a few alterations that would greatly improve them, but the queen ordered them packed up and returned to Morrighan."

And *there* they had promptly burned them, I thought. Along with an effigy of me too.

"Is something wrong?" Jeb asked.

I realized I was scowling. "Just thinking about—" I stopped my horse and turned to him. "Jeb, when you first came to my room back in the Sanctum, you said you were there to take me home. Which home did you mean?"

He looked at me, puzzled. "Why, Dalbreck, of course."

Of course.

I spoke to Rafe about it later, reminding him that we had to get to Morrighan first.

"Our first priority is to get to safety," he countered, "and that means Dalbreck's outpost. Morrighan can come after that."

THINGS REMAINED DISTANT BETWEEN TAVISH AND ME. HE was polite, but when Rafe had to attend something else, he never offered to fall back to ride at my side. It had been clear he didn't want to be alone with me.

Rafe continued to be restless and was always riding off to check on something. We'd only been on the trail a short time today when he said he was going to a lookout to see if he could spot game. He called for Sven to ride beside me, but this time Tavish offered to come. Even Rafe took note, raising a curious brow at me before he left.

At first Tavish made small talk, asking me how my back was feeling, saying he could remove the stitches in another week or so, but I sensed something else was on his mind.

"I never answered your question," he finally mumbled.

"What question?" I asked.

He looked back at the trail and then embarked on a different subject entirely. "Rafe had balked at the barrels and raft, but I promised him it would work." He paused, clearing his throat. "The moment we lost sight of you in the river, I was certain neither of you would survive. Those hours we spent searching for you were the longest—" His brows pulled together in a scowl. "They were the longest hours I've ever endured."

"It's not your fault that we fell in—"

"It is my fault," he said. "It's my job. To think of every worst scenario and have a plan to avert it. If I had—"

"If I hadn't been wearing that dress," I said, cutting him off. "If the Council meeting hadn't ended early. If the Komizar hadn't killed Aster. If only I had married Rafe in the first place like I was supposed to. I play the if game too, Tavish. It's practically a hobby of mine, but I've found it's a game of endless possibilities with no winner. No matter how great a gift or skill, it's impossible to foresee every outcome."

He didn't look convinced. "Even after we found you, I still wasn't sure you'd live. The expression on Rafe's face—" He shook his head as if he was trying to erase the memory. "You asked me if I am always certain of my skills and gifts. Prior to that day, my answer would always have been yes."

"Your plan may not have gone exactly as you wanted, but it did save us, Tavish. I say that not to spare your feelings but because it's true. With it, we had a chance. Without it, our deaths were certain, that much I know, and you must believe it too." I cleared my throat as if perturbed. "In fact, I command it," I added with a haughty air.

A hint of a smile broke his solemn expression. We rode on, this time in a more comfortable silence, my thoughts drifting to the guilt he had carried these past days, the guilt that still edged my thoughts.

"One other thing," he finally said. "I don't understand this knowing of yours, but I want to try. Is the gift ever wrong?"

Wrong? I immediately thought of Kaden's claim of a vision of us together in Venda with him carrying a baby on his hip and then remembered my recurring dream of Rafe leaving me behind.

"Yes. Sometimes," I answered.

Sometimes it had to be wrong.

CHAPTER NINE

KADEN

TRYING TO HELP GRIZ OFF HIS HORSE WAS LIKE TRYING TO wrestle a bear to the ground.

"Getcher hands off me!" he bellowed.

"*Shhh!*" I ordered for the hundredth time. His pain had made him careless. His growl echoed through the canyon. "They could still be here."

I let go of his belt and he fell, bringing me down with him. We both lay in the snow.

"Go on without me," he groaned.

I was tempted. But I needed him. He could be useful. And there was no doubt that he needed me.

"Quit your complaining and get up." I stood and put my hand out to help him. He had all the dead weight of a butchered bull.

Griz was not used to relying on anyone, much less admitting

to weakness. The gash in his side began oozing blood again. It needed more attention than my hasty bandaging job. He mumbled a curse and pressed the wound with his arm. "Let's go."

We studied the tracks outside of the cave.

Griz used his boot to crush a ridge of snow made by a horse hoof. "I was right. The old coot brought her here."

He had confessed to me that he and the so-called Governor Obraun had a history, and part of it included this cave, a place they had hidden out together when they escaped the grips of a forced labor camp.

Obraun's real name was Sven, and he was a soldier in Dalbreck's Royal Guard. Sven's deception didn't surprise me as much as Griz's. I had suspected a lot of people of being something they were not, but I had never suspected Griz of being anything but a fiercely loyal Rahtan. Not someone who sold information between kingdoms, though he hotly claimed none of it had ever betrayed Venda. Working with the enemy was betrayal enough.

I bent down and looked more closely at the muddle of footsteps and horse tracks. Some were Dalbretch horses, but others unmistakably Vendan.

"They got hold of some our horses is all," Griz said.

Or someone else had caught up with them.

I stood, my gaze following the tracks that disappeared through the pines ahead. They headed east, which meant they weren't being taken back to Venda. How did they get Vendan horses?

I shook my head.

Rafts. Stashed horses and supplies.

This was a plan that had been long in the making. Maybe

from the moment Lia set foot in Venda. The only conclusion I could draw was that she had used me from the beginning. Every tender word from her lips had served a purpose. I shuffled through them all. Our last night, when she told me her vision was of us together . . . when she asked me about my mother—

It turned my stomach inside out. Lia was the only person I had ever even whispered my mother's name to. *I see your mother, Kaden. I see her in you every day.* But now I knew all she saw when she looked at me was one of them. Another barbarian, and someone she couldn't trust. Even if she had deceived me, I couldn't believe that her affections for the people were anything but real. That much wasn't an act. It churned in me, the memory of Lia standing on a wall, sacrificing precious seconds of her escape so she could speak to the people one last time.

We checked inside the cave and found dark stains in the sandy soil, possibly blood from a slain animal—or maybe from one of their own wounds. And then I saw a scrap of fabric no bigger than my thumbnail. I picked it up. Red brocade. It was a piece of her dress—confirmation that she had made it this far. If she was able to ride, it meant she was still alive. It was a possibility neither Griz nor I had brought up. No one had found a body downstream, but that didn't mean a rocky crag hadn't hidden it from view.

"They're not far ahead," I said.

"Then what are we waiting for?"

Find her.

There was no time to waste.

I looked at Griz. What real good was he going to do me? He

could barely lift a sword, even with his good arm, and I'd be able to move faster without him.

"You can't hold them off by yourself," he said as if reading my mind.

It appeared that was exactly what I'd have to do. But Griz was at least still an intimidating figure. He could make a show of force. It might be all the edge I needed.

CHAPTER TEN

I STEPPED OUT OF THE GROTTO AND LOOKED OUT ON THE
landscape. The beauty of trees dressed in glittering white robes,
and a world as quiet and holy as a Sacrista met me—except for a
gentle wordless whisper that wove through the tree tops. *Shhh.*

The last few days had finally given me the time with Rafe I
had once prayed for when we were trapped on the other side of
the river. Of course, with an escort of four, we were never alone,
so our affections were kept in check, but at least we had time to
ride beside each other.

We talked of our childhoods and our roles in court. His role
was far more purposeful than mine. I told him how I frustrated
my aunt Cloris to distraction, never quite meeting her standards
in the womanly arts. "What about your mother?" he asked.

My mother. I wasn't even sure how to answer him. She had

become an enigma for me. "She shrugged off Aunt Cloris's admonishments," I told him. "She said it was healthy for me to run and play with my brothers. She encouraged it."

But then something changed. Where she had once sided with me against the Royal Scholar, she began to take his council; where she had never been short with me, she began to lose her temper. *Just do as I say, Arabella!* And then, almost apologetically, she would draw me into her arms and whisper with tears in her eyes, *Please. Just do as I say.* After I'd had my first cycle, I had run into her chamber to ask her about the gift that hadn't yet appeared. She was sitting by the fire with her stitchery. Her eyes had flashed with anger, and she missed a stitch, her needle drawing a bead of blood on her thumb and staining the piece she'd been working on for weeks. She stood and threw the whole thing into the fire. *It will come when it comes, Arabella. Don't be in such a hurry.* After that I only cautiously brought up the gift. I was ashamed, thinking she'd had a vision of my shortcomings. It hadn't occurred to me that she was the cause of them. "I think my mother is somehow part of all this, but I'm not sure how."

"Part of what?"

Other than the kavah on my shoulder, I didn't know what to say. "She wanted to send me off to Dalbreck."

"Only after my father proposed it. Remember, it was his idea."

"She went along easily enough," I said. "My signature on the contracts hadn't dried before she was calling for dressmakers."

A flash of surprise suddenly brightened his face, and he laughed. "I forgot to tell you. I found your wedding gown."

I stopped my horse. "You what?"

"I plucked it out of the brambles when I was tracking you down. It was torn and dirty, but it didn't take up much room, so I shoved it in my pack."

"*My dress?*" I said in disbelief. "You still have it?"

"No, not here. It was too risky to carry around in Terravin. I was afraid someone would see it, so when I got the chance, I stuffed it behind a manger stored up in the loft. Enzo's probably found it and thrown it out by now."

Berdi maybe, but not Enzo. He never did any more tidying up than he had to.

"Why in the gods' names would you keep it?" I asked.

A smile played behind his eyes. "I'm not really sure. Maybe I wanted something to burn in case I never caught up with you." A disapproving brow shot up. "Or to strangle you with if I did."

I suppressed a grin.

"Or maybe the dress made me wonder about the girl who had worn it," he said. "The one brave enough to thumb her nose at two kingdoms."

I laughed. "Brave? I'm afraid no one in my kingdom would see it that way, nor likely yours."

"Then they're all wrong. You were brave, Lia. Trust me." He started to lean over to kiss me, but was interrupted by the whinny of Jeb's horse not far behind us.

"I'm afraid we're holding everyone up," I said.

He scowled, jerking his reins, and we moved on.

Brave enough to thumb her nose at two kingdoms. I think that was how my brothers saw it too, but certainly not my parents—nor the cabinet.

"Rafe, have you ever wondered why I was the one who had to go to Dalbreck to secure the alliance? Couldn't it have been accomplished just as well by you coming to Morrighan? Why is it always the girl who must give up everything? My mother had to leave her homeland. Greta had to leave hers. Princess Hazelle of Eilandia was shipped off to Candora to create an alliance. Why can't a man adopt his wife's homeland?"

"I couldn't because I am going to rule Dalbreck one day. I can't do that from your kingdom."

"You aren't king yet. Were your duties as a prince any more important than mine as a princess?"

"I'm also a soldier in Dalbreck's army."

I remembered my mother's claim that I was a soldier in my father's army, an angle of duty she had never used before. "As I am in Morrighan's," I said.

"Really," he replied, his tone dubious. "You may have had to leave your homeland, but did you consider everything you would have gained as my queen?"

"Did you consider everything you might have gained as my king?"

"You were planning to depose your brothers?"

I sighed. "No. Walther would have made a fine king."

He asked me about my brother, and I managed to talk about him without tears in my eyes for the first time, recalling his kindness, his patience, and all the ways he encouraged me. "He was the one who had taught me how to throw a knife. It was one of his last requests to me, that I keep up my practice."

"Was that the same knife you used to kill the Komizar?"

"Yes. Fitting, don't you think? And after I stabbed him, I used it to kill Jorik. That's where I left it, stuck in the middle of his throat. It's probably for sale in the *jehendra* by now. Or Malich is wearing it at his side as a memento of his undying fondness for me."

"You're so certain that Malich is the next Komizar?"

I shrugged. No, I wasn't certain, but of the Rahtan, he seemed the most ruthless and hungry for power—at least of those who were left alive. Worry burrowed through me. How had the people in the square fared, and what did they think when I disappeared? A part of me was still there.

"Tell me more about your kingdom," I said, trying to banish my worst thoughts from my head. "Let's not waste one more word on vermin like Malich."

Rafe stopped his horse again, then shot a warning glare over his shoulder at the others to keep their distance. His chest rose in a slow deep breath, and his pause made me sit higher in my saddle. "What is it?" I asked.

"When you were traveling across the Cam Lanteux . . . did any of them—did he *hurt* you?"

There it was. Finally.

I had wondered if it would ever come. Rafe had never asked me a single question about those months I was alone in the wilderness with my captors—what had happened, how I had lived, what they had done—and he'd avoided any mention of Kaden at all. It was as if a fire burned so brightly inside him, he couldn't allow himself to get too close to it.

"Which *he* are you referring to?"

His gaze faltered. "Malich," he answered. "That's who we were talking about."

No, not just Malich. Kaden always simmered beneath the surface. This was about him more than anyone else.

"My time crossing the Cam Lanteux was hard, Rafe. Most of the time I was hungry. All of the time I was afraid. But no one touched me. Not in the way you're thinking. You could have asked me long ago."

His jaw twitched. "I was waiting for you to bring it up. I wasn't sure if it was too painful for you to talk about. All I had wanted was for you to survive so we could be together again."

I grinned and kicked his boot with my own. "And we are together."

AT NIGHT, WHEN WE COULD FIND SHELTER THAT AFFORDED some measure of comfort, I read aloud from the Last Testaments of Gaudrel. They all listened with fascination.

"It appears that Gaudrel was a vagabond," Rafe said.

"But with no colorful wagon," Jeb added.

"And none of those tasty sage cakes," Orrin mused.

"It was soon after the devastation," I told them. "She and the others were survivors just trying to find their way. I think

Gaudrel may have been a witness and one of the original Ancients."

"It's not much like Dalbreck history," Sven said.

I realized I was largely ignorant of Dalbreck history. Since it was a kingdom that had sprung from Morrighan many centuries after it was established, I had assumed their view of history was the same as ours. It wasn't. While they acknowledged that Breck was an exiled prince of Morrighan, their account of the devastation and its aftermath was different, apparently melding with the stories of nomadic tribes who gave the fleeing prince safe passage to the mesa lands of the south.

It seemed I had stumbled upon yet another history that conflicted with the Holy Text of Morrighan. Dalbreck's account, at least as Sven told it, had a precise number to the Remnant—exactly one thousand chosen survivors. They spread to the four corners of the earth, but the strongest and most courageous headed south to what would one day become Dalbreck. Breck rallied them and laid the first stone of a kingdom that would become greater than all the others. From there it was all about heroes and battles and the growing might of a new kingdom favored by the gods.

The only things all of the histories did have in common was a surviving Remnant and a storm. A storm of epic proportions that laid waste to the land.

"I had warned Venda not to wander too far from the tribe," I read aloud from Gaudrel's testament. "A hundred times, I had warned her. I was more her mother than her sister. She came years after the storm. She never felt the ground shake. Never saw the sun turn red. Never saw the sky go black. Never saw fire burst on the horizon and choke the air."

I read a few more passages, then closed the book for the night, but the descriptions of the storm lingered, and I turned Gaudrel's account over silently in my mind. Where was the truth? *The ground shook, and fire burst on the horizon.* That was a truth Gaudrel had actually witnessed.

And that was what I had seen too.

When the Komizar showed me his army city, fire burst forth as the brezalots exploded, the ground shook, and the testing fields stained the sky with copper smoke, choking the horizon.

Seven stars. Maybe all the destruction wasn't flung from the heavens.

Maybe there had been a dragon of many faces, even then.

CHAPTER ELEVEN

RAFE

LIA'S QUESTION STUCK WITH ME. *WHY IN THE GODS'* *names would you keep it?*

I had fumbled for answers because I didn't know myself. When I found the gown, I had cursed her repeatedly as I untangled it from the thorny branches. *I'm the crown prince of Dalbreck for the gods' sake. Why am I cleaning up after a spoiled runaway?* When I freed the gown and held it up, I was even angrier. I wasn't one to dwell on fabrics or fashion like Jeb, but even I could see its matchless beauty. Her complete disregard for the careful work that had gone into it only fueled my fury. But that still didn't explain why I went to the trouble to stuff it in my bag.

I knew now. It wasn't to burn it or wave it in her face. It was something I wouldn't even admit to myself at the time. It was the warrant for her arrest I had heard about. Her own father was hunting her down like she was an animal. I'd stuffed the dress in my bag because I knew eventually someone else would come. I didn't want one of them to find the dress—or her.

I finally reached a crest where I had an open view of the trail behind us. I waited, studying the landscape. How many more excuses could I conjure for Lia? This time I claimed I was scouting for the ridge that led to the valley we would reach today. I didn't want her to worry needlessly, but now there was reason to worry. I spotted what I suspected all along and rode back to tell the others.

"Go," I whispered to Tavish. "Less than a quarter mile back. Circle around to the south. There's good cover, and you'll be downwind in case the horses make noise. I couldn't see how many through the trees. I'll stay here with her."

Tavish nodded, and they rode off.

I loosened the strap on my sheath and gripped my hilt just as Lia limped back from a brief trip behind some brambles. She saw them riding away, and an annoyed crease furrowed her brow. "Now, where are *they* going?"

I shrugged. "I spotted a flock of geese, and they're all craving a juicy goose for dinner tonight."

"I don't understand. I thought we were in a hurry to get to the valley floor."

"We're making good time, and we do need to eat tonight."

Her eyes narrowed. "*All* of them needed to go?"

I turned away, using the premise of searching for something in my saddlebag. "Why not?" I said. "Orrin's not the only one who likes to hunt."

I felt the silence at my back, and I pictured her with her hands on her hips. I didn't think she'd buy it again.

When I turned, her head was angled with accusation.

"I spotted something through the trees when I was out," I explained. "It was a long way off. I'm certain it was only a herd of deer, but they're going to go check just to be sure."

CHAPTER TWELVE

I KNEW IT WASN'T DEER.

Fifteen minutes passed.

Then an hour.

"Should we go look for them?" I asked.

"No," Rafe insisted, but I saw him circling. Positioning the horses. His hand returning to his hilt again and again.

Finally we heard the ruffled nicker of a horse through the trees, and we both spun toward the sound.

Tavish emerged from the forest, leading two horses behind him. "Well, well, well," he crowed. "You were right. Look what we found."

The others followed behind him, and when Sven and his horse moved aside, I gasped.

By the gods. It couldn't be.

I hobbled forward, but Rafe stretched his hand out to stop me.

Orrin and Jeb had their bows drawn, arrows aimed with razor-sharp concentration at Kaden's and Griz's hearts as they walked them into our camp. It was as if they didn't trust a sword to bring down Griz and a safe distance was their best strategy. Sven had already relieved them of their weapons.

Rafe approached them, eyeing Kaden. Kaden returned his frigid stare. My breath froze in my chest. Nothing had changed between them. Their gazes were heavy with threat, though Kaden was in no position to threaten anyone.

"So we meet again, Prince Jaxon."

"So we do," Rafe replied, his voice as brittle as the air. "But it looks as if you've traveled a long way for nothing. *Stupid sot.*"

Kaden's nostrils flared. He hadn't missed the irony of his own long-ago words being thrown back into his face.

"What should we do with them?" Tavish asked.

Rafe stared at Kaden for what seemed an eternity, then shrugged as if it was of little matter. "Kill them," he said.

I jumped forward grabbing his arm. "Rafe! You can't kill them!"

"What am I supposed to do, Lia? Take them prisoner? Look at the size of that one!" he said, pointing at Griz. "I don't even have enough rope to go around him."

"There's rope in their gear," I countered, waving my hand at a coil hanging from the back of Griz's horse.

"And then what? Tie them up so they can wait for the opportunity to slit all our throats and take you back to Venda again? What do you think they're here for? Just to say hello?"

Kaden stepped forward, and both Orrin and Jeb yelled at him to hold his position, pulling their bows taut with threat. He stopped. "We don't want to take her back," he said. "We're only here to escort and protect her. A squad of Rahtan and First Guard are charged with hunting her down. They could be here any time."

Rafe laughed. "You, escort and protect her? Do you take me for a fool?"

A smile lit Kaden's eyes. "That's beside the point, isn't it? What's more important, your pride or Lia's life?"

"And that's why you were stalking us? To protect her?"

"We were watching for the Vendan riders, hoping to intercept them before they reached her."

"And yet, the only Vendan riders I see are *you.*"

I didn't blame Rafe for balking at Kaden's claim. I questioned his motivations as well. Escort me? When he had claimed that I belonged in Venda with him? When he had assured me at every turn that there was no way for me to escape? There clearly had been. He had found another way across the river. My distrust simmered.

I limped forward, sidestepping Rafe's efforts to stop me. I kept a safe distance but looked sternly at Griz. "Put your hands behind your back. Now."

He eyed me uncertainly, but then slowly did as I instructed. "Good," I said. "Now, after they tie you up, you must give me your word you won't try to escape, and if Kaden should try, you must promise that you'll strike him down."

"How would I do that with my hands tied?" he asked.

"I don't care how you do it. Fall on him. That should stop him. Do I have your word?"

He nodded.

Rafe grabbed my arm and began to drag me away. "Lia, we're not going to—"

I twisted my arm free. "Rafe! We are not going to kill them!" I looked accusingly back at Kaden. "Yet," I added. I ordered him to put his hands behind his back too. He didn't move, only stared, his eyes drilling into me, trying to thrust guilt back on me for deceiving him. "I'm not going to ask you a second time, Kaden. Do it."

He slowly put his hands behind his back too. "You're making a mistake," he said. "You're going to need me."

"Tie them up," I said to Tavish and Sven. Neither one moved, deferring instead to Rafe for an answer.

Rafe's jaw was rigid with anger.

"Rafe," I whispered between gritted teeth.

He relented and signaled to Sven and Tavish, then pulled me over behind the horses, his fury mounting. "What's the matter with you? Griz's word is worth nothing, and Kaden's even less. How are we going to travel with them? Griz will break his word the first time we—"

"He won't break his word."

Exasperation flashed across Rafe's face. "And how would you know *that*?"

"Because I commanded it, and he believes that I'm his queen."

CHAPTER THIRTEEN

THE VALLEY OF THE GIANTS WASN'T WHAT I EXPECTED. IN the lush basin below us, enormous boxy temples covered in green and gold snaked for miles in neat rows, like a giant's stash of moss-covered trunks. Sven said legend claimed it to be a marketplace of the Ancients. What treasures had been so grand and immense that structures of equal stature had been required? They lined a path that wound through the valley and finally disappeared behind low hills. Trees with golden leaves sprouted between them, and emerald moss and vines covered their walls. Even though some had fallen into rubble, many were eerily intact, just like in the City of Dark Magic, almost as if the Ancients still roamed there. Even from afar, I could see the remnants of signposts that had once marked the way. Why had this city been spared the ravages of the devastation and time?

It made me wonder if this was another place that Griz and his cohorts had avoided, fearing that the dark spirits of the Ancients held up the walls. He and Kaden walked ahead of us, traversing the twisting trail down the side of the mountain. Rafe wouldn't let them ride. He said it was safer to have them walk just ahead of Jeb and Orrin, who still had their bows at the ready, even though Kaden's and Griz's hands were firmly tied behind their backs.

"Would you really have killed them in cold blood?" I asked.

"It's no less than what he ordered for me."

"Tit for tat? Is that how this soldiering stuff works?"

An annoyed hiss escaped through Rafe's teeth. "No, I wouldn't have killed them on the spot. I probably would have waited for Kaden to do something stupid in the heat of the moment—which he surely will—and then I would have killed him. Oh, wait, excuse me! I forgot. We're all in good hands. Griz promised to *fall* on him if he got out of line. Do I have that right?"

I returned his sarcasm with a steely glare. "Next I'm going to order him to fall on *you*. Save your cynicism. All I needed to know was that you wouldn't kill them in cold blood."

Rafe sighed. "But it doesn't hurt for them to think that I would. I don't trust either of them, and we still have a long way until we reach the safety of the outpost."

"How long have you known they were following us?"

"I've suspected for a few days now. I saw white smoke early one morning. A campfire being doused, I guessed. What I can't figure out is how they caught up with us so fast."

"I know." As soon as the last knot was tied on his hands,

Kaden's long-ago explanation, *no other way*, pinched inside me. It was another of his lies. At the very least, he had deliberately painted a picture that made me assume things.

"Kaden led me to believe that the bridge into Venda had replaced the old footbridge that used to span the river. I'm guessing, dangerous or not, somewhere not too far from the Sanctum, it still exists. Which means if Griz and Kaden got across, others probably did too. He may not have been lying about the squad."

Rafe reached up and raked his fingers through his hair. This was news he didn't want to hear. If we had a lead at all now, it was only because the snow had covered our tracks.

Commotion broke out in front of us. The scrape of gravel, the whinny of horses, and startled shouts exploded across the air.

Whoa!

Back up!

Watch out!

The trail was suddenly bedlam as horses stumbled into one another. Rafe's sword flashed from its scabbard. I instinctively drew mine too, though I didn't know what I was defending myself from.

Orrin's horse was rearing back, and the others were trying to control their skittering horses on the narrow trail. For a few seconds, confusion reigned and then we saw what had happened. Griz had fallen, blocking the path. Kaden knelt beside him, yelling for someone to untie him so he could help Griz.

Rafe ordered everyone to hold their positions, as if he suspected a trick. He dismounted to investigate, but we quickly saw where Griz's cloak had fallen away, revealing bloody, wet fabric on his side. His face was waxy and damp, and I knew it was no trick. The wound Jorik had inflicted days ago was still bleeding.

"What happened?" Rafe asked.

"It's nothing," Griz growled. "Just give me a hand—"

"Shut up," Kaden told him. He looked up at Rafe. "It's from the battle on the terrace. He took a sword in his side. I tried to bandage it, but it keeps opening back up."

Griz snarled at Kaden and tried to rise on his own, but Rafe held him down with his boot. "Don't move," he ordered, then yelled over his shoulder for Tavish. "Come take a look at this."

Kaden was escorted several feet away by Orrin and directed to sit while Tavish examined Griz. The rest of us hovered, watching as Tavish pulled up Griz's filthy vest and shirt, and then cut away the sodden bandages.

Sven groaned when he saw the wound, and I stifled a shudder. The eight-inch gash was caked with dried black blood, and the skin around it was red and inflamed. Yellow pus oozed from the wound.

Tavish shook his head, saying he couldn't do anything about it here on the trail. It needed hot water and cleaning before he could stitch anything. "It's going to take some work."

The way he said *work*, I knew even he was doubtful about how much he'd be able to do. I knelt down beside Griz. "Do you have any thannis with you?" I asked.

He shook his head.

"I have some," Kaden called from his guarded position several feet away.

"I'm not drinking any thannis," Griz groaned.

"Quiet!" I said. "If I command you to drink, you'll drink." But what I had in mind was a poultice once we got down to the valley to help draw out some of the poison.

They untied his hands, and it took Rafe, Jeb, and Sven working together to get Griz to his feet. Several curses later, they finally loaded him onto his horse. They were no longer worried about him making sudden moves. Kaden was still forced to walk ahead of us. His status hadn't changed.

Sven rode close to Griz, and when he teetered in his saddle, Sven reached out and grabbed his arm to steady him.

Because of the delays with Griz and Kaden joining our caravan, we didn't reach the valley floor until dusk. Kaden had been walking for five hours now with his hands tied behind his back. I saw the fatigue in his steps, but strangely, instead of sympathy, my own anger and fears resurfaced. How many months had I been in that same position, a half-starved prisoner, humiliated and afraid, uncertain if I'd live another day? He hadn't suffered half as much as I had. Yet. The unsettling difference was, he had come looking for this trouble. Why was he really here?

We rode down the main avenue, surrounded by the eerie boxy giants. Many of the ancient walls and roofs were still intact. There was a quick scramble to choose a suitable shelter, which meant one that could be defended—just in case.

Rafe and Tavish conferred, and a ruin was decided upon. We all gathered armfuls of what loose and dried branches we could find and filed into the cavernous dwelling, taking the horses with us. It probably could have held an entire regiment.

As soon as a fire was roaring, I prepared a poultice, helping myself to whatever was in Kaden's saddlebag. Tavish sharpened his knife and work began on Griz. Our shelter rose several stories, and thick slabs of stone that had fallen from higher places littered the floor around us. Griz was laid out on one of them. As weak as he was and, now it seemed, slightly delirious, it took all four of them to hold him down while Tavish cleaned the wound.

Kaden was ordered to sit in an open area far from the gear and fire. I sat nearby on a large block of rock, guarding him, a sword across my lap. A strange feeling knotted inside me, like a meal that wasn't eaten properly, rushed and uncomfortable. I noted his arms, still bound behind his back. A sour taste rose in my throat.

He was the prisoner now, like the prisoner he had made me. All his actions I had sloughed off and forgotten, because I knew that in some twisted way he had also saved my life, were suddenly as fresh and hurtful as if they had happened yesterday. I felt the rope cutting into my wrists and the suffocating terror of trying to breathe beneath a black hood he had pulled over my head. I felt the shame of crying as my face was ground into the sand. My emotions weren't blinding and explosive, as they had been back then, but were now tight and contained, like an animal pacing behind the cage of my ribs.

Kaden met my stare, his eyes revealing nothing; cold, calm, dead. I wanted to see terror in them. Fear. Just as he had surely seen it in mine when I discovered he wasn't the pelt trader he had claimed to be but an assassin sent to kill me.

"How does it feel?" I asked.

He acted as if he didn't know what I was talking about. I tried to goad his fear to the surface. "How does it feel to have your hands tied behind your back? To be dragged across the wilderness, not knowing what will happen to you?" I forced a long and luxurious smile as if I was enjoying the turn of our fortunes. "How does it feel to be a prisoner, Kaden?"

"I'm not fond of it, if that's what you want to hear."

My eyes stung. I wanted far more than that. "What I want is to watch you beg for your release. To desperately bargain for your life like I had to."

He sighed.

"That's all I get? A sigh?"

"I know that you suffered, Lia, but I did what I thought was right at the time. I can't take back what I've done. I can only try to make amends."

I choked on the word. I knew bitterly the cost of trying to make amends, and how pathetically they could fall short. When Greta died, I thought it was all my fault as I tried to make *amends*, but now I realized I hadn't even known the rules of the game I'd been drawn into, nor all the players—like the traitors back in Civica. My amends would have changed nothing. The lies went on and on. Just like Kaden's lies.

"You lied to me about the footbridge," I said. "It was there all along."

"Yes. Four miles north of the Brightmist gate. It's not there anymore. We cut it down."

Four miles? We could have gotten there on foot.

I leaned back on the rock. "So what cunning story did you spin to get them to spare your lives? I'm sure it was an excellent one. You're the master of deceit, after all."

He studied me, his brown eyes as dark and deep as night. "No," he said. "Not anymore. I think that title has fallen to you."

I looked away. It was a title I would gladly embrace if it could get me what I needed. I stared at the firelight dancing across the steel of the sword, both edges equally sharp and gleaming. "I did what I had to do."

"All those things you told me? Only what you had to do?"

I stood, the sword still in my hand. I wasn't going to get wrangled down a path of guilt. "Who sent you, Kaden?" I demanded. "Why are you here? Was it Malich?"

A disgusted smirk twisted his lip.

"Say it," I said.

"In case you hadn't noticed, Lia, we were outnumbered that day on the terrace. We barely escaped with our lives. Faiwel died. So did the other guards who fought by our sides. Griz and I managed to fight our way down to a portal on the lowest level, and we sealed the door behind us. From there we hid in various abandoned passages for three days. When they couldn't find us, they assumed we had escaped on another raft."

"And just how would you know what they assumed? Or that there was a squad sent after us?"

"One of the passages we hid in was next to Sanctum Hall.

We heard the Komizar shouting orders, one of which was to find you."

My knees turned to water. I stared at Kaden, the cavern suddenly spinning with shadows. "But he's dead."

"He could be by now. He was weak, but Ulrix called for healers. They were caring for him."

My legs gave way, and I dropped to the floor. I saw the Komizar's eyes drilling into me, the dragon refusing to die.

"Lia," Kaden whispered, "untie me. Please. It's the only way I can help you." He scooted closer, until our knees almost touched.

I tried to focus but instead I was smelling the salty blood that had spilled to the terrace, seeing the shine of Aster's eyes, hearing the chants of the crowd, feeling the icy grip of the knife as I pulled it from its sheath, the day coming to life again, the disbelief that had swept over me, the seconds that changed everything, the Komizar crumpling to the ground, and my naïve hope swelling that it could really be over.

Words, dry as chalk, lay on my tongue. I swallowed, searching for saliva, and finally managed a hoarse whisper. "What happened to the others, Kaden? Calantha, Effiera, the servants?" I rattled off another half dozen names of those who had been sympathetic to me, those who had looked at me with hopeful eyes. They had expected something from me that I didn't deliver. A promise they were still waiting for.

His brow furrowed. "Most likely dead. Clans who cheered your succession in the square suffered losses. It was a message. I don't know the numbers, but at least a hundred were slaughtered. All of Aster's clan, including Effiera."

My thoughts whirled. "Yvet and Zekiah?" I asked, not sure if I really wanted to know the answer. "And Eben?"

"I don't know." But the tone of his voice held little hope. He glanced at my lap. The sword still lay across it.

Part of me wanted to untie him, to believe every word he had told me, that he was only here to help us escape, but Rafe's story didn't match Kaden's. Rafe had seen the Komizar dead. He'd told Sven he'd seen the corpse dragged away.

The cavern shuddered with a sudden bellowing scream. I heard Sven curse and the shouts of the others trying to hold Griz down. The worried flutter of birds roosting high above us sent sandy debris raining down.

Kaden looked up as if something else might lurk in the dark floors above us. "Untie me, Lia. Before it's too late. I promise you I'm not lying."

I stood, dusting off my trousers, a familiar ache blooming in my chest. *Venda always comes first.* His long-ago words burned bright. If any words were true in Kaden's heart, I knew it was those.

I lifted the sword and pressed its sharp edge to his neck. "You may have saved my life, Kaden, but you haven't yet earned my trust. I care about all these men I am traveling with. I won't have them harmed."

His eyes smoldered with frustration. Things were different now. There was far more at stake than just my life and saving it. There was everyone I loved in Morrighan, everyone I cared about in Venda, every one of the men in this company I rode with—they were threaded into every thought and movement

I made. They had to become part of his thoughts too. He had to care like I did. Venda couldn't come first for him anymore. Even I couldn't come first.

I LAY CURLED IN RAFE'S ARMS, EXHAUSTION OVERTAKING both of us. I had asked him again about the Komizar, telling him what Kaden said. He told me not to worry, that the Komizar was dead—but I saw his hesitation this time before he answered, the slack in his jaw, the barest stalled moment that told me what I needed to know. He was lying. He hadn't seen the body dragged away. I wasn't sure if I should be angry with him, or grateful. I knew he was only trying to calm my fears, but I didn't want to be calmed. I wanted to be prepared. I didn't push the point. Rest was more imperative to our survival. His eyes were lined with fatigue.

We were nestled in a dark nook of the ruin that afforded us only a small amount of privacy. A few fallen slabs separated us from the others and the glow of the firelight. Orrin had first watch. I could hear him pacing on the gravel floor just feet away. Maybe it was the rustling of birds somewhere high above us, or the distant howling of wolves that kept him on edge. Or the fact that the Assassin now slept among us. Maybe that was why none of us could sleep.

Only Griz seemed to find deep slumber, swept away into some dark dream-filled world. Tavish said if he made it through the night, he might have a chance. There was nothing more any of us could do.

CHAPTER FOURTEEN

KADEN

ORRIN'S PACING WAS DRIVING ME MAD. IT MADE IT DIFFICULT to hear other noises. Things I should listen for. I rolled to my side, trying to reach the rope around my feet, but the knots were out of my reach. My shoulder ached from lying for hours in the same position.

For a moment, when I had told her about the Komizar, I'd thought Lia would untie me. I saw the struggle behind her eyes. I saw our connection rekindle. But then a wall came down. This was a harder Lia than I had known, fierce and unbending, but I knew what had been done to her, and the horrors she had witnessed.

How does it feel?

The rope dug into my wrists. Numbed my ankles.

Familiar, I had wanted to answer. *Being a prisoner feels familiar.*

It was all I had ever been. My past held on to me today as strongly as it had when I was a child, my choices still limited, my steps still shackled. My life had been patched together with lies from the day I was born.

How does it feel?

Old. I was tired of the lies.

CHAPTER FIFTEEN

THE END WAS IN SIGHT. JUST AHEAD, THE FOOTHILLS WERE stepping back, and the last of the ruins were melting into the earth. The majesty of the Ancients bowed yet again to time, which proved itself the ultimate victor. I was relieved to see the first glimpses of open grasslands up ahead, yellow with winter. The valley had twisted on far longer than I had anticipated, though some of the length may have had to do with the company I rode between. Even when sharp words weren't bandied between Rafe and Kaden, I felt the blows of their dark glances.

If ever there were three mismatched riders, it was us—the crown prince of Dalbreck, the Assassin of Venda, and the fugitive princess of Morrighan. Sons and daughter of three kingdoms, each bent on the domination of the other two. If our situation hadn't been so dire, I would have thrown back my head and laughed at the irony. It seemed whether I was at the citadelle or in the far-flung wilderness, I was ever caught in the middle of opposing forces.

Griz had not only made it through the first night but had woken up hungry. Tavish said nothing, but I saw his relief and maybe some of his lost pride restored. Each day Griz grew stronger, and now after three days, his color was ruddy and the fever gone. Tavish asked me about the thannis poultice I applied daily. I shared what I knew about the purple weed, including its brief but deadly golden phase, when it seeded. He took the pouch that I offered him, noting he would avoid the golden flowers if he found any. Griz told him not to worry, that he wouldn't find any thannis here. It grew only in Venda. I wished now I had some of those golden seeds, if only to plant a few in Berdi's garden.

Kaden was finally allowed to ride his horse. His hands were still tied, but at least in front of him now. The squad he had claimed was hunting us down hadn't materialized, but the possibility still kept us all on edge. I believed Kaden's story. I was sure the others did too, though Rafe would admit to nothing. The fact that he let Kaden ride was admission enough. He wanted to get to the safety of the outpost as soon as possible. *Only half a day's ride to go*, he had estimated when we packed up this morning. Sven concurred.

The Marabella outpost was the closest point of safety. It was named after one of their long-ago queens. Rafe said there were more than four hundred soldiers stationed there and it was easily defendable. Once there, we could rest, stock up on supplies, change out our horses, and continue on our journey with additional soldiers. With the Komizar dead, I hadn't felt it necessary to return to Civica immediately, but now with even the slim possibility of him being alive and able to carry out his plan to annihilate Morrighan, the urgency returned. As much as I delighted in the idea of having several days of rest with Rafe, we couldn't stay long at the outpost. Morrighan had to be warned not only about the Komizar, but also the traitors who aided him.

Rafe took a long swig of water from his canteen. "Be sure to drink, Lia," he said absently as his eyes scanned the landscape ahead. He never rested. I wasn't sure he even slept most nights. The slightest noise roused him. By bringing Kaden and Griz into our company, he only had more to juggle, and the exhaustion showed on his face. He needed a good night's sleep, one where he didn't carry the weight of everyone's safety on his shoulders. He turned to me and smiled unexpectedly, as if he knew I was watching him. "Almost there." The icy blue of his gaze lingered, igniting a fire in my belly that spread down to my toes. His eyes turned reluctantly back to the trail ahead, his guard back up. We weren't there yet. He continued to talk as he watched our path. "First thing I'm going to do is take a hot bath—then burn these filthy barbarian clothes."

I heard Kaden pull in a seething breath.

Behind us there was banter on the amenities of the outpost. "First thing I'm going to do is break into Colonel Bodeen's red-eye," Sven said cheerfully, as if he was tasting the burning brew in his throat already.

"And I'll lift a few with you," Griz added.

"Bodeen keeps a fetching pantry too," Orrin added admiringly.

"*Barbarian* or not, the clothes served you well enough," Kaden shot at Rafe. "You were lucky to have them."

Rafe leveled a cool stare over his shoulder at Kaden. "So I was," he answered. "Just as you were lucky that I didn't part your head from your neck when we parried in Sanctum Hall."

Only stewing silence was returned by Kaden.

But then I noticed there was a strange brooding silence *everywhere*. My fingertips tingled. A sudden pall had fallen, as if someone had boxed my ears. Blood rushed to my temples. I turned my head, listening. And then, from somewhere faraway, the satisfied purr of an animal. *You are ours.* I looked at Rafe. Movement around me was drawn and slow, and the small hairs on my neck lifted.

"Stop," I said softly.

Rafe pulled his horse to a halt, his eyes already sharp and alert. "Hold back," he said to the others.

Our group of eight clung together uncertainly, a tight knot in the silence. Eight pairs of eyes searched the nearby ruins and the narrow spaces between. Nothing stirred.

I shook my head, thinking I had alerted everyone needlessly. We were all on edge—and tired.

And then a shrill howl split the air.

We spun to look behind us, our horses jostling and prancing for position in our constricted circle. At the end of the long road we had just come down, four horsemen sat poised, all equally spaced as if ready for a parade—or an advancement.

"Rahtan," Kaden said. "They're here."

They were too far away to identify, but they clearly wanted us to see them.

"Only four?" Rafe asked.

"There's more. Somewhere."

Orrin and Jeb unhooked their bows from their packs. Rafe and Sven slowly drew their swords.

I swept aside my cloak and pulled both my knife and sword free. "Why are they just sitting there?"

Another piercing cry rang out, bouncing off ruins and raising gooseflesh on my arms. We turned the other direction to find what was almost a mirror image of what lay behind us. Six horsemen, but these were much closer. They sat like evenly spaced statues, cold and planted as if nothing could get past them.

"Bloody hell," Sven said under his breath.

"Untie me," Kaden whispered. "Now."

"What are they waiting for?" Rafe asked.

"Her," Griz answered.

"They'd rather take her alive than drag her back dead," Kaden explained. "They're giving you a chance to give her up before they kill us."

Orrin grunted. "They're assuming we'll be the ones who are killed."

It was a reasonable assumption. I recognized two of them by their long white hair. Trahern and Iver, the vilest Rahtan. We were outnumbered, their ten healthy well-armed men against our eight, three of whom were injured, including myself.

Rafe glanced to either side, looking at the crumbled ruins, but it was apparent that none offered quick defensible positions.

"If you make the slightest move, they'll charge," Kaden warned.

"Anything else we should know?" Rafe asked.

"You don't have much time. They know we're talking."

"Keystone formation," Rafe ordered, keeping his voice low and calm. "We take the six first, then Jeb and Tavish double back with me. Only when I give the word. Griz, cut Kaden loose on my signal."

"Orrin—right," Tavish said. "Jeb—left."

The horses stamped, sensing the danger.

"Hold steady," Sven whispered.

They worked together like a smooth machine, exchanging a few more words, their chiseled focus remaining on the Rahtan as they spoke.

Rafe finally turned to me, his weariness vanished, his eyes fierce with battle. "Lia, make a show of putting your sword away. You're going to move forward as if we're giving you up." He turned to look at the riders behind us, then back to me. "Slowly. Ahead five lengths. No more. Then stop. Ready?" His eyes cut into me, a beat longer than we had time for. *Trust me. It will be all right. I love you.* A hundred things shining in his gaze that he didn't have time to say.

I nodded and moved forward. Time turned to syrup, every hoof fall amplified, one length becoming a mile. I steeled my eyes on the Rahtan ahead, as if that would keep them in place. They didn't move, waiting for me to come all the way to them. Yes,

Trahern and Iver, but now I could also recognized Baruch, Ferris, and Ghier, only cruel guards before, now elevated to ride with the Rahtan. The sixth one I didn't know. But Malich wasn't among them. If he wasn't here, maybe he was the one ruling Venda now. I had sheathed my sword as Rafe had ordered, but the knife was still in my hand, hidden behind the pommel of the saddle. Two lengths. Their horses pranced, impatient. Three lengths. They looked between one another, victorious. Four lengths. I was close enough to see their faces. Each gleamed with satisfaction. Trahern moved forward to meet me. Another step. Five lengths. I stopped my horse.

"Keep coming, girl," he called.

I didn't move.

A question crossed his face only briefly before the battle cry of a warrior prince rent the air. The ground shook with the rumble of hooves. Flesh and shadows flew past me.

The Rahtan raced forward to meet them, Trahern leading the pack. Rafe maneuvered in front of me to block him. Swords flashed and axes swung. My horse whirled in the confusion, rearing back. I worked to regain control. Arrows flew, their smooth hiss singing past my ears. The Rahtan who had been behind now raced toward us too, but then Rafe and Tavish doubled back, arrows flying in the other direction, a circle of battle with me at the center. Dust rose in clouds, and the death ring of swords clanged against the air. Griz swung mightily, even with his weak side, bringing down Iver. Kaden fought beside him, his hands free for the first time in days. Blood spattered them both, but I wasn't sure whose blood it was.

Kaden whirled on his horse, killing Baruch with a vicious stab to his throat, pulling the sword free and, in the same motion, blocking an attack from Ferris. Ghier advanced on Sven from behind, and I threw my knife, hitting him dead center in the back of his neck. I circled, the melee coming from all sides and swung my sword into another Rahtan as he attacked Orrin. The blade glanced off his leather armor, but it was enough of a distraction that Orrin was able to knock him from his horse. I drew a second knife from my belt, but then, hidden in the ruins, a flash. Color. Something else turning my eye. Movement. Charging.

A horse raced forward—with Ulrix guiding it toward me.

I raised my sword, but he was already upon me, his horse's side ramming my horse, the impact sending my animal stumbling and the sword flying. His horse was still butting mine, not giving me time to reposition or gain control, every part of us, saddle and stirrup, seeming tangled. I still had the knife tight in my grip, and I slashed out at his arm, meeting only with a leather wrist cuff. I slashed out again for something more vital, but he blocked me with his sword and yanked me onto his horse with his other hand in a single violent pull. The pommel of his saddle slammed into my stomach like a fist, punching my breath away, punching over again and over again as I straddled the horse on my stomach. I couldn't breathe, but I knew, *he was riding away. We were disappearing into the ruins.* I tried to force air back into my lungs, to roll away, free the arm pinned beneath me, I reached desperately for something to hit him with. Where was my knife? Air. I needed air. His fingers threaded through my hair, yanking my head back. "All I need is your head, Princess. The choice is yours. Submit to me or lose it."

I gasped, my lungs finally filling, and I pulled my pinned arm free, something hard still in my grasp. I slashed upward. He struck at my hand, sending the knife flying, but it was too late. The blade had left a spurting line of blood from his collarbone to his ear. He roared with pain, grabbing my arm with one hand and lifting his sword with the other. I had no leverage to move, no way to push off, no way to protect my neck from his blade— and then he was gone.

Gone.

Ulrix's crumpled body lay on the ground. His head tumbled down the incline into a rock. Rafe circled around, sheathing his bloody sword. He rode over, scooping me around the waist and pulling me sideways onto his saddle. His heart pounded against my shoulder.

His breaths were ragged from the exertion of battle. I turned to look at him. Smeared blood and sweat streamed from his face. He pulled me to him, holding me so tight there was no chance of me slipping off.

"You're all right?" he said into my hair.

My words choked in the back of my throat. "Rafe," was all I could say.

His hand stroked my head, crushed my hair, his breaths calming as he held me. "You're all right," he repeated, this time it seemed, more to himself than to me.

THE RAHTAN WERE DEAD, BUT OUR GROUP HAD SUSTAINED more injuries.

When we got back to the others, Tavish had a gash on his forehead that he waved away as unimportant, wrapping his head with a strip of cloth to keep the blood out of his eyes. Jeb was lying on the ground, his face wet and waxy. My heart clutched, but Kaden assured me it wasn't fatal. When Jeb's horse was struck by the blow of a sword, he'd been thrown and his shoulder was dislocated. Jeb shuddered as they cut away his shirt so they could see his injury.

"That was my favorite shirt, you savages," he said, trying to smile, but his breaths were strained and only agony registered on his face.

I dropped to his side, brushing back his hair. "I'll buy you a dozen more," I said.

"Cruvas linen," he specified. "It's the finest."

"Cruvas it is."

He grimaced and looked at Rafe. "Get on with it."

We all stared at his shoulder. It was more than just a dislocation. Something had ripped inside. The skin swelled purple and blue, and the previous injury that Tavish had stitched was bleeding again.

Tavish nodded at Orrin and Kaden. They held him down while Rafe rotated Jeb's arm off to the side, upward slightly, then pulled. Jeb's scream was full and guttural, echoing through the valley. My stomach turned. Afterward his eyes remained closed, and I thought he had passed out, but when his breath returned, he looked up at me and said, "You didn't hear that."

I wiped his brow. "I heard nothing but savages ripping off a perfectly fine shirt."

We made a sling for his shoulder from a dead Rahtan's bedroll, and Jeb was helped onto one of the Vendan horses, his own now dead in the road and stripped of its belongings. We were on our way again, all of us spattered in blood, Griz favoring his wounded side again, making me fear he had pulled his stitches loose. The dead Rahtan lay scattered, a gruesome scene of butchered men, some of them stripped of their needed linens. As we took the supplies we needed from their dead bodies, I felt like a scavenger—the kind Gaudrel and Morrighan had feared. I prayed there were no more Rahtan lying in wait in another ruin. It seemed we would never be out of this hell.

I cry out and fall to my knees,
unable to go on,
weeping for the dead,
weeping for the cruelties,
and a whisper calls to me from far away,
You are strong,
Stronger than your pain,
Stronger than your grief,
Stronger than them.
And I force myself to my feet again.

—*The Lost Words of Morrighan*

CHAPTER SIXTEEN

RAFE

I COULDN'T BANISH THE SIGHT OF THE BARBARIAN YANKING Lia's head back by her hair, his sword rising, and in the flash of that moment, I saw the bounty hunter in Terravin again, his knife held to her neck, but this time I knew she was going to die. I was too far away. Terror had gripped me. I would never make it in time.

But then, somehow I did. Somehow I was there. My reach longer, my advance faster than it had ever been before. She rode with me now, settled in my saddle against me. When I told the others that she would ride with me, I didn't explain why. No one asked. The extra horses were tethered behind us.

We'd only been back on the trail for an hour when we saw dust in the distance, and then a squad. They spread out. They had spotted us too. *Devil's hell.* How much more could we take on? There were at least thirty of them, and we were stuck on a wide open plain, the ruins far behind us.

I raised my hand, and our convoy stopped. I heard the rumble of murmurs behind me.

Blessed gods.

Jabavé.

Mother of demons.

What do we do now?

The order to turn around and try to make it back to the ruins was on my lips when I spotted something in the dust cloud.

"*Your Highness,*" Sven said, impatient for an order.

Something blue. And black.

"A banner," I called. "They're ours!"

Shouts of relief erupted, but then we all saw the same thing as they galloped closer. Lances pointed, weapons drawn. There was no mistaking their intent as they charged toward us. They didn't know who we were. We waved our arms, but they didn't slow.

"Something white!" I yelled. By the time they realized who we were, at least one of us would be impaled. But there wasn't a scrap of white among us to wave.

"Our cloaks," Lia said, and then louder, "Our cloaks are Vendan!"

The saddle blankets we wore were woven in Vendan colors and patterns. As far as they were concerned, we were a barbarian squad. Who else would be out here?

"Shed the blankets!" I yelled.

The patrol slowed as if they were conferring, but their

weapons were still aimed. When they were within shouting distance, we identified ourselves, with our hands in the air, as Dalbreck soldiers. They cautiously approached, then stopped six lengths away, still poised to run us through. I ordered everyone to dismount and to keep their hands in sight and off their weapons. I helped Lia down, then Sven and I stepped forward.

"You bloody fools," Sven yelled. "Don't you know your own prince when you see him?"

Between our grime and blood spattered clothes, I wouldn't have expected anyone to recognize us.

The captain squinted. "Colonel Haverstrom? *Sven?*"

I heard a collective sigh from the others. My muscles went slack for the first time in weeks. We were almost home.

"That's right, you knucklehead," Sven said, his tone full of relief.

"And, as much as I look like a stray dog, Prince Jaxon," I added.

The captain looked at me strangely, then glanced at the soldiers on either side of him. He dismounted and stepped forward to meet me. His expression was grim.

"Captain Azia," he said, introducing himself. "The entire Dalbreck army has been searching for you . . ."

Something about his expression was all wrong.

And then falling down on one knee, he added, "Your Majesty."

CHAPTER SEVENTEEN

THE MOMENT STRETCHED AS LONG AND FRAGILE AS SPIDER silk blown taut in the wind. Longer. Impossible. Sven's eyes watered. Tavish looked down. Orrin and Jeb exchanged a knowing glance. Even Kaden and Griz froze, though I wasn't sure if they understood what the captain's words meant. The young soldiers on either side of the captain looked confused. Even they hadn't known. A fierce ache gripped my heart as everyone waited to see what Rafe would do. A cruel moment. But it was his and his alone to finish.

Your Majesty.

I only had a crescent view of Rafe's face, but it was enough. He stared down at the captain as if he didn't really see him. Only the clenching of his jaw, still streaked with dirt and blood, revealed anything. And the slow curling of his fist. Every small controlled gesture told me the news hit him hard—but he was well-trained. Prepared. Sven had probably been preparing him for this moment since he was a child. Rafe would do what was required of him, just as he had when he came to Morrighan to marry me. After two measured breaths, he nodded at the captain. "Then you've done your duty."

A prince, in the turn of a moment and a few words, was now a king.

Rafe motioned for the captain to rise and said quietly, "When?"

It was only then that Sven put a hand on Rafe's shoulder.

The captain hesitated, looking at the rest of us, unsure if he could speak freely.

Rafe eyed Kaden and Griz, then asked Tavish and Orrin to take them for a walk. He may have trusted them with a sword, but not his kingdom's secrets.

It happened weeks ago, the captain explained, only a few days after the queen had died. The inner court was reeling, and it had been decided to keep the king's death a secret. With no one on the throne and the crown prince missing, the cabinet wanted to hold back the news from neighboring kingdoms that Dalbreck was without a monarch. They explained the king's lack of public appearances as mourning for the queen. The cabinet ministers ruled discreetly while a desperate search was launched for the prince. With top officers missing along with him, they assumed he was alive but ensnared in an unauthorized but well-deserved retaliation against Morrighan. The whole kingdom was still enraged over the breaking of the contract, and they wanted retribution. When they searched Sven's office, they'd found messages sent to Sven from the prince about a meeting in Luiseveque but could turn up nothing else besides Sven's orders to Tavish, Orrin, and Jeb to meet there too. They feared they'd all been found out and thrown into one of Morrighan's prisons, but careful inquiries turned up nothing. It was as if they had all vanished into thin air, but hope was never lost. Their skills were known.

When the captain finished, it was Rafe's turn to explain. "I'll fill you in as we ride," Rafe told him, saying we were tired, hungry, and some of us in need of medical care.

"And those two?" the captain asked, nodding toward Griz and Kaden in the distance.

The corner of Rafe's mouth pulled. I tensed, waiting to see what he would call them. Barbarians? Prisoners? He seemed unsure himself. I prayed he wouldn't say Rahtan or Assassin.

"Vendans," he answered. "Whom we can moderately trust for now. We'll keep a close watch on them."

Moderately trust? They had just helped save our lives. For the second time. But I knew they'd done it not for Rafe's benefit or Dalbreck's—only mine—so I reluctantly understood his caution too.

The captain's expression turned hard, and a deep line creased between his brows. "A platoon of ours has been missing now for weeks. We've been hunting down men like—"

"The platoon is dead," Rafe said flatly. "All of them. I saw their bloody weapons and valuables brought to the Komizar. Those two weren't involved. As I said, I'll explain as we ride."

The captain paled. An entire platoon dead? But he made no further comment, complying with Rafe's wish to explain as they rode. He shot a last sideways glance at me but was too polite to ask who I was. He'd surely seen me riding in front of Rafe on his horse and probably assumed something unsavory. I didn't want to embarrass Rafe or the captain with the truth at this point. We'd all heard what he said about the rage they still nursed toward Morrighan, but as the captain returned to his horse, his soldiers eyed me with curiosity too. With the remnants of my clan dress, and my skin still spattered with blood, I surely looked like a wild barbarian in their eyes. What on earth was their king doing riding with me?

The glances and stares didn't escape Rafe. He looked down and shook his head.

Yes, he had much to explain.

I DIDN'T GET EVEN A PASSING MOMENT TO HOLD RAFE. TO tell him how sorry I was. To convey any kind of sorrow at all. The convoy resumed immediately. Maybe it was just as well for Rafe to have a chance to absorb this news without words from me stirring his emotions further.

I had met his father once. Briefly. He was an old man walking up the steps of the citadelle, a limp in his gait, and he required assistance. That sight had sent terror pulsing through me. He was old enough to be my father's father. I had assumed the worst about the age of the prince, though I knew now, it wouldn't have mattered how old or young the Dalbreck king would have been.

My terror was rooted in the reality of this man arriving in Civica to sign marriage agreements. At the sight of him, I saw my choices being crushed, my voice being silenced forever in a foreign kingdom I knew little about. I was property to be bartered like a wagon full of wine, though perhaps less precious and certainly far less enjoyed. *Hush, Arabella, what you have to say doesn't matter.*

I knew this king had to have some redeeming quality for Rafe to love him and for Sven to tear up at the news, but I couldn't forget that this king also told his son, *Take a mistress after the wedding if she doesn't suit you.* Only for Rafe's sake could I mourn him.

With thirty soldiers to escort us now, I had suggested I ride my own horse farther behind in our caravan. I knew it would be a more comfortable ride for all concerned if I wasn't there as Rafe and Sven tried to explain where they had been for the last several months. How angry would Dalbreck be that I was the cause of their prince's disappearance? I'd already heard the tone with which the captain said *Morrighan*, as if it were a poison to be spat out.

The wind picked up, cool and crisp. I missed Rafe's warmth at my back, the comfort of his arms around me, the nudge of his chin at the side of my head. My hair stank of oil, smoke, and dirt, even the river that had nearly killed us both, and yet he had nuzzled close, as if it smelled of flowers, as if he didn't care if I was or ever had been a proper princess.

"Rafe seemed shocked. I take it the king's poor health was one of his lies too?"

I hadn't noticed that Kaden had come up alongside me. He

had probably been tallying the lies ever since I left him on the terrace.

I looked at him, his shoulders slumped. Spent. But the weariness I saw in his eyes came from someplace else, from words that had carved out pieces of his flesh, one calculated day after another. My words. I scrambled for a defense, but there was no more anger in his expression, and that left me hollow. It gave me nothing to push back against. I had no game pieces left to play.

"I'm sorry, Kaden."

His lip lifted in a pained expression, and he shook his head, as if to ward off any more apologies from me. "I've had time to think about it," he said. "There's no reason I should have expected the truth from you. Not when I was the one to lie and betray you first back in Terravin."

It was true. He had lied and betrayed me, but somehow my lie seemed like the greater crime. I had played with his need to be loved. I had listened sympathetically to his deepest, most painful secrets that he had never shared with anyone. He let me into a raw corner of his soul, and I used that to gain his trust.

I sighed, too weary to parse out guilt like chits in a card game. Did it matter if my pile was bigger or his? "That was a lifetime ago, Kaden. We were both different people then. We both used lies and truth for our own purposes."

"What about now?"

I saw him holding it out to me tentatively, *truth*, a treaty written on the air between us. Was truth even possible? I wasn't sure what it was anymore, or if now was the time for it.

"What is it you want, Kaden? I'm not sure why you're even here."

His blond hair whipped in the wind. He squinted into the distance, but no words were forthcoming. I saw the struggle, his search for the false calm he always painted on his face. It was beyond his grasp now.

"You're the one who just proposed truth," I reminded him.

An anguished smile pulled at his mouth. "All those years . . . I didn't want to see the Komizar for what he was. He saved me from a monster, and I became just as driven as he was. I was ready to make an entire kingdom pay for the sins of my father—a man I haven't seen in over a decade. I've spent half of my life waiting for the day he would die. I blocked out the kindnesses of every person in Morrighan that I ever met, saying it didn't matter. It was the cost of war. My war. Nothing else mattered."

"If you hated him so much, Kaden, why didn't you just kill your father? Long ago. You're an assassin. For you it would have been an easy enough matter."

He cleared his throat, and his hand tightened on the reins. "Because it wasn't enough. Every time I imagined my knife slitting his throat, it didn't give me what I needed. Death was too quick. The longer I planned for the day, the more I wanted. I wanted him to suffer. Know. I wanted him to watch everything he had denied me slip from his fingers one piece at a time. I wanted him to die in a hundred different ways, slowly, agonizingly, day by day, the way I had when I begged on street corners, terrified that I wouldn't bring in enough to satisfy the animals he sold me to. I wanted him to feel as sharp a lash as the one he took to me."

"You said it was beggars who beat you."

"They did, but only after he laid the first marks, and those were the deepest ones."

I flinched at the cruelty he had suffered, but the horror of how long he had planned and hungered for vengeance left a sickening lump in my throat. I swallowed. "And you still want this?"

He nodded without hesitation. "Yes, I still wish him dead, but now there's something else that I want even more." He turned to face me, worried lines fanning out from his eyes. "I don't want any more innocents to die. The Komizar will spare no one, not Pauline, Berdi, or Gwyneth—no one. I don't want them to die, Lia. . . . and I don't want you to die." He looked at me as if he could see death's pallor on my face already.

My stomach rolled. I thought of the last words Venda had spoken to me, the missing verses someone had torn from the book, *Jezelia, whose life will be sacrificed.* I hadn't shared that verse with anyone. Some things I had to keep tucked and secret for now. Truth was still far off for me.

"It's a whole kingdom in jeopardy, Kaden. Not just the few you know."

"Two kingdoms. There are the innocents in Venda too."

My eyes stung, thinking about Aster and those who were slaughtered in the square. *Yes, two kingdoms in jeopardy.* Anger bubbled inside me at the scheming of the Komizar and the Council.

"The clans deserve more than what they've been dealt," I said, "but a terrible threat grows in Venda, one that has to be stopped. I don't know how to make it all work, but I'll try."

"Then you'll need help. I have nothing to go back to, Lia, not as long as the Council is in power. And I'm just as hated in my birth home of Morrighan. I can't even go back to the Vagabond camps anymore. If I'm with you—"

"Kaden—"

"Don't make more of it than it is, Lia. We want the same thing. I'm offering you my help. Nothing more."

And there was the truth that Kaden was trying to believe. *Nothing more.* But what I saw in his eyes was *more.* There was still so much need in him. It would be a difficult path for me to navigate. I didn't want to mislead or hurt him again. Still, he was offering me something I couldn't turn down. Help. And a Vendan assassin in my employ was something of unquestionable value. How I would love to see the cabinet's reaction to that— especially the Chancellor and Scholar. *We want the same thing.*

"Then tell me what you know about the Komizar's plans. Who else in the Morrighese cabinet was he conspiring with besides the Chancellor and Royal Scholar?"

He shook his head. "The only one I know of is the Chancellor. The Komizar kept those details to himself—to share his key contacts would give away too much power. He only told me about the Chancellor because I had to deliver a letter to his manor once. I was thirteen and the only Vendan who could speak Morrighese without an accent. I looked like any other messenger boy to the maid who answered the door."

"What did the letter say?"

"It was sealed. I didn't read it, but I think it was a request for more scholars. A few months later, several arrived at the Sanctum."

More and more, I had been pondering just how many had conspired with the Komizar besides the Chancellor and the Scholar. I'd been thinking about my brother's death and was sure it wasn't a chance encounter. What was a whole Vendan battalion doing so far from the border in the first place? They weren't marching on an outpost or kingdom, and as soon as my brother's company was dead, they turned around and went home. They were lying in wait, perhaps uncertain when the encounter would occur, but somehow they knew my brother's company was coming. Had word been sent ahead by someone in Morrighan? The slaughter was planned. Even when I met with the *chievdar* in the valley, he never expressed surprise at running into the platoon of men. Could the treachery in Morrighan have reached even into the ranks of the military?

A sudden hard gallop clipped the air. A soldier circled his horse around to my side. "Madam?" The word was stiff on his tongue as if he wasn't quite sure what to call me. He strained to keep the innuendo out of his tone. It was obvious that Rafe hadn't told the captain everything yet.

"Yes?"

"The king wishes for you to come ride at his side. We're almost there."

The king. This new reality rattled beneath my ribs. The coming days were going to be difficult for Rafe. Besides dealing with his grief, he'd be under as much scrutiny as I would be. This could change everything. Our plans. *My* plans. There was no way around it.

I glanced back at Kaden. "We'll talk more later."

He nodded, and I followed the soldier to the front of the caravan.

I LOOKED AT RAFE BUT COULDN'T IMAGINE HIM SITTING ON a throne. I could only see him on the back of a horse, a soldier, his hair sun-kissed and windblown, fire in his eyes, intimidation in his gaze, and a sword in his hand. That was the Rafe I knew. But he was more than that now. He was the ruler of a powerful kingdom, and no longer the heir apparent. His lids were heavy, as if all his lost days of sleep were finally overtaking him. No man, not even one as strong as Rafe, could go forever on handfuls of rest.

The captain rode on the other side of him, conferring with a soldier. I didn't know how Rafe had explained his long absence. I was certain most details of Terravin had been left out. What did a captain care about a tavern maid serving a farmer?

Rafe turned, knowing I was looking at him, and smiled. "Hot baths for both of us first thing."

Was it wrong for me to wish it could be a single hot bath for us both? A few blessed hours where we could forget that the rest of the world existed? After everything we'd been through, weren't we entitled to that much? I was tired of waiting for tomorrows, hopes, and maybes.

"There she is!" I heard Orrin call from somewhere ahead of us.

I looked and saw a structure rising on a gentle knoll in the distance. Two soldiers galloped ahead of our party to announce us. This was an outpost?

"That's Marabella?" I said to Rafe.

"Not what you were expecting?"

Not at all. I expected a sea of tents. Perhaps some wooden barricades. Maybe a fortification of sod. This was the Cam Lanteux, after all, and no permanent structures were allowed here. It wasn't just an understanding—it was part of a very old treaty.

Instead what I saw was a sprawling stone structure with gleaming white walls, lithe and graceful, spreading out like beautiful swan wings from a tall gate tower. As we got closer, I saw wagons and tents huddled in groups outside those walls. A city in its own right.

"What is all that?" I asked.

Rafe explained that the outside perimeter of the outpost served as a safe haven and stopping point for traders on their way to other kingdoms. Vagabonds also took refuge close to its walls, especially in winter, when the northern climes were too harsh. Here they could set out plots and grow winter vegetables. And there were those who came to ply their trade with the soldiers too, offering food, trinkets, and diversions of various kinds. It was an ever-changing city as merchants came and went.

The sun was still high, and the rising expanse of stone wall shone bright against the dark earth, reminding me of something magical from a child's story. The gate opened and people flooded through it—not all of them soldiers. More crowded the tower walls above, eager to get a look. The news had arrived, and likely none of them could quite believe it. The lost prince was found. Curious merchants from the nearby wagons walked closer to the gates to see what the fuss was all about. A line of soldiers kept them back so the road was clear for us to enter.

It seemed that if there was one thing I was destined for, it was to make underwhelming and filthy first impressions, whether it was the first time I stepped into Berdi's tavern, my entrance into Sanctum Hall—or today, meeting Rafe's countrymen for the first time.

I felt the stickiness of my neck anew, the grit behind my earlobes, the grime smearing my face, and wished I at least had a basin to wash up in. I smoothed back my hair, but my fingers only became tangled in knots.

"Lia," Rafe said, reaching out and returning my hand to my side, "we're home. We're safe. That's all that matters."

He licked his thumb and rubbed it across my chin, as if that made a difference, then smiled. "There. Perfect. Just the way you are."

"You smudged my dirt," I said, feigning irritation.

His eyes sparked with reassurance. I nodded. Yes. We were safe—and together. That was all that mattered.

Other than the rumble of hooves, it was silent as we approached. It was as if every breath was held, all unbelieving, certain that the soldier had made an error in his message, but then murmurs of recognition rose, and someone high on the tower wall yelled, "Bastards! It *is* you!"

Rafe smiled and Sven waved. I was startled at first, then realized that it was a greeting and not a jeer—soldier to soldier, not soldier to king. Jeb, Orrin, and Tavish returned calls from other comrades. I was surprised to see that there were women among the crowd. Finely dressed women. Their mouths hung half-open and their gazes rested on me—not their new king. Once we were through the gates, soldiers waiting to lead our horses away took our reins, and Rafe helped me down. My injured leg was stiff and with my first step, I stumbled. Rafe caught me, keeping his arm around my waist. His attentions didn't go unnoticed, and there was a lull in the greetings. Certainly the soldiers who rode ahead with a hurried message of the prince's return hadn't included details of a girl in the convoy.

A tall, trim man made his way through the crowd, and everyone quickly moved aside for him. His stride was deliberate, and his bare scalp gleamed in the sun. One of his shoulders held the distinction of a wide gold braid. He stopped in front of Rafe and shook his head, his chin dimpling like an orange, and then just as the captain had when we were out on the plain, he dropped to one knee and said loudly so everyone would hear, "Your Majesty King Jaxon Tyrus Rafferty of Dalbreck. Greet your sovereign."

There was a collective hush. A few immediately dropped to their knee as well, more officers echoing *King Jaxon*, but the majority of soldiers hesitated, shocked by the news. It had been a secret—the old king was dead. Slowly the realization took root, and the crowd rippled to their knees.

Rafe acknowledged them with a simple nod, but it was

obvious to me that, beyond anything, he wished he could forgo these formalities. While he honored tradition and protocol more than I did, right now he was only a very tired young man in need of rest, soap, and a decent meal.

The officer stood and studied Rafe for a moment, then reached out and gave him a vigorous embrace, not caring that Rafe's filthy clothes were soiling his fresh tunic and crisp shirt.

"I'm sorry, boy," he said softly. "I loved your parents." He let go and held him at arm's length. "But blessed devils, soldier, your timing stinks. Where the hell have you been?"

Rafe briefly closed his eyes, his weariness returned. He was king and didn't have to explain anything, but he was a soldier first, loyal to his fellow soldiers. "The captain can answer some of your questions. First we need—"

"Of course," the man said, realizing his error, and turned to a soldier at his side. "Our king and his officers need baths and fresh clothes. And quarters prepared! And—" His eyes fell on me, perhaps noting for the first time that I was a female. "And . . ." He fumbled uncertainly.

"Colonel Bodeen," Rafe interjected, "this was the cause of my absence." He looked at the crowd, addressing not just the colonel, but them as well. "A worthy absence," he added with a hint of sternness. He lifted his hand toward me. "May I present Princess Arabella, the First Daughter of the House of Morrighan."

Every eye turned to me. I felt as naked as a peeled grape. There was stifled laughter from a few young soldiers, but then they realized Rafe was serious. Their smiles vanished. Captain

Azia gawked at me, his face flushing with color, perhaps recalling every vulgar word he'd said about Morrighan.

Colonel Bodeen's mouth quirked awkwardly to the side. "And she is . . . your prisoner?"

Considering the circumstances, the current animosity between our kingdoms, and my wretched appearance, it wasn't an unlikely conclusion.

Orrin snorted.

Sven coughed.

"No, Colonel," Rafe answered. "Princess Arabella is your future queen."

CHAPTER EIGHTEEN

A LOW GROWL ROLLED FROM GRIZ. RAFE HAD USURPED HIS claim. I knew, as far as Griz was concerned, that once he had raised my hand to the clans at the Sanctum, I was queen of one kingdom and one kingdom only.

I shot him a sharp glance, and he clutched his side, wincing as if that had been the source of his untimely noise. But Griz's growl was little compared to the pall of silence that followed. The scrutiny was smothering.

Right now it seemed that being Vendan within these out-post walls was preferable to being the impudent royal who had abandoned their precious prince at the altar.

I squared my shoulders and lifted my chin, though it surely only exposed more rings of dirt around my neck. I suddenly ached with the trying, ached for a way of belonging that was always out of my reach, ached for Pauline, and Berdi, and Gwyneth to be by my side, to hold me, a tight circle of arms that were invincible. Ached for a hundred things lost and gone, things I could never get back, including Aster, who had believed in me unconditionally. It was an ache so deep I wanted to bleed into the ground and disappear.

But the trying never ended. I stiffened my spine and set my jaw in good royal form. I wedged my voice into something firm and even, and I heard my mother speaking, though it was my lips that moved. "I'm sure you all have a lot of questions, which I hope we can answer later once we've cleaned up a bit."

A thin, whittled woman with severe cheekbones stepped forward, elbowing the colonel aside. Her raven hair was streaked with silver and pulled back in an unforgiving bun. She addressed Rafe. "Quarters will be prepared for Her Highness as well. In the meantime, she can retire to my chamber, and the other ladies and I will attend her needs."

She eyed me sideways, her thin lips drawn in a tight, tawny line.

I didn't want to go. I'd rather have cleaned up at the soldiers' showers and borrowed another pair of trousers, but Rafe thanked her, and I was escorted away with the wave of a hand.

As I left, I heard Rafe order that the guards posted at the gate be doubled, and rotations at the watchtowers shortened so soldiers were always fresh. He didn't say why, but I knew it was because he feared more Rahtan could still be out there. After so many weeks of looking over our shoulders, I wondered if we could ever stop watching. Would peace ever be ours again?

Deliberate efforts were made to step back and avoid touching me. Because of my filth or position? I wasn't sure, but as I followed this thin, angled woman, the crowd parted, leaving me wide berth. The woman identified herself as Madam Rathbone. I looked back over my shoulder, but the crowd had already seamed back together and Rafe was gone from my view.

I WAS OFFERED A STOOL IN MADAM RATHBONE'S SITTING room while we waited for a bath to be drawn. Two other ladies who had introduced themselves as Vilah and Adeline had disappeared into their own quarters, and began returning with assorted clothes, trying to find something suitable for me to wear. It was quiet and awkward as they shuffled around me, laying garments over chairs and tables, eyeing them for size rather than holding them up to me. That would require more intimacy, and I was still filthy. Their stares were too cautious, and I was too tired to try to make small talk.

Madam Rathbone sat across from me on a wide tufted settee. She hadn't taken her eyes off me. "You have blood on you," she finally said.

"By the gods, she has blood *all* over her!" Adeline snapped.

Vilah, who was probably only a few years older than me, asked, "What in the heavens did they do to her?"

I stared down at my arms and my blood-soaked chest, then reached up and felt the crackling roughness of dried blood on my face. So much Vendan blood. I closed my eyes. All I could think of was Aster. The blood all seemed to be hers.

"Are you injured, child?"

I looked up at Madam Rathbone. There was a tenderness in her voice that caught me off guard, and a painful lump lodged in my throat.

"Yes, but not recently. This is someone else's blood."

The three women exchanged glances, and Madam Rathbone muttered a long string of hot curses. She noted the slight drop of my jaw, and her brows rose. "Certainly traveling with soldiers you've heard far worse."

No. Not really. I hadn't heard many of those words since my days playing cards in back rooms with my brothers.

She wrinkled her nose. "Let's get all *this* off of you," she said. "The bath should be ready by now." She led me into a connecting room. This was apparently an officer's bungalow, small and squarely laid out, a sitting room, sleeping chamber, and a grooming chamber. The walls were smooth white stucco, elegantly adorned with tapestries. A soldier set a last bucket of steaming rinse water next to the copper tub and quickly exited through another door. Madam Rathbone dropped a bar across it.

"We can help you bathe or leave you in privacy. Which would you prefer?"

I stared at her, not sure myself what I wanted.

"We'll stay," she said.

I CRIED. I COULDN'T EXPLAIN IT. IT WAS NOT ME. BUT I WAS many things now that I had never been before. Slow tears rolled down my face as they peeled off clothes, as they unlaced my boots and pulled them from my feet, as they sponged my neck and soaped my hair. As every last bit of blood on my skin was washed into the water.

You're exhausted. That is all, I told myself. But it was like a vein had been opened that refused to clot. Even when I shut my eyes trying to stop the flow, the saltiness trickled past my lids in a slow languid line, finding the corner of my mouth, then spread across my lips.

"Drink this," Madam Rathbone said, and she set a large goblet of wine on a table next to the bath. I sipped as ordered and laid my head back on the elongated copper rim of the tub, staring up at the timbered ceiling. The women took handfuls of citrus crystals and rubbed them into my skin, buffing it clean, polishing away the grime, the scent, and the misery of where I had been. They worked longer on my hands and feet, and more gently around my stitched wounds. Another sip, and circles of numbing warmness spiraled to my fingertips, thinning my muscles, loosening my neck, pulling on my lids until they slipped closed.

Vilah held the goblet to my lips again. "Sip," she said softly. Familiarity, a field of vines, a silky sky, skins staining my fingers, velvet . . . home.

"Morrighan," I whispered.

Yes.

The caravans bring it.

The best.

Colonel Bodeen won't miss one bottle.

Much.

I didn't remember falling asleep, and only vaguely remembered standing with their assistance to rinse. I lay on thick soft blankets, where they worked on me further, massaging oils into my skin. Madam Rathbone examined the stitched scars on my thigh and back.

"Arrows," I explained. "Tavish dug them out." ·

Adeline sucked in air between her teeth.

I heard the low cluck of their voices.

Madam Rathbone rubbed a buttery balm into the scars, saying it would aid their healing. The scent of vanilla floated in the air.

A deep purple bruise had bloomed on my hip where Ulrix had slammed me onto the pommel of his horse. Their fingers were gentle, working around it. I felt myself slipping again, voices around me growing distant.

"And this?" Vilah asked, her fingertips grazing the tattoo on my shoulder.

It was no longer my wedding kavah. Maybe it never had been. I heard Effiera describing the promise of Venda . . . *the claw, quick and fierce; the vine, slow and steady; both equally strong.*

"It is . . ."

The claim of a mad queen.

The one who was weak,
The one who was hunted . . .
The one named in secret.

"Their hope." The words were so thin and gauzy on my lips I wasn't even sure I had said them aloud.

I WOKE TO WHISPERS FROM THE SITTING ROOM.

Maybe this and this together?

No, something less intricate, I think.

Do you think she knows?

Not likely.

I never thought it was right.

Do you think the prince knew?

He knew.

The fools.

Makes little difference now. Did you see the way he looked at her?

And his tone. You don't want to be on the wrong side of that.

Especially now that he's king.

And his eyes. They can cut a man down.

Just like his father.

Doesn't mean they still couldn't use her as leverage.

No, I'd say not. Not anymore, after all that's happened.

What about this one?

I think this fabric best.

And with this sash.

I sat upright, pulling the blankets around me. How long had I been sleeping? I looked at the empty goblet beside the table and then at my hands. Soft. A glow to them that hadn't been there since I left Civica months ago. My nails were trimmed and buffed to a natural shine. Why did they do this for me? Or maybe it was only for their king—the one who—what was it they said? His eyes cut through them?

I yawned, trying to shake the fogginess of sleep away, and stepped over to the window. The sun was fading. I had slept for a few hours at least. A goldish pink haze was cast over the towering white wall of the outpost. I could view only a small slice of this soldier city, but the calm of twilight gave it a serene glow. Atop the wall I saw a soldier walking the length, but even that had a strange elegance about it that seemed out of place. Golden light caught the shine of his buttons and glimmered on his neatly trimmed belt and baldrick. Everything here seemed fresh and cleanly laid out, even this whitewashed bungalow. Though it was far from the actual border, this was the world of Dalbreck, and it looked nothing like Morrighan. It *felt* different from Morrighan. Order permeated the air, and everything Rafe and I had done had gone against that order.

I wondered where he was. Had he finally gotten some rest too? Or was he meeting with Colonel Bodeen and hearing the circumstances of his parents' deaths? Would his comrades forgive him for his absence? Would they forgive me?

"You're awake."

I spun, clutching the blanket close to my chest. Madam Rathbone stood in the doorway.

"The prince—I mean, the *king*—was by earlier to check on you."

My heart leapt. "Does he need—"

The women flooded into the room, assuring me he had no immediate needs, and they proceeded to help me dress. Madam Rathbone sat me down at her dressing table, and Adeline brushed out my tangles, her fingers moving with swift assurance, threading through my hair as effortlessly as an accomplished harpist, plucking multiple strands at once, braiding it with a rhythm as easy as a whistled tune, while at the same time weaving it with a sparkling gold thread.

When she was finished, Vilah lifted a loose dress over my head, something fine and flowing and as creamy as warm summer wind. Now I knew what I'd heard about Dalbreck and their love affair with fine fabrics and clothing was true. Next came a soft leather vest that laced up the back, embossed with a gold filigree design. It was more of a symbolic gesture of a breastplate, for it covered little of my breasts. Next Madam Rathbone tied a simple black satin sash low on my hips so it flowed almost to the floor. It all seemed far too elegant for an outpost, and I imagined that if the gods wore any clothes at all, they looked something like this.

I thought they were done, and I was about to thank them and excuse myself so I could find Rafe, but they weren't ready to let me go. They moved on to jewelry. Adeline slipped an intricate lacy ring on my finger that had tiny chains on one end connecting it to a bracelet she fastened around my wrist. Vilah dabbed perfume on my wrists, then Madam Rathbone fastened a shimmering gold chain-mail belt over the black sash and—maybe most surprising of all—slipped a sharp dagger into its sheath. Last came a gold pauldron that flared out on my shoulder like a wing. Every touch was beautiful, but clearly the armor was more decorative than utilitarian. It heralded a kingdom whose history was built on strength and battle. Perhaps it was a kingdom that never forgot it began when a prince was thrown out of his homeland.

They were determined that no one would question their strength again.

But all this for dinner at an outpost? I didn't mention the extravagance, fearing I might sound ungrateful, but Madam Rathbone was perceptive and said, "Colonel Bodeen sets a fine table. You'll see."

I looked at their efforts in the mirror. I hardly recognized myself. This still seemed to be far more than just making me presentable for a dinner party—no matter how fine a meal.

"I don't understand," I said. "I rode in prepared to be met with animosity, and instead you've shown me compassion. I'm the princess who left your prince at the altar. None of you harbor resentment toward me?"

Vilah and Adeline averted their gazes as if uncomfortable with my question. Madam Rathbone frowned.

"We did. And certainly a few others still do, but . . ." She turned to Vilah and Adeline. "Ladies, why don't you go and dress for dinner too. Her Highness and I will be along."

When Adeline had shut the door behind them, Madam Rathbone looked at me and sighed. "For me it was a small omission of kindness that had accrued interest, I suppose."

I looked at her, confused.

"I met your mother once many years ago. You look so much like her."

"You've been to Morrighan?"

She shook her head. "No. It was before she ever arrived there. I was a maid working at an inn in Cortenai, and she was nobility from Gastineux on her way to marry the king of Morrighan."

I sat down on the edge of the bed. I knew so little about that journey. My mother never spoke about it.

Madam Rathbone crossed the room, replacing the stopper on the perfume. She continued to put the finishing touches on her own attire as she spoke. "I was twenty-two at the time, and the inn was in near chaos with the arrival of the Lady Regheena. She stayed only one night, but the innkeeper sent me to her room with a crock of sweetened warm milk to help her sleep."

She looked in the mirror, pulling her bun loose and brushing her long hair. Her severe features softened, and her eyes narrowed as if she was seeing my mother all over again. "I was nervous to enter her chamber, but eager to see her too. I'd never seen nobility before, much less the future queen of the most powerful kingdom in the land. But instead of finding a regal jeweled and crowned woman, I found only a girl, younger than I was, road weary and terrified. Of course, she didn't say she was frightened, and she forced a smile, but I saw the terror in her eyes and the way her fingers were tightly woven in her lap. She thanked me for the milk, and I thought to say something reassuring or cheerful, or even reach out and squeeze her hand. I stood there for the longest time, and she waited expectantly, her eyes fixed on me as if she desperately wished me to stay, but I didn't want to overstep my bounds, and in the end, I only curtsied and left the room."

Madam Rathbone pursed her lips in thought, then turned, removing a short fur cloak from her wardrobe. She draped it over my shoulders. "I tried not to think about it, but that short exchange haunted me long after she was gone. I thought of a dozen things I could have said but didn't. Simple things that might have eased her journey. Things I'd want someone to say to me. But that day and chance were gone, and I couldn't get them back. I vowed I'd never worry about overstepping bounds and never let unsaid words plague me again."

Ironically, that was exactly what gnawed at me—all the words my mother never said. All the things she had kept from me. Things that might have eased my journey. When I got back to Morrighan, one way or another, there would be no more hidden words between us.

CHAPTER NINETEEN

PAULINE

IT WAS THE FIRST TIME I HAD EVER BROKEN THE SACRAMENTS. I prayed the gods would understand as every First Daughter was called to come forward and light a red glass lantern and place it at the base of the memorial stone. Then they sang the Remembrance of the Dead for the departed prince and his fellow soldiers—the same prayer I had sung for Mikael, day after day back in Terravin. Had they all been wasted prayers, since Mikael wasn't really dead?

My nails dug into the flesh of my palm. I wasn't even certain who I should be angry with. The gods? Lia? Mikael? Or the fact that I once held an honored position in the queen's court and now I was little more than a fugitive sneaking in the shadows of a beech tree, unable to show my face to anyone, or even step forward and lift my voice to the gods? I had fallen lower than I ever thought possible.

When the last prayer was sung and the priests dismissed the First Daughters to return to their families, the crowds began dwindling. I didn't expect to see my aunt there—she would stay by the queen's side—but I looked for her just the same. I'd been afraid to ask Bryn or Regan about her. She was a stickler for rules and had drilled them into me from the time I came to live with her at the citadelle. I didn't even want to ponder how she had reacted to my complete breach of protocol or my new status as treasonous accomplice. I saw Bryn and Regan speaking with one veiled widow, then another, until finally they worked their way toward us, carefully, so no one would suspect us of being anything but mourners.

They were silent at first, shooting questioning glances at Berdi.

"You can speak freely," I told them. "Berdi's trustworthy. She loves Lia as much as we do and is here to help."

Regan continued to eye her suspiciously. "And she keeps secrets well?"

"Without question," Gwyneth said.

Berdi squinted at Regan, her head tilting to the side as she scrutinized him. "The question is, can we trust *you*?"

Regan offered her a weary smile and a slight bow. "Forgive me. These last several days have been difficult."

Berdi gave him a reassuring nod. "I understand. My condolences on the loss of your brother. Lia spoke highly of him."

Bryn swallowed hard, and Regan nodded. They both seemed lost without their brother and sister.

"Were you able to speak with your parents about Lia?" I asked.

"Not before the news came about Walther," Bryn answered. "And then Father fell ill. Between Walther and Father, our mother is devastated. She doesn't leave her room except to tend Father, but the physician says there's nothing she can do, and asked her to stay away. He says her visits only agitate him."

Berdi asked about the king's health and Bryn said he was about the same, weak but stable. The physician said it was his heart, and with rest he would recover.

"You said you had news to share?" Gwyneth asked.

Bryn sighed and brushed his dark locks from his forehead. "The soldier who brought the news of Lia's betrayal is dead."

I gasped. "I heard he wasn't injured. Only exhausted. How could this happen?"

"We don't know for sure. We asked a hundred questions. All the physician said was that it was a seizure probably brought on by dehydration," Regan answered.

"Dehydration?" Gwyneth mused. "He must have crossed a dozen streams and rivers to get here."

"I know," Regan said. "But he died before anyone could question him other than the Chancellor."

Berdi's eyes narrowed. "You think they lied about what the soldier told them?"

"What's more important," Gwyneth added, "is you think they had something to do with his death."

Regan rubbed the side of his face, frustration evident in his eyes. "We're not saying that. We're just saying that a lot is happening, and fast, and there seem to be no answers for our questions. You need to be cautious until we get back."

"Back?"

"That's the other thing we need to tell you. We're being dispatched to the City of Sacraments next week, and after we finish up there, my squad is going on to Gitos while Bryn's goes to Cortenai. We'll make stops at cities along the way."

"You're *both* leaving?" I said a bit too loudly, and Gwyneth cleared her throat as a warning reminder. I lowered my voice. "How is that possible with Walther dead and your father ill? You're the crown prince now, and Bryn's next in line. You can't leave Civica. Protocol requires at least one of you—"

Bryn reached out and squeezed my hands. "These are hard times, Pauline. The foundations of Morrighan are shaken. The Lesser Kingdoms have seen the falling-out between us and Dalbreck; the crown prince has been butchered along with the sons of great nobles and lords; my father is ill, and my sister is presumed to have joined forces with the enemy. The Watch Captain says it's not a time to hunker down and cower but to show our strength and confidence. It was decided by the cabinet. Regan and I questioned the order too, but my father confirmed this is what he wanted."

"You spoke to him yourself?" Berdi asked.

Regan and Bryn looked at each other briefly, something unspoken passing between them. "Yes," Regan answered. "He nodded affirmation when we questioned him on the order."

"He's not well!" Gwyneth said with disbelief. "He wasn't thinking clearly. That will leave the throne at risk if he should take a turn for the worse."

"The physician assured us it's safe for us to leave, and as the Watch Captain said, nothing can bolster the confidence of the troops and neighboring kingdoms like the appearance of the king's sons."

I looked at Bryn and Regan, whose expressions were sending mixed messages. They were torn. This wasn't just about restoring confidence. "It's to prove that you're still loyal to the crown, even if your sister isn't."

Regan nodded. "A divided family instills fear and anarchy. That's the last thing we need right now."

And there had been fear. In some ways their mission made sense, but it still felt wrong. I saw the worry in their eyes.

"You both still believe in Lia, don't you?"

Bryn's eyes softened. "You don't need to ask, Pauline. We love our sister, and we know her. Please don't worry. Trust us on this."

There was something about the way he said it. Gwyenth noticed too. She eyed them suspiciously. "There's something you're not telling us."

"No," Regan said firmly. "Nothing else." He looked down at my belly, barely disguised now by my loose cloak. "Promise us you'll lie low. Stay away from the citadelle. We'll return as soon as we can."

Berdi, Gwyneth, and I exchanged glances, then nodded.

"Good," Bryn said. "We'll walk to the gate with you."

The graveyard was nearly empty. Only a few mourners still lingered. The rest had returned to their homes to prepare for eventide remembrances. One young man, dressed in full warrior armor with his weapons at his sides, remained on his knees before the memorial stone, his head bent, every angle of his body bearing a deep agony.

"Who is that?" I asked.

"Andrés, the Viceregent's son," Regan answered. "He's the only one from Walther's platoon who's still alive. He was sick with fever when they rode out and couldn't go with them. He's come here every day since the stone was placed to light a candle. The Viceregent says Andrés is racked with guilt for not being there with his fellow soldiers."

"So that he could die too?"

Bryn shook his head. "So that maybe they all might have lived."

We stared at him, probably each of us wondering the same thing—could one more soldier really have made a difference?

When the brothers left, I told Gwyneth and Berdi to wait for me, that I'd be right back. I understood Andrés's guilt, the anguish of reliving moments and wondering what could have been done differently. In those weeks after Lia disappeared, I relived that morning of Kaden dragging me into the brush a hundred times, thinking I should have grabbed his knife, kicked him, done something that could have changed everything—but instead I had only trembled, frozen with terror as he pressed his face close to mine and threatened to kill us. If I had a second chance, I would do it all so differently.

Andrés was still kneeling at the memorial stone when I returned. Maybe I could pull two purposes from this moment that would help us both. If he loved the platoon and Walther so deeply, he also knew how close Walther and Lia were. He may have even been one of those who helped Walther plant false leads when Lia and I ran. When I approached him, he looked up, searching the shadows of my hood.

"They were good men," I said.

He swallowed and nodded agreement.

"No one thought so more than Lia. I'm sure she never would have betrayed them."

I watched him closely to see if he recoiled at her name. He didn't.

"Lia," he said thoughtfully, as if reminiscing. "Only her brothers called her by that name. You knew her well?"

"No," I said, realizing my error. "But I met Prince Walther once, and he spoke fondly of her. He told me at great length about their devotion to each other."

He nodded. "Yes, all the royal siblings were close. I always envied them that. My only brother died when I was small, and my half brother—" He shook his head. "It doesn't matter."

He looked up at me, peering closer, as if trying to get a better glimpse. "I don't think I caught your name. What may I call you?"

I searched quickly for a name, and my mother's came to mind. "Marisol," I answered. "My father has a candlery in the next hamlet. I came to pay my respects and heard some other mourners mention you were the lone survivor. I hope I haven't intruded. I wished only to offer you comfort. This was the work of ruthless barbarians and no one else. There was nothing you could have done."

He reached out and boldly squeezed my hand. "So others have told me too, including my father. I'm trying to believe it." I was rewarded when some of the agony in his expression lifted.

"I will keep them—and you—in my remembrances," I promised. I slipped my hand free and kissed two fingers, lifting them to the heavens before I turned and walked away.

"Thank you, Marisol," he called after me. "I hope I'll see you again."

You most definitely will, Andrés.

Gwyneth's eyes flashed with anger when I rejoined her. "Speaking with the Viceregent's son? How is *that* lying low?"

I answered her with a smug smile. "Have some faith in me, Gwyneth. Aren't you the one who said I had to stop playing nice girl? He may know something that we'll find helpful. Maybe now I'm the one who's become the spy."

CHAPTER TWENTY

RAFE

I WALKED INTO THE SURGEON'S BUNGALOW.

Tavish, Jeb, Griz, and Kaden were all laid out on cots being treated. Kaden had hidden the fact that he'd been wounded as well—a gash on his lower back. A small wound but still in need of stitches. Orrin and Sven sat in chairs across from them, their feet propped up on the patients' cots.

As soon as they caught sight of me, Tavish and Orrin let out insulting whistles like I was a swaggering dandy. Jeb approved of my transformation.

"And here we were all getting used to your ugly face," Sven said.

"It's called a bath and a shave. You should try it sometime."

Jeb's shoulder was slathered with ointment and compresses. The surgeon told me he had torn muscles and would have to keep his shoulder immobile for several weeks. No riding, no duty. Bed rest for three days. Jeb made faces behind the surgeon's back, mouthing *no*.

I shrugged as if I couldn't override the surgeon's orders, and Jeb scowled.

A few days' rest was prescribed for Griz too, but Tavish and Kaden had minor wounds that would only bring them discomfort for a day or so and required no restricted duty. The surgeon had somehow missed the news that Kaden wasn't one of ours and assumed he was another soldier.

"Those two can go shower," the surgeon said. "I'll bandage them after they've cleaned up." He went back to check on Griz.

Kaden was in the rear of the bungalow in dim light, but as he reached for his shirt, he stepped into the light from the window and I saw his back and the short line of black thread where the surgeon had stitched him. Then I saw the scars. Deep ones. He'd been whipped.

He turned and saw me staring.

His chest was equally scarred.

He paused, and then slipped his shirt on as if it was of no matter.

"Old injuries?" I asked.

"Yes. Old."

How old? I wondered, but his clipped reply made it clear he didn't want to elaborate. He was about my age, so old injuries could mean he'd been little more than a child when he acquired them. I remembered Lia mumbling that he was once Morrighese, but she was feverish and half asleep when she'd said it, and I thought the possibility was unlikely. Still, if he had been beaten that severely by Vendans, I couldn't understand how he had remained so loyal to them. He finished buttoning his shirt.

"I have some soldiers outside who will show you where the showers are. They'll give you some fresh clothes too."

"Guards, you mean?"

I couldn't let him walk around freely, not only because I still didn't trust him completely, but for his own protection as well. News of the platoon's slaughter had spread through camp. Any kind of Vendan, even one the king said could be moderately trusted, was not welcome here.

"Let's call them escorts," I answered. "You remember that word, don't you? I promise you, your escorts will be far more congenial than Ulrix and his pack of brutes were with me."

He eyed his belt and sword still lying on a table.

"And you'll have to leave those behind."

"I saved your royal ass today."

"And I'm saving your Vendan one right now."

NORMALLY WHEN I HAD BEEN ASSIGNED TO MARABELLA, I had slept in the barracks with the rest of the soldiers, but the colonel said it wasn't fitting now that I was king. *You have to start acting the role*, he insisted, and Sven concurred. They ordered a tent set up for me. Tents were reserved for visiting ambassadors and dignitaries who used the outpost as a stopping point. They were larger, more extravagant, and certainly more private than the crowded barracks that housed the soldiers.

I had ordered one set up for Lia as well, and let myself inside her tent to make sure everything was in order. A thick floral carpet had been rolled out across the floor, and her bed was fully made with blankets, furs, and a surplus of pillows. A round stove was stocked with fuel and ready to go, and an oil chandelier was hung for light.

And flowers. A small vase overflowed with some kind of purple flower. The colonel must have sent a whole squad out to scour the merchant wagons for them. A colorful pitcher of water was on a lace-covered table, along with a crock of shortbread next to it. I popped one into my mouth and replaced the lid. No detail had been overlooked. Her tent was far better appointed than mine. Of course the colonel had known I would check to make sure she was comfortable.

I spotted her saddlebag on the floor next to her bed. I'd told the stable hand to bring it as soon as her tent was ready. It, too, was stained with blood. Maybe that was why he'd left it on the floor. I emptied the contents onto the bedside table so I could take it with me to be cleaned. I wanted to erase every reminder of the day that was behind us.

I sat on her bed and thumbed through one of the books from her bag. It was one she had told me about, the Song of Venda. The one that mentioned the name Jezelia. I lay back and sank into the soft mattress, looking at words that made no sense to me. How could she be certain of what they said? She wasn't a scholar.

I remembered her expression back in the Sanctum when she tried to explain the importance of it to me.

Maybe it isn't chance that I'm here.

A chill had crept up my neck when she said those words. I'd hated the way Venda—woman or kingdom—was playing on her fears, but I remembered the crowds too, and the way they grew each day. There was something unnatural about it, something that didn't feel right to me, something that even the Komizar couldn't control.

I laid the book aside. It was behind us now. The Sanctum, Venda, everything. Including Griz's ridiculous notion of her being his queen. We'd be on our way to Dalbreck soon. I cursed the fact that we couldn't leave right away. The colonel couldn't spare an escort large enough to please Sven, but he said he expected a rotation of troops to arrive in a few days and we could leave safely with the departing troops. In the meantime, he'd ordered the falconer to send a swift trio of Valsprey to Falworth with news of my safety and my imminent return.

He said that would also give him time to update me on matters at court. *Prepare me*—those were the warning words I saw in his eyes—even if he didn't say them. My return to court was not going to be easy. I knew that. I was still trying to absorb the knowledge that my worst fears had been realized. Both my mother and father were dead, and they had died not knowing the fate of their only son. Guilt riddled through me. *But they knew I loved them. They knew that much.*

We agreed to wait until tomorrow after I was rested to discuss the details of my parents' deaths and everything that had transpired since. The cabinet would be furious when they learned where I had been and the risks I had taken. It was going to take some work to regain their confidences.

But Lia was alive, and I would do it all again if I had to. Sven and the others understood. Once the cabinet met her, they would understand too.

CHAPTER TWENTY-ONE

KADEN

I FOLLOWED THE GUARDS AS IF I DIDN'T KNOW WHERE I WAS going, but I remembered every inch of the Marabella outpost—especially where the privies and showers were. As we walked past the gate that led to the paddocks, I saw they had added another watchtower to the back paddock wall. It had been their only blind spot. A very unlikely one because of the steep, rocky access and the river below, but a blind spot nonetheless, and it had allowed me to gain entrance.

Lia had asked me once how many people I had killed. Too many to remember them all, but this one I remembered.

There.

I eyed the privy on the end. A fitting place for him to die.

"Hold up," Tavish said.

I stopped while the guards went into a supply hut.

I was sure they wouldn't be offering me a shower and fresh clothes if they knew I had slit the throat of one of their commanders. That was two years ago. I couldn't remember exactly what his sins had been, just that many Vendans had died under his command and that was reason enough for the Komizar to send me.

This is for Eben, I had told him before I slashed the blade, though I didn't know if he had anything to do with killing Eben's parents. Now I wished I knew. I wished I could remember all the reasons.

That was a lifetime ago, Kaden. We were both different people then.

"Something wrong?" Tavish asked.

The soldiers had returned with supplies and were waiting for me to follow.

"No," I answered. "Nothing's wrong."

We continued on to the showers, and I was grateful that the water was warm. It wasn't like the vagabond hot springs that had practically boiled the grime away, but it was easier on sore muscles than the ice water of the Sanctum. It felt good to wash off the blood of men who had once been my comrades, those I had ridden with only months ago—yet today I had helped kill them.

"Looks like Griz is going to be all right."

I kept my head under the water, pretending I didn't hear Tavish. Was he fishing for compliments? Just because he had stitched Griz up out in the wilderness?

When I turned to give him a cool reply, he was scrubbing under his arms and studying me. I didn't like Rafe or his deceptive friends, but the truth was, Tavish had saved Griz's life, and I did owe him thanks. Griz was still my comrade—maybe my only one.

"You're skilled with a needle," I offered.

"Only out of necessity," he answered, turning off the water. "No one else wants the job." He toweled off and began to get dressed. "Funny, Rafe won't shove a tiny piece of steel into someone's cheek, but he can bring down three men with the single swing of his sword without even breaking a sweat. But you already know that, don't you?"

A not-so-subtle warning. I remembered him watching my exchange with Rafe back in the surgeon's barracks. He obviously didn't appreciate my lack of regal respect.

"He's not my king. I won't be bending my knee to him like the rest of you."

"He's not a bad fellow if you give him a chance."

"I'd expect you to say something like that, but I'm not here for chances or to be someone's friend. I'm here for Lia."

"Then you're here for the wrong reason, Assassin." He tightened his belt and adjusted his scabbard. His eyes were hot black pools. "One other word of advice—be cautious when you use the privies. Especially late at night. I've heard they can be dangerous. Surprising, isn't it?" He turned and left, ordering the guards outside to wait until I was done.

He had been studying me more closely than I thought. It was only a simple glance at the privy, but he'd seen it and put it together. No doubt he'd be keeping a diligent eye on me—or making sure someone else did. He was probably already telling Rafe about his suspicions.

Had any of them noted that I had fought on *their* side today?

I continued to shower, in no hurry to join back up with the guards who waited for me. I wondered when and if I would see Lia again. Rafe wouldn't make it easy, especially now that he was—

I shoved my head back under the water. I hadn't even gotten used to the idea of him being a prince, and now he was a blazing king. I sputtered water out and scrubbed my chest. Did Lia really think he would traipse behind her all the way to—

I turned off the water.

He won't go to Morrighan.

But that won't stop her.

Something warm slivered into me.

I felt hope again.

He didn't know her like I did.

There were a lot of things he didn't know.

There was even the possibility that Lia was using him the way she had used me.

That same thought tumbled into another.

There were also things she didn't know about him, and maybe it was time she found out.

CHAPTER TWENTY-TWO

NIGHT FELL EARLY, AND I HEARD A DISTANT HUM. A SONG? Was it possible their eventide passed here with remembrances of the girl Morrighan too? It didn't seem likely, and yet we had all sprung from the same beginnings. How far had those beginnings diverged? The night tugged at me, a quiet pull I wanted to give in to, yet the golden lit windows of the officer's dining room lay ahead.

I followed Madam Rathbone up the steps of a large wooden structure with a wide veranda all the way around it.

"Wait," I said, grabbing her arm. "I need a moment."

A furrow lined her brow. "There's nothing to be afraid of."

"I know," I said, slightly breathless. "I'll be right in. Please."

She left and I turned, bracing myself against the railing.

I had always faced others' expectations, usually with little patience, snapping at the cabinet who pressured me in one way or another, but now I had to deal with another kind of expectation that I didn't fully understand. It was mired in complications, and I wasn't sure how to navigate them. *Your future queen.* When I walked through the door of the dining room, that was what they would see. I had told Kaden that I would somehow make it all work, but I knew I couldn't. It was impossible. Someone always came out on the losing end. I didn't want it to be me and Rafe.

I looked to the western sky and its constellations: Aster's Diamonds, God's Goblet, and Dragon's Tail. The stars that hovered over Morrighan. I kissed my fingers and lifted them to the heavens, to home, to those I had left behind, to everyone I loved, including the dead. *"Enade meunter ijotande,"* I whispered, then turned and pushed open the door of the dining room.

Rafe was the first person I saw, and I secretly thanked the gods, because it made my heart weightless, soaring somewhere high and free. He stood when he saw me, and the look in his eyes made me grateful for Madam Rathbone's, Adeline's, and Vilah's efforts. They had chosen well. His gaze made my heart settle back down, now warm and full in my chest.

I looked past officers, wives, and whoever else was there, to where he stood at the end of the long dining room table, mesmerized. It was the first time I had ever seen Rafe dressed in his own kingdom's clothing. It was strangely unnerving, a confirmation of who he really was. He wore a deep blue officer's tunic over a loose black shirt, and a dark leather baldrick embossed with

Dalbreck's crest crossed his chest. His hair had been trimmed, and his face gleamed with a close shave.

I sensed heads turning, but I kept my eyes locked on Rafe, and my feet glided over the floor to his side. This was it. I had no understanding of Dalbreck's formal customs. The Royal Scholar had tried to school me in the most basic of greetings, but I had skipped his lessons. Rafe held his hand out to me, and when I took it, I was shocked that he pulled me close and kissed me in front of everyone. A long, scandalous kiss. I felt color rush to my cheeks. If this was a custom, I liked it.

When I turned to face the rest of the guests, it was quite apparent this sort of greeting was not standard protocol. Some of the ladies had color on their cheeks too, and Sven's hand rested over his mouth as if he was trying to conceal a frown.

"My compliments and gratitude, Madam Rathbone," Rafe said, "for taking such good care of the princess." He unclasped the fur cape around my shoulders and handed it to a servant. I sat in a chair next to him, and that was when I took in exactly who was present. Sven, Tavish, and Orrin were all dressed in the deep Dalbretch blues as well, their appearances transformed with a razor, soap, and crisply pressed clothes—officers in the powerful army that Sven had told me the history of so proudly. Sven, like Colonel Bodeen, who sat at the opposite end, wore a gold braid on his shoulder too. There was nothing to distinguish Rafe and his position, but they certainly didn't keep the trimmings of a king on hand at an outpost.

Colonel Bodeen jumped in with introductions. Greetings were cordial but reserved, and then servants brought in the first of many courses served on small white porcelain plates—warm goat cheese balls rolled in herbs; finger-size rolls of chopped meat wrapped in thin strips of smoked pork; fried flat breads shaped into bite-size bowls and filled with warm spiced beans. Each course was served on a fresh plate, and we hadn't even gotten to the main course yet. *You'll see.*

Yes, I saw, though I was sure Colonel Bodeen was setting a more extravagant table tonight, to honor not only their returned comrades, but the king they had thought was lost. Jeb's absence was due to the physician's orders for rest. No one else seemed to notice that Griz and Kaden weren't present, though I was certain they would both have been extremely uncomfortable at the table. At times I felt I was in a dreamlike fog. Only this morning we had been on the backs of horses fighting for our lives, and now I was navigating a sea of porcelain, silver, glowing candelabras, and a thousand tinkling glasses. Everything seemed brighter and louder than it was.

It was a celebratory evening and I noted the effort to keep conversation light. Colonel Bodeen brought out his revered red-eye and poured Sven a glass. He announced that another celebration was in the works that would include the entire outpost. It would give all the soldiers a chance to toast their new king and—Colonel Bodeen added hesitantly—their future queen.

"Marabella parties are unmatched," Vilah said with excitement.

"It lifts spirits," Bodeen added.

"And there's dancing," Madam Rathbone said.

I assured them all I was eager to partake.

Between courses, toasts were offered, and as the wine and spirits flowed, caution was forgotten and more conversation was directed at me.

"Madam Rathbone told me you set a fine table," I said to Colonel Bodeen, "and I must admit I am quite impressed."

"The Marabella outpost is known for its exceptional food," Fiona, Lieutenant Belmonte's wife, answered, her voice filled with pride.

"The better fed a soldier, the better they can serve," Colonel Bodeen explained, as if the food wasn't an extravagance, but a battle strategy.

The memory of the Komizar's assured grin and tall shining silos shimmered behind my eyes. *Great armies march on their stomachs.*

I stared down at the plate before me. A smear of orange sauce and a pheasant leg bone lay upon it. There had been no plates of bones to pass before the meal, no acknowledgment of sacrifice. Its absence left a strange hole in me that begged to be filled. I wasn't sure what had happened to my own tether of bones. It had probably been thrown away along with my bloody and torn clothes as something unclean and savage. I discreetly slipped the bone from the plate and hid it in my napkin before the servant could take it away.

"I can't imagine what you suffered at the hands of those savages," Madam Hague said.

"If you mean the Vendans, yes, some were savage, but many others were extremely kind."

She raised her eyebrows as if doubtful.

Captain Hague threw back another glass of wine. "But you must regret your decision to flee the wedding. All this—"

"No, Captain. I don't regret my decision."

The table grew silent.

"If I had been shipped off to Dalbreck, there are valuable things I never would have learned."

Lieutenant Dupre leaned forward. "Surely there are easier ways to learn lessons of youth—"

"Not lessons, Lieutenant. Cold, hard facts. The Vendans have amassed an army and devised weapons that could wipe out both Dalbreck and Morrighan."

Dubious glances were exchanged. A few eyes came close to outright rolling. Poor delirious girl.

Rafe put his hand on mine. "Lia, we can talk about this later. Tomorrow, with the colonel and other officers." He quickly suggested we retire and excused us. As we walked past Sven and Bodeen, I eyed the near-empty bottle of red-eye.

I grabbed it from the table and sniffed. "Colonel Bodeen, do you mind if I take the rest of this with me?"

His eyes widened. "I'm afraid it's very strong brew, Your Highness."

"Yes, I know."

He looked at Rafe for approval, and Rafe nodded. I was getting quite weary of everyone deferring to Rafe before answering me.

"It's not for me," I explained, then shot an accusing stare at Sven. "We did promise Griz a glass, didn't we?" Bodeen remained gracious, but several of the dinner guests cleared their throats, and stared at Bodeen, waiting for a refusal to share the red-eye. I understood their disapproval. They had just learned of an entire platoon's demise at the hands of Vendans. Still, everyone couldn't keep ignoring the fact that Kaden and Griz had suffered injuries to help save our lives.

Rafe took the bottle from me and handed it to a sentry standing at the door. "See that the large fellow in the surgeon's barracks gets this." Rafe looked back at me and raised his brows as if to ask if the problem was solved, and I nodded my satisfaction.

"THESE ARE YOUR QUARTERS," RAFE SAID, PULLING ASIDE the curtained entry of the tent. Even in the dim glowing light of an overhead chandelier, I was met with a shock of color. A lush indigo carpet swirling with flowers covered the entirety of the floor. A blue velvet quilt, white satin pillows, and fur blankets were piled high on a canopied bed topped with finials carved in the shapes of lion heads. Elegant blue drapes were gathered back with gold cording, waiting to be pulled, and a squat stove with an intricate grill was nearby. Fresh cornflowers graced a side table, and a small dining table with two chairs was in a corner. It was more luxurious than my own chamber at home.

"And your quarters?" I asked.

"Over there."

A dozen yards away, a similar tent had been erected. A short distance that seemed so far. We hadn't slept apart since we left the Sanctum. I had grown accustomed to feeling his arm around my waist, the warmth of his breath on my neck, and I couldn't imagine him not being with me tonight, especially now that we finally had what might be called real privacy.

I smoothed back a lock from his face. His lids were heavy. "You've gotten no rest, have you?"

"Not yet. There will be time for that later—"

"Rafe," I said, stopping him. "Some things can't be put off until later. We still haven't talked about your parents. Are you all right?"

He let the tent curtain drop, blocking out the lantern light, and we were in darkness again. "I'm fine," he said.

I cradled his face and drew him closer, our foreheads touching, our breaths mingling, and it seemed tears swelled in both our throats. "I'm sorry, Rafe," I whispered.

His jaw tensed beneath my touch. "I was where I needed to be. With you. My parents would understand." Each word he spoke throbbed in the space between us. "My being with them wouldn't have changed anything."

"But you could have said good-bye."

His arms circled around me, holding me tight, and it felt like all the grief he would ever be allowed was in that grip. I could think only of the cruelty of his new position and what was immediately expected of him.

His hold finally loosened, and he looked at me, tired creases at the corners of his eyes, a smile through his exhaustion.

"Stay with me?" I asked.

His lips met mine, and he whispered against them between kisses. "Are you trying to seduce me, Your Highness?"

"Absolutely," I said, and leisurely ran the tip of my tongue along his lower lip like it was my final course of the evening.

He pulled away slightly and sighed. "We're in the middle of an outpost with a hundred eyes watching—probably right now from the dining room windows."

"You didn't seem to be worried about what others thought when you kissed me in there."

"I was overcome with the moment. Besides, kissing you and staying the night in your tent are two different things."

"You're afraid you'll taint my reputation?"

An evil grin pulled at the corner of his mouth. "I'm afraid you'll taint mine."

I punched him playfully in the ribs, but then felt the smile fade from my face. I understood protocol—especially with royals. By the gods, I had lived with it my entire life. I also knew Rafe was in an especially delicate position now, all eyes newly trained on him. But we had both nearly died. I was tired of waiting. "I want to be with you, Rafe. Now. It seems waiting is all we've ever done. I don't care what anyone thinks. What if there are no tomorrows? What if now is all we'll ever have?"

He reached up and gently pressed his finger to my lips. "Shhh. Don't ever say that. We have a lifetime ahead of us, a hundred tomorrows and more. I promise. That's what all this has been about. Every breath, every step I've taken has been for our future together. There's nothing I want more than to disappear into this tent with you, but I do care what they think. They've only just met you, and I've already disregarded every protocol expected of a prince."

I sighed. "And now you're king."

"But I can at least come in and light the stove for you. That won't take me long."

I told him I could light it myself, but he pulled aside the curtain and led me in, and I didn't protest further. He checked the flue in the tall round chimney that vented through the top of the tent, and then lit the kindling. He sat back on the side of the bed, watching to make sure the wood caught. I walked around the tent, brushing my fingers along the bed drapes, taking in the extravagance.

"This really wasn't all necessary, Rafe," I said over my shoulder.

I heard him poking at the wood. "Where else would you stay? In the soldiers' barracks?"

"Anything would be a luxury compared to where I have been sleeping." I spotted my belongings on the table. They were carefully placed in a neat pile, but the saddlebag was gone. I pulled my hairbrush from the stack and began pulling pins from my hair, undoing all of Adeline's beautiful work. "Or I could have slept in Madam Rathbone's sitting room. Though her husband might not have—"

I heard an odd thump and turned. The poker had slipped from Rafe's grasp and now lay on the floor.

It appeared I was going to get my wish after all.

"Rafe?"

He was out cold. He lay on my bed, his feet still on the floor, and his hands limp at his sides. I walked over and whispered his name again, but he didn't respond. Even a stubborn king could stay awake only so long. I pulled his boots off, and he barely stirred. Next came his belts. I couldn't wrestle with his deadweight, so the clothes would have to stay. I lifted up his legs and turned them so he was fully on the bed. He mumbled a few incoherent words about leaving and then didn't utter another sound. I removed my pauldron and jewelry and struggled to unlace the leather corset on my own. Once I extinguished the chandelier lights, I curled up on the bed beside him and pulled the furs over both of us. His face was serene, glowing in the firelight. "Rest, sweet farmer," I whispered. I kissed his cheek, his chin, his lips, memorizing every inch of his skin beneath my touch. *A hundred tomorrows.* I laid my head on the pillow next to his and slid my hand around his waist, holding him, still afraid he might slip away and our tomorrows would never come.

CHAPTER TWENTY-THREE

I SENSED HIM SLIPPING FROM BENEATH MY ARM IN THE midde of the night, but I thought he had just rolled over. When I woke early the next morning, he was gone. All I found was a servant with wary eyes and a tray of tarts, dried fruit, and cream. She set it on the table and curtsied.

"I'm Tilde. His Majesty told me to tell you he had meetings and would check on you later. In the meantime, I am to help with anything you require."

I looked down at the rumpled gown I had slept in. "Madam Rathbone is sending more clothes over soon," Tilde said. "She also wanted to know if you wanted your other belongings cleaned or . . . burned."

I knew they assumed everything should be burned. The clothing was beyond repair, but my boots, and especially Walther's baldrick, were not things I could let go, and then when I thought of it, the remains of the dress of many hands was not something I could let go of either. I told her I would clean the items myself if she would bring them to me.

"I'll take care if it right away, ma'am." She curtsied and scurried out of the tent.

I brushed my hair, pulled on the dainty slippers Vilah had lent me, and left to find Colonel Bodeen's office.

The thick walls of the outpost were bright in the morning sun. Everything about the garrison was pristine—and intimidating in its order. It exuded the confidence of a kingdom that was strong all the way down to its foundation. Even the ground between the buildings was covered with neatly raked gravel the color of marmalade. It crunched lightly beneath my feet as I approached a long building that looked similar to the dining hall, but that had only small high windows. Perhaps they wanted no one to see who met within.

The officers looked up in surprise when I opened the door, but neither Rafe, Sven, nor Colonel Bodeen was present.

"Your Highness," Lieutenant Belmonte said as he rose to his feet. "Is there something we can do for you?"

"I was told we would meet today. I came to continue our discussion of last night. About the Vendan army. You need to be aware—"

Captain Hague dropped a thick stack of papers onto the table with a loud thud. "The king has already informed us of developments in Venda," he said, and then added pointedly while surveying my rumpled dress, "while you were still sleeping."

I smoothed out my dress. "I respect what the king may have already told you, but he didn't see what I saw when—"

"Are you a trained soldier, Your Highness?"

He cut me off so sharply he may as well have slapped me. The sting hissed through the air. So this was how it was to be? I leaned forward, my palms flat on the table, and met his stare. "Yes, I *am*, Captain, though perhaps trained with a different eye than yours."

"Oh, of course," he said, sitting back in his chair, his tone ripe with disdain. "That's right. The Morrighese army does do things a little differently. It must have something to do with that *gift* of yours." He shot a grin at an officer next to him. "Go ahead, then. Why don't you tell us just what you think you saw?"

The ass. Apparently Rafe's claim of me as his future queen carried little weight with the captain—as long as the king wasn't present—but I couldn't let my pride nor contempt keep me from sharing what they needed to know. So I told them everything I knew about the army city.

"A hundred thousand armed soldiers is a staggering claim," he said when I finished. "Especially for a people as backward as the barbarians."

"They are not so backward," I countered. "And the men I rode in with, Kaden and Griz, can confirm what I've told you."

Captain Hague rose from his chair, his face splotched with sudden color. "May I remind you, Your Highness, we have just lost twenty-eight men to the barbarians. The only way we'll be gathering information from savages like them will be at the end of a knotted whip."

I leaned forward. "And it is clear you would prefer to gain it from me in the same way."

Captain Azia laid a hand on Hague's arm and whispered something to him. Hague sat down.

"Please understand, Your Highness," Azia said, "the loss of the platoon has been a bitter blow to all of us, especially to Captain Hague. One of his cousins was a soldier in the unit."

My hands slid from the table, and I stood straight, taking a calming breath. I understood grief. "My condolences, Captain. I'm sorry for your loss. But please make no mistake. I owe a debt to the men you slander, and if they are not invited to our table, do not expect to see me there either."

His wiry brows fell low over his eyes. "I will convey your wishes to Colonel Bodeen."

I was just turning to leave when a door at the back of the room opened and Colonel Bodeen, along with Sven, Rafe, and Tavish emerged. They startled when they saw me, and Rafe's eyes turned briefly sharp as if I had undermined him.

"I was just leaving," I said. "It seems you've already taken care of matters here."

I was out the door and halfway down the stairs before Rafe stepped out on the veranda and stopped me. "Lia, what's wrong?"

"I thought we were going to meet with the officers together."

He shook his head, his expression apologetic. "You were asleep. I didn't want to wake you. But I told them everything you told me."

"About the silos?"

"Yes."

"The brezalots?"

"Yes."

"The size of the army?"

"Yes, I told them everything."

Everything. There were some things even I might have held back. "The traitors on the Morrighese court?"

He nodded. "I had to, Lia."

Of course he did. But I could only imagine how it lowered their regard for Morrighan and me even further. I came from a court roiling with snakes.

I sighed. "They didn't seem to believe anything I said about the Vendan army."

He reached out and took my hand. "If they seem skeptical, it's because they've never encountered barbarian patrols that numbered more than a dozen before—but I told them what I saw too, the armed and organized brigade of at least five hundred that led you into Venda. Trust me, we're evaluating the measures that need to be taken, especially now with the deaths of an entire—"

I let out a soft groan. "I'm afraid I've gotten off to a bad start with your officers, and Captain Hague already dislikes me intensely. I didn't realize one of the dead was his cousin. He and I had a bit of a clash in there."

"Bad news or not, Captain Hague is always a pill best taken with strong ale. At least that's what Sven tells me. I know the man only in passing."

"Sven's right. He made it clear he had no respect for the Morrighese army, and he scorned the gift as well. I was as welcome in there as a skinned knee. Why in the gods' names did Dalbreck ever want me if they had no regard for First Daughters and the gift?"

Rafe seemed momentarily stunned, his shoulders pulling back as if my question unsettled him. He quickly recovered. "The captain insulted you. I'll speak to him."

"No," I said, shaking my head. "Please don't. The last thing I want is to look like an injured child who ran tattling to the king. We'll work it out."

He nodded and brought my hand to his lips and kissed it. "I'll try to wrap up these meetings as soon as I can."

"Is there anything I can help with?"

A weary grimace lined his eyes, and he told me that a lot more had transpired in his absence besides his parents' deaths. With no strong leadership, the assembly and cabinet had been warring. Certain egos had flared, generals were questioning the chain of command, and fear over the scourge that had killed the queen had affected commerce—all while they were keeping the king's death a secret from the rest of the world. There were battles waiting for Rafe on every front once he got back to the palace.

"When will that be, Rafe?" I hated to push the point, especially now, but I had no choice. "You know that Morrighan still needs to be warned. That I need to—"

"I know, Lia. Please just give me a few days to deal with all this first. Then we can talk about—"

Sven poked his head out the door. "Your Majesty," he said, rolling his eyes toward the room behind him, "they grow restless."

Rafe glanced back in my direction, lingering like he never wanted to leave. I saw the shadows that still lurked under his eyes. He'd only had a few hours of sleep when he needed a week, and had been granted only a passing moment of mourning when he needed far more. All he asked from me was a few days to juggle his new role as king, but a few days seemed like a luxury Morrighan couldn't afford.

I nodded, and he turned and disappeared behind the door with Sven before I could even say good-bye.

I HOOKED THE LAST BUCKLE OF THE BODICE AND ADJUSTED the belt. I was grateful that Vilah and Adeline had brought me more practical clothes—a split leather skirt, jerkin, and shirt—but they were no less luxurious than the gown I had worn last night. The embossed brown leather was so supple it felt like it might melt between my fingers.

The old broken and knotted laces had been replaced on my newly cleaned boots, and Walther's baldrick was snug against my chest, gleaming like the day Greta had given it to him.

"A family heirloom?" Vilah asked.

They both looked at me tentatively as if they'd read something painful in my expression when I put it on. They were as kind as Captain Hague was nasty. I smiled and nodded, trying to erase any sadness they had seen. "I'm ready."

They offered to give me a tour of the outpost, which was contained within a large oval wall. Rafe's and my tents were just outside the officers' housing and the dining room. They pointed out the rows of soldiers' barracks, as we walked, the soldiers' dining hall, the surgeon's bungalow, and tucked between them all, the cookhouse. We came to a wide gate that led to the lower level of the outpost. After pointing out the barns, paddocks, and the cook's garden, they showed me the mews where the Valsprey were caged. They were striking birds with white plumage, sharp claws, and an intimidating stare. Their glowing red eyes had a black slash of feathers above them. Vilah said they were swift flyers with wingspans of five feet. "They're able to fly thousands of miles without stopping. It's how we send messages between outposts and the capital." When I asked if they could be sent anywhere, she said they were only trained to fly to certain destinations. Their heads turned eerily, watching us as we passed.

Below the rear wall was the river that wound behind the outpost. We circled back to the upper level and they showed me the laundry house, which was enormous. That didn't surprise me given their love affair with clothes. Finally we found ourselves at the front of the outpost again, near Colonel Bodeen's offices. I looked at the small, high windows and wondered what "measures" they had discussed.

"Can we go out there?" I asked, pointing to the watchtower gate. Rafe had said that vagabonds often camped near the outpost walls. I hadn't seen Dihara's band of wagons when we had approached yesterday, but in truth I'd seen very little besides the people flooding out to meet us. Now I wondered if she and the rest could be out there somewhere in the makeshift city.

"Of course," Adeline said cheerfully. A small door in the massive watchtower gate was open, and as Rafe had ordered, soldiers four deep guarded it. Each one held a well-polished hal-berd. They let other soldiers pass through freely, but merchants were allowed only to leave messages and then were turned away.

As we approached, their halberds crossed and clicked like a well-timed machine to block us.

"James!" Adeline admonished. "What are you doing? Step aside. We're going out to—"

"You and Vi may pass," he replied, "but not Her Highness without an escort. King's orders."

I frowned. Rafe feared more Rahtan could be out there. "These ladies don't count as my escorts?" I asked.

"Armed escorts," he clarified.

I made an exaggerated point of looking at the daggers at each of our sides. We were armed.

James shook his head. Apparently our own weapons weren't enough.

IT WAS AWKWARD WALKING AMONG THE MERCHANT WAGONS with six sober-faced guards wielding sharp, pointy halberds, but we were lucky that James had rustled up even these, because none of the four at the gate would leave their posts.

The small wagon city reminded me in some ways of the *jehen-dra*. A little something for everyone and every taste—grilled foods, fabrics, leather goods, tents for games of chance, exotic brews, even a letter-writing service for soldiers who wanted to send home missives written with an elegant flair. Other merchants were there only to sell staples to the outpost and be on their way.

I was still pondering that the outpost seemed to break the treaty calling for no permanent dwellings in the Cam Lanteux. Why had Eben's family been burned out when here in the same wilderness was a structure that housed hundreds?

When I asked Adeline about this, one of the guards overheard me and answered in her stead. "There are no permanent residents here. We are regularly rotated in and out." His explanation sounded like a loophole exploited by the well-armed and powerful. I remembered Regan talking about the encampments where their patrols would rest, but I had always pictured them as temporary places of muddy ruts, shaky tents, and windblown soldiers huddling against the elements. Now I wondered if Morrighan had loopholes too and their encampments were more permanent than I had believed them to be.

I asked the whereabouts of the vagabond camps among the merchants as we walked, and I was always directed a short walk away, but none were the vagabonds I searched for. "The one Dihara leads," I finally said to an old man who was pounding designs into a leather browband.

He paused from his work and used his chisel to point still farther down the wall. "She's here. At the end." My heart leapt, but only momentarily. His wrinkles deepened into unmistakable grimness. I ran in the direction he indicated, Vilah, Adeline, and the soldiers struggling to keep up with me.

When we found the camp, I understood the old man's grim expression. The camp was tucked under expansive pine boughs, but there were no chimes hanging from them. No painted ribbons or pounded copper twirled from branches. There was no steaming kettle in the midst of it all. There were no tents. Only three scorched *carvachis*.

Reena's *carvachi* was more black now than purple. She sat on a log near the fire ring with one of the young mothers. Nearby, Tevio scraped the dirt with a sharp stick. Behind the *carvachis*, I spotted one of the men tending the horses with a child on his hip. There was no gaiety.

I turned to the guards and pleaded with them to stay back. "Please," I said. "Something is wrong." They surveyed the surroundings and reluctantly agreed to maintain their distance. Adeline and Vilah planted themselves in front of them as their own kind of safeguard—a line not to be crossed.

I approached, my chest hammering. "Reena?"

Her face brightened, and she jumped up to meet me, squeezing me against her full breast as if she'd never let me go. When she loosened her grip and looked at me again, her eyes glistened. *"Chemi monsé Lia! Oue vifar!"*

"Yes, I live. But what has happened here?" I stared at her charred wagon.

By now several others had joined us, including Tevio, who was pulling at my skirt. Reena drew me over to the fire to sit on the log and told me.

Riders came. Vendans. Ones she had never seen before. Dihara went out to meet them, but they didn't want to talk. They held up a small knife. They said helping enemies of Venda could not go unavenged. They killed half the horses, torched the tents and wagons, and left. She and the others grabbed blankets and whatever they could to beat out the flames, but the tents were gone almost instantly. They managed to save three of the *carvachis*.

From the moment she mentioned the small knife, a sick salty taste swelled on my tongue. *Natiya's knife.* When Reena finished, I stood, unable to contain my anger. *One death was not good enough for the Komizar! I wanted to kill him again!* I pounded my fist against the wooden side of the *carvachi*, rage clawing through me.

"*Aida monsé, neu, neu, neu.* You mustn't hurt yourself over this," Reena said pulling me away from the *carvachi*. She looked at the slivers in my hand and wrapped it in her scarf. "We will recover from this. Dihara said it was a season that none of us could prevent."

"Dihara? Where is she? Is she all right?"

The same grim lines spread out from Reena's eyes as I had seen on the old man.

My knees weakened. "*No,*" I said, shaking my head.

"She lives," Reena said quickly to correct my assumption, but then added, "but maybe not for long. She is very old, and in stamping out the flames, her heart failed. Its beat, even now, is weak. The outpost healer came out to see her, may the gods bless him, but there was nothing he could do."

"Where is she?"

THE INSIDE OF THE *CARVACHI* WAS DIM EXCEPT FOR A THIN blue flame flickering in a bowl of sweetly scented tallow—to keep the scent of death away. I carried a bucket of warm water floating with pungent leaves inside with me.

She was propped up on pillows in the bed at the back of the wagon, feather light, gray ash to be blown away. I sensed death hovering in the corners, looking on. Waiting. Her long silver braid was the only strength I saw, a rope that kept her moored to the living. I pulled a stool close and set the bucket down. She opened her eyes.

You heard her. Get the girl some goat cheese.

The first words I'd ever heard her speak swelled in my chest. *You heard her.*

She was one of the few who ever did.

I dipped a rag into the bucket and squeezed it out.

I wiped her forehead. "You're not well."

Her pale eyes searched my face.

"It is a long way you've traveled, and you have farther yet to go." Her breath faltered, and she blinked slowly. "Very far."

"I've only traveled far by the strength you've given me."

"No," she whispered. "It was always in you, buried deep."

Her eyelids closed as if their weight was too much to bear.

I rinsed the rag and wiped her neck, the elegant folds marking the days she had spent on this earth, the beautiful lines crowding her face like a finely drawn map, ancient, but now, in this moment, not nearly old enough. This world still needed more of her. She couldn't go. Her hand inched on top of mine, cold and papery light.

"The child Natiya. Speak to her," she said, her eyes still closed. "Do not let her carry the guilt of me. What she did was right. The truth circled and gathered her into its arms."

I lifted her thin wraithlike hand to my lips, squeezing my eyes shut. I nodded, swallowing the ache in my throat.

"Enough," she said, pulling her hand away. "I was almost eaten by wolves. Did I tell you? Eristle heard me crying in the woods. When the skies quaked with thunder, she taught me to shut out—" Her eyes opened, her pupils large black moons floating in a circle of gray, and she weakly shook her head. "No, that is my story, not yours. Yours is calling. Be on your way."

"Why me, Dihara?"

"You already have the answer to that question. It had to be someone. Why not you?"

These were the same words Venda had spoken to me. Cold fingers danced up my spine. *This world, it breathes you in . . . it* knows *you, and then it breathes you out again, shares you.*

Her eyes drifted shut, and her tongue reverted back to her native one, her voice as faint as the flickering of the candle. *"Jei zinterr . . . jei trévitoria."*

Be brave. Be victorious.

I stood to leave. It felt like it was impossible to be either.

CHAPTER TWENTY-FOUR

RAFE

SVEN TAPPED THE TABLE NEAR MY PLATE. "COLONEL BODEEN will be offended. You're not eating."

"And these are the best bison chops I've ever had," Orrin added as he sucked the last bit of sauce from a bone. "Don't tell him I said so. I claimed mine were better."

Tavish leaned back, his boots propped up on the table, scuffing the polished wood. He stared at me, not saying anything. We had taken a break from our discussions and were holed up in Bodeen's office while the other officers ate their midday meal in the meeting chamber.

Sven stood and looked out the window. "Don't worry, boy. All this will fall into place. It's a lot to take in at once."

"Boy?" Tavish said. "He's the blooming king now."

"He can strip it from my hide."

I pushed my plate away. "It's not just court matters on my mind. It's Lia. She had a run-in with Hague."

Sven grunted. "So? Everyone has run-ins with Hague. Nothing to worry about."

"What about the other officers?" I asked. "Have any of you gotten a sense how they feel about her?"

"They don't hold her kingdom against her," Tavish said flatly. "Belmonte, Armistead, and Azia were like captivated pups when they met her."

Sven squinted, continuing to look at something out the window. "That's all you're worried about? If they *like* her?"

No. That wasn't even half of it. Out on the veranda I had seen her eyes—they spoke as much as her words before I cut her off. I had avoided the subject on our way here by stressing that our only goal was to reach the safety of the outpost. But now we were here. Her questions were harder to avoid. I leaned forward, rubbing my temples. "No. That's not all I'm worried about. She wants to go home."

Sven spun back to look at me. "To Morrighan? Why would she want to do a fool thing like that?"

"She thinks she needs to warn them about the Vendan army."

"The Komizar may have conveyed his big plans to her, but that doesn't mean they were a reality," Sven said. "When was anything he said not tainted by his own ambitions?" He reminded me that even some of the governors thought he had inflated his numbers.

Orrin licked his fingers. "And a few thousand soldiers can look like a hell of a lot more when you're frightened."

"But we've known for some time that their numbers were growing," I said. "It's what helped push us toward a marriage alliance with Morrighan."

Sven rolled his eyes. "There were many motivations for that."

"And numbers aren't the same as an army with centuries of training and experience like we have," Tavish countered. "Not to mention they no longer have a viable leader."

Jeb frowned. "But there was that small flask of liquid Lia gave to Rafe to blow up the bridge. That's a weapon none of the kingdoms have."

"And it took out the main gear, which had to be twelve feet of solid iron," I said. "It's a worry."

Sven sat back down. "There are not bridges on a battlefield, and brezalots can be taken down, assuming they even march. The Council members will eat one another alive long before they ever get that bridge fixed."

Orrin reached for another chop. "You're king. You just tell her she can't go."

Tavish snorted. "*Tell her?* You don't just tell a girl like her that she can't do something," he said, then turned a long, dissecting stare at me. He shook his head. "Oh, holy hell. You already told her you'd take her there, didn't you?"

I blew out a puff of air and looked up at the ceiling. "I may have." I pushed back my chair and stood, pacing the room. "Yes! I did! But it was a long time ago, back at the Sanctum. I told her what she needed to hear at the moment, that we'd go back to Terravin. One day. I didn't say when. I was just trying to give her hope."

Sven shrugged. "So you told her what was expedient at the time."

Tavish sucked in a slow breath. "A lie. That's how she'll see it."

"It wasn't a lie. I thought that maybe someday I'd be able to take her back there, a long time from now if things change, but for the gods' sakes, there's a bounty on her head now, and the Morrighese cabinet is thick with traitors. I'd be insane to let her go back."

"She's probably facing a noose there now," Orrin agreed. He rubbed his neck. "Isn't that how they execute their criminals?"

Tavish shot him a glare. "You're not helping."

"The girl loves you, boy," Sven said. "Any fool can see she wants to be with you. Just tell her what you told us. She's a girl of reason."

Sven's words cut the deepest. I turned away, pretending I was looking at a relic hanging on the wall. I saw her struggle every day. Some part of Venda still had its claws in her—and some part of Morrighan did too. *Reason with her?* It is hard to find reason when you're being torn in two. Part of her heart was in both kingdoms and none of it was in Dalbreck.

"I heard her speaking to the clans on our last day there," Tavish said. "That's part of the problem too, isn't it?"

I nodded.

"*The one who was hunted . . .*" Orrin mused.

Their moods darkened. I realized they'd all heard it, and it disturbed them as much as it did me.

Sven shook his head. "That claw and vine on her shoulder is

the damnedest thing. The Vendan clans seemed to have a lot of regard for it."

"It's all that's left of our wedding kavah. When we first met, she said the kavah was a terrible mistake."

Somehow, I had to make her believe that again.

Be true, my sisters and brothers,
Not like the Chimentra,
The alluring creature
With two seductive mouths.
Its words flow luxurious, like a satin ribbon,
Binding up the unwary in its silken braids.
But without ears to hear its own words,
The Chimentra is soon strangled,
Caught in the trail of its beautiful lies.

—Song of Venda

CHAPTER TWENTY-FIVE

KADEN

LIA ARGUED WITH THE GUARDS POSTED AT THE DOOR AND finally pushed past them. She walked to the back of the barracks where I sat with my feet resting on the end of Griz's cot.

The first thing she did was look at the empty bottle on the floor beside me, and the second thing was to hover over me and sniff.

Her upper lip curled. "You're drunk."

I shrugged. "Only half buzzed. There wasn't much left in the bottle."

"That bottle was for Griz. Not you."

"Look at him. Does he look like he needs it? The surgeon's plying him with his own special brew to keep him flat on his back. Him too," I added, nodding toward Jeb. "The only company I have in here is their farts and snores."

She rolled her eyes. "You have nothing better to do than drink red-eye?"

"Like what?"

"Anything! Go outside and get some sunshine. Explore the outpost."

"In case you hadn't noticed, there are guards posted outside, not to mention I've had more than my share of the outdoors the last couple of weeks." I lifted the bottle and let a few last drops fall on my tongue, then kicked Jeb's foot to make sure he was completely out before I said more. "As for the outpost, I already know what it looks like. I've been here before."

She looked at me, confused. "You've been—"

She paled, realization setting in. She pushed Jeb's feet to the side and sat on the end of his cot, resting her face in her hands, trying to absorb this news.

"You had to know I wasn't always hunting down princesses," I said. "I had duties. One of them brought me here." I told her the barest details of my visit two years ago, only one man as my target, but a key one. "If it's any consolation, he deserved it. At least that's what the Komizar told me."

Deserved. The word had wormed through me all morning. The way Aster had deserved a knife in her heart? Maybe that was why I had picked up Griz's bottle. There was no doubt that countless Vendans had died brutally at the hands of other kingdoms, and probably by the hand of the man I killed too, just as the Komizar had claimed. I had witnessed the brutalities myself. But there had to be others like Aster who were killed simply to send a message. How many of them had died by my hand?

The weight of Lia's steady stare tore through me. I looked away, wishing the bottle of red-eye wasn't empty. She sat quietly for a long while. Did she still believe I was a different person?

A hiss finally escaped between her teeth. She stood and began rummaging through supplies in the surgeon's cabinet. For the first time, I noticed that the scarf she was carrying was wrapped around her hand.

"What happened?"

"Stupidity, and something that will never happen again."

She unwrapped her hand and rinsed it in a basin, then began pulling out slivers with a tweezer.

"Here, let me," I said.

"You?" she scoffed.

"It's not surgery. I'm sober enough to take out a sliver."

She sat down opposite me, and while I held her hand and worked out a sliver, she told me about Dihara and the other vagabonds being burned out.

"Natiya," I said, shaking my head. "I knew she wanted your horse to kick out my teeth, but I never thought she'd slip you a knife. Most vagabonds know better."

"Even vagabonds can put up with only so much. Especially young ones. She's suffering now. She thinks it's all her fault."

"The Komizar must have believed you when you said you stole it. Otherwise they'd all be dead."

"Well, isn't that a consolation? The great, merciful Komizar!"

Her sarcasm stung. I rubbed my thumb across the top of her hand. "I'm sorry."

Her expression turned earnest. "Is he dead, Kaden? You must have gotten a sense of something."

I knew she was desperate for me to say yes, but I repeated what I had told her before. I didn't know. He was badly wounded. He was weak. I'd heard some mumblings that didn't sound hopeful for his recovery, and after that first day until we left I hadn't heard his voice again.

Her hand relaxed in mine. It was clear she didn't think any of those who remained in the Sanctum could manage the monumental task of leading such an army. She was probably right.

A shadow crossed the door of the barracks, and I looked up to see Tavish watching us, most particularly focused on Lia's hand resting in mine. I let him look long and hard before I alerted Lia to his presence: "We have company."

CHAPTER TWENTY-SIX

RAFE

I FOUND LIA TUCKED UP IN THE CORNER OF THE SOLDIERS'
mess hall, her back to me. I uncurled my fingers, forcing them
to relax. I promised myself I wouldn't go in with accusations. I
would forget it.

But no matter how I tried to block it, my encounter with
Kaden in the surgeon's bungalow pounded in my head. *It was me
she held on to when she needed comfort. My shoulder she wept on. Don't
be so certain of the position you now hold. It was me she slept beside
every night, and trust me, she enjoyed every second of it when she kissed
me. You're only her means to an end.* It was only a taunt, I told myself, that was all, and I didn't let on that I gave it any merit. It
deserved none.

The dining hall was mostly empty between meals, except for
the five soldiers who sat at a table with her. I walked across the

room slowly, the floor creaking beneath my boots. It immediately caught everyone's attention. Except for Lia's. One by one, the soldiers looked at me and laid their cards down.

Lia didn't turn, not even when I stopped behind her stool and her hair brushed against my belt. The soldiers made to stand up, but I waved them back down.

"So, what's your stake this time?" I asked. "Something I should be worried about?"

She lifted up a bottle of red-eye, still not turning to look at me. "Every time I lose a hand, the bottle gets passed. I've only had to pass it twice." She sighed dramatically. "Colonel Bodeen really should be more careful about locking his liquor cabinet." Her head tilted as if she was weighing a thought. "Or maybe it was locked."

I took the bottle from her and set it in the middle of the table, then shoved the pile she had accumulated into the middle as well. "Gentlemen, enjoy your game."

"It's been a pleasure," she said to her new comrades, and put her hand out for me to escort her.

Neither of us said a word until we were outside.

I turned to face her, rested my hands on her waist, and then gently kissed her. "It's not like you to give in so easily."

"They were nice young men but lousy players. It was only something to pass the time."

"And taking Colonel Bodeen's red-eye was a challenge?"

"It was a more genteel stake than the one I offered last time. I was only thinking of you."

"Well, thank you for that. I think. What spawned this diversion?"

She eyed me with frustration. "It seemed everywhere I went to today, I needed King Jaxon's permission to pass. First the merchant wagons outside, then trying to access the outpost wall, and finally Tavish all but threw me out of the surgeon's bungalow—"

"What were you doing in there?"

My tone came out sharper than I meant it to, and she stepped free from the circle of my hands. "What difference does it make?"

"We need to talk."

Her expression sobered. "About what?"

"In my tent."

CHAPTER TWENTY-SEVEN

HE NEARLY DRAGGED ME ACROSS THE COURTYARD, AND MY thoughts tumbled trying to figure out what had disturbed him so. Colonel Bodeen's red-eye? Playing an innocent game of cards? Or had something happened in his meetings today?

As soon as we were in his tent, he spun. Every muscle in his face was tight with restraint. A vein twitched at his temple.

"What is it, Rafe? Are you all right?"

He walked over to a bedside table and poured a goblet of water, swilling it back in one swallow. He offered me none. He looked at the goblet in his hand, and I feared it might shatter in his grip. He set it down carefully on the table as if it held poison.

"It's probably not important," he said.

I huffed a disbelieving breath. "It clearly is. Just say it."

He turned to face me fully. There was a mountain of challenge in his stance, and I felt my shoulders bracing.

"Did you kiss him?" he asked.

I knew he could only mean Kaden. "You saw me kiss him—"

"When you were alone together in the Cam Lanteux."

"Once."

"You told me nothing happened."

"Nothing did," I answered slowly, wondering what had brought this all on. "It was a kiss, Rafe. That was all."

"Did he force himself on you?"

"No. He did not."

"Was it part of your escape strategy?"

"No."

His jaw rippled with tension. "Did you . . . enjoy it?"

I prickled at his insinuating tone. He had no right to interrogate me as if I had committed a crime. "Yes! I did enjoy it! Do you want to hear every last detail? I was scared, Rafe. I was alone. I was tired. And I thought you were a farmer I'd never see again. You had moved on without me. I was desperate for something to hold on to, but I learned that Kaden wasn't that something. It was one kiss in a lonely moment, and you can turn it into anything sordid that you like, but I won't apologize for it!"

"He said he slept beside you every night."

"*On bedrolls!* I also slept by Griz, Eben, and the whole smelly lot! And let's not forget the snakes and vermin! Unfortunately there were no private rooms available at the lovely inns on our holiday route!"

He paced the floor, shaking his head, his hands still drawn

into fists. "I knew when he said it he was taunting me, but then when Tavish told me he saw him holding your hand—"

"I hurt my hand, Rafe. Kaden was pulling out slivers. That is all." I made every effort to cool my own rising temper. I knew Rafe was under tremendous strain, and it appeared Kaden had taken advantage of that. I pulled on his arm so he had to face me. "You have to make your peace with Kaden, and he with you. You are not on opposite sides anymore. Do you understand?"

He looked at me, the line of his jaw still tight with anger, but he reached out and lifted my hands. He examined the one that was scratched and red. "I'm sorry," he whispered. He pulled my hand to his lips, kissing a knuckle and lingering there, his breath warming my skin. "Please forgive me."

I withdrew my hand. "Wait here," I said, and headed for the tent door before he could argue. "I'll be right back."

"Where are you going?"

"To the privy."

I kept my rage in check until I was outside the tent. There was far more that still needed to be settled.

There wasn't a lot of arguing this time when I told the guards to move aside. They must have seen something in my expression. Maybe everyone did. Griz and Jeb lifted their heads from pillows, but Kaden, Orrin, and Tavish all rose as I walked in. I stopped in front of Kaden, my hands shaking with fury.

His eyes narrowed. He knew exactly why I was there.

"Don't you *ever* undermine me again, or dare to insinuate things that aren't true!"

"He asked. I only told him the truth. I can't help how he twisted it in his own mind."

"You mean how you laid it out for him to twist!"

"I thought we both agreed to be honest. You kissed me. Or maybe you're leading him along too."

My hand shot out, slamming across his face.

He grabbed my arm and yanked me close. "Wake up, Lia! Can't you see what's going on here?" In almost the same movement, the hot slice of metal filled the air, and both Tavish's and Orrin's swords were at Kaden's heart.

"Unhand the princess," Tavish growled. *"Now."*

Kaden slowly released his grip, and Orrin pushed him back several steps with the tip of his sword, but Kaden's eyes never left mine.

I heard more footsteps. Rafe was walking toward us.

"There's someone else who needs to be honest besides you and me," Kaden said. "I thought you were in on the story from the beginning, but then I realized you didn't get it."

"Get what?"

"The excuse he conjured so quickly—the port and the few hills? Why do you think the Komizar bought it? You really think the marriage was only about an alliance? Dalbreck doesn't give a horse's ass about the Morrighese army. They mock you. The port was all they ever wanted, and the esteemed First Daughter of the House of Morrighan was going to be their leverage."

I had no air. I couldn't force words to my tongue. Instead, a blur whirled in my head.

There's a port we want in Morrighan and a few miles of hills.
The rest is yours.

> *The prince has grand dreams.*
> *Is it worth it to have any other kind?*

> > *. . . I never thought it was right.*
> *Do you think the prince knew?*
> *He knew.*

I turned and looked at Rafe. *Another secret?* His lips were half parted, and he looked like he'd been punched in the gut— or had been caught.

The anger burning at my temples drained away. My stomach floated loosely in my chest.

Rafe reached out for me. "Lia, let me explain. That's not how—"

I stepped back, avoiding his reach, and turned to look at everyone else. Tavish and Orrin shifted uncomfortably but met my stare; Jeb looked away. Their expressions confirmed I was a pawn in a game that was so old it was practically a joke.

The floor seemed to bob. I tried to find footing in this truth that rolled through the room like an unwelcome tide. I hugged my arms to my waist, every limb suddenly feeling awkward and out of place. I skimmed their gazes, felt the shake of my head in a distant, detached way. "How very disappointing it must have been for Dalbreck to learn I was a branded criminal in Morrighan. Being worthless to my own kingdom made me a worthless game piece to yours as well. My apologies." The wobble in my voice only added to my humiliation. It seemed I was a grave disappointment to every kingdom on the continent.

Kaden looked at me, his expression morose, as if he knew he'd gone too far. When I turned to leave, Rafe tried to stop me, but I jerked free, shaking my head, unable to speak, my throat swollen with shame as I ran out the door.

I rushed across the courtyard, the ground a sickening blur beneath me. *He knew.*

I had been so worried about the sham my parents were perpetrating, when all along, it had mattered not one whit to Dalbreck if I had the gift at all. My worth to them lay elsewhere. *Leverage.* The word cut deeply. I'd heard it so many times, the cabinet uttering it with a smug smile in regard to one lesser kingdom or another, one county lord or another, all the ways they used tactical pressure to get something, couching it in a word that appeared so diplomatic and practical, but was laced with force and threat. *It is the way these things are done*, my father had said, trying to explain it. *A little pressure and they pay attention.*

"Lia—"

I felt a tug at my elbow and whirled, yanking it loose. I didn't give Rafe a chance to say more. "*How dare you!*" I screamed, my anger returned full force.

His shoulders squared. "If you'd let me—"

"*How dare you* lay guilt on me for one stupid kiss, when all along you had this sham of epic proportions on your conscience!"

"It wasn't—"

"You and your conniving kingdom turned my entire life upside down over a port! *A port!*"

"You aren't getting the—"

"Oh, believe me, I get it! I get everything now! I—"

"Stop cutting me off!" he yelled. The steel of his eyes sparked with warning. "The least you can do is give me a chance to speak! We're going to talk!"

WE SAT ON THE OUTPOST WALL. HE HAD LED ME THERE, maybe wanting a place where no one would hear us, maybe trying to make amends knowing I had been turned away from there earlier. He had dismissed the guards in our section of the wall, saying we would keep watch. They had raised their eyebrows. The king keeping watch? But it was as natural for Rafe as his arm was on my shoulder now. Our legs dangled over the wall's edge. How far we had come. Now he joined me on precarious ledges.

He hadn't denied it or tried to justify it, but he had promised the alliance wasn't only about the port, and by the time he was done speaking, I believed him. It was about a lot of things, not the least of which was foolish pride and the need to reclaim a part of their history and what had once belonged to the exiled prince. But there was a practical side to their motivations as well. Dalbreck too had heard the reports of the growing Vendan population, and they'd had more incidents with barbarian patrols. Maintaining the Dalbreck army was the largest expense of the treasury. Of all the kingdoms, Morrighan had the next largest army. It was true that Dalbreck viewed their forces as superior to Morrighan's, but they also knew they could use resources elsewhere if they didn't have to maintain such a large military. An alliance could mean cutting back on their western outposts, and the profits from a deep-water port on the western coast would help finance the rest. After I was within their borders, they would press for the return of the port, claiming it as a dowry.

Press. Another innocuous word like *leverage.* I didn't even want to unravel all its nuances.

"So after they secured a political alliance, they set their sights on more, and I'd be the winning game piece clutched in their palms."

He stared out at the darkening horizon. "I wouldn't have let it happen, Lia."

"You're a king now, Rafe," I said, and jumped down from our perch onto the walk. "Will you devise new ways to get it?"

He followed after me and pressed his palms against the watchtower wall, pinning me between his arms. A scowl darkened his eyes. "It doesn't matter who or what I am or what the cabinet wants. You are what matters to me, Lia. If you don't know that already, I'll find a hundred more ways to show you. I love you more than a port, more than an alliance, more than my own life. Your interests are my interests. Are we going to let the conspiracies and schemes of kingdoms come between us?"

His dark lashes cut a shadow under his eyes. His gaze searched mine, and then the turmoil receded and was replaced with something else—a need that had gone too long unquenched. It matched my own, and I felt its heat spreading low in my gut. It was only Rafe and me. Kingdoms disappeared. Duties disappeared. Only the two of us and everything we had ever been to each other—and everything I still wanted us to be.

"No kingdom will come between us," I whispered. "Ever." Our lips drew closer, and I leaned in to him, wanting every part of him to be part of me too, our mouths meeting, his embrace gentle and then passionate, wanting more. His lips traced a line down my neck and then nudged my dress from my shoulder. My breaths shuddered and my hands slipped beneath his vest, my fingertips burning as they slid over the muscles of his stomach. "We're supposed to be keeping watch," I said breathlessly.

He quickly signaled a sentry below to resume his patrol of the wall and turned his attention back to me. "Let's go to my tent," he whispered between kisses.

I swallowed, trying to form a coherent answer. "You aren't worried about your reputation?"

"I'm more worried about my sanity. No one will see us."

"Do you have *anything* with you here?" I didn't want to end up in Pauline's predicament.

"Yes."

His tent was only steps away, but still almost as far as a lifetime when I knew how quickly the fates could turn on a moment and rip it away.

"We're here now, Rafe, and the watchtower is warm. Who needs a tent?"

THE WORLD VANISHED. WE CLOSED THE DOOR. PULLED THE shutter tight. Lit a candle. Threw a woolen blanket to the floor.

My fingers trembled and he kissed them, concern filling his eyes. "We don't have to—"

"I'm only afraid this isn't real. That it's only another one of my dreams that I'll wake from."

"This is our dream, Lia. Together. No one can wake us."

We lay on the blanket and his face hovered over mine, my prince, my farmer, the blue of his eyes as deep as a midnight ocean and I was lost in them, floating, weightless. His lips slowly skimmed my skin, exploring, tender, setting every inch of me on fire, the room and time disappearing, and then his eyes were looking into mine again, and his hand slipped behind me, lifting me closer to him, the yearning of weeks and months burning, and the fears that we'd never be together dissolving.

The vows we made to each other, the trust written on our souls, all of it swept past me as he brought his mouth back to mine. Our hands knotted, and the rhythm of his breaths surrounded me. Every kiss, every touch, was a promise that we both knew, I was his and he was mine, and no conspiracy or scheme of kingdoms had a fraction of the power that surged between us.

CHAPTER TWENTY-EIGHT

WE HURRIED UP THE STEPS OF THE VERANDA, NEITHER OF us feeling guilty about being late for dinner, but we were both caught by surprise when we saw Kaden and Griz among the guests. Captain Hague took particular delight in whispering, "As per your orders," as I passed him.

The timing for listening to me couldn't have been worse, and he knew it. Rafe's hand tensed in mine when he saw them. Making peace with Kaden was still a long way off for him. As uneasy as everyone at the table was with their presence, I knew none were as uncomfortable as Kaden and Griz. To Kaden's credit, he avoided saying anything that might be construed as combative. He seemed contrite even, which I hoped was a sign he regretted his method of delivering "honesty." The unsaid and the innuendo had tarnished his truth. I supposed we all needed practice at it. Truth was a harder skill to master than swinging a sword.

Even Jeb had come to dinner, refusing to be confined to bed any longer. I could only imagine the pain he'd had to endure to wriggle his arm and shoulder into the freshly pressed shirt, but he wore it with style and pride. Cruvas linen, no doubt.

Banter turned to the upcoming party plans and spirits grew lighter. Our dinner mates seemed to grow more at ease with Griz's and Kaden's presence—though even their smallest gestures were still monitored.

Rafe made it through the evening with considerable restraint, though several times during dinner, his hand strayed to my knee beneath the table. I think he enjoyed watching me stumble over my words. I returned the distraction when he was deep in conversation with Captain Azia. After having to begin the same sentence three times, he reached under the table and squeezed my hand, to stop me from drawing lazy circles on his thigh. Captain Azia blushed as if he knew the game we played.

THE NEXT DAY WAS CROWDED WITH MORE DUTY FOR RAFE. I saw the weight of it in his eyes. He'd had to muster incredible self-control back at the Sanctum, keeping up a charade day after day by playing a conniving emissary, and now he had been thrust into another new role—one that came with enormous expectation.

I was walking past his tent when I heard strained voices within. Rafe and Sven were arguing. I stooped near the curtained door to relace my boot and listen. A message had arrived saying the rotation of troops would be delayed a few days, but it also brought news of a growing rift between the assembly and the cabinet.

"That's it," Rafe had yelled. "We're going back now, escort or no escort."

Sven stood his ground. "Don't be a damned fool! The message Bodeen sent has arrived at the palace by now. It will announce you're alive and well and on your way, but you can't discount the fact that enemies will also know you're on your way. It's too big a risk. A large escort is prudent. Knowing you're alive is enough to calm the assembly until we get there." Rafe's reaction to cabinet squabbles seemed excessive, and I wondered if I had missed something, or maybe the news had simply added to his impatience.

Rafe wasn't the only one growing impatient. With each passing day, I was more certain I needed to leave. The pull grew stronger, and I had restless dreams. In them I heard pieces of the Song of Venda, a jumbled melody punctuated by my own breathless running, though in the dreams, my feet refused to move, as if they had grown into the ground beneath me, and then came the low rumble of something approaching. I felt its hot breath on my back, something hungry and determined, the refrain sounding over and over: *For when the Dragon strikes, it is without mercy.* I would startle awake, trying to catch my breath, my back stinging with the memory of sharp claws slicing into me, and then I would hear the Komizar's words as clearly as if he stood beside me. *If any royals survive our conquest, it will give me great pleasure to lock them up on this side of hell.*

After a particularly restless night, I went into Rafe's tent the next morning while he was still dressing. He was in the middle of shaving. I didn't bother with greetings.

"Rafe, we have to talk about my going to Morrighan to warn them."

He studied me in the reflection of his mirror and dipped his lathered razor in the basin to rinse it. "Lia, we've already talked about this. The Komizar is gravely injured or dead, and the Sanctum is in chaos with more dead. You saw how the Council was, like a pack of hungry dogs. They're tearing each other apart right now." He took another swipe at his neck. "And none of those left have the ability to lead any kind of army anyway."

"For now. We hope. But I can't take a chance on guesses. I need to go back and—"

"Lia, the bridge is destroyed. They can't even get across."

"Bridges can be fixed."

He dropped the razor in the basin and turned to look at me. "What about the bounty on your head? You can't just waltz back into Morrighan. We'll send word. I promise."

"Word? To whom, Rafe? There are traitors in the cabinet conspiring with the Komizar, and I don't know how many. I wouldn't know who to trust, and the Chancellor intercepts—"

He wiped his face with a towel. "Lia, I can't go back to Morrighan right now. You know that. You've seen the turmoil my own kingdom is in. I have to settle things there first. We have time to figure this out."

He didn't get what I was trying to say. I knew he couldn't go to Morrighan with me, but I saw the look in his eyes. He wanted me to trust him. Time felt like precious sips of water slipping through my fingers. His gaze was unwavering, bright, and sure. I nodded. I'd give it a few more days, out of necessity if nothing else. The physician had said Griz couldn't ride a horse or wield a weapon yet. The long neglect of his wound made it slow to heal, but the healthy flesh was beginning to knit together—if he was careful and didn't tear it loose again.

Rafe buckled on his scabbard and gave me a quick kiss before he left. The officers were riding out to observe training exercises. He seemed relieved to be doing something within the realm of his expertise—being a soldier—instead of arguing with Sven or Bodeen about court matters.

I stood in the doorway of his tent watching him walk away, wishing it was simply a matter of sending word to Morrighan, but I knew a messenger from Dalbreck probably wouldn't even make it past the border alive.

THE NEXT MORNING, VILAH, ADELINE, AND MADAM RATHBONE brought more dresses to my tent trying to find something for me to wear for the party the next evening. After much fussing, they settled on a deep blue velvet dress—Dalbretch blue—with a silver sash. "We'll put together the other accessories," Vilah said. "Unless you'd prefer to?"

I left it to them to figure out as Vilah suggested. I liked a beautiful gown as well as anyone, but it was probably obvious to all of them that I didn't fuss over the particulars of fashion.

"Do you mind if I ask—" Adeline blushed. "Never mind," she said, shaking away her question.

"Please," I said. "Speak freely."

"It seems that you and King Jaxon have genuine feelings for each other, and it just made me wonder . . ."

"Why did you run from the wedding?" Vilah finished for her.

"They claim it was a deliberate snub planned by Morrighan all along," Adeline added.

I refrained from rolling my eyes. "That is just bruised egos speaking," I answered, "and a court full of men who couldn't believe a girl could derail all their plans. The Morrighese cabinet was just as angry as Dalbreck's. My departure wasn't nearly as dramatic as a conspiracy. I simply left of my own accord because I was afraid."

Adeline twisted the silver sash in her hand. "Afraid of the prince?"

"No," I sighed. "The prince was probably the least of it. I was afraid of the unknown. I was afraid of the sham and the gift I thought I lacked. I was afraid of all the lost choices I would never be able to make, and that for the rest of my life someone would always be telling me what to do or say or think, even when I had better ideas of my own. I was afraid of never being anything but what suited others and being pushed and prodded until I fit the mold they shoved me into and I forgot who I was and what I wanted. And maybe most of all, I was afraid I would never be loved beyond what a piece of paper had ordered. That's enough fear to make any girl jump on a horse and ride away, princess or not, don't you think?"

They stared at me, and I saw the understanding in their eyes. Madam Rathbone nodded. "Enough and then some."

I WALKED, TRYING TO IGNORE THE RATTLE OF THE BELTS AND weapons of the guard escort trailing behind me. They reverberated like an entire marching army in the midst of the peaceful marketplace of wagons, but the king's orders were to be followed to the letter, six guards and not one less. I stopped to check on Dihara first, then went in search of Natiya.

Like Dihara, Natiya had been orphaned when she was a baby. Her parents' wagon had lost a wheel and tumbled down a mountainside. By some miracle Natiya had been spared, and together the tribe had raised her. Dihara, Reena, they had all been her mothers.

I found her down at the river's edge, alone, staring at the calm rippling waters, supervising a bevy of fishing lines thrown into the water. The guards hung back, and I sat down beside her, but her focus on the river remained constant, as if it flowed with dreams and memories.

"They told me you were here," she said, still staring straight ahead.

"Thanks to you," I answered. With a single finger, I gently turned her chin so she had to look at me. Her large brown eyes glistened.

"I frightened a man twice my size with that little knife. He had hurt a small child, and I threatened to cut off his nose. You took a stand, Natiya. It helped me to take one too."

She looked back at the river. "My stand didn't go well."

"Neither did mine. That will never stop me from taking them. Once we fear to take a stand, tyranny will have won."

"Then why do I feel that we've lost everything?"

I pulled in a slow, shaky breath, feeling the price she had paid. "There are more battles to be fought, Natiya. This isn't the end."

Tears trickled down her cheeks. "It is for Dihara."

A sickening twinge wrenched my chest. This was Natiya's reality—and mine. Were any losses worth the gains? I struggled with the same doubts I saw in her eyes. Dihara had sent me here to speak to her, but really, what did I have to offer? I was still trying to find my own way.

"Once, when I was feeling despair over bad fortune, Dihara told me we're all part of a greater story—one that transcends even our own tears. You're part of that greater story now too, Natiya. You listened to the truth speaking within you. It may not seem like it right now, but you're stronger today than you were yesterday. Tomorrow, you'll be even stronger."

She turned to look at me, the same defiance in her face as the day I'd left her in the vagabond camp. "I want to go with you," she said.

My stomach gripped. I wasn't prepared for this. I saw the hunger in her eyes, but I also saw Aster. It filled me with fear and renewed grief. I wouldn't let this part of the story be hers.

"Not yet, Natiya. You're too young—"

"I'm thirteen now! And a woman—the same as you!"

My blood rushed and my thoughts tumbled like a thousand tiny stones in a swollen river. "*Cha liev oan barrie*," I said. "Your time will come. I promise. For now, your family still needs you. Be strong for them."

She stared at me and finally nodded, but I was certain she remained unconvinced, and my own shortcomings seemed evident again.

A fishing line tugged, and she jumped up, giving it a sharp jerk to snag the hook deep in the fish's mouth.

I SAT ON THE WATCHTOWER WALL LOOKING OUT AT THE rolling plain. An orange ball of fire settled into the earth, the rippling line of the horizon slowly swallowing it up as if it were nothing, as if all the sun's timeless power were merely warm frosted confection. Gone in a single bite.

All that was left in its wake was an orange glow that lit the edges of spiked ruins in the distance. Rafe said legend claimed the ruins were what remained of a great stronghold that once held all the wealth of the Ancients. Now the works of the demigods were little more than scars on a landscape—reminders that even the great, with all their wealth and knowledge, can fall.

Somewhere beyond all that, on an unseeable horizon, was Morrighan and all the people who lived there, going about their lives, unaware. My brothers. Pauline. Berdi. Gwyneth. And more patrols like Walther's who would meet their deaths, as unaware as I had once been.

I want to go with you.

Where I was going was no place for Natiya. It was hardly a place for me.

CHAPTER TWENTY-NINE

RAFE

"MAY I HAVE A TURN?"

I wiped the sweat dripping from my face with my sleeve. I knew a crowd was watching my sparring exercises with other soldiers, but I hadn't known Lia was among them. I turned, following the sound of her voice. She hopped down from the paddock rail and walked toward me. I waved off the soldier who was poised to spar with me next.

I had seen her use a sword in our escape from the Sanctum, but that was in surprise attacks, and I didn't know how well she really knew how to spar. It wouldn't hurt for her to expand her skills.

"All right," I answered.

"I could use the practice," she said as she approached. "I had training with my brothers, but they emphasized dirty fighting."

"There's no other kind when you're fighting for your life. First thing, let's find a sword that's suited for you."

I walked over to the rack of practice swords, testing their weights. "Try this one." It was a lighter sword that wouldn't fatigue her arm as quickly but still had a decent reach. I selected a shield for her too.

Sven stepped forward. "Your Majesty, is this wise?"

Lia leveled a death stare at him. I knew she was already weary of every decision being deferred to me. "We'll be fine, Colonel."

"Astute move, Your Majesty," Lia said under her breath. "Or I might have had to take your steward down."

We went through a few slow thrusts and parries so she could get the feel of her weapon and then I applied more pressure.

"Don't use your sword to block or defend unless you have to," I said as our blows reverberated through the yard. "Advance! The sword is a killing weapon, not a defensive one. If you're using it to defend, you're missing a chance to kill." I showed her how to use her shield to deflect and unbalance her opponent to her best advantage, while at the same time using her sword to thrust and cut.

"Attack!" I yelled, baiting her just as I did the other soldiers. "Attack! Don't wait for me to wear you down! Keep me on the move! Let surprise be your ally!"

She did, in earnest. The dust kicked up around us.

The soldiers hooted. I had no doubt it was the first time they'd ever seen a woman sparring in the work yard—with their king, no less.

Her reflexes were fast and her concentration dogged—excellent qualities for a swordsman, but I had the advantage of height, weight, and strength, as most opponents she might face would.

To her advantage, she seemed to naturally understand the concept of movement and timing. Some soldiers planted their feet like trees, as if their sheer size would keep them upright. I had seen many of them felled by soldiers not much bigger than Lia. Her face glistened with sweat, and I was caught by a surge of pride.

"Watch your shins," someone called out. I glanced toward the crowd. Kaden. Our audience had grown.

Her sword skimmed my ribs, and cheers erupted. Like a wolf tasting blood, her thrusts became ravenous, her movement a graceful chaos that kept me increasingly alert. I advanced, pressing harder, and her strikes slowed against the pressure. I knew every sinew in her shoulder had to be burning with fire.

"Go for the kill," I yelled, "before the choice is taken from you."

She was a fast learner, using her shield well, deflecting my blows expertly, but then a piercing horn sounded, dividing her attention. I pulled back on my swing, but not before the flat of the sword caught her in the jaw and she went flying backward to the ground. The shocked groan of the crowd ricocheted through the yard, and I rushed to her side, falling to the ground.

I gathered her into my arms. "Lia! My gods. Are you all right?" Soldiers closed in around us and I yelled for someone to get the physician.

She grimaced, reaching up to hold her jaw where the redness was already turning blue. "Stupid," she hissed.

"I'm sorry. I didn't—"

"Not you. Me. Walther told me a hundred times I couldn't let in distractions." She pushed my hand away and opened her mouth, testing to see that her jaw was in working order. "I still have all my teeth. Stop fussing."

The horn sounded again. "What is it?" she asked.

I wasn't sure. "A warning or a welcome." I looked up at the watchtower, and a soldier waved the Dalbreck banner. "Our soldiers!" he yelled.

The rotation of troops had arrived.

I'd be able to leave for Dalbreck with Lia at last.

CHAPTER THIRTY

THAT EVENING, NO ONE MENTIONED MY TUMBLE, WHETHER to spare me or their king I wasn't sure. But if Sven said anything, I was prepared to point out that two of Rafe's sparring partners had fared worse—one a knot on the head, and the other a cracked knuckle. I hadn't sparred with Rafe to prove a point the way I had with Kaden. I knew a time might come when I would need greater sword skills, and I wanted to learn from the best.

With the arrival of the troops, everyone lingered over dinner, then dessert, eagerly eating up news of home from the newly arrived Officers Taggart and Durante.

While both officers were relieved to learn that Prince Jaxon had been found alive, I noticed Rafe grew quieter as the evening progressed and news was shared. Some of the reports were lackluster—betrothals, harvests, promotions in the ranks—but when it turned to the squabbles among the assembly and cabinet, and the rumblings of generals, Rafe's eyes narrowed and his fingers curled around the arm of his chair.

"We leave in two days. It will all be addressed soon enough," he said. His tense composure didn't escape the officers and further news of grumbling generals stalled on their lips.

Colonel Bodeen turned the conversation back to a lighter topic—the party that was planned for the next evening—and he noted the good timing of the troops' arrival. Apparently Officers Taggart and Durante were well-versed in Bodeen's celebrations.

"Be prepared, ladies," Taggart said. "There aren't enough of you to go around. You'll be dancing all night."

"That's fine by me," Vilah said. The other women chimed in with agreement.

"You too, Your Highness," Captain Hague said, lifting his glass to me.

This prompted another round of toasting, this time to dancing. Soon the conversation turned elsewhere and I became lost in my own thoughts, as detached from the party plans as Rafe seemed to be. I fingered the bone in my pocket, feeling a strange emptiness that a party wasn't able to fill. I had accumulated a small pile of bones back in my tent. It was a habit I couldn't let go of: the jingling tokens of remembrance and worry for those I had left behind. I feared the cruelties they would suffer at the hands of the Komizar, and worried for the greater needs that still lay ahead. Morrighan could be extinguished—snuffed from memory with only a few broken memorials to prove we were ever there.

Shouts jostled me from my thoughts. Everyone startled, looking toward the door. An angry scuffle was going on outside on the veranda. The door slivered open, and a soldier entered, apologizing profusely for the interruption. "We found one, Your Majesty, just like you said. Caught him lurking around the back wall. He's a small one, but wild. He slashed one of our guards on the arm before we could tackle him. He's demanding to see, er—" He looked down briefly as if embarrassed. "He wants to see the princess. He says he knows her?"

Rafe, Kaden, Griz, and I were all on our feet.

"Bring him in," Rafe said.

We heard more yelling, then two guards stumbled in trying to control their prisoner.

"Hold your place before I knock your head into the next world!" one guard growled.

The prisoner locked eyes with me, and my heart stopped.

It was Eben.

Though I knew better than to fawn over him, I couldn't stop myself and ran, pulling him from the guard's grip. Kaden and Griz were right behind me.

"Eben!" I drew him into my arms. "Thank the gods you're alive!"

His arms circled around me, unashamed, and I felt all the ribs and angles of his thin body. I pushed back an arm's length to look at him. His cheekbones were sharp, and his eyes hollow and circled with shadows. He was half starved and looked more like a wild animal than a boy. Dried spattered blood covered his clothing.

I saw emotion well in Griz's and Kaden's faces. Kaden stepped forward, grabbed fistfuls of Eben's shirt, and pulled him roughly into his arms. *"Drazhone."*

Brother.

Eben was their comrade. A Rahtan in training.

Griz did the same, then checked a scrape on Eben's cheek. When I turned from our tight-knit circle, I saw Rafe watching us, not with curiosity like everyone else, but with dark scrutiny. Kaden's shoulder brushed up against mine, and I stepped away, creating some distance between us.

Eben's attention shot to Rafe, and he eyed him suspiciously. He had only known Rafe as Dalbreck's emissary, and I realized he probably still didn't know Rafe's true position here. His gaze shifted to Jeb, once a filthy Vendan patty clapper, hardly recognizable now with his neatly combed hair and pristine clothing. Next he looked at Sven, the one-time governor of Arleston, who now wore a high-ranking officer's uniform, and then Orrin, the governor's mute guard, also in Dalbreck uniform, drinking from a crystal goblet.

Orrin grinned. "Surprise," he said lifting his glass toward Eben.

I made introductions.

"Fikatande chimentras," Eben said under his breath.

I looked at Rafe, wondering just how many of the choice Vendan words he knew.

"Yes, we're liars," Rafe said, answering my question. He

leaned forward, aiming a frigid stare at Eben. "We lied to save the princess's life. Do you object to that?"

Eben's chin lifted, defiant, but then he shook his head.

Rafe sat back in his chair. "Good. Now, someone bring the boy some food. We have talking to do."

Colonel Bodeen suggested it was a good time for the officers and their wives to retire for the evening. They all left except for Captain Hague.

It was more like an interrogation than talking. Rafe, Kaden, Griz, Tavish, Sven, and I all took turns asking questions as Eben wolfed down food.

He had barely escaped with his life. He had been in the far eastern paddock with Spirit when they came for him. His voice wobbled when he mentioned the name of the young foal that he had to leave behind. He was oblivious to what had happened back on the Sanctum terrace, but he saw Trahern, Iver, and Syrus—one of the tower guards—kill a paddy clapper without a word. He knew something was wrong, and when they caught sight of him, he knew he was next. He ran, hiding in stalls, barns, between stacks of hay, wherever he could as they chased him down. Finally Syrus cornered him in a loft. Eben killed him with a pitchfork in his chest. He spent the rest of the day moving from one hiding place to the next, finally ending up in an abandoned room in the South Tower, where he was trapped for two days. That was where he pieced together what had happened. Because of his close association with Griz, he had been targeted. Anyone who was known to have been intimately speaking with the princess, Griz, Kaden, or Faiwel was suspected as a traitor and systematically hunted down. He heard the screams of the slaughtered. He closed his eyes, and I thought he might not open them again. When he did, his lids were heavy and his eyes swam in his head. It wasn't terror but exhaustion undoing him. His head lolled briefly to the side. With a full stomach, he was barely able to stay conscious.

"Where did you stay in the South Tower?" Kaden asked.

"Right below the Komizar's room. I could hear almost everything through the flue."

"Do you know who he sent to hunt us down?" I asked.

Eben rattled off the names of everyone sent after us. He saw them leave from his hiding place. We had killed everyone he mentioned back in the Valley of the Giants—except for one who hadn't been among our attackers. Malich. Which meant he was still out there somewhere.

"Eben," I asked, before I lost him completely, "is the Komizar ruling now?"

Eben looked at me, fear briefly pushing aside the stupor in his eyes. He nodded as if too afraid to speak the Komizar's name. "The ghouls down in the caverns took care of him with their own potions. He's different now. He wants us all dead, and I'm the only one who didn't do anything."

"Except slash one of my men," Rafe said. "What am I going to do about that?"

"It was only a scratch on his arm," Eben chided. "Probably won't even need a stitch. He shouldn't have gotten in my way."

Rafe looked across the room at the guard who had brought in Eben. The guard nodded confirmation, and Rafe turned back to Eben, this time with a sterner gaze. "And where do your loyalties lie now, Eben?" he asked.

"Not with *your* kind," he answered, a snarl lifting his lip, but then his head bowed and he whispered, with all the misery and confusion the world could hold, "but not with the Komizar either." He'd been cut loose from the only life he knew—for a second time. His focus shifted to the far wall and then his head fell back against his chair, his eyes closed and his mouth open, finally succumbing to his exhaustion. He started to fall to the side, but Rafe grabbed him, scooping his limp body into his arms.

"I'll be right back," he said saying he was taking him to the physician's barracks to bunk, and to check on the soldier Eben had slashed.

"Be sure to post a guard on the urchin," Sven reminded him as he walked out.

Rafe's footsteps faded, and the room was heavy with silence, then a few mumbled words erupted among the officers. Unimportant words. Nothing like the ones that pounded in my head.

The Komizar rules Venda.

It was the truth I had known all along.

The truth Rafe had tried to deny.

The truth even the Komizar knew as he lay bleeding: *It's not over.*

Even Dihara whispered to me, *jei zinterr.* Be brave.

She knew it was only beginning.

He wants us all dead.

The vision I'd had of Civica when I was back in the Sanctum

seeped into the air before me again, like fingers of curling smoke that had been waiting just outside my field of vision. The citadelle was destroyed, the ruins only broken fangs on the horizon, and piles upon piles of bodies lined the roads like stacked stones in a wall. The cries of a shackled few, to be taken back to Venda as prisoners, hung in the smoky air.

Their moans wove through other voices, Rafe's, the Komizar's, the priest's, Venda's, and Dihara's too.

We'll send word. I promise.
It's my turn now to sit on a golden throne in Morrighan.
The bridge is destroyed. They can't even get across.
The Dragon knows only hunger.
Trust your gifts, Arabella, whatever they might be.
We call them our Death Steeds.
Sometimes a gift requires great sacrifice.
You'll know what you need to do.
Don't tarry, Miz.

Or they will all die. This last a knowing within me as certain as a sunrise. *They will die.*

The smoky haze before my eyes vanished, and I met the stares of everyone seated around the table.

"Your Highness?" Jeb asked cautiously, his pupils, pinpoints. Everyone else's gaze looked much the same. What had they seen in my face?

I stood. "Colonel Bodeen, I'll be leaving first thing in the morning, along with Kaden." I turned to Griz, "Once you're completely healed, you and Eben can catch up with us somewhere in Morrighan, but you can't ride yet. I need you fit and healthy—not as an added worry." I spoke quickly and firmly, not giving Griz or anyone else a chance to protest. "Colonel, we'll need our horses readied and additional supplies, including weapons if you can spare them. I promise that I'll repay—"

"What are you talking about?"

Everyone's attention turned toward the doorway of the dining room. Rafe stood there, tall and formidable, his eyes blazing. By his strained tone, it was obvious he had heard me, but I said it again anyway.

"I was just telling Colonel Bodeen that I'm returning to Morrighan in the morning. Any doubt about the Komizar and his intentions are gone now, and I—"

"Lia, you and I will discuss this later. For now—"

"No," I said. "We've already talked, Rafe, and I can't put it off any longer. I'm leaving."

He walked across the room and took hold of my elbow. "May I speak with you in private, please?"

"Talking is not going to change—"

"Excuse us, please," he said to everyone as he led me out of the dining room, his grip tight on my arm. He shut the doors behind us and turned on the veranda to face me. "Just *what* do you think you were doing in there? You can't go around giving my officers orders behind my back!"

I blinked, taken aback by his immediate anger. "It was hardly behind your back, Rafe. You were only gone for a few minutes."

"It doesn't matter how long I was gone! I return and you're shouting orders for horses?"

I struggled to keep my voice even. "I was not shouting—as you are now."

"If I'm shouting, it's because we've gone over this already, and you don't seem to be listening! I told you I need time."

"And time is a luxury I don't have. I will remind you it is my kingdom they are descending upon—not yours. I have a duty to—"

"Now?" he said, throwing his hands in the air. "Now you suddenly decide that duty matters? You didn't seem to give a devil's hell about duty when you left me at the altar!"

I stared at him, a hive of bees swarming in my chest, and I desperately tried to swallow my growing irritation. "I'm regrouping and moving forward with new information—just as some fool told me to do."

He walked across the wooden veranda and then back again, his boots punctuating his growing anger. He stopped in front of me.

"I didn't run across a whole continent and risk good officers' lives just to let you traipse back to a kingdom where you'll be killed."

"You're assuming the worst," I said between gritted teeth.

"You're damn right I am! You think one little lesson in swordplay and you're ready to take on a kingdom of traitorous cutthroats?"

Swordplay? I trembled with fury at his dismissal of my

abilities. "I will remind you, King Jaxon, that all of your fingers are intact now thanks to me. You think you'd be giving anyone sword lessons without them? I endured weeks of the Komizar pawing me, beating me, and sticking his tongue down my throat to save your miserable life. And I will also remind you I felled four men in our escape. You are not *letting* me go anywhere. Where I go and what I do is still my choice to make!"

He didn't back down, and his eyes became molten steel burning me with their heat. "No."

I looked at him uncertainly. "What do you mean, *no*?"

"You can't go."

An incredulous puff of air escaped from my lips. "You can't stop me."

"You think not?" He stepped closer, his chest as imposing as a wall. His eyes glowed like a beast's. "Have you forgotten? I am the *king* of Dalbreck," he growled. "And I decide who comes and goes here."

"You're a damn fool is what you are, and I'm leaving!"

He turned toward the end of the veranda. "Guards!"

The sentries standing at the railing immediately stepped forward. "Escort Princess Arabella back to her quarters," he ordered. "And post four guards to see that she stays put!"

I stood there, stunned with disbelief, trying to find my voice. "Are you saying I've gone from being the prisoner of one kingdom to being the prisoner of another?"

"You can twist it into whatever warped thing you choose, which I'm sure you will, but you're going to your tent and staying there until you come to your senses!"

I looked back at the guards. They stared at me anxiously, not sure how to proceed until Rafe told them, "If she doesn't follow willingly, you have my permission to drag her."

I glared at him and spun, stomping down the steps with the guards hot on my heels.

CHAPTER THIRTY-ONE

KADEN

WE HEARD EVERY WORD.

When the shouting began, Sven stood halfway up as if to leave. "Maybe we should give them some privacy—" Then he seemed to realize that the only exit led right into their argument. He sat back down. The only other option would have been to sneak out single file through the cook's entrance, which would be even more awkward, an admission that we were hearing their raging argument.

So we sat there listening, wondering how it could get worse.

Words like *devil's hell, damn fool,* and *I decide* raised eyebrows, but *prisoner* was a word that sucked in breaths. Tavish groaned, and Jeb mumbled a curse. Sven leaned forward, his face in his hands like he wished he could counsel his charge in the rules of a proper argument. I heard him mumble *drag her?* beneath his breath.

Griz was surprisingly silent, and I realized he was enjoying listening to the king dig his grave. Griz believed in Lia in a strange, fierce way that I was only just grasping. It didn't matter that she planned to leave him behind. The king was showing his true royal colors, and Griz was savoring every word.

I tried to savor the warm kernel of satisfaction growing in my gut too, but I also knew the rage I heard in Lia's voice came from a place of deep hurt. My satisfaction turned cold. After my promise of honesty, I had dispensed only portions of the truth to Rafe about my kiss with Lia, knowing it would enrage him, but she was the one who had shouldered the brunt of the pain it had caused. I didn't want to hurt her any more.

It was quiet outside on the veranda, and Sven finally broke our silence. "What else could he do? It's not safe for her to go back to Morrighan."

"She asked me once about going home," Jeb said. "I always assumed she meant Dalbreck."

"Dalbreck is not her home," I told him.

"It's going to be," Tavish said, shooting me a dark glare.

"Nothing to worry about." Orrin poured himself more ale. "She'll come to her senses."

Tavish snorted. "Sure she will."

"Her worry is valid," I said. "The Komizar is going to march against Morrighan and the other kingdoms."

"Which kingdom first?" Sven asked.

"Morrighan."

"And you know that with certainty, probably because he *told* you."

Sven's point was clear. The Komizar wasn't the best source for any truths, and I knew how he could hold back information, pitting one governor against another for his own purposes. The Komizar wanted Morrighan, but he wanted Dalbreck too. He wanted them all.

"Yes," I answered. "Certain." But now I wasn't.

Bodeen grinned. "March with his supposed army of a hundred thousand?"

Griz cleared his throat. "Not exactly," he said, finally speaking up. "I'm afraid the princess didn't get the numbers quite right."

No, she didn't. I remembered when I returned to the Sanctum and asked the Komizar how the plans were going. *Better than I hoped.* His army had grown significantly in the last few months.

Sven's eyes were sharp beads on Griz, as if he knew there was more coming.

"There you go!" Hague said waving his hand in the air. "Confirmation right out of the big barbarian's mouth. Maybe he's the one who should speak to the princess."

Griz swilled back a shot of red-eye and set the glass down with a loud thud. "The numbers are actually closer to a hundred and twenty thousand. All well armed. He motioned to Sven to pass the bottle to refill his empty glass. "That's about twice the size of your forces, isn't it, Captain?"

Jeb sighed. "Three times."

Hague said nothing. His mouth gaped like a fish dangling from a hook. Griz tried to restrain a smile.

Orrin and Tavish shook their heads, and Sven passed the bottle to Griz, scrutinizing him for signs of a lie.

It was the truth. That was what the Komizar was so heavily pressuring the governors for—more supplies to sustain his expanding army.

"They're only wild barbarians! Not a trained marching army. The numbers mean nothing!" Hague finally sputtered, dismissing the matter.

Bodeen sat back in his chair. "While the size and abilities of a Vendan army remain in question," he interjected, "the king's concerns do not. His worry is valid too. I understand there's a bounty for the princess's capture, and thanks to the Komizar and his rumors, probably something much worse awaits her by now. I think I heard King Jaxon describe her as 'the most wanted criminal in Morrighan'? That's a perilous position to be in."

Stalemate. That was true too, and I knew in their view it made Griz and me look callous and unconcerned for Lia's well-being.

Bodeen quirked his head to the side, listening, and then stood, finally judging it safe to leave. "What was that last thing she growled as she went down the steps? *Jabavé*?"

"It's a Vendan word for—"

Sven coughed, cutting me off. "It's not a term of endearment," he offered. "The king knows what it means. That's all that matters."

My kernel of satisfaction warmed again, in spite of myself.

> *It is in the sorrows.*
> *In the fear.*
> *In the need.*
> *That is when the knowing gains wings.*
> The black wings of knowing fluttered beneath my breast.
> He was gone, and he would not come back.

> —*The Lost Words of Morrighan*

CHAPTER THIRTY-TWO

I PACED IN MY TENT, TRYING TO CONTROL MY RAGE. MY blood raced faster than a whipped horse. I was certain that at any moment he would come, his head bowed in shame, begging forgiveness for his appalling behavior.

My head throbbed, and I rubbed my temples as I wore a path on the carpet. Come to *my* senses? Did he even hear himself? *Dear gods, had the entire camp heard us?* The dining room veranda was far from the soldiers' barracks, but the officers' quarters were within earshot. I squeezed my eyes shut, imagining all the ears pressed to windows. I knew Rafe was under strain and the additional news today of dissent back home only piled on more stress, but I was under pressure too. I hissed a frustrated breath between clenched teeth. Maybe in some small way I had gone behind his back, but it was only because I wanted to get my intentions out before he returned, making them clear and public and certain so he couldn't discount them the way he had before. Maybe he could construe it as usurping his authority, especially at a time when he was trying to gain the confidence of those around him, but acting like an ass was no way to gain respect.

I decide. I was not a subject of Dalbreck. He would decide nothing.

Minutes passed and then an hour with still no sign of him. Was he sulking? Too ashamed to come and apologize? Maybe he was commiserating with his men over his ill-spoken words. Or contemplating what Eben had shared. Rafe wasn't stupid. With the Komizar alive and moving forward with his plans, he had to know we were all at risk. Keeping me alive for now meant nothing if in the end we were all dead or imprisoned. Just because Morrighan was the Komizar's first target didn't mean that Dalbreck wouldn't be next.

I grabbed a pillow from my bed and punched it, then threw it against the headboard.

Swordplay! I could still hear his sarcastic emphasis on *play.* Maybe that was what hurt most of all. His lack of belief in me, only valuing his kind of strength and not the kind I possessed. The kind that had helped save both of our necks. Kaden had earned a healthy knot on his shin when he had done the same. It wasn't too late for me to give Rafe a knot too. Maybe he needed one on his head.

The sides of the tent shivered with the wind, and a low, distant rumble sounded as if the skies had been drawn into our tempest. I added wood chips to the stove. *Where was he?*

I threw aside the curtain of the tent entrance. Two guards stepped forward to block my path, crossing their halberds in front of me.

"Please, Your Highness, step back inside," one of them asked. A wrinkle curled across his brow. He looked genuinely frightened. "I really don't want to—" He was unwilling to finish his thought.

"Drag me back to my quarters as the king ordered?"

He nodded. The other guard fretted with the shaft of his halberd, refusing to meet my gaze. Surely they'd never had to guard a prisoner like me before, one who had been a guest of the king only hours before. For their sakes alone, I stepped back and snatched the curtain closed, growling as I did.

I snuffed the chandelier lights, and the room glowed dimly with the embers from the stove. I seethed that he hadn't already come in here begging on bended knee. I flopped onto my bed taking off one boot, then another, then threw them across the room. Both smacked the tent wall, each small thud pathetically unsatisfying.

Anger stabbed in my throat like a painful bone I couldn't swallow. I didn't want to go to sleep this way. I brushed at my wet lashes, blinking away tears. Maybe I should have explained it to him in private. Could I have made him understand? But I thought of all our miles traveling from the Sanctum to here, all the times he had skillfully turned the conversation away from Morrighan. *We just have to reach the outpost for now.* He had done it time and time again, so smoothly I hadn't even noticed.

Tonight he hadn't bothered to be smooth. All I got from him was a curt, arrogant dismissal. *No.* No chance for discussion—

"Lia?"

I jumped up from my bed, sucking in a startled breath.

It was his voice. Just on the other side of the curtain. Low and quiet. Contrite. I knew he'd come to work this out.

I walked to the end of the bed, quickly wiping my face with my palms. I pressed my back against the wide bedpost column and took a deep cleansing breath. "Come in," I said softly.

The curtain parted, and he stepped inside.

My stomach twisted. Only two hours had separated us, but it had felt as long as my trek across the entire Cam Lanteux. The dark crystal pools of his eyes warmed my blood in a way that made me feel lost to everything else in the world but him. His hair was tousled, as if he'd been out for a brisk ride to work off his pent-up frustrations. His face was calm now, his eyes soft, and I was sure a well-practiced apology waited on his lips.

He searched my face, his gaze tender. "I just wanted to check on you," he said quietly. "Make sure you had everything you needed."

"Now that I'm a prisoner."

Hurt flashed in his expression. "You're not a prisoner. You're free to move about the camp."

"As long as I don't leave."

He stepped closer, stopping only inches away. The heat of his body surrounded me, filled the tent, filled my head.

"I don't want it to be this way between us," he whispered. He reached out and touched my hand. His fingers slowly slid up my arm to my shoulder, and his thumb traced a slow, lazy circle over my collarbone. Hot embers burned in my chest. He knew

I wanted him, that I wanted nothing more than to reach out and close the hurtful space between us.

Almost nothing more. "Are you here to apologize?" I asked.

His hand slipped behind my back, drawing me closer, his hips meeting mine, and his lips brushed my earlobe. "I have to do what I think is best. I can't let you go, Lia, not in good conscience. Not when I know the danger you'd be heading into." He loosened the laces of my dress. My breaths skipped through my chest, uneven, singeing my thoughts.

His lips skimmed a burning line from my temple to my mouth and then he kissed me, hard and deep, and I wanted to melt into the feel and taste and scent of him, the wind in his hair, the salt on his brow, but another need—a greater one—flamed brighter, blazing and persistent.

I wedged my hands between us, gently nudging him away.

"Rafe, haven't you ever felt something deep in your gut? Or heard a whisper you had to listen to against all reason?"

The tenderness receded from his eyes. "I am not going to change my decision, Lia," he said. "I need you to trust me. You're not going back for now. Maybe later when it's safer."

I stared into his eyes, praying he'd see the urgency in mine. "It will never be safer, Rafe. It's only going to get worse."

He stepped back, sighing, everything about his stance conveying impatience. "And you think you know this because of an ancient text?"

"It is true, Rafe. Every word is true."

"How do you know? You're not a scholar. You may not have even translated it properly." His boorish skepticism snapped the last of my patience. There would be no more explaining or groveling.

"We're done."

"Lia—"

"Get out!" I yelled, shoving him away.

He stumbled back and stared at me, stunned. "You're throwing me out?"

"No, I don't think it's possible to throw *you* out. You are after all *King* Jaxon, and you decide who comes and goes here—or so I've been told. But I suggest you leave before I find another way to dispatch you." I placed my hand at my side over my sheathed dagger.

Pure rage flushed his face.

He turned and stormed off, nearly ripping the curtain from the door.

We'd see which of us came to our senses first.

MADAM RATHBONE APPEARED AT MY TENT EARLY THE NEXT morning, along with Vilah and Adeline. Curiously, Madam Hague accompanied them, though she never had before. Inwardly I sighed. Yes, the officers and all their wives had heard our ugly argument, and certainly Madam Hague was hoping for additional juicy details, even if the official purpose of their visit was to deliver the accessories to go with my dress for the party that evening. Adeline held up a silver chain-mail belt encrusted with sapphires. Once again, I marveled at the extravagance, especially here at this remote outpost. Next Vilah laid out a jeweled silver pauldron, embossed with an intricate pattern.

"Tell me, have Dalbretch women ever actually worn these in battle?"

"Oh, yes!" Vilah answered. "That's why they're part of our traditional dress. Marabella was a great warrior before she was a queen."

"But that was hundreds of years ago," Madam Hague added, raising her brows in distaste. "Our ladies and queens don't go to battle anymore. It's unnecessary now."

Don't be so sure, I was tempted to say.

Madam Rathbone took a last inventory of everything laid out on the table and said, "We'll be by early to help you dress."

"And do your hair," Adeline said.

"With silver cording," Vilah added clasping her hands together in anticipation.

I heard a strained eagerness in their voices, as if they were trying to erase the dark pall of last night's argument. "You'll all be busy getting ready yourselves," I answered. "I can manage on my own."

"Really?" Madam Hague asked doubtfully. "Is that how it's done back in Morrighan? No one to attend you?" Her lip lifted with patronizing pity.

"Yes," I sighed. "We're nothing but savages in Morrighan. It's a wonder your king would arrange a marriage with one of our kind at all."

Her lashes fluttered downward and she left with a faint apology that she had much to do that day, but with no apology for her insult. Perhaps now that her king had lashed out at me, she felt free to do the same.

SIX GUARDS ARRIVED AT MY TENT A SHORT TIME LATER. Percy, their leader, informed me they were my escorts for the day. So, this was Rafe's version of being free to go where I wished? Six guards—even within the walls of Marabella. I supposed I should take it as a compliment that Rafe held my skills in higher regard than he would admit. I immediately decided I had many places I would need to go today, not only so the entire outpost could share in the amusement of six guards trotting behind me, but also because, one way or another, I would be leaving and I needed to attend to details.

First I went to the lower paddock, checking on our Vendan horses, now also in the custody of the king. I eyed the lower gate where horses came and went. It was heavily guarded. We'd never get past that, but at least I knew where the horses and tack were. I'd figure out the rest later. Next I went to the cook's pantry. The cook was not pleased with my intrusion, saying he would gladly bring something to my tent. I pretended I wasn't sure what I wanted, then perused the shelves and cold cellar. Unfortunately, nearly everything was stored in large bulky bags or containers. I took one of his bowls and filled it with handfuls of pine nuts, hard soda bread, and some dried sweet figs. He eyed my strange assortment of food and glanced at my abdomen. I smiled sheepishly, letting him draw his own conclusions.

Next I trudged over to the physician's barracks to consult

with the surgeon. Kaden and Eben were gone to the showers, but the surgeon was in the middle of examining Griz's wound. He showed me that it was healing nicely in most places, but one section of flesh was slower to knit. He said he felt confident that it would heal, then shot a stern glance at Griz. "With a little more *rest*."

Griz balked, saying he was fine now.

"But you won't be if you're lifting heavy saddles on and off a horse twice a day," I said. "Or, the heavens forbid, if you should have to swing your sword."

Griz smiled, his eyes twinkling with mayhem. "Anywhere you'd like me to swing it in particular?"

My stomach burned. He had heard our argument too, which meant everyone in the dining room had. Surely Kaden gloated over this development, but when I saw him in the work yard later, there was only concern in his eyes.

He spoke in Vendan so the guards wouldn't understand us. "You're all right?" he asked.

I nodded, trying to ignore the knot swelling in my throat again.

He grinned. "And Rafe's shins?"

I knew he was trying to lighten my mood, and for that I was grateful. "Fine for now, but this isn't over."

"I never thought it was."

His vote of confidence in me was like cool water on a parched throat. I wanted to hug him, but that would only have brought him additional scrutiny.

The guards became nervous with this conversation they

couldn't understand, as if they suspected we were conspiring—which we were. I stepped closer to Kaden and whispered to really give them something to worry over. "When we leave, Eben will have to stay behind with Griz. It will just be the two of us—with Malich out there somewhere. Are the odds against us?"

"He'd have been there with the others in the Valley of Giants if he was sent to kill you. I think he's on his way to Civica with a message."

"That I'm dead?"

"That you've escaped. They won't count you as dead until they have a body—and they'll know exactly where you're headed."

Which meant the Chancellor and his coconspirators would be waiting for me. Probably watching every road leading into the city. The element of surprise was no longer mine. I didn't need anything to be harder than it already was.

Out of the corner of my eye, I saw Tavish and Orrin sauntering up to us shoulder to shoulder. They circled, stopping on either side of me. "We're here to relieve the guards, Your Highness," Tavish said, casting a withering stare at Kaden.

"Off you go, Percy," Orrin added, with a shooing motion. "Colonel wants you all back at his office. Go."

Tavish gave a respectful nod toward me. "We'll be your escorts for the rest of the day."

"By whose orders?" I asked.

Tavish smiled. "Ours."

Neither Tavish nor Orrin spoke Vendan, so I quickly spoke

a few last Vendan words to Kaden. "We'll talk more later. We need to gather supplies."

Tavish cleared his throat. "And Jeb will be joining us shortly."

His message was clear. Jeb spoke Vendan. I sighed. This was more than loyalty to a king—it was loyalty to their friend.

CHAPTER THIRTY-THREE

THE MORRIGHESE ARMY CAME INTO BEING CENTURIES BEFORE any of the others had so much as set a cornerstone to the foundation of their realms. It was yet another thing the Holy Text emphasized—that the Holy Guardians, the fierce warriors who accompanied Morrighan on her trek through the wilderness had unmatched strength and wills of steel bequeathed by the heavens themselves, to ensure the survival of the chosen Remnant.

Aldrid, who was to become her husband and the revered father of the kingdom, was one of those guardians. His warrior blood ran through all of us. The citadelle even had some of the Holy Guardians' swords displayed in the throne room—reminders of our greatness and the anointing of the gods.

Throughout history, the Morrighese army had remained

great, and its soldiers were courageous and honorable. But as I watched the Dalbretch troops going through their exercises and training from my vantage point on the outpost wall, I was struck by their daunting precision. Their halberds were braced with formidable timing, their shields were interlocked with the ease of a perfected dance. Confidence emanated from every meticulously orchestrated move. They practically glowed with intimidation. Their strength and discipline were like none I had ever seen. I understood why they believed in their power. But they couldn't see what I did—their numbers.

Even with an army forty thousand strong, they were no match for the terrible greatness of Venda. After Morrighan fell, Dalbreck would be next.

My gaze rose to the wide expanse above the troops where a crescent moon shared the sky with the departing sun. Another day was gone, fewer still remaining. Time moved forward, circling, repeating, another devastation coiling like a poisonous serpent that had awakened, ready to strike. It was coming, and hidden forces in Morrighan were helping it in the most insidious way—from within—feeding it with power that would destroy us all.

There had to be a way.

Jezelia, whose life will be sacrificed for the hope of saving yours.

A different way.

I wrestled with Venda's words. Sacrifice my life for mere hope? I would have preferred more than that—like certainty. But hope was at least something, and as unsure as it was, it was all I had to offer Natiya and so many more. Not even Rafe could take that away. Like the stories that Gaudrel had fed Morrighan, hope was nourishment for an empty belly.

Jeb interrupted my thoughts, saying it was time to get ready for the party. Tavish and Orrin stood several paces behind him, staring at me curiously. I looked out at the practice fields, and all the soldiers were gone. A handful of stars were already lighting the sky. Orrin shifted, sniffing the air, but they all waited for me to make the first move to leave. The three of them had maintained a respectful distance all day, vanishing with skill, just as they had at the Sanctum, but still always there, still always watching.

It wasn't by their own volition they had taken on the task of escorts, as they claimed. I was certain it was by Rafe's orders. He was trying to shed his own embarrassment about having a parade of anonymous guards follow me. He knew I cared about these three—we had a history together—even if it was short. Nearly losing your lives together had a way of deepening bonds and lengthening time. I studied their faces. No, not guards. Their eyes were filled with the concern of friends, but no doubt if I saddled a horse to leave, they would become something else. They would stop me. Even under the guise of friendship, I was still a prisoner.

I gathered my skirts and got down from the wall. For the first time, I sniffed the scent of roasted meat in the air, and then re-membered the lanterns being strung in the lower field earlier today, the canopy set for the head table, silk streamers draped be-tween poles in anticipation of a party eagerly awaited by almost everyone. Jeb fell in by my side, and Tavish and Orrin walked just behind us.

Jeb picked at his shirt. Smoothed the sleeve. Pulled at his collar.

"Say it Jeb," I told him. "Before you worry holes into your shirt."

"His throne is being challenged," he blurted out, voiced like a plea for his friend.

I heard Tavish and Orrin groan behind us, obviously not pleased with Jeb's loose tongue.

I rolled my eyes, unmoved. "Because of cabinet bickering? What else is new?"

"It's not the cabinet. One of his generals has begun proceedings to claim the throne."

A coup d'état? My steps slowed. "So the Dalbreck court has traitors too?"

"The general isn't a traitor. It's within his rights. He's charging Prince Jaxon with abdicating, which everyone knows is a false claim."

I stopped and faced Jeb. "His mere absence is interpreted as abdication?"

"Not by most, but it could be construed that way, especially with the general bandying even stronger terms around, like desertion. The prince has been gone for months."

I bristled. "Why didn't Rafe tell me?"

"Both colonels advised him not to tell anyone. Dissent breeds doubt."

I wasn't just anyone, but maybe Rafe didn't want me to doubt him most of all.

"Now that the general knows Rafe is alive, surely he'll stop those proceedings."

Jeb shook his head. "A general tasting power? He probably has an appetite now for the full-course meal. But Rafe has the overwhelming support of the troops. Their respect for him has only grown. It shouldn't take long to quell the challenge once he arrives back at the palace—but it's one more worry on his shoulders."

"And that's suppose to excuse his behavior of last night?"

"Not excuse," Tavish said from behind me. "Just to explain it and give you a fuller picture."

I spun around to face him. "Like the full picture you gave to Rafe when you caught Kaden holding my hand? Maybe *everyone* in Dalbreck needs to be sure of their information before they run off feeding it to others."

Tavish nodded, accepting his culpability. "I made a mistake, and I apologize. I only reported what I thought I saw, but news of the challenge comes directly from the cabinet. This is not a mistake."

"So Dalbreck has a usurper. Is that supposed to sway me? Why are Dalbreck's worries so much more important than Morrighan's? The Komizar rages with enough venom to make your general look like a whimpering kitten."

My patience unraveled. The urgency, the long miles to Morrighan, the temptation to say yes when no still blared in my head, the needs of so many compared to the enormous lack within me—it all picked at every last shred of confidence I had until I felt like a frayed rope ready to snap—the last pull of weight coming from Rafe himself. If the person I loved the most in this world didn't believe in me, how would anyone else? My eyes stung, and I blinked back any show of weakness. "If anything, you'd think Rafe's situation would give him empathy and help him understand why I have to get back to Morrighan—but it doesn't seem he's given that a passing thought."

"It's not his head he's thinking with," Tavish said. "It's his heart. He fears for your safety."

His words stabbed into my tender underside. "I am not a thing to be protected, Tavish, any more than he is. My choices—and my risks—are my own."

There was nothing he could say. I was right.

They dropped me off at my tent. Percy and the other soldiers were already stationed there to take over.

"See you soon," Jeb said, offering a hesitant smile. "First dance."

"That will be reserved for the king," Tavish reminded him.

Maybe not. Maybe there would be no dancing at all. At least not between Rafe and me. Kings and prisoners did not share dances, at least not in any world I wanted to be part of.

I LAY ACROSS MY BED, STRIPPED DOWN TO THE SOFT COM-fort of my chemise, writing down the verses from the Song of Venda that had been ripped from the book. After so many years, I was finally returning her original words where they were meant to be. They squeezed onto the back side of the torn page.

Betrayed by her own,
Beaten and scorned,
She will expose the wicked,
For the Dragon of many faces
Knows no boundaries.

And though the wait may be long,
The promise is great,
For the one named Jezelia,
Whose life will be sacrificed
For the hope of saving yours.

I remembered every word she had spoken that day on the terrace, though at first I had only been preoccupied with the phrase *whose life will be sacrificed.* Now another phrase caught my attention: *She will expose the wicked.*

I fingered the burned edges of the book, and then the furious jagged tear of the last page that attempted to rip the words from existence.

I smiled.

Someone hated me very much or, maybe better, feared me, believing I would expose him—or her.

Fear. Anger. Desperation. That was what I saw in these burned edges and torn page. I would find a way to fuel that fear, because even though I knew desperation could make people dangerous—it also made them stupid. Exposing the highest players in this conspiracy was essential. If I fanned their fears, maybe they would choke and show their hands.

With Malich on his way to tell them about me, I had already lost the advantage of surprise. They would be fortified and waiting—now I'd have to turn that knowledge, at least in some small way, to my favor.

I set the book aside and fluffed some pillows, leaning back against them, contemplating how I would go about this without exposing myself. I had to stay alive at least long enough to find out who might be conspiring with the Chancellor and Royal Scholar. Maybe one of the county lords? Their influence was limited, but if I was lucky, I might be there in time for when the winter conclave assembled. Or maybe it was others in the cabinet? The Watch Captain? The Trademaster? The Field Marshal? The Timekeeper had always eyed me suspiciously, and he jealously guarded my father's schedule. Was it to keep him out of the way? I avoided the obvious—my father, who had posted the bounty for my arrest. He was many things, but he wasn't a traitor to his own people. He would have nothing to gain by conspiring with the Komizar—but was he an unwitting puppet? The solution seemed to be getting past the minions who surrounded his movements to speak directly to him—but that was a thorny problem too. Would it be safe?

I buried my fingers in the sable blanket at my side, balling the softness into my fist. There was the matter of his anger to deal with. I remembered Walther's words. *It's been almost a month, and he's still blustering around.* Even the much-adored Prince Walther had to sneak behind my father's back to help me when he planted the false trail for trackers. The several months that had passed would not have diminished my father's anger. I had undermined his authority and humiliated him. Would he even listen to anything I had to say without a shred of evidence to support it? I was branded an enemy of Morrighan, just like his nephew, whom he had hung. With only my word against a Chancellor who had worked with devotion at his side for years, why would he believe me? Without evidence, the Chancellor and Royal Scholar would turn my claims to make me look like a coward trying to wheedle out of my own culpability. The last time I had aimed even a mild insult at the Chancellor, my father became enraged and ordered me to my chamber. Would they use other, more permanent ways to silence me this time? My chest tightened with possibilities I couldn't untangle. Could I be wrong about everything? Rafe thought I was.

My brothers were my only hope for inroads, but they were young like me, only nineteen and twenty-one, and still low-ranking soldiers in the military. But if both of them pressed my father, maybe they could sway him to listen to me. And if not listen willingly, perhaps help me use more forceful ways to persuade him. Nothing felt beyond me right now, with so much at stake.

A second round of music drifted up from the lower pasture—the party was well under way. It was beautiful, urgent music, the ringing conversation of a thousand strings, a chorus of rebuttals, satin strummed gauntlets laid down again and again, the tone similar to our mandolins but with a deeper, lustier reverberation. The *farache*, Jeb had called it when he came to pick me up—the battle dance. I had sent Jeb along without me, saying I wasn't quite ready. Once he was gone, I told my guards I wasn't going at all and encouraged them to go and enjoy themselves, giving them my solemn oath I wouldn't leave my tent. I kissed two fingers and lifted them to the heavens as sincere evidence of my promise—then silently asked the gods to forgive my small lie. The godless oafs didn't budge, not even when I commented on how delicious the roasted meats smelled and their eyes danced with visions of suckling pigs.

I was nibbling on the pine nuts I had taken earlier when I heard the rattle of halberds outside my tent and the curtain was swiped aside. It was Rafe, dressed in elegant full regalia, his black jacket draped with the gold braids of his station, his hair pulled back, and his cheekbones burnished with a day in the sun. His cobalt eyes flashed brightly beneath his dark brows, and waves of anger rolled off him. He stared at me like I had two heads.

"What do you think you're doing?" he said between gritted teeth.

The warmth that had leapt beneath my breastbone when he entered quickly shriveled to a cold rock in my stomach. I glanced at the bowl next to me and shrugged. "Eating nuts? Is that against the rules for prisoners?"

His attention shifted to my scant attire, and his jaw grew impossibly more rigid. He turned, searching my room until his eyes landed on the midnight blue dress Vilah had hung on the dressing screen. He strode across the tent in three steps, snatched it down, and threw it at me. It landed in a heap in my lap.

His finger stabbed toward the tent door. "There are four hundred soldiers down there, all waiting to meet you! You are a guest of honor. Unless you want all of their opinions of you to match Captain Hague's, I suggest you get dressed and make the small effort of an appearance!" He stomped toward the door, then spun with one last order. "And you will not utter the word *prisoner* one time if you choose to attend!"

And then he was gone.

I sat there, stunned. My first thought when he had walked in the door was that he looked like a god. I wasn't thinking that anymore.

If you choose?

I grabbed my dagger and prayed for Adeline's forgiveness as I altered the dress she had lent me, and Vilah's forgiveness too as I pried free a long piece of chain from her chain-mail belt. I would attend the party just as he had asked, but I would attend as the person I was—not the one he wanted me to be.

CHAPTER THIRTY-FOUR

RAFE

I SLUMPED AGAINST THE PADDOCK RAIL, WHERE THE torchlights from the party didn't reach, and stared at the ground.

Quiet footsteps stopped near me. I didn't look up, didn't speak. It seemed every time I opened my mouth, I said stupid things. How was I going to lead an entire kingdom if I couldn't even sway Lia without losing my temper?

"She's coming?"

I shook my head, closing my eyes. "I don't know. Probably not after—"

I didn't finish. Sven could put it together without my rehashing every detail. I didn't want to remember everything I'd said. It was getting me nowhere. I didn't know what to do.

"She's still set on going back?"

I nodded. Every time I thought about it, fear gripped me.

More footsteps. Tavish and Jeb came up on my other side and leaned on the rail beside me. Jeb offered me a mug of ale. I took it and set it on the post, not feeling thirsty.

"I wouldn't let her go back either," Tavish finally said. "We understand your position, if it helps."

Jeb mumbled agreement.

It didn't help. It didn't matter how many agreed with me if Lia didn't. As sure as I was that I couldn't let her go, she was certain she had to leave. I thought about when I'd found her on the riverbank, half dead, and all the hours I carried her through the snow, all the times I pressed my lips to hers to make sure she was still breathing, all the steps and miles where I thought, *If only I had answered her note, if only I had honored her simple request.* But this time it wasn't a simple request. This time it was different. She wanted to head straight into danger—and she expected to do it with Kaden.

I grabbed the mug of ale and swallowed it dry, slamming it back down on the post.

"You two are at cross purposes," Sven said. He leaned back against the paddock rail studying me. "What was it about her that caught your attention in the first place?"

I shook my head. What difference did it make? "I don't know." I wiped my mouth with my sleeve.

"There must have been something."

Something. I thought about when I had walked into the tavern. "Maybe it was the first time I saw her, and I—"

A memory surfaced. No. It was long before that. Before I ever laid eyes on her. The note. The gall. A voice demanding to be heard. The same things that angered me now had intrigued me back then. But even that wasn't what had captured my imagination. It was the day she had left me at the altar. The day a seventeen-year-old girl had been brave enough to thumb her nose at both my kingdom and her own. A refusal of epic proportions because she believed in and wanted something else. That was what had first captivated me.

It was her bravery.

I looked up at Sven. He stared at me as if he could see the unsaid words behind my eyes, as if I were a horse he had just forced to drink from a dirty trough of my own making.

"It doesn't matter." I snatched the empty mug from the post and walked back to the party, feeling his scrutiny on my back.

SHE WAS DANCING WITH CAPTAIN AZIA WHEN I RETURNED to the head table, smiling and enjoying his company. He clearly enjoyed hers too. Next she danced with a pledge who was no more than fifteen. He was unable to hide his infatuation and had a ridiculous smile pasted on his face. And then there was another soldier and another. I saw a few on the perimeter of the dance area staring at her bare shoulder, her kavah in plain view. She had cut away a sleeve and part of one shoulder on her dress to expose it, undoubtedly a message for me. The Morrighese vine tangled around the Dalbretch claw, holding it back. How differently I saw the kavah now.

And then I spotted the bones.

My fingers curled into my palms. I thought she had left the miserable practice behind us in Venda.

Where she had gotten so many bones I didn't know, but against her fine blue velvet gown, a long chain of them dangled, swinging through the air as she danced like a disjointed skeleton. She avoided my gaze, but I knew she was aware of my presence. Whenever she paused between dances, she fingered the monstrosity hanging at her side and smiled like it was as precious as a jeweled belt of gold mail.

Another round of the *farache* began, and I watched her dancing with Orrin, stamping her foot toward him, retreating back. They circled and clapped their hands high over their heads, and then slapped them together, the sound ringing through the field, echoing off the high walls. Orrin laughed, oblivious to my stare or her maneuvers, and I marveled at how he lived so fully in the moment. Whether it was dancing, cooking, or pulling back his arrow for the kill, only the moment mattered. Maybe that was why he was such a skilled archer, and a fearless one. I didn't have the luxury of living only in a single moment. I had to live in a hundred fractured moments that held our futures in the balance. I had a new understanding of my father—my mother too—and the decisions they had to make, sometimes compromising something they wanted for the greater good of something else.

The dancers sidestepped to the right, a new partner circled back from the opposite end, and I saw Lia matched with Kaden. I had been so focused on her, I hadn't even noticed him farther down in the line of dancers. Their hands clapped overhead, and then when they circled, I saw words pass between them. Only words. She had spoken with Orrin too, but this time the unheard words burned through me.

"Your Majesty?"

Vilah caught me by surprise. I sat up from my slouched position. She curtsied, her brown cheeks blushing warmer, then she held her hand out to me. "You haven't danced all night. Do me the honor?"

I took her hand, trying to shake my flustered state, and stood. "I'm sorry. I've been—"

"Occupied. I know."

Instead of me escorting her to the dance floor, she led the way, and instead of going to the end of the line, she squeezed in to Lia's right. I reluctantly took my place opposite her, realizing how easily she had duped me. I raised a questioning brow, and she smiled, stamping toward me to begin our dance. I stamped back. We circled, we clapped, and it seemed it was only seconds before it was time to move to the right—to a new partner.

Lia and I stood opposite each other. She dipped her chin in cursory acknowledgment. I did the same. The rest of the dancers were already moving toward one another. We worked to catch up. She stamped forward, and I retreated. When it was my turn to move toward her, she didn't retreat.

"Tired?" I asked.

"Never. I'm simply not fond of that step."

We circled, my back brushing hers.

"Thank you for coming," I said over my shoulder.

She snorted.

I reminded myself not to speak.

At our last overhead clap, just as our hands touched, the music immediately changed to the *ammarra*—the midnight dance of lovers. Someone was conspiring with Vilah. My hand squeezed around Lia's, slowly lowering it, bringing it to my side. My other hand circled her waist, and I pulled her close—as the dance dictated. I felt the stiffness of her back, but kept my hold firm. I breathed in the scent of her hair and felt the softness of her fingers between mine.

"I don't know this dance," she whispered.

"Let me show you." I tucked my chin near her temple and pulled her hips close to mine as I leaned her back, then swept her to the side, bringing her upright as we circled around.

The muscles in her back loosened, and she relaxed in my arms. The night suddenly seemed darker, the music more distant, and though the air was cool, her skin was hot against mine. I searched for something to say, something that wouldn't take our conversation to places I didn't want to go.

"Lia," I whispered against her cheek. It was all I could utter, even though other words crowded my mind. I wanted to tell her about Dalbreck, its beauty and wonders, the people who would love and welcome her, all the things she would marvel at, but I knew, no matter what I said, it would lead her back to Morrighan, and for me it would lead back to the traitors and noose she would face there.

The music slowed, and she lifted her head from my shoulder. Only shallow breaths separated our lips for a long-drawn moment, but then her back tightened again, and I knew it was far more than a breath that lay between us. We stepped apart, and her eyes searched mine.

"You never intended to take me back to Morrighan, did you?" she asked.

There were no more creative dodges left in me. "No."

"Even before you knew that your parents were dead. Before you knew any of your troubles back home."

"I was trying to keep you alive, Lia. I said what I thought you needed to hear at the time. I was trying to give you hope."

"I have hope, Rafe. I've had it all along. I never needed false hope from you."

Her expression betrayed no emotion, except for the glisten in her eyes, but that was enough to hollow me out. She turned and walked away, the bones jingling at her hip, the claw and the vine on her shoulder glaring back at me.

CHAPTER THIRTY-FIVE

KADEN

I WAS IN THE MIDDLE OF RUINS.

Turning my head. *Listening.*

Something was there.

They were coming.

A high-pitched howl split the air, but I couldn't move.

And then the world spun and I was flying through the air, tripping, stumbling. The fabric of my shirt cut into my neck as someone balled it into their fists. This part was real, not a dream. I instinctively grabbed for my knife, but of course, it wasn't there. My eyes adjusted to the darkness. It was Rafe. He was dragging me from my bed toward the door.

He threw me out of the barracks, then slammed me up against the wall, the night watch stepping aside, ready to let him tear me to pieces.

Even in the darkness, his face glowed with rage. "So help me, if you so much as lay a hand on her, if you drag her back to that godforsaken kingdom, if you do anything—"

"Are you mad?" I asked. "It's the middle of the night!" The fury in his eyes made no sense. I had done nothing. "I've never harmed her. I would never—"

"We leave an hour past dawn. Be ready," he said between clenched teeth. There was ale on his breath, but he wasn't drunk. His eyes were wild and bright like a wounded animal.

"You woke me to tell me that? I already knew when we were leaving."

He glared at me, freeing my shirt from his grip, giving me one last shove against the wall. "Well, now you know again."

He walked away, and I got my bearings. The rest of the camp was silent, asleep in their quarters, and for a brief moment, I wondered if he'd had a walking nightmare. It wasn't just anger I had seen in his expression. There was fear too.

Griz and Eben poked their heads out the door, their eyes still full of sleep, and the night watch stepped forward. Eben was still under close watch.

"What was that all about?" Griz grumbled.

"Go back to bed," I said. I pushed Eben's shoulder, and he went back in. Griz and I followed, but I couldn't get to sleep, trying to puzzle out what had prompted Rafe's attack. *If you do anything.* What did he think I was going to do with two hundred soldiers surrounding us on our way to Dalbreck? I was skilled, maybe even foolhardy at times, but I wasn't stupid, especially knowing they kept a suspicious watch on me too. I rubbed my jaw. Somewhere along the way, when he dragged me from my bed, he must have planted his fist in my face.

DAWN WAS JUST LIGHTING THE EASTERN HORIZON. MIST IN the distance hovered close to the ground in soft layers like a downy blanket. It made the morning even quieter. The only sound was my boots swishing against the dew-covered grass. I had managed to elude my escorts at least temporarily. This was not a quest for which I wanted company. I reached the end of the merchant wagons near the back wall of the outpost and spotted the charred *carvachis*—and Natiya.

Her eyes met mine, and she drew a knife—and I knew she meant to use it. I stared at her, not sure she was even the same person. She'd gone from a soft-spoken girl with an eager smile who used to weave presents for me to a fierce young woman I didn't know.

"I'm going in to see Dihara. Step aside," I told her.

"She doesn't want to see you. No one wants to see you." She lunged at me, the knife blindly slicing the air, and I jumped back. She came at me again.

"You little—"

On her next lunge, I grabbed her wrist, spinning her around so the knife was at her own throat. With my other arm, I held her tight against my chest so she couldn't move. "Is this really what you want?" I hissed in her ear.

"I hate you," she seethed. "I hate you all."

The endless depth of her hatred extinguished something in

me, something I had nursed like a weak ember, the belief that I could go back, could somehow undo these last months. But to her I was one of them and that was all I would ever be. One of those who had tied up Lia and forced her to leave the vagabond camp; one of those who had torched her *carvachi* and burned out her quiet way of life.

"Let her go," Reena ordered. She had returned with two buckets of water in her hands. She set them down slowly and looked at me with large worried eyes as if I would really slit Natiya's throat. She glanced at a poker near the fire pit.

I shook my head. "Reena, I would never—"

"What do you want?" she asked.

"I'm leaving with the outpost troops. I want to see Dihara one last time."

"Before she *dies*," Natiya said. Her tone was sharp with accusation.

I pried the knife from her hand and pushed her away. I looked at Reena, trying to find words to convince her I hadn't been part of what had happened to them, but the fact was, I had been. I had lived by the rules of the Komizar, even if I didn't live by them anymore. I had no words to erase my guilt.

"Please," I whispered.

Her lips pursed in concentration, weighing her decision. She was still wary. "She has good days and bad," she finally said, nodding toward the *carvachi*. "She may not know you."

Natiya spat on the ground. "If the gods are merciful, she won't."

⁓ 257 ⁓

WHEN I SHUT THE DOOR OF HER *CARVACHI,* I COULDN'T SEE her at first. She folded into the rumpled bedclothes, like a threadbare blanket, barely there. In all the years I had known her, she'd either been hoisting a spinning wheel on her back or butchering a deer or, if it was late in the season, taking down tent poles and rolling up rugs for the trip south. I'd never seen her like this, or expected to. It had seemed she would outlive us all. Now she looked as fragile as the feathers she once wove into her ornaments.

I'm sorry, Dihara.

She was the oldest member of their tribe and had fed generations of Rahtan like me in her camp. I understood Natiya's rage. Dihara might have gone on forever if not for the attack.

Her eyes fluttered open as if she had sensed my presence. Her gray eyes stared at the small swelling her feet created beneath the bedclothes, and then her head turned and she looked at me with surprising clarity.

"You," she said simply. Her voice was weak, but she managed a frown. "I was wondering when you'd come. And the big one?"

"Griz was injured. Otherwise he'd be here too." I pulled a stool close to her bed and sat beside her. "Natiya and Reena weren't happy to see me. They almost didn't let me in."

Her chest rose in a labored wheeze. "They're only afraid. They thought they had no enemies. But we all have enemies, eventually." She squinted. "You still have all your teeth?"

I stared at her, thinking she was no longer lucid, but then I remembered Natiya's blessing—her send-off to Lia as we left the vagabond camp. *May your horse kick stones in your enemy's teeth.* Dihara's body may have given out, but her mind still held a world of history in it.

"So far," I answered.

"Then you are not the princess's enemy. Nor ours." Her eyes closed, and her words became even fainter. "But now you must decide what you are."

She was asleep again, and I guessed straddling two different worlds, maybe traveling between both, much as I did.

"I'm trying," I whispered and I kissed her hand and said good-bye.

If I saw her again, I knew, it wouldn't be in this world.

CHAPTER THIRTY-SIX

I WAS TOLD TO WAIT.

The king himself would escort me to the caravan. The guards outside my tent were dismissed, which made me suspicious. A trick? Something was not right.

Rafe was late, and his tardy minutes seemed like hours. It gave me too much time to think. After our dance at the party, he had disappeared. I saw the shadows swallow him up as his long strides catapulted him through the arched paddock gate to the upper work yard. He never returned, and strangely, I found myself worrying about him. Where had he gone when this party had been so ridiculously important to him? And then I was angry at myself for worrying, and angrier still when later I was lying in bed and my thoughts drifted to the soft touch of his lips on my cheek. It was madness.

I desperately needed something from Rafe that he couldn't give to me. Trust. His lack of faith cut me to the core. His disregard for the future of Morrighan cut me deeper. In spite of what he claimed, Dalbreck and its interests were all that mattered to him. How could he not see that the survival of both kingdoms was at stake?

When the party was over, Sven had walked me back to my quarters. He was more reserved than usual, offering me a stiff bow when we reached the door of my tent.

"You do know he has to go back. His kingdom needs him."

"Good night, Sven," I answered curtly. I hadn't wanted to hear any more pleas for Rafe. I wished to hear someone plead for me and Morrighan for once.

"There is something else you should know," he added quickly, before I disappeared inside. I stopped and frowned, waiting for another petition on Rafe's behalf. He looked down as if embarrassed. "I was the one who suggested the marriage to the king. And I also planted the enticement of the port."

"You?"

"Along with someone from your kingdom," he hastily added. He spilled it out in one long breath as though he'd been holding it in for a very long time. "Years ago, when the prince was fourteen, I received a letter. Even he doesn't know about it. It came while I was out in the field training cadets, and it had the seal of the kingdom of Morrighan.

"Needless to say, it caught my attention." His brows rose as if he'd been caught by surprise all over again. "I'd never received any missive directly from another kingdom, but it was clear that somehow, someone there knew of my relationship with the prince. It was from the minister of archives."

"The Royal Scholar?"

"Presumably. From his office at least. The letter proposed a betrothal between the young prince and the Princess Arabella. Effective immediately on our agreement, she would be sent to Dalbreck to be raised in the palace and groomed for her position there. The only stipulation was that the official proposal had to come from Dalbreck. They asked that I destroy the letter. A great deal of money was offered to me if I honored these requests. The whole thing was ludicrous, and I tossed the letter into the fire. I thought it a prank at first, played by my own troops, but the seal had appeared genuine, and I couldn't shake the urgency in it. There was something worrisome in those words that I couldn't quite put my finger on. Still, I ignored the request for weeks, but then when I was back at the palace and alone with the king, I thought of the letter again. Just to get it out of my mind, I threw the idea out, an alliance with Morrighan by way of a betrothal between the young prince and princess. When he balked and dismissed the idea, I added the incentive of the port, which I knew he wanted. I never thought anything would come of it, and the king continued to reject the idea—until years later."

My mind was already jumping from the content of the letter to who had written it. "Tell me, Sven, do you remember anything about the handwriting?"

"Strangely, I do. It was neat and clear as I would expect from a minister, but excessive too."

"The scrollwork? It was elaborate?"

"Yes. Very," he said, squinting his eyes as if could still see it. "I remember being quite taken with the *C* in *Colonel,* written as if to impress me, and it did. Maybe that was it. There was a certain desperation to keep me reading, to play every card at their disposal, even playing to my vanity."

The Royal Scholar may have sent the letter, but he didn't write it. My mother's handwriting was distinct—and impressive. Especially when she was trying to make a particular point.

How long had the conspiracy to get rid of me been in the making? If Rafe was fourteen, I was only twelve—the very year the Song of Venda seemed to have come into the Royal Scholar's possession. *She will expose the wicked.* My stomach turned, and I grabbed a tent pole to steady myself. *No.* I refused to believe my mother had been conspiring with him all along. It was impossible.

"I'm sorry, Your Highness. I know you're set on going back, but I wanted you to know there are people in your own kingdom who have wanted you gone for a very long time. I thought maybe that knowledge would ease your discontent about going to Dalbreck. You'll be welcomed there."

I looked down, still thinking about the long-ago letter, and felt unexpected shame that Sven had to deliver this news to me. Discontent did not begin to describe the range of emotions charging through me.

"We're leaving just after dawn," he added. "Someone will be by to help you gather your things."

"I have no things, Sven. Even the clothes on my back are

borrowed. All I have is a saddlebag, which, as wretched as I am, I'm still capable of carrying myself."

"No doubt, Your Highness," he answered, his tone filled with compassion. "Nevertheless, someone will be by."

I stared at the saddlebag laid out on my bed now, ready and waiting. It was a wonder that it had survived at all—that I had survived. *May the gods gird her with strength, shield her with courage, and may truth be her crown.* The prayer my mother had uttered pinched in my throat. Had the prayer helped me survive? Was there any heart behind it for the gods to hear? Or was it a rote verse said by a queen for the sake of those who watched? She had been so distant in those last weeks before the wedding, like someone I didn't even know. Apparently she had been playing a deceptive role in my life for years.

She may have conspired and deceived but she was also the mother who had laid her skirts out in the meadow for Bryn and me to sit on as she interpreted the birdsong for us, making us laugh at their silly chatter; the mother who shrugged at my shiner when I scuffled with the baker's boy and then tamped down my father's scowl; the mother who told me just before an execution that I could turn away—that I didn't have to look. I wanted to understand who she really was or what she had become.

My eyes blurred, and I longed for that distant meadow and my mother's warm touch again. It was a dangerous thought because it tumbled into more longings, for the laughter of Bryn and Regan, the sound of Aunt Bernette humming, the echoing chimes of the abbey, the aroma of Tuesday buns filling the halls.

"You're ready."

I spun. Rafe was waiting near the door. He was dressed, not as an officer, nor as a king, but as a warrior. Black leather pauldrons tipped with metal widened his already broad shoulders, and two swords hung from his sides. His expression was hard and scrutinizing, like that long-ago day when he had first walked into Berdi's tavern. And in the same way it had that day, his gaze took away my breath.

"Expecting trouble?" I asked.

"A soldier is always expecting trouble."

His voice was so controlled and distant, it made me pause for a second look. His dark expression didn't waver. I grabbed my saddlebag from the bed, but he took it from me. "I'll carry it."

I didn't argue. It sounded like the stubborn declaration of a king rather than a proffered kindness. We walked through the camp in silence except for the jingle of his belts and swords, which made his footsteps seem more ominous. With each step, he seemed larger and more impenetrable. The camp was buzzing with activity, supply wagons rolling toward the gates, soldiers still carrying gear to their horses, officers directing troops to their squad positions in the caravan. I spotted Kaden, Tavish, Orrin, Jeb, and Sven clustered on their own horses just inside the outpost gates. Two more horses waited beside them, which I assumed were for Rafe and me.

"Find your places in the middle of the caravan," Rafe told them. "I'll help the princess. We'll catch up." *The princess*. Rafe wouldn't even say my name. Kaden looked at me oddly, a rare flash of worry in his expression, then turned his horse, riding away with the others as ordered. Dread snaked through me.

"What's wrong?" I asked.

"Everything." Rafe's tone remained flat, frighteningly absent of the lively sarcasm he had favored lately. He stayed busy, his back to me, taking an excessive amount of time to strap on my saddlebag.

I noted that my horse was heavily laden with supplies and gear.

"My horse is a pack animal?" I asked.

"You'll need the supplies." Another dose of his distant coolness plucked at my ire.

"And you?" I asked, looking at his horse, which had none.

"Most of my gear and food will be in the wagons that follow."

He finished with my horse and moved to his own. A sword sheathed in a plain scabbard hung from the pommel of my saddle, and a shield was strapped to the pack behind it.

I ran my hand along the horse's soft muzzle. Rafe saw me examining the plain leather noseband. "None of your tack denotes a kingdom. You can become whoever you choose as the need arises."

I turned, not certain what he was saying.

He refused to look at me, checking his own bag and cinch again. "You're free to go where you wish, Lia. I'm not going to force you to stay with me. Though I would suggest you travel with the caravan for the first twelve miles. At that point, there's a trail that veers west. You can take it if you choose to."

He was letting me go? Was there a catch to this? I couldn't go anywhere without Kaden. I didn't know the way. "And Kaden is free to go with me as well?"

He paused, stone still, staring at his saddle, his jaw clenched tight. He swallowed but still didn't turn to look at me. "Free," he answered.

"Thank you," I whispered, though it didn't seem like the right response at all. I didn't know what to say. Everything about this threw me off.

"Don't thank me," he said. "It might be the worst decision I've ever made. Get up." He finally turned to me, his voice still cool. "And you're free to change your mind about leaving any-time during those twelve miles."

I nodded, feeling disoriented. The day I had laid out in my head had suddenly vanished and was replaced with a new scenario. I wouldn't be changing my mind, but I wondered why he had changed his. He got up on his horse and waited for me to do the same. I looked at my horse, a fine-boned runner, sturdy but swift like a Morrighese Ravian. I unsheathed the sword, testing its feel, the cynical tone of Rafe saying *swordplay* still ringing in my ears. The sword was of medium weight, well-balanced for my arm and grip. There was no doubt he had chosen every de-tail of my tack and weapons—from horse to shield. I buckled the sheathed sword to Walther's baldrick and swung up on my horse.

"There's one condition I would like to add," Rafe said.

I knew it.

"I'd ask that you ride beside me—alone—for those twelve miles."

I glanced warily at him. "So you can talk me out of it?"

He didn't answer.

THE CARAVAN SET OUT. RAFE AND I RODE IN THE MIDDLE with twenty yards between us and the riders ahead and behind—clearly a calculated margin that everyone had been fore-warned not to breach. Was it to keep others from overhearing us if our voices should become raised?

Surprisingly, he said nothing, and the silence weighed on me like blankets used to sweat out a fever. He stared straight ahead, but even from the side, I could see the storm in his eyes.

It was going to be the longest twelve miles of my life.

Didn't he think I had doubts and fears about going myself? *Damn his stubbornness!* Why was he trying to make this even harder for me? I didn't want to die. But neither did I want others to die. Rafe didn't know the Komizar the way I did. Maybe no one did. It wasn't just that he had laid claim to my voice or that his knuckles had slammed across my face. The scent of the Komi-zar's lust still clung to my skin. His desire for power would not be stopped by a damaged bridge—nor even a knife in his gut. Just as he had warned me, it was not over.

After a mile, the silence broke me. "I'll send a note once I'm there," I blurted out.

Rafe's eyes remained fixed ahead. "I don't want any more notes from you."

"Please, Rafe, I don't want to part this way. Try to under-stand. Lives are at stake."

"Lives are always at stake, *Your Highness*," he answered, his tone ripe with sarcasm once again. "For hundreds of years, kingdoms have battled. For hundreds more, battles will be waged. Your going back to Morrighan won't change that."

"And likewise, Your Majesty," I snapped back, "cabinets will always bicker, generals always threaten rebellion, and kings will always prance home all lathered and puckered to appease them."

His nostrils flared. I could almost see words blazing in his eyes, but he held them back.

After a long silence, I stirred the conversation again. I needed resolution before I was gone, and I'd heard the way he had bandied *Your Highness* at me as if it meant just the opposite. "I have a duty too, Rafe. Why should your duty be any more important than mine? Just because you're a *king*?"

A frustrated breath hissed through his teeth. "It's as good a reason as any of the ones you've offered, Princess."

"Are you mocking me?" I eyed my canteen, remembering it could be useful for more than just drinking.

He didn't answer.

"A storm brews, Rafe. Not a skirmish or a battle. A war is coming. A war like the kingdoms haven't seen since the devastation."

Anger rose off him like heat on a skillet. "And now the Komizar is even able to pluck stars from the heavens? What spell has Venda cast on you, Lia?"

This time it was I who didn't answer. I looked away from the canteen, my fingers itching to swing it. We rode on, but he was only successful at being quiet for a short while. When he lashed out, I understood why there was such a great distance between us and the other riders. He abruptly stopped his horse, and I heard a succession of *halt*s and *whoa*s behind us, the whole caravan grinding to a sudden stop behind us.

His hand slashed through the air. "Do you think I'm not concerned about the Vendan army? I'm not blind, Lia! I saw what that small flask of liquid did to the bridge. But my first duty is to Dalbreck and to make sure our own borders are safe. To make right the shambles of my capital, and to make sure I even have a kingdom to go back to. I owe that much to every single citizen there. I owe it to every single soldier riding here with us today, including the ones who helped save *your* neck." He paused, his eyes fiercely locked on mine. "How can you not understand that?"

His scrutiny was desperate and demanding. "I do understand, Rafe," I answered. "That's why I never tried to stop *you* from going."

A reply stalled on his lips, as if I had punched the air from his arguments, then he angrily snapped his reins to move forward again. He couldn't accept that what was right might also come with a cost to both of us. I heard the creaks and moans of wagons starting to roll again, heard my own heartbeat pounding in my ears. Minutes passed, and I wondered if he was acknowledging the allowance I had afforded him that he couldn't quite give to me.

Instead, he uttered another complaint. "You're allowing a dusty old book to control your destiny!"

A book controlling me? Heat shot to my temples. I shifted in my saddle to face him fully. "Understand this, *Your Majesty*, there's been a lot of effort to control my life, but it hasn't come from books! Look a little further back! A kingdom that betrothed me to an unknown prince controlled my destiny. A Komizar who commandeered my voice controlled my destiny. And a young king who would force protection on me thought he would control my destiny. Make no mistake about it, Rafe. *I* am choosing my destiny now—not a book, nor a man or a kingdom. If my goals and heart coincide with something in an old dusty book, so be it. I choose to serve this goal, just as you are free to choose yours!" I lowered my voice and added with cold certainty, "I promise you, King Jaxon, if Morrighan falls, Dalbreck will be next, and then every other kingdom on the continent until the Komizar has consumed them all."

"They're only stories, Lia! Myths! You do not have to be the one to do this."

"It has to be someone, Rafe! Why not me? Yes, I could turn away and ignore everything in my heart. Leave it to someone else! Maybe hundreds have! But maybe I choose to step forward, instead of stepping back. And how do you explain this?" I asked, angrily pointing to my shoulder where the kavah still lay beneath my shirt.

He looked at me, his expression unmoved. "The same way you explained it when we first met. It's a mistake. Little more than the marks of grunting barbarians."

I heaved a deliberate, grumbling sigh. He was being impossible. "You're not even trying to understand."

"I don't want to understand, Lia! And I don't want you to believe any of it. I want you to come with me."

"You're asking me to ignore what's happened? Aster took a risk because she wanted a chance for a future for herself and her family. You're asking me to do less than a small child? I won't."

"Do I need to remind you? *Aster is dead.*"

He may as well have added *because of you.* It was the cruelest blow he could have dealt to me. I was unable to speak.

He looked down, his mouth pulled in a grimace. "Let's just ride and not talk before we both say something we'll regret."

My eyes burned with misery. It was already too late for that.

THE SUN WAS HIGH, MIDDAY, AND I KNEW WE HAD TO BE getting close to the point where Kaden and I would leave the caravan. Whatever landscape we passed, I saw none of it. My insides were raw—shredded from one end to the other by someone who I had thought loved me. Yes, it was the longest twelve miles of my life.

Orrin, Jeb, and Tavish rode ahead, and when they pulled out of the caravan, for the first time I noticed that their horses were as heavily laden with supplies as mine was. They stopped about thirty yards away between two low knolls. Kaden joined them. Waiting. And that's when I understood—they were coming with us.

I couldn't bring myself to tell Rafe thank you. I wasn't even sure if their added presence was protection or a trick.

He motioned for me to pull off the trail, and we stopped

halfway between Kaden and the caravan. We both sat there waiting for the other to speak, seconds stretching as far as the horizon.

"This is it," he finally said. His tone was subdued, weary, as if all the fight was gone out of him. "After all we've been through, this is where we part ways?"

I nodded, meeting his stare with silence.

"You choose a duty you once scorned over me?"

"I could turn that right back on you," I answered quietly.

The blue of his eyes grew deeper, like a bottomless sea, and they threatened to swallow me whole. "I never scorned my duty, Lia. I came to Morrighan to marry you. I sacrificed everything for you. I put my own kingdom at risk—for you."

The bloody furrow inside me tore wider. What he said was true. He had risked everything. "Is that my debt to you, Rafe? Do I have to give up all that I am and everything I believe in to pay you back? Is that really who you want me to be?"

His eyes locked on mine and it seemed there was no air left in the universe. Time stretched impossibly, and he finally looked away. He eyed my pack and weapons—the sword, the knife at my side, the shield, all the supplies he himself had carefully selected. He shook his head as if it wasn't enough.

His attention turned toward the waiting trio. "I will not risk their lives again by sending them into a hostile kingdom. Their only duty is to escort you safely back to your border. After that Dalbreck is done with Morrighan. Your fate will be in your own kingdom's hands, not mine."

His horse stamped as if sensing his frustration, and Rafe cast one last look at Kaden. He turned back to me, the anger drained from his face. "You've made your choice. It's for the best, then. We're each called somewhere else."

My stomach turned queasy, and a sick salty taste filled my mouth. I felt him letting go. This was it. I forced myself to nod. "For the best."

"Good-bye, Lia. I wish you well."

He turned his horse before I could even offer my own last farewell, riding off without so much as a backward glance. I watched him go, his hair blowing in the wind, the shine of his swords glinting in the sun, and a memory flashed in my mind. My dreams rushed back, large and crushing like a wave, the dream I'd had so many times back at the Sanctum—a confirmation of the knowing that I didn't welcome—Rafe was leaving me. Every detail I had dreamed was now laid out before my eyes, stark and clear: the cold wide sky, Rafe sitting tall on his horse, a fierce warrior dressed in garb I had never seen before—the warrior dress of a Dalbreck soldier with a sword at each side.

But this wasn't a dream.

I wish you well.

The distant words of an acquaintance, a diplomat, a king.

And then I lost sight of him somewhere near the front of the caravan where a king should ride.

CHAPTER THIRTY-SEVEN

WE RODE HARD. I FOCUSED ON THE SKY, THE HILLS, THE rocks, the trees. I scanned the horizon, the shadows, always watching. I planned. I devised. No moment was left without purpose. No moment left for my mind to steep in dangerous thoughts that would consume me. *What if . . .*

Doubt was a poison I couldn't afford to sip.

I rode faster, and the others worked to keep up. The next day, I did the same. I said my remembrances morning and evening without fail, remembering Morrighan's journey, remembering Gaudrel and Venda, remembering the voices in the valley where I had buried my brother. Every memory was another bead on a necklace strung somewhere inside me. I fingered them, squeezed them, held them, polished them bright and warm. They were the real and true. They had to be.

And when fatigue washed over me, I remembered more. The easy things. The things that could pull another mile, another ten, out of me and my horse.

My brother's face, desolate and weeping as he told me about Greta.

The shine of Aster's lifeless eyes.

The traitorous grins of the scholars in the caverns.

The Komizar's promise that it wasn't over.

The endless games of courts and kingdoms that traded lives for power.

Each bead of memory that I added helped me move forward.

On the first night, when I had unloaded the pack on my horse, the necklace of carefully polished beads suddenly snapped and spilled to the ground. It was the simplest of things that broke it loose. An extra blanket tucked inside the bedroll. A change of riding clothes. An additional belt and knife. They were only the basics for a long journey, but I saw Rafe's hand behind it all, the way he folded a blanket, the knots he made to secure it. He had chosen and packed each piece himself.

And then his last words struck me.

Cruel words. *Aster is dead.*

Words that piled on guilt. *I sacrificed everything for you.*

Parting words. *It's for the best.*

I had clutched my stomach, and Kaden was immediately at my side. Jeb, Orrin, and Tavish stopped what they were doing and stared at me. I claimed it was only a cramp, and I willed the pain twisting in me into a small hard bead and knotted my resolve with it. It wouldn't undo me again.

Kaden reached out. "Lia—"

I shook him loose. "It's nothing!" I ran down to the creek and washed my face. Washed my arms. My neck. Washed until my skin shivered with cold. What I left behind would not jeopardize what lay ahead.

Over the next few days, Jeb, Orrin, and Tavish regarded me carefully. I guessed they were not comfortable with their quest. Before, they had been leading me away from danger, and now they were depositing me on its doorstep.

In the early evening, when there was still light, I practiced with knife and sword, ax and arrow, not knowing when or where I might need any of them. Since it was his specialty, I enlisted Jeb to teach me the silent art of breaking a neck, and he reluctantly agreed, then showed me more methods to dispatch an enemy without a weapon—though many of those methods were not exactly silent.

Later, when it was dark and there was nothing left to do but sleep, I listened for the sounds of the Rahtan—howls, footsteps, the sliding of a knife from a sheath. I slept with my dagger on one side of my bedroll and my sword on the other, ready. There was always a thought, a task, another bead to polish and add to my string, and then when there was only silence, I would wait for the veil of darkness to overtake me.

The one thing I couldn't control were my moments of restless half sleep, when I rolled over and my arm searched for the warmth of a chest that was no longer there, or my head tried to nestle in the crook of a shoulder that was gone. In that netherworld, I heard words trailing behind me, like wolves stalking their prey, waiting for it to weaken and drop, strings of words that would pounce. *How can you not understand?* And, maybe worse, the bite of words that were never said.

CHAPTER THIRTY-EIGHT

KADEN

I KNEW SHE WAS HURTING. IT HAD BEEN THREE DAYS. I wanted to hold her. Make her stop. Slow down. I wanted her to look into my eyes and answer a question I was too afraid to ask. But trying to make Lia do anything right now was the wrong course of action.

On the first day when she had joined us on the trail and Tavish had asked if she was all right, I had watched her turn to stone. She knew what Tavish was implying, that she was weak or wounded by Rafe's departure.

"Your king is where he should be, tending to the needs of his kingdom. And I'm doing what I need to do. It's as simple as that."

"I know he made promises to you about Terravin."

She hadn't answered him. She'd only looked back at the

disappearing caravan and tugged on her gloves, flexing and shoving her fingers deeper into them and said, "Let's ride."

Rafe's expression on that last night when he threw me up against the barracks wall stayed with me. He had been wild with fear—afraid to let her go—but he did. Something I hadn't done, no matter how many times she'd asked me to free her as we crossed the Cam Lanteux. The thought turned in my head over and over again.

WE WERE CAMPED IN A THIN SCRABBLE OF BEECH, TUCKED up close to an outcropping of boulders. A shallow brook ran close by.

Lia sat off by herself, but not too far from the camp. We all still looked over our shoulders and slept with our weapons ready. We knew there could be more out there. Eben's account of who he had seen leave the Sanctum, while helpful, could not include who he might not have seen.

I knew what would come next. Once she finished her re-membrances, she would sharpen her knives, check her horse's hooves for stones, scan the trail behind us, or scratch in the soil with a stick, then erase the marks with her boot. I wondered what she drew. Words? Maps? But when I asked her, she only said, *Nothing.*

I had thought this was all I ever wanted. To be with her. On the same side. *She's with you Kaden. That's all that matters.*

"I'm going to start dinner," Orrin said, casting a wondering glance Lia's way. He walked over to the firewood I had gathered and set his spit, spearing the pheasant he'd already gutted and cleaned.

Tavish returned from washing up in the brook. His thick black ropes of hair dripped with water. He followed my gaze, looking at Lia, and offered a quiet grunt. "I wonder what drill she'll put one of us through tonight."

"She wants to be prepared."

"One person alone can't take on an entire kingdom."

"She has us. She's not alone."

"She has you—and that's not saying a lot. The rest of us turn around once we reach the Morrighese border." He shook out his hair and pulled his shirt over his head.

The first few days riding with Rafe's loyal trio had been tense, but for Lia's sake, I held back my tongue, and a few times my fist, too. Now they seemed to accept that I wasn't along to whisk Lia back to Venda and that I had retired my former title of Assassin, at least until Lia was back in Morrighan. Whether I wanted to admit it or not, they were useful too. I knew hundreds of trails along this southern route, but every Rahtan knew them too. These three had surprised me with a few trails that wound through hidden box canyons where I had never traveled before. And with Orrin along, we never had to eat snake. He was able to draw an arrow and bring down game from his saddle while barely slowing his pace. His skill and passion were perfectly matched.

"Have you noticed," Tavish asked as he shook out his saddle blanket and hung it over a low branch, "every dusk when she says her remembrances, the wind stirs?"

I had noticed. And wondered. The air seemed to thicken and come alive, as if she were summoning spirits. "Could just be the natural shift of air as the sun goes down."

Tavish's eyes narrowed. "Could be."

"I didn't think you Dalbretch were the superstitious sort."

"I saw it back at the Sanctum too. I was there watching from the shadows, and I heard everything she said. Sometimes it felt like her words were touching my skin, like the breeze was carrying every single one past me. It was a strange thing." I had never heard Tavish ruminate on anything beyond trails and suspicions of my true motivations, which had almost brought us to blows. He blinked as if catching himself. "My watch," he said, walking away to relieve Jeb. He stopped after a few steps and turned.

"Just curious. Is it true you used to be Morrighese?"

I nodded.

"That's where you got all the scars? Not in Venda?"

"A very long time ago."

He eyed me as if trying to figure out how old I must have been.

"I was eight the first time I was whipped," I said. "The beatings lasted for a couple of years until I was taken to Venda. It was the Komizar who saved me."

"Being the fine fellow that he is." He studied me, chewing the corner of his lip. This revelation probably didn't improve his regard for me. "Those are deep scars. I'm guessing you remember every lash. And now you suddenly want to help Morrighan?"

I leaned back on my elbows and smiled. "Always suspicious, aren't you?"

He shrugged. "Tactician. It's my job."

"Tell you what, I'll answer your question if you'll answer one of mine."

His chin dipped in agreement, waiting for my question.

"Why are you really here? Your king could have sent any squad to escort the princess to the border of her kingdom. Why his top officers? Was it only so you could escort her back to Dalbreck once she came to her senses? And if she didn't, to force her back?"

Tavish smiled. "Your answer isn't so important to me after all," he said, and left.

As Tavish walked away, I watched Lia stride toward me, with dusty riding leathers and a smudged face. Three weapons hung from her sides, and she looked more like a soldier than a princess, though in truth, I wasn't even sure what a princess should look like. She had never fit any image I had conjured of one. *Royal.* How easily I had disparaged the title when the only nobility I had ever really known was my father, the esteemed Lord Roché of County Düerr. His line went all the way back to Piers, one of the first Holy Guardians, affording him an elevated status and special favor among nobility, if not the gods themselves. My mother had told me of my ancestry once. I had worked hard to forget it and prayed I had gotten all of her blood and none of his.

Lia paused, lifting Walther's baldrick over her head and laid it down on her bedroll, then unbuckled her other belt that held two knives, dropping it with the rest of her gear. She stretched her arms overhead as if she was working a knot loose in her back, then surprised me by plopping down beside me. She gazed across the hills and woods that obscured the horizon and setting sun, as if she could see all the miles that still lay ahead of us.

"No knives to sharpen?" I asked.

Her cheek dimpled. "Not tonight," she said, still gazing out at the hills. "I need to rest. We can't keep this pace up, or the horses will give out before we do."

I looked at her skeptically. Jeb and I had said almost those exact same words to her this morning, and she had only answered us both with a scathing look of contempt.

"What's changed since this morning?"

She shrugged. "Pauline and I were terrified when we rode from Civica, but eventually we stopped looking over our shoulders and started looking for the blue bay of Terravin. That's what I need to do now. Only look forward."

"It's that simple?"

She stared through the trees, her eyes clouded in thought. "Nothing is ever simple," she finally said. "But I have no other choice. Lives depend on it."

She shifted on the blanket and faced me fully. "Which is why we need to talk."

She shot questions at me, one after another, a methodical urgency to them. Now I knew at least some of what occupied her thoughts as she rode. I confirmed her suspicion that the Komizar would begin marching after first thaw. As I doled out answers, I realized how little I actually had to give her. It made me see that, for all of my conspiring with the Komizar, he had kept me in the dark more than he had confided in me. I had never been a true partner in this plan of his, only one of many to help him accomplish it.

"There must be other traitors besides the Chancellor and Royal Scholar. Didn't you deliver any other messages?"

"I only delivered the one message when I was thirteen. He mostly kept me out of Civica altogether. I tracked down deserters, or he sent me to deliver retribution to outlying garrisons."

She chewed on her lip for a moment, then asked me something odd. She wanted to know if we would pass any place where messages could be sent.

"Turquoi Tra. There's a relay post of messengers there. They're fast but costly. Why?" I asked.

"I might want to write home."

"I thought you said the Chancellor would intercept all messages."

A fierce glint shone in her eyes. "Yes. He will."

CHAPTER THIRTY-NINE

ON THE FOURTH DAY, WE HADN'T GOTTEN FAR WHEN KADEN said, "We have company."

"I saw," I answered sharply.

"What do you want to do?" Tavish asked.

I kept my eyes straight ahead. "Nothing. Just keep going."

"She's waiting for an invitation," Jeb said.

"She's not going to get one!" I snapped. "I told her she couldn't come. She'll turn around."

Orrin smacked his lips. "If she made it through three nights alone, I doubt she'll give up that easily."

I growled with all the fury of Griz, and snapped my reins, turning my horse around to gallop back toward Natiya. She stopped her horse when she saw me coming.

I came alongside her. "What do you think you're doing?"

"Riding," she said defiantly.

"This is no holiday, Natiya! Turn around! You can't come with me!"

"I can go where I want."

"And it just happens to be in the same direction I'm going?"

She shrugged. Her audacity appalled me. "Did you steal that horse?" I asked, trying to shame her.

"It's mine."

"And Reena said you could come?"

"She knew she couldn't stop me."

She was not the same girl I had met in the vagabond camp. I hated what I saw in her expression. Her cheerful innocence was gone and replaced with alarming hunger. She wanted more than I could give her. I needed her to go back.

"If you come along, you're probably going to die," I told her.

"I heard you're going to do the same. Why didn't that stop you?"

Her eyes were clever and sharp like Aster's, and I looked away. I couldn't do this. I wanted to strike her, shake her, and make her see how very much she was not welcome here.

Kaden rode over. "Hello, Natiya," he said, and nodded like we were all out for a spring ride.

"Oh, for the love of gods! Tell her she has to go back! Make her listen."

He smiled. "The way you listen?"

I looked back at Natiya, a bitter gall climbing up my throat. She met my stare, unblinking, her decision shining in her eyes. Moisture sprang to my face and I was afraid I might lose my morning meal. She was so young. Almost as young as Aster and far more naïve. What if—

I wiped the sweat from my upper lip.

"Come along!" I snapped. "And keep up! We aren't going to coddle you!"

Journey's end. The promise. The hope.

Is this the place of staying Ama?

A vale. A meadow. A home.

A scrabble of ruins we can piece together.

A place far from the scavengers.

The child looks at me, her eyes full of hope. Waiting.

For now, I tell her.

The children scatter. There is laughter. Chatter.

There is hope.

But there is still no promise.

Some things will never be as Before.

Some things you cannot bring back.

Some things are gone forever.

And other things last just as long.

Like the scavengers.

One day, they will come for us again.

—*The Last Testaments of Gaudrel*

CHAPTER FORTY

RAFE

THE SUN.

Had I mentioned the sun?

Maneuver your opponent so the sun is in his eyes, not yours.

Dodge and undercut. I hadn't gone over that. But it wasn't as if she didn't already have good sword fighting skills. *Maybe I should have given her a lighter sword.*

There were so many things I could have said—and not just about swords.

I knew I was second-guessing myself. I had been for most of the journey.

"Your Majesty, we're almost there. I've been talking for twenty minutes, and you haven't heard a word I said."

"I heard you say it yesterday, Sven. And the day before. Kings do this, they don't say that. They listen, they weigh, they act.

They take, but they give. They push but aren't pushed. Does that sum it up? You're acting as if I didn't grow up in court."

"You didn't," he reminded me.

I frowned. For the most part, he was right. Yes, I'd had weekly meals with my parents, and I was included as a matter of protocol in most official functions, but for the many years I was under Sven's tutelage, I had lived with cadets, pledges, and most recently, with other soldiers. Dalbreck's kings were soldiers first, and I had been raised no differently from how my own father had been raised, but in the last year, he had been pulling me closer into the fold. He had me sit in on high-level meetings and counseled me on them afterward. I wondered if he had seen his reign coming to an end.

"We're still a good ten miles out," I said. "I'm ready, I promise you."

"Maybe," he begrudged me. "But your mind is elsewhere."

My hands tightened on my reins. I knew he wouldn't let this go.

"You did what you had to do," he went on. "Letting her go was an act of courage."

Or stupidity.

"She's on her way to a kingdom riddled with traitors who want her dead," I finally blurted out.

"Then why did you let her go?"

I didn't answer. He knew. He'd already said it. Because I had no choice. And that was the biting irony. If I had forced her back to Dalbreck, I'd have lost Lia just the same. But as long as Sven had opened the door to what occupied my mind, I ventured further, asking a question that had circled in my head like a mad crow pecking at my flesh.

"I know the Assassin loves her." I swallowed, then added more quietly, "Do you think she loves him?"

Sven coughed and shifted in his saddle. He grimaced. "That's not my area of expertise. I can't advise you on—"

"I am not asking for advice, Sven! Just your opinion! You seem to have one on everything else!"

If he had knocked me off my saddle it would have been within his rights. And it wouldn't have been the first time. Instead, he cleared his throat. "Very well. From what I observed at the Sanctum, and the way she interceded on his behalf when we captured him, I would say . . . yes, she does care for him. But love? Of that, I'm not so sure. The way she looked at you was—"

A trumpet sounded. "Troops!" the flag bearer called.

We were too far out to be greeted by a squad yet, but when Sven and I pushed our horses forward for a better view, there it was. Not just a squad but what looked like a whole Dalbretch regiment heading our way. Double the numbers in our caravan. To stop us, or escort us in? It was not customary for outpost caravans to be greeted this way—but then challenged kings were not usually part of a returning caravan.

"Arms ready," I called. The order rolled back along the caravan like a war chant. "Move forward."

As we got closer, Captain Azia shouted more orders and the caravan spread out, creating a wide, formidable line. Shields were raised. We were facing our own—not exactly how I had envisioned beginning my reign. The kingdom was more divided than

I'd thought. Sven rode on one side of me, and Azia on the other. Faces came into view, General Draeger foremost among them.

"I'm not liking this," Sven grumbled.

"Let's give him a chance to do what's right," I said. I turned and yelled, "Hold!" to those behind me, then moved forward with my officers to meet him and his officers.

Several yards from one another, we all stopped.

"General Draeger," I said firmly, and dipped my head in acknowledgment, trying to avoid a bloody outcome.

"Prince Jaxon," he returned.

Prince. The heat rose on my neck. My eyes locked onto his.

"You've been out too long in the field, General," I said. "You must not be aware, my title has changed—and yours has not."

He smiled. "I think you're the one who's been gone too long."

"Agreed. But I'm here now to take my rightful place on the throne."

He returned my stare, neither correcting himself nor backing down. He was a young man for a general, no more than forty, and had been in the highest military position for three years, but perhaps he felt he had already outgrown it. He glanced at Sven and Azia, then briefly to the long line of soldiers behind us, assessing their numbers, and possibly their resolve.

"And now you think you're here to stay put and rule?" he asked.

I answered him with an icy stare. He was pushing his limits and mine. "I am."

He made a move, reaching for the pommel of his saddle, and Azia's hand went to his sword.

"Steady," I said.

The general swung down from his horse, and the troops behind him did the same. He looked into my eyes, sure and unafraid, and nodded. "Welcome home then, King Jaxon." He dropped to one knee. "Long live the king," he called. The soldiers both before and behind me, echoed his shout.

I looked at him and wondered, was he a truer subject to Dalbreck than any of us, willing to challenge me and risk his life to ensure stability for his kingdom, or had he judged the loyalty of those behind me against those behind him and decided to take the more prudent action? I would believe the former for now.

He rose and embraced me, and after some quickly offered condolences, the caravan continued, General Draeger riding between me and the captain. Tension still ran high. I saw Sven eyeing the general and exchanging glances with the officer on his right. *Keep an eye on him. Stay close. Be aware.* All the hidden messages I had learned to read in Sven's eyes from years under his tutelage.

As we neared the gates, the general rode ahead to direct his troops, and I turned to Sven.

"Here," I said, reaching behind me into my pack, rustling blindly through the contents until I found what I needed. "Take this to Merrick at the chanterie first thing. Judging by Draeger's greeting, I'm not going to get a chance to slip away for several days. It's a little something I lifted. Don't show it to anyone else, and don't tell anyone else. Merrick will know what to do."

Sven looked at me incredulously. "You stole this?"

"You of everyone, Sven, should know that kings don't steal things. We simply make acquisitions. Isn't that in your bag of royal maxims?"

Sven sighed and mumbled almost to himself. "Why do I feel that this acquisition is only going to bring trouble?"

It already has, I thought, and now I was hoping it might bring the opposite, some sort of peace. I wondered if, in the list of royal truths, a king was allowed hope.

CHAPTER FORTY-ONE

LESSONS WERE LEARNED, MILES COVERED, MESSAGES SENT, days of rain endured, arguments settled, weapons mastered. Natiya was exhausted, as she should have been. I had promised her that this would be no holiday, and I made sure it wasn't. At times she stared at me with loathing, and other times I held her while she choked back sobs. I taught her everything I knew and made sure everyone else did the same. She had as many bruises, knots, and blisters as I did. Her arms ached from throwing a knife. I made her use both until one arm's aim was as good as the other's—and then I prayed she'd never have to use any of her newly acquired skills.

Natiya made an uneasy peace with Kaden, because I told her she must if she was to ride with us. I saw how it needled Kaden. The small bit of tranquillity and acceptance he had found in the vagabond world was forever lost to him. At times, he seemed lost to everything, his eyes squeezing shut when he thought no one was looking as if trying to see where he fit in with a different kind of eye, but then he would speak about some part of Venda, a part that didn't belong to the Council or the Komizar, and I saw the strength in his gaze again.

Dihara's death came when we were two weeks out. I had just finished my remembrances when I saw her on the crest of a winter brown hill. She sat at her spinning wheel, the treadle clicking the air, tufts of fur and wool and flax turning, long tendrils swirling, lifting on the breeze. They became the dusky colors of sunset, pink, amethyst, and orange fanning out above me, a warm blush coloring the sky, brushing my cheek, whispering, *Greater stories will have their way.*

Then others gathered on the hill, watching her. Those I had seen before, their numbers growing each time they came. It began with my brother and Greta. Then a dozen clanspeople on either side. Effiera and the other seamstresses. A platoon of soldiers. Then Venda and Aster—*Don't tarry, Miz*—the faces I had seen and the voices I had heard many times these past weeks. All of them little more than a rustle of air, a glint of lost sunlight, and a hush beating through my veins. A madness, a knowing, circling, repeating, a swath cutting deep into my heart.

It had to be someone. Why not you?

Voices that wouldn't let me forget.

They are waiting.

A promise, a vow spilled from my lips in return.

No one else saw them. I didn't have to ask. The routine sounds of making camp missed no beats. No heads ever turned. No steps faltered.

Ah, you again, Dihara said, turning to face me. The spinning wheel still whirred, the gifts swirled, the tendrils reached. *Trust the strength within you, and teach her to do the same.*

I looked over my shoulder at Natiya, just loosening her boots, ready to fall into her bedroll. I walked over and grabbed her hand. "We're not done."

"I'm tired," she complained.

"Then go make camp elsewhere. Let the pachegos eat you right now."

"There's no such thing as pachegos."

"When they're chewing off your foot because you're not prepared, you may think differently."

I WAS SURPRISED AT HOW LITTLE NATIYA UNDERSTOOD THE gift. How was that possible when she had lived with Dihara? But I remembered what Dihara had told me. *There are some who are more open to the sharing than others.*

"The knowing is a truth that you feel here and here," I told Natiya. "It is connection. It is the world reaching out to you. It flashes behind your eyes, it curls in your belly, and sometimes it dances along your spine. The truths of the world wish to be known, but they won't force themselves upon you the way lies will. They'll court you, whisper to you, slip inside and warm your blood, and caress your neck until your flesh rises in bumps.

That is the truth whispering to you. But you have to quiet your heart, Natiya. Listen. Trust the strength within you."

After a few quiet moments, she yelled in frustration, "I don't understand!"

I grabbed her by the wrist as she turned to storm off. "It is survival, Natiya! A whisper that could save you! Another kind of strength the gods have blessed us with. The truth you need doesn't always come at the end of a sword!"

She glared at me. I could see in her eyes that, for now, sharp-edged steel was the only kind of power she sought. I felt something give within me. I could understand that kind of truth too.

"It is good to have many strengths, Natiya," I said more gently, remembering the cold fullness of the knife in my hand as I plunged it into the Komizar's gut. "Do not sacrifice one kind of strength for another."

ONE NIGHT, WHEN NATIYA AND I WERE BOTH TOO SPENT TO practice anything, and I sensed it might be our last camp before reaching Morrighan's border, I emptied out my saddlebag to get the ancient texts I had packed away. It was time to teach her about what had come before, not just what we were heading into. All I found was the Last Testaments of Gaudrel. I ruffled through the contents again, shaking out my folded shirt and chemise. The Song of Venda was gone. I went on a rampage, asking who had gone through my bag. I knew I had carefully tucked both thin books into the bottom.

"You sure you packed them?" Tavish asked.

I glared at him. "Yes! I remember when—" I caught my breath. The bag had been in my possession for the entire journey—except at the beginning when I'd handed it to Rafe. He'd insisted on carrying it. It had been less than a few minutes while we walked, but then I had looked away while I checked my horse and supplies. He had *stolen* it? Why? Did he think stealing it would make the truths disappear too? Or that it would shake my resolve?

"Lia?" Natiya looked at me with worried eyes. "Are you all right?"

Stealing the book would change nothing. "I'm fine, Natiya. Come help me make a fire. I have some stories to tell you, and I expect you to remember them word for word in case anything happens to me."

Jeb looked up from what he was doing, the same worried expression crossing over his face. "But nothing is going to happen," he said firmly, his eyes locked on mine.

"No," I answered to reassure him. "Nothing." But we both knew that was a promise that couldn't be made.

———◦———

WE REACHED THE SOUTHERN BORDER OF MORRIGHAN—AT least according to Kaden. There were no markers. We were still in the wilderness.

Tavish had looked down at the ground. "I don't see a line. You see a line, Orrin?"

"Not me."

"I think the border's a little farther ahead yet," Jeb added.

Kaden and I exchanged a glance, but we traveled on with them for several more miles before I decided to get our doubts out in the open. All three had made not-so-subtle pleas for my return to Dalbreck when we were out of Kaden's earshot. They had made the same stern suggestions privately to him, in what seemed an effort to divide and conquer. I stopped my horse and looked all three squarely in the eyes. "Was there another purpose to your escort besides protection in the Cam Lanteux"—I tipped my head in acknowledgment toward Orrin—"and keeping us well fed? Did your king charge you with forcing me to return if the long ride didn't change my mind?"

"Never," Jeb answered. "His word is true."

Not entirely, I thought.

Jeb sat back in his saddle and surveyed the barren hills ahead of us as if it roiled with vipers. "What do you plan to do when you get there?" he asked.

Exactly what the traitors had always feared. I had practice at this, only this time I would do it better—but I knew my plans would not soothe Jeb's misgivings. "I plan to stay alive."

He smiled.

"It's time for you to return home. I can assure you, this is Morrighan," I said. "I see the line even if you can't, and I don't want it to be a regrettable one that you cross. You have your orders from your king."

Jeb looked stricken, and I was afraid he wouldn't turn back.

Tavish glanced at Kaden, then stared solemnly at me. "You're sure about this?"

I nodded.

"Any messages you'd like me to take back to the king?"

A chance for last words. Probably the last he would ever hear from me. "No," I whispered. As the king had already said, it was for the best.

"Hang me, I say we take her back anyway."

"Shut up, Orrin," Jeb ordered.

Orrin swung down from his saddle and secured a hare he had snared to Natiya's pack. He cursed under his breath and returned to his horse.

And that was it. We said our good-byes, and they left. Now, as Rafe had so ardently pointed out before we parted, my death would be on my own kingdom, not his.

Some last words should never be said.

CHAPTER FORTY-TWO

KADEN STOPPED HIS HORSE. "MAYBE I SHOULD HANG BACK?"

I looked at him, confused. We had come into Terravin on a back trail and were on the upper road that led to Berdi's inn. Since Terravin was on the way to Civica, we had decided it would be our first stop. It would give us a place to clean up and properly wash our clothes, which reeked of smoke, sweat, and weeks on the trail. A distant whiff of us alone could attract attention, and that was something we didn't need. More important, I owed Pauline and the others a visit so they could have some assurance after all these months that I was all right. They might have news to share too that could be useful—especially Gwyneth, with her questionable cadre of contacts.

"Why hang back now?" I asked. "We're nearly there."

Kaden shifted uncomfortably in his saddle. "So you can let Pauline know I'm with you. You know, prepare her."

For the first time, I thought I glimpsed fear in Kaden's face. I drew my horse closer. "Are you *afraid* of Pauline?"

He frowned. "Yes."

I sat there stunned. I wasn't sure what to say to this admission.

"Lia, she knows I'm Vendan now, and the very last words I said to her threatened her life—and yours. She's not going to forget that."

"Kaden, you threatened Rafe's life too. That didn't make you afraid of him."

He looked away. "That was different. I never liked Rafe, and he never liked me. Pauline's an innocent who—" He stopped short, shaking his head.

An innocent who had once thought highly of him. I had seen the kindnesses exchanged between them, and their easy conversation. Perhaps seeing her one-time regard for him plummet into hate was a last straw he couldn't bear. He had already experienced that with Natiya, who while civil now, was still cool toward him. She would never forget the Vendan attack on her camp, nor that he was one of *them*. It seemed Kaden was in much the same position as me—there were only a handful of people on the entire continent who didn't want to see him dead. I remembered the terror in Pauline's eyes when Kaden dragged us into the scrub, and then her pleas for him to let us go. No, she wouldn't forget, but I prayed she hadn't nursed the terror of that day into hatred during all these long months.

Kaden took a drink from his canteen, draining the last sip. "I just don't want to risk creating a scene inside the tavern when she sees me," he added.

It was more than worry over a disturbance, and we both knew it. It was strange to see him rattled by a simple encounter with someone as harmless as Pauline.

"We'll go in through the kitchen door," I said to appease him. "Pauline is reasonable. She'll be fine once I explain. In the meantime, I'll keep myself between you, her, and the kitchen knives." I added the last part as a jest to lighten his mood, but he didn't smile.

Natiya spurred her horse forward beside mine. "What about me?" she asked. "Shall I help you protect the trembling Assassin?" She said it loud enough for Kaden to hear, her eyes sparkling with mischief. Kaden shot her a warning look to be careful how far she pushed him.

My heart fluttered with anticipation as we got closer, but as soon as the tavern came into view, I knew something was wrong. Fear jumped between the three of us like fire. Even Natiya sensed something was amiss, though she'd never been here before.

"What is it?" she asked.

It was empty. Silent.

There were no horses tethered at posts. No laughter or conversation came from the dining room. There were no tavern guests, and it was the dinner hour. The sickening pall of quiet held the inn like a shroud.

I jumped from my horse and ran up the front steps. Kaden was right behind me, telling me to stop, yelling something about caution. I flung open the door, only to find chairs stacked on tables.

"Pauline!" I yelled. "Berdi! Gwyneth!" I traversed the dining room in leaps and pushed open the kitchen door, sending it slamming against the wall.

I froze. Enzo stood behind the chopping block, a cleaver in hand, his mouth gaping as wide as the fish he was about to behead.

"What's going on?" I asked. "Where is everyone?"

Enzo blinked, then took a harder look at me. "What are you doing here?"

Kaden drew his knife. "Set it down, Enzo."

Enzo looked down at the cleaver still poised in his fist, first surprised and then horrified to see it there. He dropped it, sending it clattering to the butcher block.

"Where is everyone?" I asked again, this time with threat.

"Gone," he answered, and with shaking hands, he waved Kaden and me to the kitchen table to explain. "Please," he added when we didn't move. We pulled out chairs and sat. Kaden kept his knife drawn, but by the time Enzo was done explaining, I rested my head in my hands, and could only stare at the scarred wooden table where I had eaten so many meals with Pauline. She had left weeks ago to try to help me. All of them had. I couldn't hold back the groan swelling in my throat. They were in the heart of Civica. Dread gripped me.

Kaden put his hand on my back. "She's with Gwyneth. That's something."

"And Berdi," Enzo added. But both of their reminders seemed

only to confirm our fears. Pauline was trusting—and a wanted criminal just like me. She could already be in custody. Or worse.

"We have to go to them," I said. "Tomorrow." There would be no resting up.

"They'll be all right," Enzo said. "Berdi promised me."

I looked up at Enzo, hardly recognizing him as the shiftless boy who could barely be relied upon to show up for work at all. His expression was earnest, one I had never seen on him before.

"And Berdi left *you* to run the inn?"

He looked down, brushing an oily strand of hair from his face. I hadn't tried to disguise my suspicion. Pink colored his temples. "I know what you're thinking, and I don't blame you. But that's what Berdi did, left me in charge, keys and everything." He rattled the ring of keys hanging from his belt, and I saw something akin to pride in his eyes. "Really. She said it was long past time for me to step up." He suddenly startled, twisting his apron in his hands. "That other fellow could have killed me. He nearly did. He heard me and—"

He swallowed, and the large apple of his skinny throat bobbed. He stared at my neck. "I'm sorry. It was me who told that bounty hunter about you walking on the upper road. I knew he was up to no good, but all I could see was that handful of coin in his palm."

Kaden sat forward in his chair. "You?"

I nudged Kaden back in his seat. "The other fellow?" I asked.

"That farmer who was staying here. He cornered me and threatened to cut out my tongue if I ever said your name to anyone again. Said he'd stuff it down my throat along with the coin.

I thought for sure he was going to. I thought about how close I'd come to—" He swallowed again.

"I knew I was running out of chances. Last thing Berdi said to me before she left was that she saw something good in me, and it was time I find it too. I'm trying to do better." He rubbed the side of his face, his hand still shaking. "I'm not doing all this half as good as Berdi, course. All I can manage is to keep rooms clean for the boarders, make a pot of parritch in the morning and a pot of stew at night." He pointed to the wall at the far end of the kitchen. "She left me directions. For everything." There were at least a dozen pieces of paper tacked to the wall scribbled with Berdi's handwriting. "I can't serve dinner for a whole dining room yet. But maybe if I hire some help."

Natiya came into the kitchen, her sword strapped to her side, a dagger in her hand, a new swagger to her stride. She leaned back against the wall. Enzo glanced at her but said nothing. We had come full circle, and I saw the worry in his eyes. He knew we saw him as a possible threat.

"So you know who I really am?" I asked.

For the briefest moment, I saw denial rush through his eyes, but he shrugged it off and nodded. "Berdi didn't tell me, but I heard about the princess being wanted."

"And just what did you hear?" Kaden asked.

"Any citizen can kill her on sight and collect a reward. No questions asked."

Kaden hissed and pushed away from the table.

"But I won't tell anyone!" Enzo quickly added. "I promise. I've known for a long time and had plenty of chances to tell the magistrate. He's come around twice, wondering what happened to Gwyneth, but I've never said a word."

Kaden stood and ran his finger along the flat side of his knife blade, turning it to catch the lantern light, then squinted at Enzo. "Even if the magistrate offers you a fistful of coin?"

Enzo stared at the blade. His upper lip beaded with sweat and his hands still trembled, but his chin jutted upward in uncharacteristic courage. "He already did. Didn't change my answer. I told him I didn't know where Gwyneth went."

"Lia? A moment?" Kaden nodded toward the dining room. We left Natiya to guard Enzo.

"I don't trust him," Kaden whispered. "He's a greasy little weasel who traded coin for you once. He'll do it again the minute we leave if we don't quiet him."

"You mean kill him?"

He answered me with a steady stare.

I shook my head. "He didn't have to tell us he was the one who informed the bounty hunter. People can change."

"Nobody changes that fast, and he's the only one in Morrighan who knows we're here. We want to keep it that way."

I walked in circles, trying to think it through. Enzo was a risk, no doubt, with a proven record of unreliability, if not greed. But Berdi had trusted him with her whole life's work. And people could change. I had. So had Kaden.

And for the gods' sakes, Enzo was making stew. *Stew.* And there wasn't a single dirty dish in the sink waiting to be washed. I turned to face Kaden. "Berdi trusts Enzo. I think we should too. And he still seems shaken by the farmer's threats. If you have to brandish your knife a few times as a reminder, so be it."

He stared at me, still unconvinced, and finally let out a long sigh. "I'll do more than brandish it if he so much as looks at any of us sideways."

We went back in the kitchen, and made sleeping arrangements. Natiya and I washed out clothing and hung it to dry in the kitchen near the fire, since time was short. We scoured the cottage I had shared with Pauline for more concealing clothing, turning up two loose work shifts and some shawls. I also spotted Pauline's white mourning scarf. Natiya wouldn't have to hide her face while in Morrighan, but I would, and nothing could turn away suspicion faster than respect for a widow. Kaden took care of the horses and then we all raided Berdi's pantry, finding food to pack. From here on out, there would be no more campfires for cooking. As Enzo helped us pack our bags with food, I was surprised to hear braying.

"That's Otto," he said shaking his head. "He misses the other two."

"Otto's still here?" I grabbed the widow's scarf and threw it over my head in case any of the boarders were about and ran out the door to the paddock.

I fawned over Otto, scratching his ears and listening to his complaints, each haw and whinny sounding like a note of music. It took me back to the day Pauline and I had arrived in Terravin, riding our donkeys down the main street thinking our new life here would last forever. Otto nudged me with his soft muzzle, and I thought about how lonely he must be without his companions.

"I know," I said softly. "Nove and Dieci will come back soon. I promise." But I knew my promise was empty, born only of convenience and—

Rafe's words dragged through me again, a tangled line pulling me under to a place where I couldn't breathe. *I said what I thought you needed to hear at the time. I was trying to give you hope.*

I turned away from Otto, my bitterness surging. Rafe had given me false hope and wasted my time. I walked inside the barn and stared at the ladder to the loft, then finally climbed it. The loft was dim, a few stray beams of light slipping through the rafters. Two mattresses still lay on the floor, never stored after our hasty departure. A forgotten shirt hung from the back of a chair. A dusty carafe was perched on a table in the corner. At the far end were stacks of crates—and an empty manger. My heart hammered as I walked toward it. *Don't look, Lia. Leave it alone. You don't care.* But I couldn't stop myself.

I inched the manger forward so I could see behind it. It was there, just as he had told me, a pile of soiled white cloth. My tongue bloomed thick and salty, and the room grew suddenly stuffy, making it hard to breathe. I reached down and lifted it from its hiding place. Bits of straw rained to the floor. It was torn in several places, and the hem was stained with mud. Brick-red blood smeared the fabric. His blood. That was where he'd gotten the nicks on his hands, ripping it loose from the thorny brambles where I had thrown it. *The dress made me wonder about the girl who had worn it.* The same dress I had torn so hatefully from my back and tossed away. My knees buckled, and I dropped to the floor. I held the dress to my face, trying to block Rafe out, but all I could see was him tearing it from the brambles, stuffing it in his bag, wondering about me the way I had wondered about him. But I had wondered all the wrong things.

I had imagined him only as a gutless papa's boy. Not as—

"Lia? Are you all right?"

I looked up. Kaden was standing at the top of the ladder.

I scrambled to my feet and threw the dress behind the manger again. "Yes, I'm fine," I answered, keeping my back to him.

"I heard something. Were you—"

I wiped my cheeks, then ran my hands down the front of my shirt before I turned to face him. "Coughing. The dust is thick up here."

He walked over, the floor creaking beneath his steps, and he looked down at me. He swiped his thumb along my wet lashes.

"It's only the dust," I said.

He nodded, and his arms slipped around me, holding me close. "Sure. Dust." I let myself lean against him. He stroked my hair, and I felt the ache in his chest as strongly as I felt it in my own.

IT WAS LATE. NATIYA WAS ALREADY TUCKED INTO BED IN THE cottage, and Enzo was asleep in Berdi's room. Kaden and I sat in the kitchen while I grilled him on any other details he might know of the Komizar's plans, but I sensed he was occupied with other thoughts. I was grateful he hadn't brought it up again, but I knew our moment in the barn weighed on him. It had been only a passing tired minute that caught me off guard. That was all. After a bowl of fish stew that was surprisingly almost as good as Berdi's, I felt fortified, ready to move forward.

Now Kaden patiently endured questions I had already asked. His answers were the same. He knew only of the Chancellor. Maybe he and the Royal Scholar were the only traitors in the cabinet. Was that possible?

My relationships with all of the cabinet members were rocky at best, except perhaps for the Viceregent and the Huntmaster. Those two had usually offered a smile and kind word when I entered a room instead of a dismissive scowl, but the cabinet post of Huntmaster was mostly ceremonial, a vestige from an earlier time when filling the larder was foremost among cabinet duties. Most of the time, he didn't even sit in on cabinet meetings. The royal First Daughter was granted a ceremonial seat as well, but my mother had rarely been invited to the cabinet table.

My thoughts jumped back to the Viceregent. "Pauline will go to him first," I told Kaden. "Of all the cabinet, he's always had the most sympathetic ear." I chewed on my knuckle. Frequent travel was part of the Viceregent's job, visiting other kingdoms, and I worried that he might very well be gone. If so, Pauline would go straight to my father instead, not quite comprehending his temper.

Kaden wasn't responding to anything I said, instead staring blankly across the room. Suddenly he stood and went to the pantry, rifling through supplies. "I have to go. It's not far from here. Only an hour west of Luiseveque in County Düerr. We won't lose time." He named a rendezvous point where he would meet Natiya and me north of here tomorrow and told me to take a woodland trail. "No one will see you. You'll be safe."

"Leaving now?" I stood, and pulled a sack of jerky from his hands. "You can't ride at night."

"Enzo's asleep. It's the best time to trust him."

"You need to rest too, Kaden. What—"

"I'll rest when I get there." He took the jerky from me and began rearranging his bag.

My heart sped up. This was not like Kaden. "What's so urgent in County Düerr?"

"I need to take care of something, once and for all." The muscles in his neck were like tight cords, and he kept his gaze averted from mine. And then I knew.

"Your father," I said. "He's the lord of the county there, isn't he?"

He nodded.

I stepped away, trying to remember the county lords. There were twenty-four of them in Morrighan, and I didn't know most of their names, especially not those down here in the southern counties, but I knew this lord might not be alive much longer.

I sat down on a stool in the corner, the same one where Berdi had once tended my neck. "Are you going to kill him?" I asked.

Kaden paused, then finally pulled out a chair and straddled it, facing its spindled back. "I don't know. I thought I just wanted to see my mother's grave. See where I had once lived, the last place where I was—" He shook his head. "I can't just let it go, Lia. I have to see him at least one more time. It's something unfinished inside of me, and this might be my last chance to make some sense of it. I won't know what I'm going to do until I see him."

I didn't try to talk him out of it. I felt no sympathy for this lord who had whipped his young son, then sold him like a piece of trash to strangers. Some betrayals ran too deep to ever forgive.

"Be careful," I said.

He reached out, squeezing my hand, and the storm in his eyes doubled. "Tomorrow," he said. "I'll be there. I promise."

He rose to leave, but then stopped at the kitchen door.

"What is it?" I asked.

He turned to face me. "There's something else that's unfinished. I need to know. Do you still love him?"

His question knifed through me—I hadn't expected it, though I should have. I saw the wondering in his eyes every time he looked at me. He knew when he held me in the loft that it wasn't dust I had choked on. I stood and walked to the chopping table, unable to look him in the eye, and brushed imaginary crumbs away.

I hadn't even allowed myself to dwell on this thought. Love. It felt foolish and indulgent in light of everything else. Did it really matter? I remembered Gwyneth's cynical laugh when I told her I wanted to marry for love. She already knew what I hadn't yet grasped. It never ended well for anyone. Not for Pauline and Mikael. My parents. Walther and Greta. Even Venda was proof, riding off with a man who had ultimately destroyed her. I thought about the girl Morrighan, stolen from her tribe and sold as a bride to Aldrid the scavenger for a sack of grain. Somehow they had built a great kingdom together, but it wasn't built on love.

I shook my head. "I'm not even sure what love is anymore."

"But it's different between us than it was with—" He left his question dangling as if it was too painful to say Rafe's name.

"Yes, it's different between us," I said quietly. I lifted my gaze to meet his. "It always has been, Kaden, and if you're honest with yourself, you've always known it too. From the beginning, you said that Venda came first. I can't explain exactly how our destinies became entwined, but they did—and now we both care for Venda and Morrighan, and want a better end for them than the one the Komizar has planned. Maybe that's what brought us together. Don't underestimate the bond we share. Great kingdoms have been built on far less."

He stared at me, his eyes restless. "On our way here, the things you scratched into the dirt, what were they?"

"Words, Kaden. Only lost unsaid words that added up to good-bye."

He pulled in a deep, slow breath. "I'm trying to find my way through this, Lia."

"I know, Kaden. I am too."

His gaze remained fixed on me. He finally nodded and left. I walked to the door, watching him ride off, the moonless night swallowing him up in seconds, and I ached with his want, ached with what I couldn't give him. His need reached deeper and farther than me.

I returned to the kitchen and blew out the lantern but

couldn't let the night go. I leaned against the wall tacked with paper—lists that tried to hold on to the life that Berdi had traded for another decades ago. In the dim light, the faint edges of her kitchen became a distant world of twists, turns, and unmapped choices, the ones that had woven together and defined Berdi's life.

Do you regret not going?

I can't think about things like that now. What's done is done. I did what I had to do at the time.

My hands pressed against the cool of the wall behind me.

What was done was done.

I couldn't think about it anymore.

EARLY THE NEXT MORNING, I RAIDED BERDI'S WARDROBE AND found only part of what I required.

"Natiya, are you good with a needle?"

"Very," she answered. I'd suspected as much. To rip out a hem, conceal a knife in a cloak, and then sew it up again in a few precious minutes required a skill that I certainly didn't have—much to my aunt Cloris's chagrin.

I asked Enzo for coin. I had used all the money Rafe had packed in my bag for messengers in Turquoi Tra. Enzo didn't hesitate, and pulled a sack from the potato barrel in the pantry. He threw me the whole thing. It wasn't much, but I gladly took it and shoved it into my pack, nodding my thanks. "I'll tell Berdi you're doing a fine job here. She'll be pleased."

"You mean amazed," he added sheepishly.

I shrugged, unable to deny it. "That too. And remember, Enzo, you've never laid eyes on me."

He nodded, an understanding passing through his eyes, and I wondered at his transformation. Rafe's threats had no doubt gotten his attention, but I was certain it was the magic of Berdi's trust that had changed him. I just had to pray that the change was lasting.

We snuck out, quiet as night, careful not to wake any boarders.

THE CLERK AT THE MERCANTILE WAS HAPPY TO SEE US. WE were her first customers of the day—and the only ones. I saw her squinting, trying to peer through the gauzy cover of the white scarf draped over my face. I asked if she had any red satin, and she didn't try to hide her surprise. Most widows would be asking for more somber, respectful fabrics.

Natiya surprised me with her quick explanation. "My aunt wishes to make a tapestry honoring her departed husband. Red was his favorite color."

I added a quick sob and nod for effect.

In minutes we were on our way, with an extra yard thrown in by the sympathetic clerk.

We had one more stop. What I needed there couldn't be bought with the usual kind of currency. I only hoped I had the kind I needed.

CHAPTER FORTY-THREE

RAFE

MY TRANSITION FROM SOLDIER TO KING HAD BEEN ABRUPT,
and it seemed every baron in the assembly wanted a piece of my
hide. I knew their bravado was posturing to secure my ear and
attention, which I assured them they had. The eight officers of
the cabinet were the most demanding, but then they were the
ones who had worked the most closely with my father.

I was welcomed of course, but behind every welcome came
an admonishment—*Where were you?* And a warning—*The upheaval
is widespread. It will take time to heal.*

The court physician offered me the most painful reminder.
*Both of your parents asked for you on their deathbeds. I promised them
you were on your way.* I wasn't the only one who offered false hope
and expedient lies, but I had little time to dwell on my guilt.

If I wasn't in sessions separately with the assembly, cabinet, or the court of generals, I was with them all at once. General Draeger spoke up often, and being the governing general of the capital, his voice held sway. He made his opinions known—a message to me as much as to everyone else that he was keeping a close watch. His hand was still in this, ready. He was going to make me pay for my absence.

They all felt the need to test this untried king, but as Sven had advised, I listened, I weighed, I acted. But I would not be pushed. It was a dance of give and take, and when they pushed too far, I cut them short. I was reminded of my dance with Lia when she would not step back, her foot stamping down and staying put.

It was during that dance that I had known she wouldn't be pushed any further. I was losing her. *No, Rafe, not losing. Lost. She's gone for good. It's for the best,* I reminded myself. I had a troubled kingdom that needed my undivided attention.

When the court of generals balked at my first order as king, I held my position and let them know this decision was not under advisement. Reinforcements were to be sent to all northern border outposts and the vulnerable cities in between, and troops at southern outposts were to be split between the eastern and western borders. Trouble was brewing, and until we knew the exact extent of it, this was a necessary precaution. The barons protested, saying it would leave little protection here in the capital.

"But first they would have to get past the borders," I told them.

"Our borders are already well fortified based on your father's and his advisers' assessments," General Draeger interjected. "You'd further disrupt the kingdom because of one *unreliable* girl's claim?"

The chamber grew instantly silent. *Unreliable* flicked off the general's tongue with a hundred insinuating nuances. Rumors and questions about the princess and my relationship with her had surely run through the assembly like wildfire. No doubt they knew of my bitter parting with her too. This was the first time anyone had dared bring her up. *One girl?* As if she was chaff. Weightless and disposable. It was another gauntlet thrown down. A test of my loyalty. Perhaps they even secretly laughed if they knew I had claimed her as my future queen before my troops. Looking at the faces staring into mine, I suddenly saw myself through Lia's eyes, how I had questioned something she so desperately believed. I saw myself as one of them. *Rafe, haven't you ever felt something deep in your gut?*

I wouldn't bite at the general's bait and bring Lia into this. "My decision is based on what I observed, General Draeger, and nothing else. My duty is to keep Dalbreck's citizens safe and the realm secure. Until we have further information, I expect my orders to be carried out immediately."

The general shrugged, and the assembly grudgingly nodded. I sensed they all wanted more from me, to denounce Lia before them all as another Morrighese conniver who couldn't be trusted. They wanted me to be fully and completely one of their own again.

There was a rushed coronation, and my father's funeral pyre

was built at last. He'd been dead for weeks, his body preserved and wrapped, but until I was found, his death had to remain a secret and he couldn't receive a proper release to the gods.

When I lifted the torch to light his pyre, I felt oddly inadequate, as if I should have understood the gods more. I should have listened more. Sven hadn't been strong on tutoring me in the heavenly realms. Most of that had been left to Merrick during my infrequent visits to the chanterie. I remembered Lia asking me which god I prayed to. I had been at a loss to answer her. They had names? And according to Morrighese tradition, there were four of them. Merrick had taught me there were three who ruled from a single heavenly throne and rode on the backs of fiercesome beasts while they guarded the gates of heaven—that is, when they weren't throwing stars to the earth. *It is by the gods that Dalbreck is supreme. We are the favored Remnant.*

I watched the flames engulf my father's shroud, the fabric dissolving, the stacked tinder falling down around him to disguise the realities of death, the flames bursting higher as a revered soldier and king left one world and entered another, a whole kingdom looking on, watching me as much as the pyre. The weight of every gaze pressed with expectation. Even now I had to be an example of strength for all of them, assurance that life would go on as before. I stood between the towering pillars of Minnaub, an ancient warrior carved in stone on one side of me, and his rearing warhorse carved on the other, two of a dozen sculpted memorials that guarded the plaza, sentinels of a glorious history, and one of many of Dalbreck's wonders I had wanted to show Lia.

If she had come.

My face grew hot with the blaze, but I didn't step back. I remembered Lia telling me that Capseius was the god of grievances, the one I had brazenly shaken my fist at when I was back in Terravin, and I thought he was probably looking down at me now, laughing. The flames crackled and snapped, hissing their secret messages to the heavens. Black smoke rose and hovered over the plaza, and instead of offering up prayers for the dead, I dropped to my knees and offered them for the living, and I heard the gasps and whispers of those around me, wondering at a Dalbreck king falling to his knees.

The funeral hadn't been behind me three days before cabinet officers, barons, or other nobles began stopping in with their marriageable daughters conveniently in tow as they dropped off insipid messages that could have waited until our assembly meetings. "You remember my daughter, don't you?" they would say, and then they'd offer an introduction and a not-so-subtle résumé of her virtues. Gandry, the chief minister and my father's closest adviser, saw me roll my eyes after a baron left with his daughter and told me I needed to give marriage serious consideration, and quickly. "It would help quell doubts and add stability to your reign."

"There are still doubts?"

"You were gone for months without word."

Strangely, my guilt over my absence was gone. Regret, yes, that I hadn't been here when my parents died, and the extra worry it must have brought them, but I had done what no Dalbreck king or general before me had—set foot on Vendan soil and lived with its people for several weeks. It gave me a unique understanding of Vendan minds, needs, and machinations. Maybe that was why I felt the support of the troops, if not of the upper echelons of the court. I had led a mission of five soldiers who were able to outmaneuver thousands. It somehow felt necessary instead of reckless, but translating that feeling into something measurable for the cabinet and assembly to appreciate was another matter.

I closed the ledger on my desk and rubbed my eyes. The funds in the treasury were at an all-time low. I was to tour with the secretary of commerce tomorrow and meet with key merchants and farmers in an effort to increase trade—and coffers. I stared at the worn leather cover of the ledger. Something else still turned inside me. Or maybe it was many things, each so faint I couldn't articulate any one of them, and they pulled in different directions.

The office closed in on me, and I pushed back my chair and walked out onto the veranda. I still thought of it as my father's office, and his presence was evident in every corner, mementos of a long life and reign. These had been his meeting chambers since I was a child. I remembered when he called me in to tell me I'd be going to go live with Sven in just a handful of weeks. I was only seven, and I hardly understood what he was saying—I only knew I didn't want to go. I was afraid. Sven was invited in to meet me, stern and imposing and nothing like my father. Meeting him didn't help calm my fears, and I struggled to hold back my tears. Now, after all these years, I wondered if my father had done the same, each of us trying to be strong for the other. How many hard decisions had he had to make that I never knew about?

It was a rare moment for me to be alone. Every night, meetings ran into the dinner hour. I felt less like a king and more like a harried farmer trying to herd a field of loose greased pigs into a pen. I leaned against the thick stone rail, feeling the cool breeze ruffling through my hair. The night was brisk, the lit pillars of Minnaub glowing in the distance, the capital asleep, the thousand stars of the sky blinking over the dark silhouette of the city. The same view my father had looked upon countless times when he wrestled with the demands of his court, but his worries had been different from mine.

Is she there yet?

Is she safe?

And then, unexpectedly, *was she right?*

Was that what continued to nag at me? Even back at the Marabella outpost, Colonel Bodeen and the captains had doubted her claim. In truth, I'd seen no evidence of a massive army, not in my tours of the city with Calantha and Ulrix or heard of it in the loose chatter in Sanctum Hall.

But I *had* seen the brigade of five hundred who escorted Lia into the city. That alone had been startling and unexpected, but it could have been the whole of their so-called army.

Except there were the tithes. I'd heard the governors grumbling, and yet they still came through with them. Was it just out of fear—or expectation of reward? There was no doubt that, like the Komizar, they wanted more. I'd seen it in their eyes when they looked upon the booty of the slain Dalbretch soldiers.

And then there was the flask, a strange, powerful liquid that had been able to damage an immense iron bridge with a single blast. That didn't fit with the image of a crude, impoverished city. A lucky fluke, Hague had called it, the result of poor Vendan craftsmanship. Maybe. There were a dozen maybes, no single one was so compelling that it pointed to the impossible—that a poor barbarian kingdom had raised up an army powerful enough to quash all the others combined. I had already pushed the limits of logic with the assembly when I dispatched troops to border outposts.

I heard the door to my meeting chamber open and shut, and then the rattle of a tray being set on my desk. Sven always anticipated what I needed. I thought about all the grief I had caused him in our early years together. All the times I had kicked his shins and run and he had scooped me up and tossed me over his shoulder, throwing me in a trough of water. *I am raising you up to be a king, not a fool, and kicking someone who can crush you in a single blink is the height of folly.* I was dunked more than once. His patience was greater than mine.

I kept my eyes fixed on the city, the seven blue domes of the chanterie barely visible. Another thump. A stack of papers. Sven brought me an itinerary each evening for the next day.

"A full day tomorrow," he said.

As they all were. This was not news. This was more like the bang of a gavel proclaiming another day set in stone.

He joined me at the rail looking out at the city. "Beautiful, isn't it?"

"Yes. Beautiful," I answered.

"But?"

"No buts, Sven." I didn't want to go into it, the worry I couldn't let go of, the vague something that didn't feel right in my gut.

"I'm afraid you'll need to squeeze in one more meeting tonight that's not on the schedule."

"Move it to tomorrow. It's late—"

"Merrick has the information you wanted. He'll be here within the hour."

BEFORE MERRICK SAT DOWN, BEFORE HE EVEN ENTERED MY chambers, I knew what he would say, but I let it play out. *It is true, Rafe. Every word is true.* But I still held out hope for a fraud, an epic hoax penned by some sick mind in Morrighan. After pleasantries and a few explanations about his surprise at the age of the document, he pulled the worn leather sleeve from his satchel and returned it to me, then handed me another paper covered with his perfect scrolled lettering. An experienced scholar's translation.

Merrick accepted a small glass of the spirits Sven offered to him and sat back. "May I ask where you acquired this?"

"It was stolen from a library in Morrighan. Is it genuine?"

He nodded. "It's the oldest document I've ever translated. At least a couple of thousand years, or more. The word usage is similar to two dated documents in our archives—and the paper and ink are unquestionably from another era. It's in remarkably good shape for its age."

But did it say what Lia claimed it did?

I read his translation aloud. With each word and passage, I heard Lia's voice instead of my own. I saw her worried eyes. I felt her hand squeezing mine, hopeful. I heard the murmurs of the clans in the square, listening to her. Word for word, it was the same as her translation. My mouth was suddenly dry when I got to the last verses, and I paused to drink some of the wine that Sven had poured me.

For the Dragon will conspire,
Wearing his many faces,
Deceiving the oppressed, gathering the wicked,
Wielding might like a god, unstoppable,
Unforgiving in his judgment,
Unyielding in his rule,
A stealer of dreams,
A slayer of hope.

Until the one comes who is mightier,
The one sprung from misery,
The one who was weak,
The one who was hunted,
The one marked with claw and vine,
The one named in secret,
The one called Jezelia.

"An unusual name," Merrick said. "And if I recall correctly, it's the princess's name as well."

I looked up from the page, wondering how he knew.

"The marriage documents," he explained. "I saw them. You probably never even looked, did you?"

"No," I said quietly. I had signed and ignored them, just as I had ignored her note to me. "But I'm told these are only the babblings of a madwoman?"

He pursed his lips as if thinking it over. "Could be. They're certainly cryptic and odd. There's no way to know for sure. But it's curious that a madwoman could accurately describe such specific things thousands of years ago. And the brief Morrighese notes that were tucked in with it confirm it was uncovered more than a decade after Princess Arabella was born. Early nomadic text in Dalbreck's historical record suggested something similar, in nearly identical phrasing—from the scheming of rulers, hope would be born. I always assumed it meant Breck, but perhaps not."

The steadiness of his gaze told me more than his commentary. He believed every word.

I felt a beat like a warning, the juddering that crawls through your bones when a horse is galloping toward you.

"There's a little more on the next page."

I looked down at the papers and shuffled the top one aside. There were two more verses.

Betrayed by her own,
Beaten and scorned,
She will expose the wicked,
For the Dragon of many faces
Knows no boundaries.

And though the wait may be long,
The promise is great,
For the one named Jezelia,
Whose life will be sacrificed,
For the hope of saving yours.

Sacrificed?

This Lia had never shared with me.

Had she known all along?

Rage shot through me, and right on its heels, gutting fear.

It is true, Rafe. Every word is true.

I stood and walked to one end of my chamber and back again, circling around my desk, my head pounding, trying to make sense of it. *Betrayed by her own? Beaten and scorned? Sacrificed?*

Dammit, Lia! Damn you!

I grabbed tomorrow's schedule and threw it against the wall, papers flying to the floor.

Merrick stood. "Your Majesty, I—"

I brushed past him. "Sven! I want General Draeger in my chamber first thing in the morning!"

"I believe he already has—"

"Here! By dawn!" I yelled.

Sven smiled. "I'll see to it."

CHAPTER FORTY-FOUR

KADEN

I USED TO GO TO MARKET WITH MY MOTHER. ISOLATED ON the estate, I didn't get to see much of the world, so the market was a place of wonder to me. We traveled on this same road in the wagon with the cook. My mother bought supplies for my lessons with my half brothers—paper, books, inks, and small bags of candied peels as rewards for a week of diligent study.

She always bought something just for me too. Strange small gifts that fascinated me—trinkets of the Ancients that had no purpose or meaning anymore, thin shiny disks that caught the sun, brown coins of worthless metals, battered ornaments from their carriages. She told me to imagine their greater purpose. I kept them on a shelf in the cottage, carefully arranged treasures that held my imagination and took me to places beyond the grounds of the estate, objects that grew in wonder and helped me imagine a greater purpose even for myself—until one day my eldest brother snuck into the cottage and stole them all away. I caught him just as he was dumping them down the well. He wanted me to have nothing. Less than I already did.

It wasn't the last time I cried. A year later, my mother died.

Less was all I'd ever had, or been. Even now. I was nothing. A soldier without a kingdom, a son without a family. A man without—

The day Lia and Rafe had parted churned in my thoughts again, as it had so many times before, like a piece was missing, something I didn't understand. When she'd left Rafe to join us on the trail, her face was like a piece of stone sculpture with a thousand tiny cracks in it, a sightless stare, her lips parted, frozen the same way a statue might be. In the past months, I'd thought Lia had looked at me with everything her eyes could hold—hatred, tenderness, shame, sorrow, vengeance—and what I'd thought might be love. I'd thought I knew the language of Lia, but the look she'd had in her eyes the day she left Rafe behind, I had never seen.

Yes, it's different between us. It always has been, Kaden, and if you're honest with yourself, you've always known it too. . . .

We both care for Venda and Morrighan. . . . Don't underestimate the bond we share. Great kingdoms have been built on far less.

Maybe with Lia, less could be more, the greater purpose my mother had always hoped for.

Maybe less could be enough.

THE ROAD TO THE MANOR WAS THICKER WITH TREES THAN I remembered. Branches hung overhead like a twisted-fingered canopy. For the first time, I wondered if I'd misremembered the way. I couldn't imagine the grand and powerful Lord Roché living down this unassuming, remote lane. I had never been back. The beggar's threats to a child had lodged somewhere in my skull, *he will drown you in a bucket.* Even once I was Venda's Assassin, the one the rest of the Rahtan had feared, the memory of that threat could still make my heart beat faster. It still did, every scar resurfacing as if I were eight years old again. Would killing him change that? I'd always thought it would. Maybe today I would find out.

And then I saw it, a glimpse of the white stone through the trees. I hadn't forgotten the way. As I drew closer, I saw that the grounds had fallen into disarray. The green clipped lawns were only stubble and dirt now, and the once-sculpted shrubs were overgrown and choked with vines. The sprawling manor, set far back from the road, looked unkempt and abandoned, but I spotted a thin trail of smoke rising from one of its five chimneys. Someone was there.

I circled around so no one would see me, and first I went to the cottage I had shared with my mother. It was once white too, but most of the paint had flaked away long ago. There was no doubt that it was uninhabited. The same vines that choked the shrubs crept over the porch and front window. I tied up my horse, and the warped door gave way under my shoulder. When I walked inside, it seemed smaller than I remembered. The furniture was all gone, probably sold to beggars too, disposable things just like me. The cottage was simply a dusty hull now that held no trace of my mother or the life I had when I was loved. I looked at the empty hearth, the empty mantel above it, the empty room that used to hold my bed, the emptiness that pervaded it all. I spun and walked out. I needed fresh air.

I leaned on the porch rail, staring at the quiet manor, the scent of jasmine strong in my memory. I pictured him sitting inside, stiff-backed in a chair, his trousers neatly pressed, a bucket of water at his side. Waiting. I couldn't be drowned anymore. I stepped off the porch and walked to the eastern part of the estate, remaining out of sight. There was one place where I knew I would find my mother. Only the gravedigger and my father had been present when we buried her. Not even my half brothers, whom she had tutored and treated kindly, bothered to come and say a few last words. No marker had been made for her grave, so I had found the heaviest stones I could carry and laid them like a blanket atop the mounded dirt, fitting them together until my father told me to stop.

I searched for the mound of stones now, but it was gone too. There was nothing to mark where she lay in the earth—but there were other graves not far away—two of which had large chiseled headstones. I pulled away the vines, hoping I had forgotten where she lay and that one of these was for her. Neither was. One was for my eldest brother. He had died only a few weeks after I left. My stepmother, if I could even call her that, had died a month later. An accident? A fever?

I looked back at the house and the smoke curling from the chimney. Was it possible that my father was a sickly broken man now? That would explain the state of the grounds he had once taken so much pride in. My other half brother would be twenty-two now, strong and able to fight back—but he probably wouldn't recognize me after all these years. I loosened the strap on my scabbard, feeling the position of my knife at my side. It was what the Komizar had always dangled in front of me—justice—and one day I would be the one to deliver it. I walked toward the house and knocked on the door.

I heard shuffling inside, something slamming, a call to someone and a curse, and then finally the door swung open. I recognized her even though her hair had gone white and she was twice the size she had once been. It was the manor housekeeper. I had remembered her as pinched and made of angles and sharp knuckles that had frequently rapped my head. Now she was round and ample. A large iron pot dangled from her hand.

She squinted at me. "Yaaap?"

The sound of her voice crawled over my skin. That hadn't changed. "I'm here to see Lord Roché."

She laughed. "Here? What rock have you been hiding under? He hasn't been here in years. Not more than in passing now that he has his big important job."

Gone? For years? It didn't seem possible. My memory of him lording over the estate and county was frozen here and in all my imaginings since.

"What job would that be?" I asked.

She hissed through her teeth like I was an oblivious jackass.

"He's at the citadelle working for the king. One of those fancy cabinet jobs. Got no need for this place nomore. Barely tosses me coin to keep it up. Shame how it looks now."

He's in Civica? Part of the king's cabinet?

"Wait a minute," the housekeeper said, leaning closer and wagging her finger at me. Disbelief shone in her eyes. "I know who you are. You're that bastard boy." In an instant, her disinterest flamed to hatred. Her finger poked my chest, but my head was still reeling with this new information. *My father was in Civica?* A far more deadly thought gripped me. Did the Komizar know? Had he guessed who my father was—was this why he kept his sources so closely held? Had he been working with the man I sought to destroy all along?

I turned to leave, but the housekeeper grabbed my arm. "You and your gift!" she snarled. "You said the mistress would die a horrible death, and she did. You miserable little beast—"

I heard a noise behind me and spun toward it drawing my knife at the same time, but then felt an explosion across the back of my head and the world tumbled as I fell forward.

WHEN I WOKE, I WAS PERCHED OVER THE WELL. TWO MEN held me. A cord cut into my hands, which were tied behind my back. The housekeeper grinned. "This is where the boy died," she said, "but you know that, don't you? Drowned. Someone pushed him in. We know it was you. You always hated him. Jealous you were. Mistress went crazy, dying slowly day by day, and finally slit her wrists a month later. A slow, horrible death, just like you predicted. Seeing her firstborn pulled from a well all clammy and bloated was the worst thing that could have happened to her. Nothing was the same around here after that. Not for any of us. Now it's your turn, boy."

The world swam in front of me. I guessed that instead of her knuckles, this time her pot had met my skull. She nodded to the men holding me. It was a deep well. Once I was thrown down, there would be no climbing out. The men lifted me under my arms, but my legs were still free. I shook off the dizziness and struck out at them both almost simultaneously. One of my boots shattered a kneecap, and I jammed the other man in the groin. When he doubled over, my knee cracked his neck. I rolled away, grabbing my knife from the dead man's side and sliced the cord behind my back. The man with the crushed knee screamed in pain but limped forward, thrashing at me with his machete. With one swipe of my blade, his throat lay open and he fell dead next to the other man. The housekeeper stared at me, horrified, and ran toward the house.

My head throbbed, and I bent over, trying to get my bearings, the world still spinning, then I ran too. I didn't know how long I'd been out. I stumbled to my horse, still tied behind the cottage, pain splitting my head in two, blood running down my neck, my back wet and sticky, and I rode, hoping Lia hadn't left without me, hoping I wouldn't pass out before I reached her. I knew at least one more traitor in the Morrighese cabinet, because if anyone had no concept of loyalty, it was my father.

CHAPTER FORTY-FIVE

DRIZZLE FELL LIGHTLY. I PULLED MY CLOAK CLOSER. THE wind circled, gusted, a hiss to its voice. Mist stung my cheeks with a thousand warning whispers. This was either the beginning or the end.

The universe sang your name to me. I simply sang it back.

For how many centuries had the name circled? How many had heard and turned away? Even now, the choice was still mine. I could turn away. Wait for someone else to hear the call. I was suddenly hit with the enormity of what I had to do. I was only Princess Arabella again, inadequate, voiceless, and, maybe most of all, unwelcome.

But time was running out.

It had to be someone.

I pressed two fingers to my lips. For Pauline. Berdi,

Gwyneth, my brothers. For Walther, Greta, Aster. I lifted my hand, giving my prayers flight. *And Kaden. Let him be alive. And Rafe. Let*—But there was nothing to ask for. He was where he needed to be.

Horses stamped behind me, their snorts muffled in the heavy air. I looked back at Father Maguire waiting beside Natiya for my signal. He nodded, his hair dripping with the damp, his eyes fixed on mine, as if he had always known this moment would come. *Seventeen years ago, I held a squalling infant girl in my hands. I lifted her up to the gods, praying for her protection and promising mine. I'm not a fool. I keep my promises to the gods, not men.* His promise to the gods was a currency worth more than gold to me now.

I stared at my old life sprawled across hills and valleys in a patchwork of memories—the misshapen ruins, the white-capped bay, the leaning spire of Golgata, the hamlets nestled outside the city walls, the village streets, the towers of the citadelle, the abbey where I was to be married—the same place where a young priest had lifted a baby girl to the gods and promised his protection, while others had conspired against her from the very beginning.

This was Civica.

The heart of Morrighan.

I was entering a city that reviled me.

Guards posted along the roads would be on the lookout for Princess Arabella. But a veiled widow traveling with her young daughter and accompanied by a priest? We wouldn't suffer much scrutiny.

"Do you think Kaden's dead?" Natiya asked.

"*No*," I answered for the third time. Natiya was betraying

what she had worked so hard to deny, even to herself. I understood that denial of feelings. Sometimes it was necessary.

"He'll be here," I reassured her.

But I wondered too. Where was he?

A week ago, when he hadn't shown at our rendezvous point by midday, I scratched the word *millpond* into the dirt and left. I had no other choice. Now that I knew Pauline was in Civica, I was worried about the danger she was in, whom she might go to for help, and that she might underestimate my father's anger.

I was also worried about the messages I'd sent before I knew she and the others would be here. I knew they'd add a reckless danger to the city, both delivered by messengers from outside Morrighan, which made them untraceable. The first message had probably arrived a few days ago.

I am here.
Watching you.
I know what you've done.
Be afraid.

—Jezelia

Of course, it would be read by the Chancellor first, but news of the message would spread like the plague among his coconspiritors. My first task was to simply get in. If they thought I was already in the city, they wouldn't be watching the roads leading into it as closely. Once I was in, there were many places to hide. I knew every dark alleyway and alcove. The added benefit I hoped for was that the notes would add to the traitors' anxiety.

Now I wouldn't be the only one watching my back—they'd be nervously looking over their shoulders too. And the notes were my trademark, after all. I wanted them to think I was just as confident and unafraid as I had been when I left the note months ago in the Royal Scholar's hidden drawer. Walther had told me how it had sent them into a mad search of the citadelle looking for the missing books. A careless search. Even the servants had noticed. I hoped these notes would help them make stupid mistakes again. Just as Walther had noticed, Bryn and Regan would too. I needed the highest players exposed, or at least more visible.

The second message would probably arrive any day, that one addressed to the Royal Scholar.

I've returned your books.
I hope you find them before someone else does.
Be afraid.

—Jezelia

I pulled out the mourning scarf and adjusted it over my head and face. I was already well-padded to fill out Berdi's cloak and disguise my form.

"Are you ready?" Natiya asked.

I had no choice but to be ready. "Yes," I answered.

We traversed down the steep hillside and were about to emerge from a copse onto the road when I was struck with the obvious. I stopped my horse, my head pounding, the shadows of trees spinning around me. *How had I not considered this before?* "Dear gods. Pauline is in Civica."

Natiya pulled up close to me, alarmed. "I don't understand. You knew that already."

But I was so worried about her safety, I hadn't put it together. *Mikael.* What if he was in Civica too? What if she saw him? What would it do to her?

"Arabella?" Father Maguire asked from behind me.

I tried to push the worry from my mind. Maybe if I was lucky, Mikael really was dead by now. "It's nothing," I said, and I snapped my reins, trotting out onto the road to Civica.

Just before the first outlying hamlet, there was a barricade and checkpoint. Two soldiers were stopping wagons and travelers.

"Your reason for coming to the city?" a soldier asked when it was our turn to pass through.

"Business at the abbey," Father Maguire answered.

One soldier gave a cursory peek into our bags, and another motioned to my face. "Your veil, madam?"

The priest flew into an immediate rage. "Has it come to this?" he yelled, rolling his eyes heavenward. "I can vouch for this widow and her daughter, as can the gods! Have you no respect for the mourning?"

The young soldier was sufficiently shamed that he waved us on through. There were no more checkpoints. Just as I'd thought, they suspected I was already within the gates of the city. My first note had done the trick. When we passed through the last hamlet and rode into Civica, I breathed with relief. I was in.

The first task was accomplished. We dismounted, and I used a cane as an additional disguise as I walked through the crowded street. My relief was momentary.

Only minutes later, chatter revealed that the king was gravely ill. My steps faltered with this revelation. I interrupted the two women I'd overheard as they surveyed a plump dumpling squash in a market bin, and I fished for more information. "But I heard the king had only a minor passing ailment?"

One of the women grunted and rolled her eyes to her friend, noting with disapproval that I was eavesdropping. "Then you heard wrong. My cousin Sophie works in the citadelle, and she said they're keeping a vigil."

The other woman shook her head. "And they don't keep vigils for passing coughs."

I nodded and moved on. Natiya and Father Maguire looked at me with questioning eyes, but I maintained my focus. The plan hadn't changed. Much. I gave Natiya my horse to be stabled and told her to go on to the abbey with the priest and complete the task I had set before her—find Pauline. She was to go to every inn and say she had information for the lady who had inquired about a midwife. They would either send her on her way if there was no guest in such need, or they'd lead her to Pauline. Once she found her, she was to send her and the others to the millpond. Pauline would know which one. There was only one that was abandoned. Father Maguire nodded over Natiya's head. He had made another promise to me—to protect Natiya if events should spiral out of my control.

I left for the citadelle, my face covered and my footsteps as quick as I dared. Two daggers were concealed beneath my cloak. I had tried to conceal a sword, but it was too bulky, and I couldn't take a chance on detection.

My father had been healthy when I left. Yes, a few extra pounds around his middle, but robust. I didn't overlook that it might well be a trap. It probably was. Draw the princess out. Appeal to her sentimental side. If that was the case, they had played the wrong card. I couldn't afford a sentimental side anymore.

When I turned the corner and saw the citadelle, my throat tightened. I stared at the steps, where I had stood countless times with my family, impatiently waiting for a procession, ceremony, or important announcement—always tucked safely between my brothers. My father's hand would rest on my shoulder, my mother's hand on Bryn, usually to keep us still. I fought the urge to run up the steps, call for Bryn and Regan, to run through the hall and greet my aunts, find my mother, to race into the kitchen for something fresh from the oven.

Now citadelle guards were posted on the perimeter. Though they were trained at the soldiers' camp, their uniforms were a stark contrast from soldiers. Guards wore highly polished black boots, long red capes, and helmets of pounded metal. More stood back in the shadows of the portico, their halberds crossed at the front entrance I'd been instructed to use on my wedding day. My stomach rolled over as I remembered my frantic last minutes stealing out the servants' door instead—the moment the sun flashed in my eyes and the day split in two creating the before and the after of my life.

I was cautious in my approach, slowing my steps and hunching my shoulders like a true grieving widow. I had bought a posy on my way.

I walked up the center of the steps, and a guard came forward to meet me. I lowered my voice, adding a slight northern accent. "For the king," I said, holding out the posy to him, "along with my prayers for his recovery."

He took the small bouquet of primroses from me. "I'll see that he gets them."

"And Prince Regan?" I added. "My prayers for him too. Is he preparing to take the throne?"

The guard cast an annoyed frown at me but quickly corrected himself. I was a widow, after all, and perhaps the widow of a soldier. "Prince Regan is away attending his duties—as is Prince Bryn. The king isn't so ill that anyone has to worry about succession."

A ploy, just as I thought. There was no vigil. But my brothers away from Civica?

"Both princes are traveling?" I asked.

"Attending kingdom business, like I said." His patience was spent. "Ma'am, I need to return to my post."

I nodded. "Bless you, son."

On my way back to the abbey, I used a little more digging to find out where Bryn and Regan had gone. More citadelle guards, easily spotted by their long red capes, were positioned on street corners and were happy to accept gifts of sweet frosted buns from a bent widow. Both princes, along with their squads, had gone to the City of Sacraments. It wasn't far, only a few days' ride, but still my spirits sank. I needed them, not just as my brothers who would back me, but as soldiers I could trust. As I walked away, I thought it odd. Cabinet members—not soldiers—were usually sent on kingdom business.

When I approached a group of soldiers, I recognized one of them. I had played cards with him in one of my late-night escapes—we had jested and laughed together. My confidence rose, and I boldly teased out more details of Bryn and Regan's purpose in going to the City of Sacraments. I learned they were to dedicate a memorial stone for the crown prince and his fallen comrades. The soldier said their presence was necessary to soothe doubts about family allegiance that the betrayal by Princess Arabella had sown.

Another of the soldiers said, "She killed her own brother, you know? Plunged the sword into Prince Walther's chest herself."

I stared at him, unable to stay hunched over my cane. "No, I didn't know."

His utter contempt rang in my ears. *Her own brother.* His comrades echoed his hatred. Princess Arabella was a traitor of the worst kind. I walked away, dazed, trying to understand how the Komizar's terrible lie about my decision to marry him could transform into something even uglier. How could anyone believe I would kill Walther? But they did, and they harbored a seething revulsion toward me.

I felt the Komizar's hands creeping down my arms, owning me, knowing me, still playing the game from far away—*there's always more to take*—knowing how best to undo me.

My stomach rose into my throat, and I ducked behind a stall. I tore my scarf away and doubled over, vomiting, tasting the Komizar's poison. I spat and wiped my mouth. What if it wasn't just these soldiers who believed the lie?

What if everyone did?

What if even my own brothers did?

I'd never convince anyone of anything.

CHAPTER FORTY-SIX

PAULINE

I HAD TOLD BERDI AND GWYNETH I WAS GOING TO THE cemetery to see if Andrés was there. Though little information had been forthcoming, no harm had come from my visits with him either. All I had learned was that he was as surprised by the death of the soldier who had brought the news of Lia's betrayal as Bryn and Regan had been. The soldier was a close comrade, and Andrés mourned his death too. When I asked if the soldier's hurried comments about Lia before he died could have been misinterpreted, he said he didn't know but that his father, the Viceregent, was distressed by the news and found it hard to believe. I wanted to go speak to the Viceregent myself, but I remembered Bryn's words. *Lie low. Stay away from the citadelle.*

I would for a little longer, but there were some things I couldn't put off. Whether it was prudent or not didn't matter.

With every passing day, it burned through me. I had to know, one way or the other.

"Hello, Mikael."

He stopped mid-stride in the narrow alley behind the pub, a girl with beautiful auburn curls still clinging to his arm. He shook her loose and told her to go on, that he would meet her later.

He stared at me, my face still hidden in the shadows of my hood. But he knew my voice.

"Pauline."

Hearing my name on his lips sent shivers swirling down my spine, every timbre of his voice as sweet and buttery smooth as I remembered.

"You didn't come," I said, barely able to form the words.

He stepped toward me, and I clutched the basket I held in front of my belly tighter. His expression held worry and remorse. "I had to reenlist, Pauline. I needed the money. My family—"

"You told me you had no family."

He paused, looking down, but only briefly, as if ashamed. "I don't like to talk about them."

My heart tugged. "You could have told me."

He changed the subject from family to us. "I've missed you terribly," he said and took another step toward me, his hand reaching out, as if he'd already forgotten about the auburn-haired girl. I set the basket down and pushed back the cloak from my shoulders.

"I've missed you too."

He stopped and stared at my rounded belly, the shock registering in his expression, the moment drawing out as long as a final breath, and then a short awkward puff of air escaped from his mouth. His arms that had just been reaching out to me folded neatly across his chest. "Congratulations," he said, and then more carefully, "who's the father?"

In those few words, for a fleeting moment, I wasn't seeing Mikael at all, but Lia, her long hair disheveled around her shoulders, her eyes glistening, her breaths coming in frightened gulps, her voice as fragile as spring ice. *He's dead, Pauline. I am so sorry, he's dead.*

Mikael stared at me, waiting for a response. I was a virgin when he met me. He was well aware that he was the only one. His lips pressed tight, and his pupils shrank to sharp beads. I could see his thoughts spinning, smooth, silky, already renegotiating whatever I would say.

"He's no one you'd know," I answered.

His chest rose in a relieved breath.

And I turned and walked away.

CHAPTER FORTY-SEVEN

BY THE END OF THE DAY, NATIYA STILL HADN'T FOUND PAU-line. There weren't more than a dozen inns in Civica, and Natiya claimed she had gone to them all. All she got were shrugs to her inquiries. By my calculations, Pauline's belly should be round with eight months of baby by now—an innkeeper would notice that.

My mind raced with something I hadn't considered. What if she had lost the baby? Enzo hadn't mentioned her condition back in Terravin. What if—

And then another possibility.

What if she couldn't be found because she was already in prison?

"You're looking drawn," Father Maguire said as I absorbed Natiya's news. "Have you eaten?"

I shook my head. What little I had nibbled was now on a Civica street. He sat me down at a table in a room no larger than a closet. It contained a table, a chair, a narrow cot, and single hook on the wall. The room was on the abbey grounds and meant for single traveling priests when they visited the archives and for nothing more. Natiya and I couldn't stay here long. It would draw attention. I had gone to the millpond cottage today to see if Kaden had shown, but there was still no sign of him. Cold fingers had gripped my spine. *Please let him be all right.*

I rested my head in my hands. With Natiya's lack of success already discussed, the priest asked me how my day had gone. I answered with silence and reviewed the news in my head.

My father was ill with an unknown ailment brought on by the wickedness of Princess Arabella's betrayal. No one had seen the queen since my father took ill, and in fact, the whole of the queen's court had gone into seclusion, mourning the lost company of soldiers. I couldn't even get to my aunt Bernette. The citadelle was guarded as if it held every last treasure on the continent. My brothers, whom I desperately needed to see, were away—along with the squads I had counted on for support. Pauline couldn't be found. And Prince Walther was believed to have been killed by his treacherous sister's hand.

I closed my eyes.

It was only my first day here.

I had been driven, ignoring obstacles, until the very things that drove me suddenly made me weak. I was tied to Civica in ways I had dismissed. Yes, I felt rage at the traitors in the cabinet, but there were still people here whom I cared about, and what they believed about me mattered—the village baker who always had a warm sample for me to taste; the Stable Master who taught me how to groom a horse; the soldiers who grinned when I beat them at cards. I cared what they believed about me. I remembered my first day in Sanctum Hall and the Komizar studying me from afar. Calculating. No one in the Morrighese cabinet ever knew me as well as he had. I saw his orchestrating hand in this.

I pressed the heels of my hands into my eyes, refusing to give in to the desolation welling in me.

It is not over.

Father Maguire set a warm bowl of broth in front of me and I forced down a bite of bread with it. Walther was dead. I couldn't change that, nor what people believed about me.

"Did you take care of the notices?" I asked.

He nodded. "All written and ready, but an official seal would help credibility."

"I'll see what I can do."

"I have some hesitation about the message though. It's risky. Maybe we—"

"It's insurance. Just in case. It will buy me time."

"But—"

"It's the only announcement that will get guzzled faster than a free jug of ale."

He sighed but nodded, and then I gave him another task. I asked him to inquire discreetly and see if any more scholars had gone missing.

I grabbed my cloak from the hook, examining Natiya's needlework hidden on the inside lining. In the dim light of twilight, it would work. It might be a few days before my brothers returned from the City of Sacraments and could help me, but there was still work to be done.

THE CITADELLE WAS A LARGE SPRAWLING STRUCTURE. IF THE architecture of Venda was a dress pieced together with rags, then the architecture of Morrighan was a sturdy practical work dress of counted stitches and ample seams for expansion.

It had grown over the centuries, just as the kingdom had, but unlike the Sanctum, it had grown in a more orderly fashion. Four main wings radiated from the original grand hall at its center, and multiple towers and outbuildings had sprung up on the grounds around them. Connecting passages between wings and other structures made for a multitude of convenient corners and hallways for a young princess to slip from the clutches of her tutors. I was intimately familiar with every drape, closet, nook, and ledge in the citadelle in a way that only a child desperate for freedom can be. And then there were the secret passages no one was supposed to know about, dusty forgotten escapes built in darker times, but my prowling had led me to discover those too.

The Royal Scholar was well aware of my skills, but his traps to catch me had, for the most part, been pathetically weak. I saw them coming before a tutor lying in wait could grab my shoulder, before I tripped a silk thread strung with a warning bell, before any obstacle laid across my path could slow me down. If nothing else, his persistence had proved a challenge for me and contributed to my stealth. He became an unwitting tutor of another kind.

The gardens behind the citadelle provided their own unique form of subterfuge. My brothers and I had burrowed through passages in the loosely trimmed hedges, some of the tunnels so large we could all nestle into an earthen den and eat the warm sweet cakes that one of us had nicked from the kitchen ovens.

I used one of those dens now, waiting for the right moment, then made opportunity bloom by throwing a carefully aimed stone. A rustle in the distance. When the guards turned toward the noise, I darted to the shadows of a covered walkway.

I was in. From here they couldn't stop me.

THERE WAS SOMETHING DANGEROUSLY EXHILIARATING about slipping through the hallways. Even as my heart pounded in my ears, every sense within me burst to life, alert and bright. It was all familiar, the sounds, the scents, but then my awareness was suddenly pricked by something else. Something that had a name now. It slithered past me, a beast clothed with the scent of treachery. I felt its underbelly rippling over my skin. I heard its heartbeat in the walls. I caught its taste, sweet and cunning, swirling in the air. It was settled, comfortable—it had been here for a very long time. And it was hungry.

Maybe that was why I had always preferred running free with my brothers in the openness of the meadows and forests. I had sensed it, even as a child, but had no name for it then. Now the truths whispered to me, betraying the secrets and collusions of the guilty—they were here. They owned the citadelle. Somehow I had to get it back.

I crept down the hall in my bare feet, hugging the shadows, stepping behind cabinets, and into nooks whenever I heard footsteps. There were only four prison cells, dank, secure rooms on the lowest level of the citadelle for those about to suffer the judgment of the highest court. As soon as I saw there were no guards in the passage leading to the rooms, I knew Pauline wasn't there. I checked anyway, whispering her name into the darkness, but there was no answer. That brought me only minor relief. It didn't mean she wasn't being held somewhere else. I returned to the upper level, skulking my way to the third floor.

I looked down the dark east hallway that held the suites of the royal family. The massive arched entrance that I had never given a second thought to before looked like a gaping mouth to me now, and the huge white keystone at its apex like a blade ready to fall.

Two guards were positioned at the entrance. No one was coming or going. The wing had gone mysteriously silent. It was strange that I hadn't even seen Aunt Cloris bustling about. She was always hurrying somewhere, usually with a complaint about one chore or another not being done properly. For her even the protocol of mourning would have its shortcomings. She was a woman of daily tasks, but of no lingering, no laughter, no dreams. Sadly, I understood her better now. Maybe protocol didn't matter so much to her anymore—grief was its own taskmaster.

I moved on and was heading for the portico lookout when I heard something louder than the beat of treason.

He's dying.

I stopped.

They are killing him.

My heart went still. *Killing him?* My thoughts immediately jumped to Rafe. He was facing a coup at home. Or was it Kaden? He was still missing. Or was it only that the hallways I once walked with Walther triggered the memory of watching him die? I forced in a deep steady breath. *Walther.* I wasn't the only one who ached with his loss. I sensed the many hearts that bled. Though I knew I had to move forward, my feet moved elsewhere against my will.

I STOOD BACK IN THE SHADOWS. SOMETHING DARK AND clawed and needy, like a wounded animal, curled in my gut. I watched my mother pull pins from her hair, an irritation to her movements. With the last pin out, her silky black hair spilled to her shoulders.

"He died in battle," I said. "I thought you should know. I saw it all happen."

Her back stiffened.

"His sword was raised for Greta when he was killed. I dug his grave and sang the required blessings over his body and his fellow soldiers. I wanted you to know. He had a proper burial. I made sure they all did."

She slowly turned to face me, and the gods help me, in that moment all I wanted to do was run into her arms and bury my face in her shoulder. But something held me back. She had lied to me.

"I have the gift," I said, "and I know what you did to me."

She stared at me, her eyes glistening, but they held no surprise. She swallowed.

"You don't seem shocked to see me, Mother," I said. "Almost as if someone told you I was here."

She started to step toward me. "Arabella—"

"Lia!" I snapped, and I put my hand out to halt her. "For once in your life, call me by the name you branded me with! The name you knew—"

And then a taller, darker figure stepped out from her dressing chamber. "I was the one who told her you were here. I got your message." It was the Royal Scholar.

I stumbled back, stunned.

"We need to talk, Arabella. You can't—" he said.

I drew my dagger and stared at my mother in disbelief. Pain stabbed my throat. "Please don't tell me that while I was burying my slain brother and his comrades, you were here conspiring with the Royal Scholar."

She shook her head, her brows drawing together. "But I was, Arabella. I've been conspiring with him for years. I—"

Her chamber door swung open, and a guard stepped in. I looked between the Royal Scholar and my mother. *A trap?* The guard immediately eyed me and my dagger and drew his sword, advancing toward me. I fled through the window I had entered, stumbling onto the ledge, and nearly tumbled to the ground below. My vision was blurred with tears, and my path danced in front of me like a loose rope bridge. I ran along the ledge, trusting my footfalls to find solid stones, sensing them more than seeing them. I heard shouts from the window behind me, orders being yelled—*stop her*—and the scuffle of their footsteps, but I had chosen my window and path carefully. In seconds I was gone from their view and headed for the opposite side of the citadelle. I wouldn't have much time, but the night was not over. Especially not now.

Especially not with the misery that raged through me.

The truths wished to be known, and it was time my mother began delivering them—a few words at a time. Who better to sway the people than Regheena, the revered First Daughter of the House of Morrighan?

Desperation grew teeth.
Claws. It became an animal inside me
That knew no bounds.
It tore open my darkest thoughts,
Letting them unfurl like black wings.

—*The Lost Words of Morrighan*

CHAPTER FORTY-EIGHT

RAFE

THE GENERAL WAS AN HOUR LATE. I WAS SPITTING WITH FURY when he finally arrived, but he came with his young daughter in tow. I bit back my curses, but not my anger. "We need to speak privately."

"She's trustworthy."

"It is not a matter of—"

He brushed past me, walking toward my desk. "Colonel Haverstrom explained your requests." He turned to face me. "Leaving so soon? Seems like you just got here. I thought we already had this conversation. I seem to recall your pledge to stay, and now you've changed your mind already?"

I shoved him into a chair, nearly tipping it over. His daughter sucked in a frightened breath and stepped back against the wall.

"I didn't ask for an account of what I did or didn't say, and these are not requests, General Draeger. They are orders."

He settled back into the seat. "And ones that I'm afraid won't be easy to fulfill. You might remember that it was by *your* insistence that companies in Falworth were sent to outlying posts. Our resources here in the capital are spread quite thin. Besides, what can a hundred men do?"

"For my purposes, far more than an entire brigade that would be seen and stopped at the borders."

"All for this *princess*?"

I held my fist at my side, vowing to myself that I wouldn't break his jaw in front of his daughter. "No," I said firmly. "For Dalbreck. What serves Morrighan will serve us tenfold."

"We have no alliance with them. This seems to be nothing more than impetuous folly."

"Their court is in jeopardy. If they fall, so will we."

He shrugged, making a flamboyant show of his doubt. "So you say, and I do respect your position as king. Still, a hundred men outfitted to your specifications could take a while. It would require much effort on my part."

"You have until tomorrow morning."

"I suppose that might be possible with the *right* motivation." He pulled some papers from his coat and threw them on my desk.

I only had to glance at them briefly. I stared back at him in disbelief. "I could have your head for this." It wasn't an idle threat.

"Yes, you could," he agreed. "But you won't. Because I'm the only one who can get you what you need as quickly as you want it. Behead me, and you'll have to reach out to other garrisons much farther away. Think about it. For all the urgency that you claim, do you really have that much time to spare, Your Majesty? And you're still on very shaky ground. This would add stability to your reign. I'm thinking of the realm."

"Devil's hell you are. You're an ambitious opportunist trying to wheedle your way into a position of power one way or another."

I looked at the girl, her eyes wide with terror. "Dammit, General! She's just a child!"

"She's fourteen. Surely you can wait until she's of age? And you must admit, she is a beauty."

I looked at the girl cowering against the wall. "You agreed to this?" I roared.

She nodded.

I turned away, shaking my head. "This is extortion."

"It is negotiation, Your Majesty, a practice as old as the realm—and one your father was well versed in. Now, the sooner you sign the documents, the sooner the betrothal can be announced and I can execute your orders."

I glared at him. *Execute* was an appropriate word choice. I turned and walked out of the room, because all I could see was his neck squeezed between my bare hands. I had never felt like I needed Sven's tempered counsel more than I did now.

CHAPTER FORTY-NINE

PAULINE

I WAS ON MY WAY BACK TO THE INN, NIGHT CLOSING IN AND blind to my path because Mikael's relieved smile continued to loom in my vision. His question—*who's the father?*—clanged in my head like a cow bell, overpowering my thoughts.

But then I sensed something. I felt a presence as strongly as a hand on my arm, and I looked up. She was a small figure perched high on the portico balcony overlooking the plaza. The royal red satin trim of her cloak shone in the fading light. *The queen.*

I stopped as a few others had, most hurrying home to their own eventide remembrances, shocked to a standstill by the sight of the queen sitting on a balcony wall. Outside of official ceremonies, I couldn't remember ever having seen her say remembrances publicly, especially not perched so precariously on a balustrade, but now her voice carried eerily over our heads, swirling like the air itself and slipping inside us just as easily.

She quickly drew more onlookers, and a stillness fell over the plaza.

At times it seemed her words were more sobbed than sung, more felt than said, and they scuttled through me with their haphazard delivery, some phrases skipped and others repeated. Maybe the rushed anguish was what held us all in a breathless grip. Nothing was by rote, only by her need. Every word was raw and true, and I heard it in a new way. Her face was hidden in the shadows of her hood, but I saw her reach up, wiping at what I was sure were tears. And then she said remembrances I had never heard before.

"Gather close, my brothers and sisters. Hear the words of the mother of your land. Hear the words of Morrighan and her kin.

"Once upon a time,
Long, long ago,
Seven stars were flung from the sky.
One to shake the mountains,
One to churn the seas,
One to choke the air,
And four to test the hearts of men.
Your hearts are to be tested now.
Open them to the truths,
For we must not just be ready
For the enemy without,
But also the enemy within."

She paused, choking on her words. Silence clutched the plaza, everyone waiting, mesmerized, and then she continued.

"For the Dragon of many faces,
Dwells not just past the great divide,
But among you.
Guard your hearts against his cunning,
Your children against his thirst,
For his greed knows no bounds,
And so shall it be,
Sisters of my heart,
Brothers of my soul,
Family of my flesh,
For evermore."

She kissed two fingers and lifted them to the heavens, a heavy sadness to her movement.

"For evermore," the crowd echoed back, but I was still trying to comprehend it all. The words of Morrighan and her kin? Seven stars? A dragon?

The queen stood and looked behind her as if she had heard something. She jumped down from the wall and hurried away, disappearing into the darkness as easily as night. Seconds later, the balcony doors burst open and the Watch Captain stepped out on the empty balcony with several guards. It was then that I saw the Chancellor standing only a few feet to my right. He was still staring up at the balcony, perhaps trying to understand the queen's unexpected appearance. I turned, tugging on my hood, and hurried away, but in spite of the danger, something compelled me to return the next night. The queen's urgent prayer still stirred within me. Again, she spoke just as the veil of darkness fell, and this time from the east tower.

The next evening, Berdi and Gwyneth came with me. The queen was on a wall below the western turret. I worried for her, perched so uncertainly on ledges and roofs, and I wondered if her grief had made her reckless. Or mad. She said things I had never heard before. The crowds grew, but it was her haunting words that prodded us to return. On the fourth night, the queen appeared in the abbey bell tower. *Open your hearts to the truth.*

"Are you certain that's the queen?" Gwyneth asked.

A nagging doubt that had prowled behind my breastbone was set free by her question. "She's impossible to see from here," I answered, still trying to puzzle it out, "but she does wear the royal cloak."

"What about her voice?"

And that was the strange part. Yes, her voice was like the queen, but it was also a voice that seemed like a hundred I had known, a timeless sound, like the wind in the trees. It passed through me as if it held a truth of its own.

Gwyneth shook her head. "That's not the queen up there."

Then Berdi voiced the impossible, what we were all thinking. "It's Lia."

I knew it was true.

"Thank the gods she is alive, but why is she posing as the queen?" Gwyneth wondered aloud.

"Because the queen is revered," Berdi answered. "Who would listen to the most wanted criminal in Morrighan?"

"And she is preparing us," I said. But preparing us for what, I didn't know.

CHAPTER FIFTY

ONLY A MIDNIGHT MOON GAVE CONTOUR TO THE ROOM. DIM
gray defined the lines of the ornate pewter goblet in my hand. I set
it back in the curio cabinet, alongside other mementos from years
of service. A medallion from Eislandia, a gilded sea shell from
Gitos, a sculpted jade bear from Gastineux. Unique tokens from
every kingdom on the continent, except of course Venda, with
whom there were no diplomatic relations. The Viceregent's
duties as consul took him on many long trips. I hadn't seen him
complain, but the pleasure he expressed upon returning home
had said much about the hardships of his travel.

I closed the door of the cabinet and sat in a chair in the corner.
Waiting. The darkness offered quiet comfort. I could almost forget where I was, except for the sword lying across my lap.

I was running out of options. It was getting harder to sneak through the citadelle, and by the fourth evening, I'd had to switch to the abbey. The citizens found me there. No doubt the cabinet would have guards stationed at the abbey tonight too.

The first night I had said remembrances over the portico, it was a miracle that I had gotten away at all. I was more careful now, but that night I was reckless and undone. My stomach had twisted into knots. All my carefully planned words had vanished. After seeing my mother with the Royal Scholar, grief had slashed through me like a sharp knife, shredding everything I had hoped for: A tearful reunion. A long-earned explanation. A misunderstanding. *Something.*

Instead I found the Royal Scholar standing at my mother's side, and got an admission of conspiracy and a guard drawing his sword. Thirty mad seconds with her became a betrayal of the worst kind, and the most painful and perplexing thing of all was, *I still ached for her.*

I heard footsteps in the outer chamber. I adjusted my grip on the sword. I had nothing to lose by this meeting and maybe something to gain, however small. I'd already searched the Chancellor's and Royal Scholar's offices, hoping to turn up some sort of evidence. A letter. Anything. The rooms were suspiciously clean and orderly, as if they'd already been scoured and emptied of anything incriminating. I even searched the ashes of their hearths, knowing that was how they'd tried to make things disappear in the past, and found small bits of charred paper but nothing more.

The Viceregent's office was cluttered, his desk a busy sea of papers clamoring for his attention, a half-finished letter to the trade minister, and some commendations ready for his signature and seal. Nothing had been scoured here.

The footsteps drew closer and the office door opened, a triangle of yellow briefly illuminating the floor before it was shut out again. He crossed the room, his footfalls light, and a faint scent swept in with him. Cologne? I had forgotten about the perfumed and pampered smells of court. In Venda the Council mostly smelled of sweat and sour ale. I heard the soft whoosh of the thickly upholstered chair as he sat, and then he lit a candle.

He still didn't see me.

"Hello, Lord Viceregent."

He startled and began to stand.

"No," I said softly but firmly. "Don't." I stepped into the light so he could see my sword casually resting over my shoulder.

He eyed the weapon and returned to his seat, saying simply, "Arabella."

His expression was solemn, but his voice was low and even, unpanicked as I'd thought it would be. The Timekeeper would have been spinning in circles and screaming by now, but the Viceregent wasn't prone to hysterics like some in the cabinet. He was never in a hurry, never rushed. I sat down in the chair across from him.

"Are you going to point that thing at me the whole time?" he asked.

"It's not pointed. Believe me, if it were, you would know it—and feel it. I'm actually affording you a bit of grace. I always liked you more than the other members of the cabinet, but that doesn't mean you're not one of them."

"One of what, Arabella?"

I tried to gauge the innocence of his response. At this moment, it didn't matter if he had ever been kind to me. I hated that I couldn't take a chance even on kindness. I could trust no one.

"Are you a traitor, Viceregent?" I asked him. "Like the Chancellor and Royal Scholar?"

"I'm not sure what you're saying."

"Treason, Lord Viceregent. Treason at the highest levels. I think the Chancellor has grown tired of the baubles on his fingers. And who knows what the Royal Scholar's stake in this is. One thing I've learned from our dear Komizar is it all comes down to power and an insatiable hunger for it." I told him about the Morrighese scholars in Venda, helping the Komizar arm and build a massive army. As I explained, I carefully watched his eyes, his face, his hands. All I saw was surprise and disbelief, and possibly a certain level of fear, as if I were insane.

When I was finished, he sat back in his chair, his head shaking slightly, still absorbing everything I had said. "A barbarian army? Scholars in Venda? Those are rather . . . fantastical claims, Arabella. I don't know what to do with them. I can't go to the cabinet armed only with accusations against esteemed members, especially from, I'm sorry to say, *you*. I'd be laughed out of the hall. Do you have any evidence?"

I didn't want to admit that I had none. I thought of Kaden, who had actually seen the army, the scholars in the caverns, and intimately knew of the Komizar's plans—but the word of a Vendan Assassin would be as laughable as mine.

"I may," I answered. "And then I'll expose the Dragon of many faces."

He looked at me, confusion wrinkling his brow. "A dragon? Now what are you talking about?"

He wasn't familiar with the phrase. Or at he least pretended not to be. I shook his question away and stood. "Don't get up—and that's not a polite request."

"What do you want from me, Arabella?"

I looked at him, scrutinizing every angle of his face, every flutter of his lashes. "I want you to know there are traitors in your midst, and if you are one of them, you will pay. You'll pay as dearly as my brother did. I wasn't the one who killed him. It was those fools who conspire with the Komizar."

He frowned. "The conspiring fools again. If they exist, as you claim, they've managed to hide it from me, so maybe they're not as foolish as you think."

"Trust me," I said, "they're not half as cunning as the Komizar, nor half as intelligent. They're fools to believe he'd keep any agreement they've struck with him. The Komizar shares nothing, least of all, power. Whatever he has promised—and I'm guessing it's the throne of Morrighan—they will never see it. Once he uses them for his purposes, they're done. As are we."

I turned to leave, but he quickly leaned forward, the candle-light illuminating a stray blond wisp falling over his brow. His eyes were earnest. "Wait! Please, Arabella, stay. Let me help. I'm sorry I didn't more vigorously defend you. I've made mistakes in the past too—ones I deeply regret." He stood. "I'm sure we can straighten this out if—"

"No," I said, raising my sword. The scent wafted again, a flutter so faint it was hardly there, but it unsettled me in a deep distant way. It was jasmine. The thought burrowed deeper. *Jasmine.* In the same breath, I saw a little boy clinging to the trousers of his father, pleading to stay.

Jasmine soap.

I was jolted with the impossible. I gaped at the Viceregent, staring as if I were meeting him for the first time. His white-blond hair. His calm brown eyes. The smooth tremor of his voice floating through my head. And then another voice of a similar timbre. *I was a bastard child born to a highborn lord.*

My breath froze in my lungs. How had I never seen it before?

Heard it before?

The Viceregent was Kaden's father, a man as cruel as the Komizar, beating his son and selling him to strangers for a copper.

He stared at me, waiting, hopeful.

But was he a traitor?

I've made mistakes in the past too—ones I deeply regret.

Worry flashed through his eyes.

Worry over me?

Or worry that I had discovered his secret?

"Why would I ever trust a man who threw out his eight-year-old son like a piece of garbage?"

His eyes widened. "Kaden? Kaden's alive?"

"Yes, alive and still very scarred. He has never healed from your betrayal."

"I—" His face crumpled as if he was overwhelmed, and he leaned forward, his head braced in his hands. He mumbled quietly to himself then said, "I searched for him for years. I knew I'd made a mistake the minute it was done, but I couldn't find him. I assumed he was dead."

"Searched for him after selling him for a copper to strangers?"

He looked up, his eyes wet. "I did no such thing! Is that what he told you?" He leaned back in his chair, looking weak and spent. "I shouldn't be surprised. He was a grieving child who had just lost his mother. I've wanted to take back that decision a hundred times, but I was grieving too."

"And what decision was that?"

His eyes squeezed shut as if a painful memory tormented him. "I was trapped in a loveless marriage. I didn't mean for the affair with Cataryn to happen, but it did. My wife tolerated the arrangement well enough because she had no use for me and Cataryn was good to our sons, but after Cataryn died, she'd have no part of Kaden. When I tried to move him into our house, she beat him in a rage. I didn't know what else to do. For his own good, I contacted Cataryn's only relative, a distant uncle who agreed to take him in. I was the one who gave him money for Kaden's care. When I went to visit Kaden, the uncle and his family were gone."

"That's a far different story than the one Kaden tells."

"What else can you expect, Arabella? He was only eight years old. In only a few days, his world was turned upside down—his mother died, and his father sent him to live with strangers. Where is he? Here?"

Even if I had known where Kaden was, I wouldn't have revealed it to the Viceregent—yet. "Last I saw him, he was in Venda—an accomplice of the Komizar."

Disbelief shone in his eyes, and I left before he could ask me another question.

CHAPTER FIFTY-ONE

I PACED THE CARETAKER'S COTTAGE ON THE EDGE OF THE millpond, listening to the rain. I had already stoked a fire and wiped down the sparse furniture that filled it—a battered table, three rickety chairs, a stool, a rocker that was missing one arm, and the wooden frame of a bed, still sturdy, but its mattress eaten by mice long ago.

The cottage and the mill that sat across from it on the other side of the pond were abandoned decades ago for a deeper, larger pond farther east of Civica. Only bullfrogs, dragonflies, and raccoons visited here now—and occasionally young princes and a princess fleeing the scrutiny of court. Our names were carved in the wide door frame, along with those of dozens of other village children—at least those brave enough to venture here. It was said to be haunted by the Ancients. Bryn and I may have had something to do with that rumor. I suppose we wanted it all to ourselves. Even my father's name was carved here. Branson. I ran my fingers over the rough letters. It was hard to imagine that he'd ever been a carefree child running through the woods, and I wondered at the way we all change, all the outside forces that press and mold and push us into people and things we hadn't planned to be. Maybe it happened so gradually that by the time we noticed, it was too late to be anything else.

Like the Komizar. Reginaus. A boy and name snuffed out of existence.

I fingered my name in the wood, the lines crooked, but deep. *LIA.* I took my knife out and squeezed in four more letters in front of it. *JEZE.* And I wondered at who I had become— someone I had never planned to be.

Pauline's name wasn't carved in the wood, and as far as I knew, she had never been here. By the time she arrived in Civica, the cottage had lost some of its magic for me and my brothers and we rarely came anymore. Besides, such wanderings were off limits, and Pauline followed the protocol of the queen's court to the letter—well, almost to the letter, until she met Mikael.

Where was she? Had Natiya misunderstood, or spoken to the wrong person? Maybe the rain had delayed her? But it was only a light rain, and we were used to that in Civica.

Today when I returned to my room, my mind had still been reeling with my late-night revelation. The Viceregent had seemed our best possibility of someone to trust in the cabinet. I had tried to test for his truthfulness, and everything he had said seemed genuine—even his claim about deep regrets. Was it possible he had changed in the eleven years since he threw Kaden out? Eleven years was a long time. I had changed in far less. So had Kaden. The Viceregent was already in a high position of power, second in command to my father. What more would he have to gain?

I was so occupied with these thoughts that Natiya had had to grab my arms and shake them, then repeat her news. She claimed she'd found Pauline. She said Pauline's head was bowed and covered so she couldn't see her hair, but she knew a pregnant belly when she saw one, and Natiya had chased after her just outside the cemetery gate. When she was close enough, Natiya called her name. Pauline seemed fearful, but she agreed to come.

I prayed she wasn't afraid of *me*. Surely she couldn't believe the lies. Or maybe she was only being cautious. She didn't know Natiya, and perhaps she suspected a trap. But she knew the millpond had once been a favorite haunt of mine. A stranger wouldn't have suggested it.

Maybe Berdi and Gwyneth had delayed her. Gwyneth was suspicious of everything, and here in Civica, rightly so. I should take that as a good sign.

But still my anxiety grew.

I paced the cottage and finally pulled out a chair and sat staring at the cottage door, my hands kneading my thighs. Bit by bit, I was losing everything. If I lost Pauline too, I wasn't sure what I would do. What if she—

The handle rattled and the door eased open cautiously, its creak the only sound. As a quick afterthought, I put my hand on my dagger, but then Pauline stepped in, her hair dripping in wet strands, her flushed cheeks shimmering with rain. Our gazes met, and her eyes told me what I had feared. She knew. There was a condemning sharpness in them I had never seen before. My stomach floated even as my heart sank.

"You should have told me, Lia," she said. "You should have told me! I could have dealt with it. You didn't even give me a chance."

I nodded, words stuck in my throat. She was right. "I was afraid, Pauline. I thought I could bury the truth and make it go away. I was wrong."

She stepped toward me, hesitant at first, then earnest, throwing her arms around me, a fierceness in her grip. Angry. Her fists curling into my clothes, demanding, shaking, and then she leaned into me, sobbing. "You're alive," she cried into my shoulder. "You're alive." My chest shook, and I cried with her, the months and lies between us vanishing. She told me how frightened she'd been, the agony of waiting with no word, and the relief she felt when she saw me impersonating the queen. She, Berdi, and Gwyneth had been discreetly looking for me since then. "I love you, Lia. You are my sister, by the gods, a sister as true as blood. I knew what they said about you were lies."

I wasn't sure who held up whom, each of us heavy in the other's arms, our cheeks wet against each other. "My brothers?"

"Bryn and Regan are well, but worried about you."

Now it was my fists that curled into her clothes, and I choked back tears as she told me they hadn't stopped believing in me either. They had asked a lot of questions trying to get at the truth and promised that as soon as they returned, they would find it.

She said Berdi and Gwyneth were here with her and she told me where they were staying. I understood now why Natiya hadn't been able to find them. It was a small tavern down an alley that let rooms above the shop. I remembered it. There was no sign. You had to know it was there. No doubt Gwyneth had found that one.

I finally stepped back and wiped my cheeks, surveying her girth. "And you're well?"

She nodded, rubbing her hand over her belly. "I spotted Mikael weeks ago, but I only had the courage to confront him recently." A bittersweet smile creased her eyes, and we sat down at the table. She talked about him, recalling her dreams for their future that she thought had been his dreams too, all the times they held hands and talked, and planned, and kissed. She went over memories and details as if they were flower petals she was plucking one at a time and then letting them go in the wind. I listened, feeling a part of me break.

"He'll never be this child's father," she finally said. She told me with calm resignation about the girls on his arm, his denial, and all the doubts she'd carefully tucked away that came to life before her eyes when they spoke. "I knew what he was like when I met him. I thought I was that one girl special enough to change him. I was a happy fool living in a fantasy. I'm not that girl anymore."

I saw the change in her. She was different. Sober. The dreams she'd had were swept from her eyes. I saw all the reasons I had lied to her, thinking if her fantasy stayed alive, maybe mine could too.

"You were never a fool, Pauline. Your dreams gave flight to my own."

She pressed her hand to her back as if trying to counter the weight of the baby pulling against her spine. "I have different aspirations now."

"We all do," I answered, feeling the tug of lost dreams.

She frowned. "You mean Rafe."

I nodded.

"He showed up at Berdi's inn looking for you. When I told him about Kaden, he started giving orders, saying more men would come to help, and they did, but none of them ever returned. At first I feared something had happened to them, but then I wondered if he had deceived us just like Kaden. Berdi guessed that Rafe wasn't really a farmer, which only fueled my worries that he couldn't be trusted—"

"Berdi was right. Rafe wasn't a farmer," I said. "He was a soldier—and also Prince Jaxon of Dalbreck—the betrothed I left at the altar."

She looked at me like I had lost my mind back in Venda.

"But he's no longer a prince," I added. "Now he's the king of Dalbreck."

"Prince? King? None of this makes sense."

"I know," I said. "It doesn't. Let me start at the beginning."

I tried to tell her everything in the order that it had happened, but very quickly she interrupted. "Kaden put a hood over your head? Then dragged you across the entire Cam Lanteux?" I saw the hatred in her eyes that Kaden had feared she would harbor.

"Yes, he did, but—"

"I don't understand how he could share a holy feast with us at Berdi's table in one moment and threaten to kill us both in the next? How could he—"

We both froze. We heard the whicker of a horse. I put my finger to my lips. "Did you ride here?" I whispered.

She shook her head. Neither did I. It was a short walk, and it was easier to slip through the woods unseen on foot.

"Could someone have followed you?"

Her eyes widened, and I was shocked to see her draw a knife. She had never carried one before. I drew mine as well.

Heavy footsteps scraped on the stone steps outside the door. Pauline and I both stood and then the door opened.

CHAPTER FIFTY-TWO

KADEN

I SAW THE BLADE BEFORE I SAW HER. IT FLASHED PAST ME, slicing my shoulder just as I slammed her up against the wall.

And then I saw that it was Pauline.

Lia was yelling at both of us. "Drop the knife, Pauline! Drop it! Kaden! Let her go!"

The knife was still firm in her grip, her hand straining against mine. "Stop!" I yelled.

She seethed. "Not this time, barbarian!"

I felt the sting where the blade had cut me and the warmth of blood spreading across my shoulder. "What's the matter with you? You could have killed me!"

Her eyes held no apology, only hatred that I didn't think it was possible for Pauline to possess.

"Stop!" Lia said firmly, and she pulled the knife from

Pauline's hand. She nodded for me to let Pauline go. I took a chance and released her, moving out of her reach, waiting for her to come at me again. Lia stepped between us.

"I told him to come, Pauline," she said. "He's here to help. We can trust him."

But Pauline was incensed and still not listening. "You lied to us! We treated you with nothing but kindness and then—"

Lia continued to try to explain and calm Pauline down.

I stood there, not knowing what to say, because every word she flung at me was true—true as Pauline always was. I had traded on her kindness and trust.

"He's changed, Pauline! You have to stop and listen to me!"

She stared at me, her eyes like glass, her chest heaving, and then suddenly she doubled over, clutching her stomach. Lia grabbed Pauline's arm to steady her. Water seeped to the floor around her feet. Pauline groaned and then was clutched with a stronger spasm. I ran to her other side, and Lia and I both kept her from falling. Even in her pain, she tried to wrench free of me.

"The bed!" Lia yelled.

I scooped Pauline into my arms and carried her to the bare wood frame in the corner. "Get the bedroll from my horse!"

Lia ran out the door, and Pauline ordered me to put her down.

"I will," I said. "Believe me, nothing will give me greater pleasure, as soon as Lia returns."

Lia was back in seconds, shaking out the roll, and I laid Pauline on top of it.

"It can't be time," Lia said to Pauline. "You still have a month to go."

Pauline shook her head. "It's time."

Lia stared at Pauline's swollen belly, not trying to hide her alarm. "I don't know anything about this. I've never—" Her gaze shot to me. "Do you—"

"No!" I said, shaking my head. "Not me. I've never done it either. I've seen horses—"

"I am not a horse!" Pauline screamed. She leaned forward in another spasm. "Berdi," she groaned. "Go get Berdi."

I started for the door. "Tell me where—"

"No," Lia said, cutting me off. "Berdi would never come with you, and I can find her faster. Stay here."

Pauline and I both protested.

"There's no other choice!" Lia snapped. "Stay! Keep her comfortable! I'll be right back!"

She left, slamming the door behind her.

I stared at the door, not wanting to turn and face Pauline. Babies took hours, I told myself. Sometimes days. It wasn't more than a twenty-minute walk into town. Lia would be back within the hour. I listened to the rain, coming down louder and harder.

Pauline moaned again, and I reluctantly turned. "Do you need something?"

"Not from you!"

An hour passed, and I alternated between silently cursing Lia and worrying about what had happened to her. *Where was she?* Pauline's pains were becoming stronger and more frequent. She swatted my hand away when I tried to wipe her brow with a cool cloth.

Between pains, she leveled a scrutinizing stare at me. "Last time I saw you, Lia was ordering you to go straight to hell. What dark magic did you weave to make her trust you now?"

I looked at her glistening face, damp strands of her blond hair clinging to her cheek, a loss in her eyes I had never seen before. "People change, Pauline."

Her lip pulled up in disgust, and she looked away. "No. They don't." Her voice wobbled, full of unexpected sorrow instead of anger.

"You've changed," I said.

She glared at me, her hands passing over her belly. "Is that supposed to be a joke?"

"I meant in other ways—most notably the knife you were flashing in my face."

Her eyes narrowed. "Betrayal tends to familiarize one with weapons."

I nodded. *Yes*, I thought. *Sadly, it does.*

"It looks like someone's taken a weapon to your head too," she said.

I reached behind, feeling the crusted gash on my scalp. "It would seem so," I answered. I had passed out and slept for two straight days on the trail after vomiting up half my insides. The throbbing had eased, but it was probably what had dimmed my judgment enough to walk into an unknown cottage without my own weapon drawn. Perhaps that was a good thing, or Pauline might be lying dead on the floor now.

I walked over to the window and opened the shutter, hoping to see a glimpse of Lia and Berdi. The downpour obscured the forest beyond, and thunder rumbled overhead. I gently pressed on the back of my head, wondering how bad the gash was. Beneath the crusted patch of blood, there was still a sizable lump. It was ironic that a housekeeper armed only with an iron pot had nearly done in the Assassin of Venda.

How the Rahtan would laugh at that.

The name dug into me with a surprising sting—and longing. *Rahtan.* It brought back the familiar, the feeling of pride, the one place in my entire life where I had felt like I belonged. Now I was in a kingdom that didn't want me and in a cottage where I wasn't welcome. I didn't want to be here either, but I couldn't leave. I wondered about Griz and Eben. Surely Griz was healed and they were on their way by now. They were the closest thing I had to family—a family of poisonous vipers. The thought made me grin.

"What's so amusing?" Pauline asked.

I looked at the severity in her gaze. Had I done this to her? I remembered all of her kindnesses back in Terravin—her gentleness. I had thought that the young man she so earnestly waited for couldn't possibly deserve her and then when I learned he had died, I had hoped it wasn't by a Vendan hand. Maybe that was what she saw when she looked at me, a Vendan just like the one who had killed her baby's father. Though my smile had long faded, her gaze remained fixed on me, waiting.

"Nothing's amusing," I answered, and looked away.

Another hour slipped by, and it seemed one labor pain hadn't subsided before another began. I dipped the rag into the bucket of cool water and wiped her brow. She didn't resist this time, but closed her eyes as if trying to pretend it wasn't me. I was getting a bad feeling about this. She was racked with another spasm.

When the pain finally passed and she relaxed again against the makeshift pillow I had made for her, I said, "We may have to do this alone, Pauline."

Her eyes shot open. "You deliver my baby?" A smile broke her face for the first time, and she laughed. "I promise you, the first hands that touch my little girl won't be a barbarian's."

I ignored her barb. It didn't hold the same venom as an hour ago. She was getting tired of fighting me. "You're so sure it's a girl?"

She didn't get a chance to answer. She was seized with a pain so strong, I was afraid she wasn't going to breathe again, and then on its heels came a sobbing scream. "No," she said, shaking her head. "No. I think she's coming. Blessed gods. Not now." The next moments were hot and blurred, her anguished wails tearing through me. She cried. She begged. I held her shoulders, and she bent forward in pain. Her nails dug into my arm.

My heart pounded furiously with every scream. It was coming. There was no more waiting. *Dammit, Lia!* I eased Pauline back against the pillow, lifted up her dress, then pulled her underclothes free before I could think too much about what I was doing. A head crested between her legs. She said a hundred things to me between each pain, a breathless one-way conversation of pleas to the gods and curses. She fell back crying, too tired to push.

"I can't," she sobbed.

"We're almost there, Pauline. Push. I see its head. It's coming. Just a little more."

She cried, a weak happiness briefly washing over her face before it vanished and she screamed again. I cupped the head, more of it emerging.

"One more push!" I yelled. "One more."

And then the shoulders came, and with a last quick whoosh, it was in my hands, wet and warm, its tiny body arching, a small hand waving past its face. A whole baby, in my hands, slivers of eyes already peering out at the world. Peering at me. A gaze so deep, it carved a hole in my chest.

"Is it all right?" Pauline asked weakly.

The baby cried, answering her question.

"He's perfect," I said. "You have a beautiful son, Pauline." And I laid him in her arms.

CHAPTER FIFTY-THREE

IT WAS ALMOST LIKE A FULL TAVERN, SO MANY CROWDED into one place.

I tried to imagine it as Terravin.

Except there was no ale. No stew. No laughter.

But there was a baby.

A beautiful perfect baby. Berdi sat on the end of the bed, crooning over him as Pauline slept. Gwyneth, Natiya, and I sat at the table, and Kaden lay sleeping on the floor in front of the fire. He was shirtless, his shoulder freshly bandaged, and his head rested on a folded blanket that Natiya had brought.

The rain poured down relentlessly. We were lucky the roof held. A bucket caught a single leak in the corner.

When I had tracked down the room Pauline had directed me to in the village, I'd found it empty and ransacked, with the windows flung open in spite of the rain. *They fled*, I thought, *through a window*. That was a very bad sign. The innkeeper claimed he'd seen nothing and didn't know where they'd gone, but I heard the terror in his voice—and then I saw the fearful curiosity as he peered into the shadows of my hood. In my haste, I had left the mourning scarf behind.

I pulled the hood farther down over my face and ran to the abbey grounds. I instructed Natiya to go the cottage with our horses and supplies while I hunted down Berdi and Gwyneth. I searched the streets and peered through tavern windows, hoping to catch a glimpse of them somewhere, but then the innkeeper's terror registered with me again. He had been as afraid of me as of whoever had ransacked the room and was eager for me to leave. I ran back to the inn. Berdi and Gwyneth would never have left without Pauline. I found them hiding in the kitchen.

It was a tearful, but hasty reunion. Gwyneth said she'd seen the Chancellor and soldiers outside her window and heard their brisk demands to the innkeeper to be led to Pauline's room. They were baffled at how the Chancellor had known Pauline was there. They confirmed the innkeeper was trustworthy—and he had stalled as long as he could, giving her and Berdi a chance to flee. When I told them of Pauline's condition, the innkeeper sent us on our way with food and supplies that we packed onto Nove and Dieci.

Natiya had been able to find the cottage but said Kaden had already delivered the baby by the time she got there, and had wrapped him in his shirt. She had bandaged the cut on his shoulder, which I knew was inflicted by Pauline, but she had also tended a gash on the back of his head. He'd told Natiya he had received a heavy blow from an iron pot. From whom? I wondered. That was why he hadn't shown at our rendezvous point, and perhaps explained his heavy sleep now. He never stirred when we walked into the cottage.

I watched his even breaths. It was strange, but I wasn't sure I'd ever seen him sleep before. Whenever I was awake, he was awake. Even that one rainy night months ago when we'd slept in a ruin and his eyes were closed, I'd known a part of him still watched me. Not tonight. This was a deep sleep that worried me. It made him seem more vulnerable. I hadn't even had a moment to express relief when he had walked into the cottage this morning, but now I stared at him, emotion welling in me. I kissed two fingers and lifted them to the gods. *Thank you.* He was injured, but he was alive.

"I think I still have a few leaves of thannis in my pack, Natiya. Will you steep them and make a poultice for his head?"

"Thannis?" Berdi asked.

"A foul-tasting weed that has some helpful uses beyond drinking. It grows only in Venda. Good for heart, soul, and growling stomachs when food is scarce—except when it seeds and turns from purple to gold. Then it becomes poison. It's the one thing they have in abundance in Venda."

The mere mention of the weed made an unexpected yearning swell in me. Memories that I had buried tumbled loose. I thought of all the proffered cups of thannis—the humble gifts of a humble people.

Gwyneth angled her head at Kaden sleeping by the fire and frowned. "So how did all"—she twirled her hand in the air—"*this* come about? How does one go from being an Assassin to being your accomplice?"

"I'm not sure *accomplice* is the right word," I said, snapping beans and adding them to a kettle. "It's a long story. After we eat."

I looked over my shoulder at Berdi. "Which reminds me, I promised Enzo I'd tell you he hasn't burned down the inn yet. Boarders are fed, and the dishes are clean."

Berdi's brows shot up. "Stew?"

I nodded. "Yes, even stew. And not half bad."

Gwyneth rolled her eyes with genuine surprise. "The gods still perform miracles."

"No one was more surprised than I was when I saw him in the kitchen wearing an apron and cleaning a fish," I said.

Berdi huffed, her face beaming with pride. "Knock me dead. I told him he had to step up. Could have gone either way, but I had no choice. I had to take the chance and trust him."

"What about that farmer?" Gwyneth asked. "What became of him? He never returned to the inn as promised. Is he dead?"

That farmer. I heard the suspicion in how she described him. Berdi and Natiya both eyed me, waiting for my answer. I hardened my expression, adding a slab of salted pork to the kettle before I put the lid on and hung it over the fire. I sat back down at the table.

"He returned to his own kingdom. He's fine, I assume." I hoped. I thought about the general who was challenging him back in Dalbreck. I couldn't imagine Rafe not prevailing, but I remembered the gravity of his expression, the lines that etched near his eyes every time one of the officers brought it up. There were no guarantees in such things.

"Dalbreck. That's where he's from," Natiya interjected. "And he's no farmer. He's a king. He ordered Lia to—"

"Natiya," I sighed. "*Please*. I'll explain."

And I did, as best as I could. I skimmed over details, emphasizing the major events in Venda and what I had learned there. There were some details I couldn't relive again, but it was hard to skim past Aster. She was still a deep bruise inside me, purple and swollen, and painful to the touch. I had to stop and recompose my thoughts when I came to her role in this.

"Many people died that last day," I said simply. "Except the one person who deserved to."

When I was finished, Gwyneth leaned back in her chair and shook her head. "*Jezelia*," she said, musing about the Song of Venda. "I knew that claw and vine was there to stay. No kitchen brush was going scrub it from your back."

Berdi cleared her throat. "Kitchen brush?"

Gwyneth stood as if the ramifications had finally sunk in. "Sweet mercy, are we ever thick in it now!" she said, circling the room. "The first time I laid eyes on you, Princess, I knew you were going to be trouble."

I shook my head apologetically. "I'm sorry—"

She stepped close and squeezed my shoulder. "Hold on. I didn't say it wasn't the kind of trouble I like."

My throat swelled.

Berdi stood, the baby still cradled in one arm, and walked over and kissed the top of my head. "Blazing balls. We'll figure this out. Somehow."

I leaned against Berdi's side and closed my eyes. Everything inside me felt like a rush of tears, sick and feverish, but on the outside, I was dry and numb.

"All right, enough of that," Gwyneth said, and sat down opposite me. Berdi took the remaining chair. "This is a whole different game now. The Eyes of the Realm seem to have set their sights on more than order. What's your plan?"

"You're assuming I have one."

She frowned. "You do."

I had never voiced it out loud. It was dangerous, but it was the only way I could ensure that my voice would be heard by the whole court and those who were still loyal to Morrighan—if only for a few minutes.

"Something I've done before. But not successfully. A coup d'état," I said. I explained that I had led a rebellion with my brothers and their friends into Aldrid Hall when I was fourteen. It hadn't gone well. "But I was armed only with righteous indignation and demands. This time I intend to go in with two platoons of soldiers and evidence."

Berdi choked on her tea. "Armed soldiers?"

"My brothers," I answered. "I know when they return that they and their platoons will back me."

"Two platoons against the whole Morrighese army?" Berdi questioned. "The citadelle would be surrounded in minutes."

"Which is why I need evidence. The hall is defensible for a short time with the cabinet as hostage. All I need is a few minutes, if I can expose at least one of the traitors with evidence. Then the conclave might listen to everything I have to say."

Gwyneth snorted. "Or you'd get an arrow in your chest before you got a chance to say anything at all."

It was well known that during conclave sessions, guards in full regalia, armed with bows and arrows, were posted in two gallery towers that overlooked Aldrid Hall. An arrow had never been shot by them. It was ceremonial, another tradition held over from earlier times, when lords from across Morrighan convened—but the guards' arrows were real, and I presumed they knew how to shoot them. The last time I had stormed in, I'd known they wouldn't shoot the king's daughter. This time I didn't have that assurance.

"Yes, it's possible I could get shot," I agreed. "I can't figure everything out at once. Right now I just need to find evidence. I know the Chancellor and Royal Scholar are involved, but when I searched their offices, I turned up nothing. They're so clean not even a dust mote dared to hang in the air. There is also—"

I stopped. *My mother.* These two small words I couldn't force loose. *No. Not her.* They were a wall inside me, unscalable even after what I had seen. I couldn't say her name in the same breath as the other traitors'. She would never have put Walther at risk. She loved him too much for that. Some things were true and real. They had to be. I closed my eyes, seeing the sky full of stars and the rooftop she'd led me away from. *There's nothing to know, sweet child. It's only the chill of the night.*

I had seen her with the Royal Scholar myself, and I knew he was mired in this. His favored scholars worked in the Sanctum caverns. Berdi and Gwyneth reached across the table and squeezed my hands and I opened my eyes.

"Hey, can I get in on some of that?"

I looked up. Pauline was awake. I went to her bedside and sat on the edge, and we all took turns kissing and congratulating her before Berdi nestled the baby into her arms.

Gwyneth helped Pauline get the baby latched and feeding at her breast, then stood back proudly with her hands on her hips. "Look at that. He takes to it like a champion."

"Have a name for him yet?" Berdi asked.

A brief cloud passed through Pauline's eyes. "No."

"Plenty of time for that later," Berdi said. "I'll see if we have something better than that old torn shirt to wrap him in."

"Maybe one of those two-headed sweaters you knitted?" Gwyneth winked, and she and Berdi went to the opposite corner and began unpacking the bag they had brought.

I reached out and touched a tiny pink toe that peeked from Kaden's swaddling shirt. "He's beautiful," I said. "How are you feeling?"

"Well enough," she answered, rolling her eyes, "considering I just paraded my lady parts to a killer barbarian." She sighed. "But I suppose, compared to what you've been through, it's a small indignity to bear."

I smiled at the baby. "And look at the prize. He was worth it, no?"

She beamed at her son, gently running her finger over his cheek. "Yes," she said. "I still can't quite believe it." She looked over at Kaden, her smile fading. "What happened to him?" she whispered. "His scars?"

Kaden lay curled on his side, his back to us. I had become used to his scars, but I was sure they had been shocking to the others.

"Betrayal," I answered.

And I told her about who he had been and what he had endured.

WHEN KADEN WOKE, HE AWKWARDLY STOOD, HIS HAND skimming his bare chest, and he said hello to Berdi and Gwyneth.

Berdi frowned, her hands on her hips. "Well, you've got all kinds of surprises in you, don't you, *pelt trader*?"

"I suppose I have a few," he answered, a slight blush tinging his temples.

Gwyneth snorted. "Not the least of which is delivering babies."

Kaden turned, looking at Pauline. "How is he?"

"Fine," she answered quietly.

He walked over, a smile pulling at the corner of his mouth, and gently nudged the blanket aside so he could see the baby's face. Pauline leaned back, lifting the baby protectively to her chest. Kaden noticed her retreat, and his smile disappeared. He stepped away, a small movement that stung with disappointment, and my heart ached for him. But I understood Pauline too. After all she had been through, trust was as slippery as hope.

"Anything else you plan to surprise us with?" Berdi asked.

He looked at me. "Lia, I need to speak with you privately."

"Not so fast, soldier," Gwyneth intervened. "Anything you have to say to her, you can tell us all."

I nodded. At some point, we all had to start trusting one another.

He shrugged. "Have it your way. I know another one of your traitors. My father is no longer lord of County Düerr. He sits on the king's cabinet."

Pauline drew in a sharp breath. Kaden didn't have to say a name. It was immediately apparent to her, much as it was to me. There was no one else in the cabinet with Kaden's white-blond hair, or his warm brown eyes. Even the sound of his calm steady voice was the same. Everything that should have been obvious had eluded us and I realized there were assumptions we made about people, and once we did, that was all we could see—Kaden was a barbarian assassin, the Viceregent a respected lord descended from the Holy Guardians, and surely one could have nothing in common with the other.

Berdi and Gwyneth didn't know the Viceregent and remained silent, but Kaden glanced from me to Pauline, wondering at her reaction. "Lord Roché," he added to confirm his assertion.

For a moment I planned to lie to him, say there was no Lord Roché in the cabinet, afraid that he would storm off and get his head bashed in again, but he was already reading my eyes.

"Don't lie to me, Lia."

I braced myself, knowing he wouldn't take this well. "I know who he is. I met with him two days ago. He's a member of the cabinet as you said. He may have been a terrible father Kaden, but there's no proof he's a traitor."

CHAPTER FIFTY-FOUR

I HAD WATCHED KADEN STOMP TOWARD THE MILL TO CHECK on the animals. I could almost see the steam rising from his shoulders.

It's a lie! I have no relatives. My mother was an only child. The people who took me in were professional beggars.

I saw the rage in his face, but I also remembered the genuine grief in the Viceregent's eyes. *He was only eight, a grieving child who had just lost his mother.*

If there was one thing I had learned, it was that time could twist and shred truth like a forgotten sheet battered in the wind. Now I had to piece the shreds together again.

I told Natiya I had another job for the priest, and at the first break in the weather, she was to go to him. A record of trained governesses was kept in the archives. Somewhere there had to be some information on one named Cataryn.

DIECI'S EARS TWITCHED WITH SATISFACTION AS I SCRATCHED between them. I gave Nove equal affection and wondered if they missed Otto. The mill was dry, but one wall had tumbled away long ago, leaving the old building cold and drafty. Owls roosted in the high rafters. Natiya sat in a far corner, drawing a whetstone over her sword. We had sparred this morning. She was the one who had reminded me of the need to keep our skills sharp. The habits I had taught her across the Cam Lanteux remained deeply ingrained.

Pauline had watched with what I thought was a doubtful eye and later questioned me again about the Komizar's army.

"They're going to destroy Morrighan," I said, "and traitors here are going to help them do it. We have to be ready."

"But, Lia—" She shrugged, her expression full of skepticism. "That's impossible. We're the favored Remnant. The gods have ordained it. Morrighan is too great to fall."

I looked at her, not sure what to say, not wanting to shake her world further, but I had no choice.

"No," I said. "We aren't too great. No kingdom is too great too fall."

"But the Holy Text says—"

"There are other truths, Pauline. Ones you need to know." And I told her about Gaudrel, Venda, and the girl Morrighan, who was stolen from her family and sold to Aldrid the scavenger for a sack of grain. I told her about the histories we never knew and the thieves and scavengers who were the bricks and mortar of our kingdom—not a chosen Remnant. The Holy Guardians were not holy at all. Saying it aloud to her felt cruel, like I had snatched a cherished piece of crystal from her hand and smashed it beneath my foot, but it had to be said.

She stood, dazed, walking around the cottage, trying to absorb this news. I saw her mind ticking through texts.

She whirled. "And how do you know the histories you found are true?"

"I don't. And that's the hardest part. But I know there are truths that have been hidden from us, Pauline. Ones we each have to find with our own hearts. Truth is as free as the air and we all have the right to breathe as deeply of it as we wish. It cannot be held back in the palm of any one man."

She turned away and stared into the loft where the owls roosted. With each shake of her head, I knew she was trying to dismiss it, weighing my truths against the only other truth she had ever known—the Morrighese Holy Text.

Scavengers.

If it was true, this history robbed us of our elevated status among kingdoms. As I watched her, I understood with clarity why the Royal Scholar had hidden Gaudrel's history away. It undermined who we were. What I didn't understand was why he hadn't just destroyed it. Someone had tried to once.

Pauline took a deep breath and wiped her hands on her skirt, smoothing it out. "I have to get back to the cottage," she said. "It's time for the baby's feeding."

CHAPTER FIFTY-FIVE

PAULINE

DURING THE NIGHT, AFTER FEEDING THE BABY, I HAD LAIN on my side for a long while, watching Kaden sleep, still wondering at his scars. Now when he looked in a mirror, he would see another mark—the one I had left—alongside the ones his father had laid. Back in Terravin, a simple shirt and a few kind words had covered up everything about who I had believed he was. Mikael had done the same, but he covered up his true nature with a few flowery words. I let those words wheedle into me until they were all I saw.

Was it possible to ever really know anyone, or was I simply the worst judge of character in all of history? I rolled over, looking at the shadows flickering on the ceiling. His seeing my lady parts was the least of my distress. I was still haunted by his expression when he first held the baby in his hands. That seemed real. His eyes were filled with wonderment, but then as he reached out and laid the baby on my chest, he faltered, as if he already knew I would never allow this child in his arms again. One part of me knew I needed to thank him for helping me, but another part was still angry, and a greater part, afraid. How could I be sure if any of his kindness was real this time? What if he was still using us for another purpose the way he had before? I knew Lia trusted him. That should have been enough for me, but trust was out of my reach.

I knelt on the porch, scrubbing the crate he had found in the mill. *It might make a passable cradle for now,* he had said when he offered it to me this morning. He hadn't met my gaze. He just set it on the porch and walked away. He was almost out of earshot before I called after him. When he turned I said, "Thank you." He stood there, studying me, then finally nodded and left.

It had poured for four days straight, rivers of water rushing down hillsides, more leaks sprouting in the cottage roof. I wasn't sure if the deluge had been blessing or curse, trapping us in such small quarters, but it also forced Lia and Kaden to work out the argument between them: Kaden wanted to go to the Viceregent himself. Confront him. Lia said no. Not until the time was right. I was surprised that he listened to her at all. There was a strange bond between them that I still didn't understand. But when she implied there was the possibility that the Viceregent had changed, that eleven years could change a man, and she pointed to Enzo as proof, Kaden became incensed. I got a glimpse of the Assassin he had been. Maybe the Assassin he still was, and I understood that when he said "confront," he didn't mean talk. "People don't change that much!" he yelled and stormed out into the rain. He returned an hour later, soaked, and they didn't speak of it again.

I had said myself that people didn't change, but I pondered the possibility. Lia had changed. She had always been fearless, oblivious to threat when something rankled her greatly, impulsive sometimes at cost to herself, but I saw a calculating, colder steel in her now that hadn't been there before. She had suffered. All my months of worry for her well-being weren't unfounded. She tried to brush past details, but I saw the scars where arrows had pierced her back and thigh. She had nearly died. I saw the thin line on her cheekbone where the Komizar had beat her. But there were other scars that couldn't be seen on her skin. Those were the ones I worried about—a vacant stare, a curled fist, a defiant lip twisted at some memory—deeper scars from seeing people she loved murdered and knowing more had died after her escape. I saw that she cared about the Vendan people. She often spoke in their language with Kaden, and her remembrances included their traditions as well.

"Are you one of them now, Lia?" I had asked her.

She looked at me, surprised at first, but then some memory flickered in her eyes, and she didn't answer. Maybe she wasn't sure herself.

It was her remembrances that had changed the most. She didn't say them by grudging obligation anymore but with a zealous power that stilled the air, calling up not just the gods, but it seemed the stars and generations too. A fullness grew in the air as if the breaths of the world kept time with our own, and I saw her stare into the darkness, her eyes focused on something the rest of us couldn't see.

She didn't fear the gift any longer but embraced it. She coaxed, demanded, trusted. She spoke of the gift in ways I had never heard before, its ways of seeing and knowing, and trusting, ways that made me reach deeper inside myself.

I had seen a glimpse of her brokenness too. She hid it well, but when Natiya began describing to Berdi and Gwyneth what the Dalbreck army and outpost were like and she merely mentioned Rafe's name, Lia walked out onto the porch as if she couldn't bear to listen. I followed and found her leaning against a post watching the downpour.

"She seems fascinated with the Dalbretch army," I said. "She's very young to be carrying all those weapons. I didn't think vagabonds—"

"They don't carry weapons," Lia said. "Natiya tried to help me by sewing a knife into the hem of my cloak. Her camp paid dearly for it."

"And now she wants justice."

"The very people she had welcomed into her camp betrayed her. Her way of life—and her innocence—have been robbed. One she may get back, the other, never."

I tried to gently nudge the conversation. "She thinks highly of the king of Dalbreck."

Lia didn't respond.

"What happened between you two?" I asked.

Her cheekbone glowed with light from the cottage window and she faintly shook her head. "Whatever happened was for the best."

I touched her shoulder, and her gaze met mine. The best wasn't what I saw in her eyes.

"Lia, it's me. Pauline. Tell me," I said softly.

"Leave it. Please."

She tried to turn away, and I grabbed her arms. "I will not. Pretending you aren't hurting won't make the pain disappear."

"I can't," she said. Her voice was hoarse. Her eyes puddled, and she angrily swiped at her lashes. "I can't think about him," she said more firmly. "There's too much at stake, including his life. I can't afford distractions."

"And that's all he was? A distraction?"

"Surely you of all people know these things don't always work out."

"Lia," I said firmly, and I waited.

She closed her eyes. "I needed him. But so did his kingdom. That is a reality that neither of us can change."

"But?"

"I thought he'd come," she whispered. "Against all reason. I knew he couldn't. He shouldn't even, but I still found myself looking over my shoulder, thinking he would change his mind. We loved each other. We made vows. We swore that kingdoms and conspiracies wouldn't come between us—but they did."

"Tell me everything from the beginning. Tell me the way I told you about Mikael."

We talked for hours. She told me things she hadn't shared

before, the moment she first realized who he really was, the tense minutes before they crossed into Venda, the note he had carried in his vest all those months, the way she'd had to pretend to loathe him when all she wanted was to hold him, his promise for a new beginning, the way his voice kept her pinned to this world when she felt herself slipping into another—and then their bitter argument on parting.

"When I left him behind, I marked every day between us by writing his last words to me in the soil—*it's for the best*—until I finally believed them to be true. Then I found my wedding dress where he had hidden it in the loft at the inn, and it tore everything loose inside of me all over again. How many times do I have to let go, Pauline?"

I looked at her, unsure how to answer. Even after everything Mikael had done, every day I had to let go again. He was a habit in my thoughts, not any more welcome than a rash, but I'd find myself thinking of him before I even realized what I was doing. Banishing him from my thoughts was like learning to breathe in a new way. It was a conscious effort.

"I don't know, Lia," I had answered her. "But however long it takes, I will be here for you."

I sat back and looked at the crate. The wood was smooth and sturdy. I stood and hung it from the porch rafter to dry. *Yes, Kaden is right. Once a soft blanket is added, it will be quite passable.*

A scream splits the air.

The pachegos have captured something,

The children cry,

The darkness too deep,

Their stomachs too empty,

The howls of the pachego too close.

> *Shhh,* I whisper.

> > *Tell them a story,* Jafir pleads.

> > *Tell them a story of Before.*

But Before was never mine to know.

I search my memory for Ama's words.

The hope. The journey's end.

And I desperately add my own words to them.

> *Gather close children,*

> *And I will tell you a story of Before.*

> *Before the world was brown and barren,*

> *When it was still a spinning blue jewel,*

> *And sparkling towers touched the stars.*

The scavengers around me scoff.

But not Jafir.

He is as starved for a story as the children.

—*The Lost Words of Morrighan*

CHAPTER FIFTY-SIX

RAFE

"SHE'S HOLED UP IN A LITTLE COTTAGE NOT FAR FROM THE citadelle with three women and Kaden. A vagabond girl too," Tavish said.

"You disobeyed orders."

Jeb grinned. "You knew we would."

"And you're glad we did," Orrin added.

"What are those for?" Jeb asked, nodding toward the handler and three caged Valsprey.

"In case things don't go well for us. A parting gift from General Draeger. He insisted on them. He doesn't want us to fall off the edge of the continent again without any word."

Tavish surveyed the details of our company with a suspicious eye and turned to Captain Azia, perhaps figuring he'd get more information out of him. "How'd you get so many horses with Morrighese tack?"

Sven cleared his throat, preempting an answer from Azia. I knew the question created as sour a taste on his tongue as it did mine. "It's a long story," he answered.

"I'll explain later," I told Tavish. "Ride back and tell the rest it's time to split off to the eastern and northern roads into the city. And to stay in groups of no more than three or four. We can't all descend into the city at once."

We were farmers, merchants, tradesmen, not a battalion of a hundred armed soldiers. At least that was what we wanted them to think.

CHAPTER FIFTY-SEVEN

HEAVE.

Heave.

I threw off my blanket and sat up, my skin hot and cold all at once. The synchronized chants, the squeal of gears, the sickening metallic clang still rang in my ears. I looked around, reassuring myself that I was still in the cottage. It was dark and silent except for Berdi's gentle snores. *Only a dream,* I told myself and lay down, struggling to get back to sleep. I finally dozed in the pre-dawn hours, then slept late, but when I finally woke, I knew—the sounds and chants were real. The bridge was fixed. They were coming.

I looked around. The cottage was empty except for Gwyneth dozing in the rocker with the baby in her arms. I noticed that the melody of drips falling into buckets and bowls had stopped at last. Finally I could slip back into town. The streets would be busy again and I could pass unnoticed—and Bryn and Regan could be back. I quietly dressed, putting on my protective riding leathers and strapping on every weapon I had. If all went well, I might be leading my brothers and their comrades into Aldrid Hall by this afternoon. First I'd scour the citadelle one last time for evidence, but with the bridge fixed, confronting the cabinet couldn't wait any longer. I threw on my cloak and tiptoed quietly outside to find the others. I found Pauline at the end of the porch, lifting a crate and hanging it from a nail on a porch timber.

"Are you sure you should be doing that?"

"I had a baby, Lia, not an accident. I'm actually feeling quite well. First time I haven't had a foot pressing on my bladder in weeks. Besides, cleaning a crate is easy enough work. Kaden got it for me from the mill. He just went back over there to let out the animals. The oats are gone. They need to graze."

I hoped that was all he was doing. I knew he still wanted to confront his father.

I looked around, walking to the other end of the porch. "What about Berdi and Natiya? Where are they?"

"They went to town while there was a break in the weather for more supplies." She ran her hand along one side of the crate. "It will make a decent enough cradle for now—at least when there aren't arms to hold the baby."

"It seems there will always be plenty of those available. Gwyneth has hardly let the baby out of her grip."

Pauline sighed. "I noticed. I hope it's not painful for her. I'm sure it stirs memories in her of all the times she didn't get to hold her own baby."

"She told you?" I asked, surprised that Gwyneth had shared what I'd thought was a closely guarded secret. I had only guessed because I'd seen the way she looked at Simone back in Terravin. A tenderness had sprung to her face that she had for no one else.

"About Simone?" Pauline shook her head. "No, she refuses to talk about it. She loves that little girl more than air itself, but at the same time, that love is what grips her with fear. I think that's why she keeps her distance."

"Fear of what?"

"She desperately doesn't want the father to find out that Simone even exists. He's not a good man."

"She told you who he was?"

"Not exactly. But Gwyneth and I have found this strange place of truth. There's a lot that we share without ever saying a word." She untied her damp apron and hung it to dry beside the crate. "The Chancellor is Simone's father."

My jaw dropped. I knew Gwyneth had some unsavory con- nections, but I never suspected one of them to be so high in the food chain. She had good reason to be afraid. I turned, cursing in Vendan to spare Pauline's ears and a penance.

"You can curse in Morrighese," she said. "No penance re- quired. I've probably said the same thing myself. Or worse."

"You, Pauline?" I grinned. "Wielding knives *and* cursing? My, how you've changed."

She laughed. "Funny, I was just thinking the very same about you."

"For better or worse?"

"You are who you needed to become, Lia. We've both changed out of necessity." A wrinkle darkened her brow. She noticed my riding leathers beneath my cloak for the first time. "Going somewhere?"

"Now that the rain has let up, people will be in the streets again. I can pass unnoticed, and Bryn and Regan are surely back by now. I want to—"

"They won't be back yet."

"The City of Sacraments is only a few days' ride, and dedicating a memorial stone doesn't take but a day. Bryn and Regan won't—"

"Lia, I think you misunderstood. They're going to more cities after that, and then on to the Lesser Kingdoms. Regan to Gitos and Bryn to Cortenai. They're on a diplomatic mission ordered by the Field Marshal."

"What are you talking about? Princes don't go on diplomatic missions. They're soldiers."

"I questioned it too, especially with your father ill. It doesn't follow protocol. But Bryn thought it was important, and your father approved it."

All the way to the Lesser Kingdoms? My heart plummeted. That could mean weeks of waiting that we couldn't afford. But I couldn't march into the conclave without them.

I shook my head. *A diplomatic mission.* I knew how Bryn and Regan hated such things. I could picture Regan rolling his eyes. The only part he would like was riding in the open—

My throat tightened.

They were asking a lot of questions, trying to get at the truth.

Just like Walther had. *I'll discreetly nose around.*

Which made them a liability.

"What's wrong?" Pauline asked.

I grabbed the porch post to steady myself. A visit to a Lesser Kingdom would mean days of traveling across the Cam Lanteux. They'd be unsuspecting and easy targets. My heart went cold. They weren't on a mission. They were headed into another ambush. The princes were being eliminated—along with their questions.

My father would never have approved this. Not if he knew.

"It's an ambush, Pauline. Bryn and Regan are headed into an ambush—the same as Walther. They have to be stopped before it's too late. I have to go tell my father. Now."

And I ran for the citadelle, praying it wasn't already too late.

CHAPTER FIFTY-EIGHT

KADEN

"HELLO, ANDRÉS."

I had promised Lia I wouldn't confront my father. I'd said nothing about my brother.

I'd heard Pauline wonder aloud to Gwyneth if it could have been Andrés who had followed her to the inn and alerted the Chancellor to where they were staying. Pauline hadn't revealed her identity to Andrés, but she recalled that he'd asked her a lot of questions. Once she learned what the Viceregent had done to me, it made her wonder if his questions hadn't been so innocent after all. I was sure they weren't innocent. He was his father's son.

I surprised him at the cemetery gate just after he walked in, quickly hooking one arm over his shoulder like we were old friends, my other hand holding a knife discreetly pressed to his side. "Let's go for a walk, shall we?" He got the message right away and fell into step with me.

I led him to Morrighan's crypt in the center of the cemetery, a place of cobwebs, spirits, dim light, and thick walls. Once we were down the stairs, I pushed him away. He stumbled forward and turned.

His head angled to the side as he finally got a good look at me. The dawning came fast. I guessed that I looked far too much like our father. Andrés took after his mother, ashy coloring, a round cherub face, better suited to begging on street corners—but he wasn't the bastard son.

"Kaden?" I saw his fingers twitch as if to reach for his weapon. "I thought you were dead."

"I think that was the point. It didn't turn out that way."

"I know you have reason to be angry for what he did to you, Kaden, but it's been years. Father has changed."

"Sure he has."

He glanced at my knife, still gripped at my side. "What do you want?" he asked.

"Answers. And maybe a bit of blood to pay for all that I've lost."

"How did you know where to find me?"

"Marisol told me," I answered.

He frowned. "You mean Pauline."

"I figured you knew."

"The belly threw me off, but her voice—I met her once. She didn't remember me. I guess I didn't make much of an impression, but she made one on me. Is she—"

"She won't be back," I said firmly, so he'd know that whatever sights he'd set on Pauline were a thing of the past. "Tell me, Andrés, how is it that you were the only one who didn't ride with Prince Walther's platoon the one time they encountered a Vendan brigade?"

His eyes narrowed. "I didn't ride because I was ill."

"I don't recall you as the sickly sort. This happen often, or was it just a coincidence that staying home saved your neck?"

"What are you implying, brother?" he sneered.

"Do I really need to say it?"

"I was ill for a week, mostly delirious. The court physician can confirm it. When I came to, Father said I'd been sick with a fever."

"You were with him when you fell ill?"

"Yes. I'd had dinner with him and a few cabinet members at his apartments the night before I was to ride out, but as I was leaving, I got dizzy and fell. Father's servants helped me to bed. I don't remember much after that. What difference does it make? No one knew what Walther and the others were headed into!"

"Sure, someone knew. And that someone didn't want his only remaining son going into a massacre that he had planned. I'm guessing the son was happy to play along."

He drew his sword. "You're talking treason."

His eyes were wide and crazed, his voice desperate, and it occurred to me that he might actually be telling the truth. Pauline had said he was grieved by the platoon's death. If his grief wasn't real, why else would he come here to mourn every day? I studied him, wondering about some other kind of motivation, but I saw only anguish in his eyes, not deceit.

"Put it away, Andrés. I'd rather not kill you."

He lowered his sword. "Who are you?" he asked, as if he sensed I was not just his little discarded brother anymore.

"No one you want to know," I told him. "Who else was there the night you fell ill?"

He thought for a moment, then said that, besides his father, he had also dined with the Chancellor, the Watch Captain, and the court physician.

CHAPTER FIFTY-NINE

MY PARENTS SHARED A MARRIAGE CHAMBER, BUT THERE WAS a private suite next to the physician's office for royal family members when they were ill or in need of care. It was the chamber where my mother had given birth to us all. If my father was truly ill, and maybe even if it was a ruse, that was where he would be.

I walked into the outer chamber, my hair tucked into a cap, and my face bowed into a stack of towels piled high in my arms. A flask dangled from my hand. I shuffled forward with indifference, while my feet burned to run. Even my father, no matter how angry with me, would still be raw with Walther's loss. A glimmer of doubt was all it would take for him to rescind his order. I'd make him listen if I had to hold a blade to his throat and take him hostage.

"I'm here to sponge the king with a tincture ordered by the physician," I said in a thick Gastineux brogue, sounding like my aunt Bernette when she was angry. The sleepy nurse sitting in a chair by the door perked up.

"But no one—"

"I know, I know," I grumbled. I swallowed and forced my words out in an annoyed drawl. "No one ever tells us anything until the last minute. Here I was about ready to go home. Maybe I can talk you into doing this? If I were to—"

"No," she said, thinking the better of it. "I've been stuck here for hours. I could use the break." She glanced at the guard standing by the open door to the inner chamber. "Need his help?"

"Pfft. Ain't doing much more than his brow. Don't need help for that."

She stood with relief and was out the door before I could say anything else.

The inner chamber was dim. As I passed the guard, I asked him to close the door behind me since my arms were full. "Protocol," I chided when he hesitated.

The door gently shut behind me, and I faced the large bed on the opposite wall. I almost didn't see my father in it. He was small and sunken, like he was being eaten up whole by pillows and blankets. His eye sockets were shadowed, and the skin thin over his cheekbones. He was someone I didn't know. I set the towels and flask on a table and stepped closer. He didn't stir.

He's dying.

They are killing him.

My pulse raced. The citadelle had already whispered this

truth to me. I'd thought it meant everyone but him, not the man who had always been bluster and power—all that I had ever known.

"Father?"

Nothing.

I dropped to his side and took his hand in mine. It was limp and warm. What was wrong with him? I desperately wanted to see him loud and angry in all the ways that Walther had described him, the way he had always been, but not like this.

"Regheena?"

I startled at his weak voice. His eyes remained closed.

"No, Father. Mother is busy elsewhere. It's Arabella. You must try to listen to me. It's important that you order Bryn and Regan home immediately. Do you understand what I'm saying?"

He frowned. His eyes slivered open. "Arabella? You're late. And it's your wedding day. How will I explain it?"

My throat pinched. A misty fog filled his gaze. "I'm here now, Father." I lifted his hand to my cheek. "All will be well. I promise."

"Regheena. Where is my Regheena?" His eyes drifted closed again.

My Regheena. My mother's name was tender on his lips. Even my name had been spoken with tenderness, a gentle reprimand, not an angry one.

"Father—" But I knew it was no use. He couldn't issue an order for a drink of water, much less make a demand for Bryn and Regan's safe return. He had already floated back to his unconscious world. I laid his hand on his chest and pressed my fingers to his neck. His pulse was firm and steady. If it wasn't a weak heart that had laid him low, what was it?

I stood and went to the bureau, my fingers carelessly running through the mountain of tinctures, syrups, and balms—all remedies I recognized. My mother had given them to me and my brothers many times. I opened the bottles and sniffed. The scents brought back memories of stuffy heads and fevered brows. I rifled through a box of herbs and liniments and then moved on to the bureau drawers. I didn't even know what I was looking for—an ointment? Liquid? Something that pointed to his true ailment? *They are killing him.* Or maybe they weren't treating a simple illness properly. I looked elsewhere in the room, searching behind a mirror, a pedestal that held a tall vase of flowers, in his bedside table, and even slid my hand beneath the mattress, but turned up nothing.

I went to the door of the adjoining physician's office, pressing my ear to it. When I judged the room to be empty, I gently eased open the door and searched there too, but short of tasting every elixir and waiting to see the effect, I had no way of knowing what may have caused my father's weak and confused state. Maybe it was his heart. Maybe I had broken it just as the rumors said. I returned to his chamber, and my eyes lit on the box of herbs and liniments again. The physician had always disdained the cook's kitchen remedies. When Aunt Bernette made tea from rapsi blossoms for Aunt Cloris's headaches, he would shake his head and smirk. I searched through it again, more carefully this time.

Beneath the other bottles, I found a small vial no bigger than my little finger. It was filled with a golden powder I'd never seen. An herb for the heart the nurse was neglecting to give him? I pulled the cork from the vial, but could detect no herbal scent and began to lift it closer to my nose. *No. Don't.* I held it at arm's length, examining the shimmering gold, then replaced the cork and set it back with the others, shutting the lid.

"Your Highness."

I spun. The Chancellor stood there in all his glory, his crimson robes flowing, his knuckles glittering, his arrogant tight-lipped smile beaming with triumph. Two guards with drawn swords stood behind him. "How amusing that your note said I should be afraid," he said, his tone cheerful. "I think, my dear, it is you who should be afraid."

I glared at him. "Don't be so sure." I shrugged off my cloak so my weapons were easier to draw and looked past him to the guards. I didn't recognize them. Had he changed the guard who kept the citadelle secure? Still, they wore the Royal Guard insignia. "Lay your weapons down," I told them. "By all that is holy, do not defend this man. He's a traitor who's sending my brothers into an ambush. Please—"

"Really, Princess," the Chancellor said, shaking his head, "I thought groveling was beneath you. We all know who the real traitor is. You're a declared enemy of the realm. Your blood runs so cold that you killed your own brother—"

"I did not kill him! I—"

"Seize her," the Chancellor said, stepping aside.

The guards came at me, but instead of running away, I lunged forward, and in a blurred second, one of my arms had hooked the Chancellor's neck, while the other held a knife to his throat.

"Get back!" I ordered.

The guards paused, swords ready to strike, but they didn't retreat.

"Step back, you fools!" the Chancellor yelled, feeling the sting of my knife pressing into his flesh.

They backed up cautiously, stopping against the opposite wall.

"That's better," I said, then whispered in the Chancellor's ear, "Now, what were you saying about being afraid?" Though I loved the feel of his racing heart beneath my arm, I heard footsteps pounding down the hallway toward us. More guards had already been alerted, and I probably had only seconds before all my exits would be blocked. I pulled him back with me toward the physician's door, and when it was only a step behind me, I shoved him so he stumbled forward. I slipped inside the room, barring the door behind me. In seconds the guards were ramming against it, and I heard the Chancellor screaming on the other side to break it down.

I went to the window and threw open the shutter, but there was no ledge for escape. I looked down to a balcony directly beneath the window—it was a twenty-foot drop onto hard stone, but I couldn't see any other option. I eased myself out, hanging from the window by my fingertips, then let go. I rolled with the fall, but the impact still sent splitting pain up my leg. I fled, limping as I ran, my route now a wild and haphazard one, darting into rooms, hallways, redirecting my steps when I heard the pounding of footsteps in pursuit. I raced down a dark servant's stairway, and then an empty hall, the shouts getting weaker, their search still confined to the upper floors. I was at the back of the citadelle, heading down a long dark passage for the rarely used servant's entrance that Pauline and I had escaped through. I had just slid the latch open when I heard a metallic *chink*, and I spun toward the sound. A strange keening whir filled the air and then a loud *thunk, thunk, thunk*.

A hot jolt exploded in my arm. My vision flashed with pain so bright I couldn't focus. When I tried to pull away, my breaths shuddered in my chest. I couldn't move. I looked to my left. Two long iron bolts were embedded high in the door, but a third had pinned my hand to the wood, piercing the center of my palm. Blood dripped to the floor. I heard footsteps and tried frantically to pull the bolt loose, but the least movement sent sickening pain convulsing through me. The footsteps grew louder, closer. I looked up and saw the silhouette of a figure walking leisurely toward me. I recognized the swagger. My knife lay on the floor at my feet. I drew my sword, a pathetic gesture, because I knew I couldn't fight with one hand pinned to the door. His face came into view.

Malich.

A crossbow unlike any I had ever seen dangled from one of his hands. I trembled with pain as he drew closer. Every sound was amplifed, his footsteps, the tip of my sword scraping the floor, my own breath wheezing in my throat.

"So nice to run into you, Princess," he said. "I understand

Kaden is here too. I never should have let him slip away from me that day when we fought on the terrace."

The smug grin. The one I'd sworn he would pay for.

"I wish I could say it was nice to see you too, Malich." I lifted my sword as a threat, but even that small movement magnified the painful stab in my hand. I tried to mask my agony.

He easily knocked my sword away with his crossbow, sending it clattering across the room. The jerking twist of my body sent blinding jolts shooting up my arm, and I couldn't restrain a scream. He grabbed my free hand and pressed his body against mine.

"Please," I said. "My brothers—"

"Just the way I prefer you, Princess, begging and with both of your hands restrained." His face still bore the lines of my attack, and his eyes glowed with vengeance. He leaned closer, and his free hand circled my throat. "The bolts are courtesy of the Komizar. He's sorry he couldn't be here to deliver them himself. Sadly, you must settle for me." His hand slid from my throat to my breast. "And after I'm finished with you, I'll carve up your face with marks like the ones you gave me. He doesn't care what you look like when I hand you over."

His grin widened and that was all I could see, all I could feel, the assured expression that said he owned the world. It was a grin that churned memories to the surface. I saw my brother weeping. I saw the arrow in Greta's throat. I saw a baby's lace cap burning and curling into ash. *That was easy*, he had boasted. Killing her was easy.

His breaths were heavy in my ear as his hand slid lower,

fumbling with my belt, jerking at the buttons of my trousers. *Easy.* I felt the crunch of bone as I forced my pinned hand to twist, turn, grab hold of the bolt. Blood rushed down my arm. Groans shuddered up from my throat like animal sounds, thick and wild. I used the pain the way a fire consumes fuel, burning hotter and hotter, and with my hand gripped around the bolt, I forced my arm to shove against it, loosening it. My fingers burned like they'd been set ablaze, the iron bolt becoming rage in my hand, and I pulled, loosening it further, my groans only adding to Malich's satisfaction. His eyes gleamed, looking into mine as if he already knew where he would carve the lines. *Easy.*

"No fainting on me now, Princess," he said as he jerked the last button of my trousers free. His hand slid beneath the leather, down along my hip, his grin widening. "I keep my promises, and I told the Komizar that you would suffer."

I yanked on the bolt, twisting it as it sprang free, the sudden release adding velocity to my swing, and it plunged into Malich's neck, the pointed end emerging through the other side. His eyes widened.

"And I keep my promises too," I said.

His lips parted as if to say something. He was unable to speak, but I saw it in his eyes. For a few glorious seconds, he knew—he was a dead man, and it was by my hand. While he could still hear me, I whispered, "I hate that it feels so good and so easy to kill you, Malich. Rest assured I will never beg you for anything ever again." I pulled the bolt free and blood spurted from his neck before he thudded to the ground. Dead.

I stared at his crumpled body, the blood running slowly from his neck, trickling into lazy red rivers across the cobbled floor. His eyes stared blankly at the ceiling.

His grin was gone.

It was then that a thunder of footsteps closed in from all sides. Six guards surrounded me—again ones I didn't recognize. The Watch Captain stood among them. He was the member of the cabinet who oversaw the citadelle guards.

He looked down at Malich's body with recognition and shook his head.

A nauseous wave rushed through me. "Not you too," I said.

"I'm afraid so."

"Captain, don't do this," I pleaded.

"Believe me, Princess, if I could reverse time, I would, but I'm in much too deep to turn back now."

"It's not too late! You could still save my brothers! You could—"

"Take her."

I stepped forward and swung, the bolt still in my hand, but my knees gave way and I hit the floor.

Two guards scooped me up by my arms, and another pulled the bolt free. Blood spurted, and my head swam as they dragged me. I tried to keep track of where they were taking me, but all I saw were blurred shapes swirling in front of me. *Stop the bleeding, Lia.* But with their hands clamped on my arms, there was no chance of that. Instead I pleaded to their loyalties, trying to convince them that the Watch Captain was the vilest of traitors. Even my words seemed slurred, distant, and one of the guards repeatedly told me to shut up, but I didn't stop. He finally cracked me in the jaw. The soft flesh on the inside of my cheek sliced into my teeth, and the salty tang of blood filled my mouth. The passageway faded in and out, and floor and ceiling spun into each other. But it was a word a guard muttered just before he threw me into a dark room, that slammed into me harder than his fist.

Jabavé.

There was a reason I hadn't recognized the citadelle guards. They were Vendan.

CHAPTER SIXTY

JUST A LITTLE FARTHER, LIA.

Hold on.

Hold on for me.

I smelled a river, glimpsed the weighty bowed pines of a forest, saw frosty breaths swirling the air above me, and heard the steady determined beat of boots crunching in snow.

I felt warm lips brushing mine.

Just a little farther.

For me.

My eyes drifted open—I wasn't dead yet. The snowy world, the blinding whiteness, and the scent of pine vanished. Instead I was in a black windowless room, but I still felt the arms that had held me, the fingers that had brushed back strands of my hair, the chest that had been a warm wall against the cold, and I heard the voice that wouldn't let me go.

Keep your eyes on me. The fiery blue that had demanded I stay.

I tried to focus, search the blackness. The cell was stuffy, the air as old as the walls themselves. It smelled of dirt and rot. I pulled my hand close to my stomach, pressing it tight to stop the bleeding, but the pressure sent a blinding stab through me.

I sucked in air, forcing my lungs to breathe.

I couldn't accept that it was over.

That there would be no word sent to save my brothers.

That the traitors wouldn't be exposed.

That the Komizar had won.

Seeing Malich dead was suddenly a very small victory. The satisfaction trickled away, like his blood across the floor. His death only gave me an ending—it didn't give back what had been taken.

The path here was a blur and I wasn't sure where I was, but it wasn't the citadelle. Maybe one of the outbuildings? Why would they chance dragging me out in the open when the citadelle prison had been only steps away? I didn't think they had taken me as far as Piers Camp, but I couldn't be sure.

I tried to stand to search the room for something to use as a weapon, but my injured leg buckled under me, and my face slammed into the dirt floor. I lay there like a wounded animal. *Do we understand each other at last?* I choked back angry tears. *No!* I pushed with my one good hand, trying to get up. I'd thought the situation couldn't get any worse, but I was wrong. I heard footsteps, muffled shouts, and squinted against the sudden bright light as the door swung open. More prisoners were flung inside, the door slammed, and the room plunged back into darkness.

He is near my children,
His lips brush my neck,
His spittle wets my cheek,
His caress crushes my breaths,
More than swords,
More than fists,
My words frighten him.
I see my end,
But the words I have given you,
I pray, those he cannot take.

—Song of Venda

CHAPTER SIXTY-ONE

RAFE

ONLY A FEW OF US RODE THROUGH THE WOODS. THE REST remained in town, dispersed so as not to attract attention—but ready. As we got closer to the cottage, I put my hand up, a wordless order for everyone to stop. They heard it too. An angry squalling. A cat perhaps, or—

We broke into a gallop. As we neared, I spotted Kaden running from the woods toward the cottage. He saw us but kept running. "Pauline! Lia!" he yelled as he ran. We piled through the cottage door, only to find it empty—except for the howl of a baby. We all looked at the bed at the same time, and Kaden bent down, pulling a bundle from beneath it.

"It's Pauline's," he said as he cradled the baby in his arms. He pulled aside the blanket to make sure it wasn't hurt. "She would never leave her baby like this." And then, as if he'd finally registered our presence, he asked, "What the hell are you doing here?"

Before I could answer, Berdi and a young girl burst through the door. Berdi yelled warnings and threats before finally demanding the baby be handed over. It was pandemonium and confusion as questions were hurled until Orrin rushed in and said there were fresh horse tracks outside that weren't ours.

"Someone took them," Kaden said. "She hid the baby beneath the bed so they wouldn't take him too."

The girl with Berdi darted for the door. "I have to get to the abbey!"

Both Kaden and Berdi yelled for her to stop, but she was already gone. I got on my horse and ran her down, unsure of her motives. She drew a knife to hold me off. That was when she told me about the notices.

CHAPTER SIXTY-TWO

THE THREE OF US SAT SIDE BY SIDE, LEANING AGAINST THE stone wall. I imagined they stared into the black void, just as I did. I was grateful that I couldn't see Pauline's face as she recounted the betrayal. Her voice was still filled with disbelief and wobbled in a soft, dangerous way between misery and cold rage. Just when I thought she would break, a terrible quietness roared up in her, one that was feral and sharp and thirsty for revenge.

Gwyneth told me that before they were taken, she had heard Pauline call her from the cottage porch. She had looked out the window, and when she saw the soldiers coming, she wrapped the baby in a blanket and laid him beneath the bed, where he wouldn't be seen.

Pauline's voice turned thin and fearful again. "Kaden will find him. Don't you think, Lia?"

Gwyneth had already reassured her that Kaden would hear him crying when he returned from the mill. I'd started to add my own affirmation when Pauline reached out for my hand and felt the bloody mess of it. I groaned at her touch.

"Dear gods, what happened?"

We had embraced when they were thrown into the room, but in the darkness she hadn't seen my hand.

I had already explained my encounter with my father, the Chancellor, and the guards who dragged me here, but now I told them about my unfortunate encounter with Malich and the bolt.

Pauline was horrified and immediately began tearing a strip from the bottom of her skirt for a bandage. Gwyneth stood and felt her way through the corners of the room, and when she had found a handful of cobwebs, she stumbled back toward me and wrapped them around my hand. Though the court physician would have disapproved highly of such kitchen remedies, it helped slow the steady ooze from my hand.

"Was it hard?" Pauline asked. "To kill him?"

"No," I answered. It had been easy. Did that make me little more than an animal? That was what I felt like now, a knot of teeth and claws ready to kill anything that walked through the door.

"How I wish I'd had a bolt in my hand when Mikael came and pointed us out." Pauline mimicked his voice as she recounted his words again. "It was my *duty* to turn you in, he said. I'm a soldier, and you're a wanted criminal of the kingdom. I had no other choice." She tied off the bandage. "Duty! When I saw the magistrate toss him a bag of coin, Mikael shrugged, like he hadn't known about the bounty."

"How did he know you'd be at the caretaker's cottage?" I asked.

"I'm afraid he knows me far better than I know him. I'm guessing he was the one who followed me to the inn and alerted the Chancellor. When he didn't find me there, he thought of another place I might go. The cottage was where we used to—" She sighed and didn't finish her thought. She didn't need to.

"And I was just the lucky bonus in the whole bargain," Gwyneth said cheerfully. "Wait until the Chancellor finds out I'm involved. That should be ugly. I learned a long time ago how delightfully vicious he can be." And then, for the first time, she opened up about Simone. Maybe when you're about to die, secrets don't seem so important to keep.

She sighed with an air of disgust that I think was directed at herself. "I was nineteen when I met him. He was older, powerful, and showered me with attention. I found him charming, if you can believe that, but the truth is, even then I knew he was dangerous on some level. I thought it was exciting compared to my dreary life as a chambermaid in Graceport. He wore expensive clothes and spoke so properly, and it made me feel like I was somehow just as important as he was. I passed information on to him for almost a year. Because of the port, a lot of lords and wealthy merchants frequented the inn. It wasn't until two patrons I had given him information about turned up dead in their beds that I grasped how dangerous he was. He told me they had become a *liability*. Everything that I had thought was exciting about him suddenly became terrifying."

She said by that point she was already pregnant. She made up a story for him that she'd found a job elsewhere and would have said or done anything to get the baby away from him. He didn't try to stop her from leaving. He wasn't happy about the child, and she was still afraid he might do something to her or the baby. She kept Simone for only a few months. She had run out of funds, had no one to turn to, and was worried the Chancellor might track her down. Passing through Terravin, she spotted an older couple who doted on some children in the square. She learned they were childless and followed them to a home that was neat and tidy. "They even had red geraniums in pots on their windowsill. I held Simone in my arms for two hours, staring at those flowers. I knew they'd make good parents." She paused and I heard a swiping sound, like she was brushing tears from her cheeks. "After I left her there, I didn't come back to Terravin for over two years. I was still afraid someone would make the connection, but not a day went by that I didn't think about her. They're good people. We don't ever talk about it—I guess they know I don't want to—but they know who I am, and they make room in their lives for me. She's a happy and sweet little girl. Nothing like me, thank the gods. Or him." Her voice cracked as if she knew she might never see her daughter again. Hearing the steely Gwyneth break squeezed the air from my chest.

"Stop!" I said. "We'll get out of this."

"Damn right we will!" Pauline growled.

Gwyneth and I sucked in startled breaths, then laughed. I pictured Pauline gripping a bolt in her fist with Mikael's name engraved on it. Gwyneth reached out and held my good hand. I hung my other hand over Pauline's shoulder and pulled her close. We leaned into one another, our arms tangled, forehead to cheek, chin to shoulder, tears and strength binding us.

"We'll get out of this," I whispered again. And then we shared the silence, knowing what was coming.

Gwyneth pulled away first, leaning back against the wall again. "What I can't figure out is why we're not all dead already. What are they waiting for?"

"Confirmation," I said. "The conclave is back in session, and someone who's a deciding factor in this little conspiracy is otherwise occupied. Maybe the Royal Scholar."

"The conclave breaks for midday meal," Pauline said.

"Then we have until midday," I replied.

Or maybe longer if my backup plan worked out, but as every minute passed and I listened for the sound of the abbey bells ringing, I became more certain that plan had been thwarted too.

My anger spiked. I should have stabbed the Komizar again. Carved him up like a holiday goose, then brought his head back skewered on a sword and showed it to the crowds as proof that I had no love for the tyrant.

"Why did they believe the lies?" I asked. "How could a whole kingdom believe I would marry the Komizar and betray a company of soldiers, including my own brother?"

Gwyneth sighed. "They were cut to the quick," she said,

"grieving and desperate. Thirty-three of their finest young men were dead, and the Chancellor stepped forward and provided them with an easy outlet for their rage—a face and name they knew that had already turned her back on them once. It was easy for them to believe."

But if I hadn't run away, I never would have found out about the Komizar's plans—or the traitors. I'd be blissfully living in another kingdom with Rafe, at least until the Komizar turned his attention toward Dalbreck. And the young Vendans who were barely big enough to lift a sword would get the worst of it all, sacrificial lambs the Komizar would place on the front lines, probably to storm the gates of the city. He would use the children to prick the consciences of Morrighese soldiers. Neither my brothers nor their comrades would ever strike down a child. They would hold their weapons, hesitate, and then the Komizar would move in with his arsenal of destruction.

Pauline gently laid her hand on my thigh. "But not everyone believed the lies. Bryn and Regan didn't believe a word of it."

Maybe that was why they were on their way to their deaths now. They had asked too many questions.

WE SAT THERE IN THE DARK, EACH OF US LOST TO OUR OWN thoughts, my hand throbbing in time with my heart, the strange tingle of the cobwebs against my skin running up my arm like a thousand tiny spiders. *A kitchen remedy.* Something the court physician would never use. *Not on his own.* The blackness swirled in front of me, and the thousand tiny spiders became a field of golden flowers. A face rose out of them, calm and sure. *He never asked me about the gift because he knew I had it.* It was what had made him afraid of me all along. *She will expose the wicked.* And I saw a wide continent of kingdoms, each with their own unique gifts, the face receding, and fields of flowers rippling in the breeze until they became spiders again, resting in my palm.

The door opened, and we were blinded by the sudden light. I heard the Chancellor's haughty sigh before I saw him.

"Gwyneth," he said, drawing her name out in exaggerated disappointment, "I thought you were smarter than this." He clucked his tongue. "Conspiring with enemies."

Gwyneth shot him a withering stare, and he returned it with a smile. Then his eyes met mine. I got to my feet and limped toward him. He resisted stepping back, not wanting to show any fear. I was, after all, injured, weaponless, and a prisoner. But I saw a brief flicker in his eyes, a heartbeat of doubt. It confirmed he'd read the Song of Venda. *She will expose the wicked.* What if I did?

He eyed my bloodied bandaged hand. His arrogant sneer returned. I didn't look so mighty now. I was only the nuisance that had forever plagued him, one with a name he couldn't quite explain, but I was not a threat. The small doubt that ate at him vanished.

"Don't do this, Lord Chancellor," I said. "Don't kill my brothers."

A satisfied puff of air escaped his lips. "So that's what did it, what made you finally run to your father."

"If my father dies—"

"You mean *when* your father dies. But I wouldn't worry, it won't come as soon as your own death. We need him a little longer—"

"If you surrender now, I will spare your life—"

The back of his hand swung, his jeweled fingers meeting my jaw, and I stumbled into the wall. Gwyneth and Pauline jumped forward. "Stay back!" I ordered.

"You spare my life?" he sneered. "You're insane."

I turned to face him again and smiled. "No, Chancellor, I only wanted to give you a chance. Now my obligation to the gods is done." I briefly fluttered my lashes, as if the gods were speaking to me.

The doubt trailed through his eyes again, like a stalking animal he couldn't quite shake.

"Take off your jacket," he ordered.

I stared at him, wondering about his motive.

"Do it now," he growled, "or I'll have them do it for you."

I pulled it off, letting it fall to the ground.

He nodded to the guards and they grabbed my arms and turned my back toward him. One of them yanked at my shirt, ripping the fabric from my shoulder. The silence stretched, marked only by his slow restrained breaths. I could feel his hatred burning into me.

The guards let go, pushing me forward, and the Chancellor

said, "Kill them. Once it's dark, take the bodies far outside the city and burn them. Make sure no trace of that thing on her shoulder is left." As he turned to leave, the guards moved toward us, drawing thin silk ropes taut between their hands, a silent, bloodless way to dispose of us. But then there was a sound—the distant ringing of bells.

"Listen, Chancellor!" I said quickly, before he could leave. "Do you hear that?"

"The abbey bells," he snapped with irritation. "So what?"

I smiled. "It's an announcement. An important one from your office, no less. You didn't happen to notice your seal was missing? The last of the bills are being posted. Citizens from all over the city are reading them as we speak. Princess Arabella has been captured. All citizens are invited to the trial and hanging tomorrow morning in the village plaza. It would be a shame indeed if you didn't produce her. Embarrassing, even. How would you ever explain your incompetence?"

I watched a splotchy red patch on his neck spread to his cheeks and temples, like flames in a wildfire, out of control and consuming. "Wait!" he said to the guards, and ordered them out. The door slammed shut behind all of them, and I heard him yelling for the bills to be ripped down. But it was too late. He knew it was too late.

"Well done, sister," Gwyneth said. "But tomorrow morning? You couldn't have put the trial off a week?"

"And give them more time to find a way to dispose of us quietly? No. We'll be lucky if we last until morning. They would never give me a chance to speak at trial. All this does is buy us a few more hours, but at least now they will be frantic, and perhaps making stupid mistakes."

I felt my way along the wall until my foot nudged Gwyneth's leg. "Get up," I said. "Both of you. In the meantime, I need to show you some moves I learned from a Dalbreck soldier—ways to kill a man without using a weapon for when the guards come back."

CHAPTER SIXTY-THREE

FOOTSTEPS TRAMPED DOWN THE STONE PASSAGEWAY ONLY an hour later. I'd thought we'd have more time. They were loud and hurried. Angry. We all stood, braced against the opposite wall waiting for the door to open, dirt gathered into our fists, ready to fling into their eyes.

"When the door opens, give your eyes a chance to adjust to the light," I said. "We only get one chance at this. Make your aim count."

Pauline whispered prayers while Gwyneth uttered curses. They had ripped several strips from Gwyneth's dress and woven them into a tight thin rope, knotting the ends so they would each have a good grip on it. The guards wouldn't be the only one with garrotes. My left hand could do little, but I could still do plenty of damage to a windpipe with the knuckles of my right hand.

I had told Gwyneth and Pauline the weak points I had noted on the guards. Besides their eyes, their groins, noses, and knees were all vulnerable—and their throats. They wore only weapons, no armor. At some point in our planned melee, I hoped to secure the weapon of at least one of the disabled guards.

The footsteps stopped outside the door.

Keys rattled.

The lock rattled.

Muffled curses. More rattling. *Hurry.*

My grip tightened on the dirt in my hand. *Hurry!* Something about it didn't sound right.

An angry jangle of keys.

Dammit! Stand back!

A crash shook the door. And another. The *crack* of splintering wood juddered off the walls.

A hole breached the door, then a ray of light, and the silver tip of an ax.

The ax tip disappeared momentarily, and there was another loud crack as it broke through again. The door swung open, and I was ready to lunge, but then—

Bright eyes and a grin.

Black ropes of hair.

Sights I didn't expect to see.

"Wait!" I shouted, putting my hand out to stop the others.

Kaden stood on the other side of the splintered door, the ax still gripped in his hand. Sweat glistened on his brow, and his chest heaved with exertion. Jeb and Tavish stepped past him, and I told Gwyneth and Pauline they could be trusted. Jeb extended his hand. "Thank the gods that we found you. This way," he said. "We don't have much time."

I dropped my fistful of dirt, thinking how close I'd come to crushing his windpipe. Jeb smiled. "You remembered."

"Did you doubt me?"

"Never."

Pauline ran toward Kaden, slamming her hands against his shoulders. "The baby!"

"He's fine," Kaden answered. "Berdi has him and fetched a wet nurse. I told her to go to the abbey to hide."

"Hurry. This way," Tavish ordered. He turned and led us down a passageway. I recognized where we were now—the citadelle armory—one of the outbuildings. It was small compared to the armory at Piers Camp, meant only to arm the citadelle guards. They must have been holding us in one of its storage rooms, but this only confirmed my suspicions—while the citadelle guards might be complicit in the traitors' schemes, it didn't mean soldiers in the ranks were. I heard a battery of shouts ahead. Jeb, who brought up the rear, noticed my slowing steps and said, "Don't worry. They're ours."

Ours? I tried to make sense of it as I ran.

We poured through a door that emptied into the main supply room, and in the center of it were five men, partially dressed in various stages of pulling on uniforms. A half dozen more lay facedown, their hands shackled behind them, the tips of swords held to their necks by just as many plain-cloaked men. Sven ripped shirts into strips and called Jeb and Tavish to help him gag the shackled men.

"Are you all right?" Kaden asked, taking another look at me and reaching for my hand.

"I'm fine," I said, pulling away. "The Watch Captain is in on it, and at least some of the citadelle guards are Vendan too. They speak flawless Morrighese. It seems the scholars were busy tutoring in languages too."

Anger flashed in Kaden's eyes. There was so much the Komizar had never told him, but that was the Komizar's way, using many people like puppets, but never sharing too much information with a single one. The power had to remain all his. Kaden grabbed a strip of cloth. "Let's wrap it a little more," he said, lifting my bloody bandaged hand.

He saw me blanch with pain. "How bad is it?"

"I'll live," I said. "Malich not so much. He's dead. The Komizar and his writhing nest of cavern worms have developed another interesting weapon—a crossbow that shoots multiple iron bolts at a time. Luckily only one of them got me."

He gently wrapped the strip of fabric around my hand. "Hold your breath," he said, before pulling the fabric tight. "A little pressure will help stop the bleeding."

The pain jolted through me and then pulsed up my arm.

"I'll get you a cloak," he said. "You can't walk out of here looking like that without drawing attention. And then there's more I need to tell you." He went over to a jumbled pile on a table, the discarded clothes of the half-dressed men, I presumed, and sorted through them.

Father Maguire came up behind me, startling me with his attire. A sword was belted at his side, almost hidden by his robes.

"You know how to use one of those?" I asked.

"I'm about to learn," he answered, and then he told me he had finally found the information in the archives that I had asked for. "There were no relatives."

I nodded. This was only further confirmation—another piece of the blurred picture that had come into focus in the darkness of the cell.

Gwyneth and Pauline had already stepped into the middle of the room, taking in the bustle of activity and becoming part of it—a plan in the making that I was beginning to grasp. At the far corner the room, I spotted Orrin pulling halberds from a rack and then Natiya carrying an armful of baldricks, all tooled with the Morrighese insignia. She handed them to the half-dressed soldiers and crossed the room to Gwyneth and Pauline, a chatter of noise and explanations I only half heard because in the opposite corner, something else caught my eye.

A warrior. Someone swinging a flanged mace to break the lock on another weapon cabinet. The lock flew into a wall, and the cabinet banged open, but then he stopped, seeming to sense me at the same time. He turned, his eyes finding mine, and then his attention dropped to my bandaged hand. Looking down, I saw that my trousers and shirt were covered in blood. He crossed the room, his steps measured. *Calculation.* For all his zeal in shattering the lock, there was restraint in his movements as he approached me.

The stiffness of his stride.

The pull of his shoulders.

Holding back.

That's what I saw in his movement, but not what I saw in his gaze when he stopped in front of me. In his eyes I saw him drawing me into his arms, his lips lowering to mine, a kiss that would never end, holding me until the kingdoms vanished and the world stood still, being everything we had ever been to each other. *Before.*

I waited. Expected. Wanted.

Some things last. The things that matter.

And yet he held back. Distant. A king. A soldier calculating his next move.

"There isn't time to explain," he said.

"I don't need an explanation. You're here. That's all that matters."

He glanced at my hand. "We can wait and regroup, or move forward now. It's your decision."

I surveyed his soldiers in the room. "How many do you have?"

"A hundred, but they're—"

"I know," I said. "They're the best."

There were only hours left before the last session of the conclave ended and the lords dispersed back to their homes. Now was my last chance to speak to them all. Minutes counted.

"My brothers are headed into an ambush. My father's dying. And the Komizar is on his way. There's no more time to wait."

"The Komizar? The bridge is fixed?"

I nodded.

He lifted my chin, turning my face toward the window. "You're pale. How much of this blood is yours?"

Most of it, but I heard a perilous edge to his voice and

decided against the truth. "Most is Malich's. He got the worst of it. He's dead."

"Then you're able to carry a weapon?"

"Yes," I said, sheathing a sword Kaden handed me, feeling like my movements had already become their movements.

The others had finished their preparations and gathered behind Rafe, waiting for my answer too. Six of Rafe's men, including Jeb, were now outfitted as citadelle guards. The rest of them wore the plain rough-spun cloaks favored by the local farmers and merchants, all in different shades and styles so as not to draw attention. Tavish and Orrin wore similar garb, as did Sven. Pauline and Gwyneth were belted with weapons and had donned cloaks too.

This was it, I thought, and terror rose in my throat.

"She stays," I said pointing to Natiya.

She flew forward, enraged.

Kaden grabbed her from behind pinning her to his chest. "Listen to her, Natiya," he said. "*Listen*. Don't make her look over her shoulder with worry for you. She will. We all have our weaknesses, and you will be hers. Please. Your day will come."

Her eyes puddled with tears, and her gaze locked on mine. "Today is my day." Her voice wobbled with anger. She understood little of the workings of the court, nor who had betrayed whom. She knew only that she wanted justice, but even today could not give her back what she had lost.

"No," I said, "not today. I see many tomorrows for you, Natiya, days I will need you at my side, but this is not one of them. Please, go back to the abbey and wait with Berdi."

Her lip trembled. She was thirteen years old and ready to fight the world, but she saw I wouldn't be moved and angrily turned away, leaving for the abbey.

I looked back at Rafe.

He nodded. "Let's go get some traitors."

WE CIRCLED BEHIND THE OUTBUILDING, WALKING THROUGH the village, Rafe on one side of me, Kaden on the other. A wagon trudged alongside us, a wheelbarrow pushed a little farther ahead, and still more followed behind with burlap sacks slung over shoulders, their supposed wares spilling over the top. Our boots tapped an uneven beat on the cobblestones; the wagon wheels creaked and bumped; our cloaks flapped in the wind, every noise sounding like a herald announcing our approach and yet somehow we blended in with citizens going about their business.

As we walked, more fell into step with us, waiting and ready, looking like merchants headed for the marketplace, and I wondered how Rafe had been able to assemble such a squad—not just soldiers but performers as well, perceiving the smallest of cues. He had said they numbered a hundred strong. I thought about what the six of us had been able to do in Venda, but then we had been running away from the enemy, not trying to settle into their dark den. How long could a hundred soldiers hold off the Morrighese army? There were at least two thousand troops stationed at Piers Camp, only a short distance away.

My heart pounded. This was no childhood rebellion. This

was a coup, and in the eyes of Morrighese law, the most unfor-givable crime. I had received an extensive lecture on it when I was fourteen. Back then, my punishment had been banishment to my chamber for a month. Today if we failed, the rebellion would be grounds for a mass hanging of epic proportions. I tried not to think of the shortcomings of our small army—only what was at stake. Everything.

The front of the citadelle was in sight, and for the first time, Rafe's steps faltered. "I can't promise that Morrighese soldiers won't die."

I nodded. I had told Rafe and his men that I wanted as little blood spilled as possible. While there were Vendans among the citadelle guards, some of them were still Morrighese and surely believed they were only following orders.

He still didn't move forward, a scowl pulling between his brows. "You don't have to go in, Lia. We can go first, and once the hall is secure, we can send for you." He and Kaden exchanged a glance. A knowing glance.

"If either of you try to stop me, you will die. Do you understand?"

"You're injured, Lia," Kaden said.

"One hand is injured," I answered. "My strengths are not your strengths."

We reached the plaza, and the men disguised as citadelle guards walked up the steps to the string of guards stationed at the entrance. Jeb, his Morrighese pitch-perfect, told them his squad was there to relieve them. The center guard looked confused, not recognizing Jeb or the others, and balked, but it was too late for them to act. Rafe's men were quick and assured and their short swords cut the air with a single united *shing*, just as quickly pressing them to the guards' chests. They pushed them back into the dark recess of the portal, taking their weapons while the rest of us flooded up the steps, shedding cloaks and unfurling more weapons from wagons and sacks.

Taking the next line of guards wasn't as bloodless. They spotted us from the end of the passageway. Two of them moved to close the heavy hallway doors while the rest charged shoulder to shoulder toward us bearing halberds that far outreached our swords. Rafe's archers stepped forward, shouting a warning order to stop. They didn't, and multiple arrows flew beneath the guard's shields and into their legs. When they stumbled, they were overtaken, and we charged the doors before the other guards were able to bar it. As one of them began to shout a warning, Sven knocked him unconscious.

The last two guards, posted outside the closed doors to Aldrid Hall, were ceremonial at best. Their purpose was to turn away uninvited visitors, not defend against attackers. Their hair was silver, their stomachs paunchy, and their armor consisted only of a leather helmet and breastplate. They drew their swords uncertainly.

I stepped forward, and they recognized me.

"Your Highness—" The guard caught himself, unsure what to call me.

"Lay down your weapons and step aside," I ordered. "We don't want to hurt you, but we will. The kingdom and my brothers' lives are at stake."

Their eyes bulged with fear, but they stood their ground. "We have our orders."

"As do I," I answered. "Move. Now. Every second you delay puts lives at risk."

They didn't budge.

I looked at the archers who stood to my right. "Shoot them," I commanded.

When the guards shifted their attention to the archers, Rafe and Kaden moved in from the left, striking the swords from their grasps and slamming both men against the wall.

Before the doors were opened, we implemented the last of our plans. Other than myself, only Pauline knew the layout of the citadelle, and I sent her off with precise instructions about what she was to bring back to me. Jeb and Captain Azia went with her. "The guard posted at the door is Vendan," I said. "You may have to kill him."

Kaden left with two of the soldiers dressed as citadelle guards. His quest was more uncertain, though I told him exactly what to look for. Gwyneth was sent in yet another direction with the rest of the soldiers dressed as guards. With the whole cabinet convened in Aldrid Hall, I prayed the passageways would be mostly empty.

My head pounded with the sound of their receding footsteps, a lifetime of voices awakening within me.

Hold your tongue, Arabella!
Quiet!
This matter is finished!
Go to your chamber!

Rafe and Tavish looked at me waiting for the signal that I was ready.

Other voices sounded in my head.

Don't tarry, Miz.
Trust the strength within you.
Nurse the rage. Use it.

That was easy to do. I drew my sword and nodded. The doors were opened, and I went in with Rafe on one side, Tavish on the other, Orrin and his best archers flanking us, Sven leading the lines of shield bearers before us, and more soldiers pulling up the rear, soldiers willing to lay their lives down for another kingdom and an uncertain cause.

CHAPTER SIXTY-FOUR

RAFE

UP UNTIL THIS POINT, EVERYTHING HAD BEEN PLANNED WITH precision. From here forward, Sven said it was another half-assed plan, but he also noted that he was becoming more comfortable with military strategies that were half-assed. Tavish had snorted at the word *strategy*. As we stormed the hall, we had skill and surprise on our side, and little else. What the next minutes and hours would bring were uncertain, but I knew we were running out of time. I knew it the minute Lia had walked into the armory. There was already a war going on—the traitors against Lia—and right now it looked like the traitors were winning.

Tavish muttered under his breath as we rushed in, eyeing the long upper gallery and balcony that overlooked the hall. Lia had said it was accessible only from the royal wing, but if archers flooded it before we could secure it, we would be like fish in a barrel waiting to be speared one at a time. We guarded Lia's back and one another's. Lords and ministers gasped, too startled to grasp what was happening, as my men filled out the perimeter. Guards posted at the dais stayed their hands when our archers targeted them in their sights. Tavish and I kept close to Lia, our shields raised, watching, turning, scanning the room. Orrin flanked us with his men, their arrows already aimed at the two towers ready to return attacks.

Lia stopped in the center of the room and yelled that no one should move, promising they wouldn't be hurt. She lied. There would be blood spilled. I saw it in her eyes, her face, her lips, the hungry rage. I thought it might be all that kept her standing. Her eyes were circled with shadows, her lips pale. I knew she had lied to me back at the armory. She'd lost a lot of blood. But I also understood the rush of battle and the surge of strength that kept dead men on their feet. Along with her desperate fury, it kept her going now.

I ordered the doors barred and the guards relieved of their weapons.

A lord who had been addressing the cabinet remained frozen on the large semicircular step at the front of the hall, unable to speak or move. I motioned to him with my sword. "Sit down."

He scrambled back to his seat, and Lia walked up the steps, taking his place.

Her scrutiny passed over the cabinet, and she addressed each one, nodding her head as if in greeting, but I saw the fear in their eyes. They knew it was no greeting. Every one of them saw the thin line she walked, and the multiple weapons strapped to her side.

The Chancellor jumped to his feet. "This is preposterous!"

An echo of agreement rumbled around him, chairs scraping back as if to escort the insolent princess to her chamber.

Before I could say anything, Lia threw her dagger. "I told you not to move!" she yelled. The blade nicked the Chancellor's sleeve and lodged in a carved wooden wall behind him.

A hush returned to the hall. The Chancellor held his arm, blood seeping between his fingers. His head shook with rage, but he returned to his seat.

"That's better," she said. "I don't want you dead *yet*, Lord Chancellor. You'll hear me out first."

He may have sat, but he wasn't silenced. "So you throw knives to muzzle the cabinet and have a ragtag collection of sword-wielding rebels whom you've compelled to follow you," he said. "What are you going to do? Hold off the entire Morrighese army?"

I stepped forward. "As a matter of fact, yes, we are."

The Chancellor skimmed the length of me, taking in my rough-spun clothes. His lip lifted in disgust. "And you would be?"

For someone in his precarious position, he showed no signs of backing down. His arrogance made mine blaze.

"I would be the king of Dalbreck," I answered. "And I can assure you, my ragtag collection can hold off your army for an amazingly extended period of time—at least long enough to see you dead."

The Watch Captain snickered. "Fool! We've met the king of Dalbreck, and you are not him!"

I closed the space between us and reached across the table, grabbing him by the front of his tunic. I jerked him to his feet. "Are you willing to bet your life on that, Captain? Because even though you've never seen me, I saw *you* from the cloister of the abbey on the day of my thwarted wedding. You nervously paced with the Timekeeper, cursing as I recall."

I let go of his tunic, shoving him back in his seat. "My father has passed. I'm king now—and I've yet to behead anyone in my new capacity, though I'm eager to see what it's like."

I stared, pinning him to his seat, then looked at the rest of the cabinet, scanning as Lia had done, wondering which hand had struck her, which had torn the shirt from her back, and worse, which of her own had betrayed her and every other kingdom on the continent by conspiring with the Komizar, trading our lives for their greed. Other than the Chancellor and the Watch Captain, the rest had remained curiously silent, and I found their quiet brooding just as disturbing as the outbursts. They plotted.

I looked at Lia. "Speak, Princess. You have the floor as long as you like."

She smiled, a frightening hardness to her lips. "The floor," she repeated savoring the words as she turned, her arms held out to her sides. "Forgive me, esteemed ministers, for the state of my"—she looked down at her bloodstained clothes, then at her exposed shoulder—"my appearance. I know it doesn't follow court protocol. But there's some comfort in it too, I suppose. *Beaten and scorned, she will expose the wicked.* She paused, the smile slipping from her face. "Do those words frighten you? They should."

She turned, her gaze traveling over the lords, then she stopped and looked up at the empty gallery. Every eye followed her stare. The silence grew long and uncomfortable, but for now the memory of her knife flying across the room seemed to keep their tongues quiet. My pulse raced, and Tavish and I exchanged a worried glance. She seemed to have forgotten where we were or what she was doing. I followed her gaze. There was nothing there. Nothing, at least, that I could see.

CHAPTER SIXTY-FIVE

THE AIR CHANGED, HANGING ABOVE US, THE COLOR SOFT and muted, like aged parchment. The room grew larger, dreamlike, becoming a distant world where a fourteen-year-old girl charged with her brothers by her side. More who believed in her followed close behind. They were all dead now, killed on a nameless battlefield. Walther whispered, *Be careful, sister.*

I heard the girl yell that no one should move, and she promised they wouldn't be hurt. She knew that wasn't true. Some would die, though she didn't know which ones or when, but their deaths already clouded behind her eyes. She saw two men charging with her, watching, turning, archers flanking her with arrows drawn. And then her eyes landed on the cabinet, the faces, the empty seat of her father. The air snapped sharp, the colors brilliant, and fear vibrated against the walls in waves. The girl was gone. It was only me. Facing them. And today, no one would be banishing me to my chamber.

The Viceregent, the Chancellor, the Watch Captain, the Trademaster, the court physician, the Timekeeper, the Field Marshal, the Huntmaster, and of course, the Royal Scholar, who looked the most troubled of all by the turn of events. Notably absent was the First Daughter and the king himself, but one of them would be here soon. The Timekeeper fiddled nervously with the buttons on his jacket, pulling and fretting until one popped off. It clattered to the floor, rolling across the polished stone.

I knew who the mastermind behind this was, the architect who craved power just as much as the Komizar. Maybe even more, risking everything for the whole prize—the continent. I looked at him, slow and steady. It was obvious now. The scales of his true nature gleamed beneath his robe. The dragon who had as many faces as the Komizar.

When the Chancellor disobeyed the first of my orders, my dagger flew. It took all of my will not to aim straight for his heart. In my days crossing the Cam Lanteux, every time I practiced throwing my knife into the trunk of a tree, I had marked his heart as the target in my mind's eye, but his death would come later. For now he might still be of some use to me, and I would use every piece of him, finger by finger, if that was what it took to save my brothers.

He sat but seethed, now throwing insults at Rafe.

I watched him and the others, one by one, down the line—for a conspiracy was only as good as its weakest link—and now that link was being tested.

The citadelle closed in, contracting, squeezing the treachery into something hard and alive, its heartbeat wild, resisting, its beastly roar echoing, but beneath it all I heard another sound, a fragile thrum as persistent as hope, and I saw someone step out on the balcony.

It was a girl. She leaned over the rail, her wide dark eyes fixed on mine. *Promise*, she said.

I nodded. "I promised long ago."

And then she was gone, the world shifting, the air sharp and bright again.

The lords waited, their attention whittled to a point, ready to snap.

I told them of traitors in their midst, of dragons with unquenchable thirst, and still another, the Komizar of Venda, who was on his way here with an unstoppable army to destroy them all, helped by the same traitors who had sent Crown Prince Walther to his death. "I ran from the wedding because I was afraid, but I did not betray Morrighan, and I did not betray my brother. I watched him die, but at the hands of Vendans who were lying in wait for him. He was sent into an ambush by traitors here in this room. The same ones who have sent Princes Regan and Bryn to die."

The Royal Scholar leaned forward. "Wouldn't this be better discussed in—"

But the Viceregent cut him off, holding up his hand. "Let's not interrupt the princess. Let her have her say. We can give her that much." He eyed me as if recalling every word we had spoken in his office. *Do you have any evidence?* He knew my word wasn't enough.

I glared, slow and steady, at the Royal Scholar, a warning—*your time will come*—and turned to the Field Marshal, who was the cabinet liaison to the troops. "My brothers need to be tracked down and brought home immediately. With my father ill, they never should have been sent away to Gitos and Cortenai in the first place. How do you explain this flagrant breach of protocol, Lord Commander?"

He shifted uncomfortably in his seat and shot a hard glance at the Watch Captain. The Royal Scholar watched them all as if ready to jump from his seat.

"I didn't want to send them," he answered, a scowl darkening his face. "In fact, I argued against it. But I was swayed to believe it was for the good of the realm."

"And your brothers heartily agreed," the Watch Captain added.

I stormed across the dais, slamming my sword onto the table inches from his hand. "They agreed to be slaughtered?"

The Watch Captain gawked at his hand as if making sure all his fingers were still there. His gaze shot back to me, his eyes glowing with anger. "The girl is insane!" he shouted to Rafe's soldiers standing near him. "Lay down your weapons before she gets you all killed!"

The rumble of footsteps echoed in the south hall, the vibration of a hundred boots pounding toward us. Soldiers had been alerted. I looked back at the cabinet.

The Dragon.

A smile.

One that no one else could see.

A voice no one else could hear.

More. It is mine. You are mine.

The grind of teeth.

A gluttonous swallow.

A satisfied breath.

I turned to Rafe as the rumbling footsteps got louder. He held my gaze and nodded, confident. *Keep going.*

A lord in the back of the hall, apparently emboldened by the sound of soldiers, stood. "The only traitor we see in this hall is you! If there were other traitors, you would name them! The Watch Captain's right—the girl is mad!"

The Viceregent sighed, tenting his hands in front of him, and frowned. "We've allowed you your say, Arabella, but I'm afraid I must agree with Lord Gowan. You can't make these accusations without providing evidence, and we don't see any."

I could name many traitors, possibly half of the cabinet, but my only evidence, if Pauline was able to secure it, would be construed as something I had planted. I needed someone else to point the finger.

"You'll have your evidence," I promised, stalling for time. *Where was Pauline?* She was coming from the north hall, but what if her way was already blocked? "And you'll get your names. But we haven't discussed—"

A hand pounded on the north entry door and a shout blared through it. *"Lia!"*

The bar was lifted, and Pauline rushed across the room, nervously taking in the scrutiny of the cabinet and the lords. She walked up the steps to meet me with a box clutched in her arms.

There was another clatter of footsteps, and our men posing as citadelle guards rushed to the gallery rail. Gwyneth joined them and nodded to me. More footsteps. Soft. Hurried. A swish of skirts. Aunt Bernette, Aunt Cloris, and Lady Adele, the queen's attendant, appeared, their hands gripping the rail as their eyes skimmed the room. Their gazes passed over me, and a knot swelled in my throat. I wasn't the same girl who had left here so many months ago, and they didn't recognize me. When they finally realized who I was, Aunt Cloris gasped, and tears flowed down Aunt Bernette's cheeks, but Gwyneth had coached them well. They were not to speak, only bear witness, and they all held their tongues. And then there was a flash of blue, and my lungs squeezed. The queen stepped forward between my aunts, a shadow of who she had once been. She looked down at me, her eyes dark hollows, her gaze searing into mine. *There's nothing to know. . . . It's only the chill of the night.* But now we both knew it was far more than a chill.

"Welcome, Your Majesty," I said. "We were just about to discuss the king's health."

I turned back to the cabinet. They fidgeted, waiting for me to say something, the Watch Captain's hands safely tucked beneath the table.

"The king doesn't seem to be recovering," I said. "Can you tell me why?"

"The news of your betrayal struck him to the core," the Chancellor growled. "There is no instant cure for a heart ripped from a man's chest."

A few of the lords mumbled agreement. I heard the gentle cries of Aunt Bernette.

"Hmm. So I'm told." My eyes landed on the court physician. "Come join me here on the step," I said, "so everyone can hear you report on my father's health." He didn't move, glancing at the other cabinet members as if they could save him. "It is not a request, Lord Fently." I held up my bandaged hand. "As you can see, I have a grave injury. Don't make me drag you over here." I sheathed my sword, and he reluctantly stood and walked over.

"Arabella," the Royal Scholar interceded, "don't—"

I turned sharply. "I have no qualms about cutting out your tongue, Your Eminence. In fact, after all the years I had to endure your condemning lectures, it would give me the greatest pleasure, so I would advise that you hold your tongue while you still possess one."

Hold it. Just like all the times you made me hold mine. His eyes narrowed, familiar. Afraid. *Worried.* But not for his tongue. For the truth?

My anger burned brighter, and when the physician stopped in front of me, I grabbed his shoulder, forcing him to his knees. "What is wrong with my father?" I asked.

"His heart, Your Highness! As the Chancellor said!" he

answered quickly, his tone high and earnest. "But his other ailments are many! It is a tricky thing, treating so many conditions. It will take time, but I have the highest hopes for his recovery."

I smiled. "Really. That is reassuring, Lord Fently." I nodded to Pauline, and she opened the box. "And these are some of the medicines you're treating him with?"

"Yes!" he said, his tone thick with pleading. "These are only simple remedies to make him more comfortable!"

I reached in and pulled out a small bottle of dark amber elixir. "This?"

"Only to ease aches and pains."

My fingers fumbled, stiff and tingling, to remove the cork with my injured hand. The effort of twisting it free made blood gush warm again beneath the bandage. I sniffed the bottle. "For pain? I could use some of this." I took a hearty swig and shrugged. "There, now. I think I'm feeling better already."

He smiled, his face a strained smear of anguish and fear. I put the elixir back and drew another bottle, this one filled with creamy white liquid. "And just how does this one help my father?"

"His stomach, Your Highness! It helps settle it."

I held the bottle up, swishing it in the light, then took a drink. I smiled. "Yes, I remember this from my childhood." I leveled a glare at the Royal Scholar. "I often suffered from stomachaches."

I put it back and shuffled through the box, then drew out the small vial filled with golden powder. "And this one?"

He swallowed. His skin was pasty, and a bead of sweat

trickled near his ear. A half smile rippled across his lips. "It is for agitation. Just to calm jittery nerves."

"Jittery nerves," I repeated. "Well, I guess you can all see, I certainly have those." I pulled the cork, began to lift it to my mouth, and hesitated. "Does it matter how much I take?"

"No," he said, a measure of relief finally reaching his eyes. "You may take as much as you like."

I lifted it to my lips again. He watched me, his mouth hanging open, waiting for me to take a hefty dose, as I had with the others. I paused and returned his earnest attention. "It seems, Lord Fently, that you're in need of this far more than I am. Here, take some."

I moved it toward his lips, and he quickly turned his head away. "No, I don't need any."

"But I insist."

"No!"

He jerked away, but I drew the knife from my boot and held it to his neck. "See how jittery you are, my lord?" I lowered my voice to a growl. "I insist you take some. *Now.*" My knife pressed harder against his throat, and lords gasped as a thin line of blood sprang up beneath the blade. I brought the golden vial slowly to his lips. "Remember," I whispered, "you may take as much as you like."

The glass brushed his lower lip. "No!" he cried, his eyes glazed with terror. "It's him! He's the one who gave it to me! It was by his order!"

He pointed at the Viceregent.

I lowered the knife, pushing the physician free. Silence crushed in as all eyes turned to the favored cabinet member. I smiled at the Viceregent. "Thannis," I said. "Good for the soul. Good for the heart. A unique token found only in Venda. Something an ambassador such as yourself probably discovered years ago on one of your clandestine visits." I walked toward him. "Perfectly deadly, but a few tiny grains? They might be just enough to keep a king out of the way while you finalized your plans—because if he died, there were so many of those troublesome princes in line for the throne who might appoint a new cabinet."

The Viceregent stood. "The man's a liar. I've never laid eyes on the substance before."

A voice called from the back of the hall. "Then how do you explain this?" Footsteps echoed, boots on stone, a slow beat that demanded attention.

Heads turned. Breaths were held for only a moment, then hushed whispers erupted into the air like a startled flock of birds. There was something about him. Something familiar—but foreign too. Something that didn't belong. They quieted again as Kaden walked down the center aisle toward us, another golden vial in his hand. "I found this in your apartment, tucked in a locked drawer." He moved forward in a slow, deliberate line, soldiers stepping aside. "Probably the same vial you used to keep Andrés—your legitimate son—out of harm's way." I saw the strain in Kaden's face, his effort at control. The impact of seeing his father shook him like a storm. His eyes glistened, the calm destroyed, a thousand cracks in his voice. The boy who wanted only to be loved. Kept. Watching him struggle to hold back made his agony even more evident, and the depth of his pain swelled in me.

The Viceregent stared as if seeing a ghost. "Kaden."

"That's right, *Father*," he answered. "Your son, back from the grave. Seems the Komizar was playing both of us. I was his Assassin." Kaden stopped, the cracks in his composure deepening, a quiver in his lip that tore through me as he spoke again. "He trained me up for years, and for every one of them, I waited for the day I would kill you. Seems now there are a few in line ahead of me to do the job."

"This is madness! It is—" The Viceregent turned, seeing the eyes fixed on him, his lies closing in, inescapable. He lunged, pulling a knife from beneath the table, and held it to the Timekeeper's throat, dragging him to his feet and using him as a shield. They both stumbled backward toward the wood panel on the rear wall of the chamber, and the Viceregent's hand groped behind him. *A little to the right,* I thought as his fingers fumbled over the carved wood. *There.* He pressed, and a passage appeared, one known to every king—and the children who spied on him. He shoved the Timekeeper away and disappeared into the passage.

The Chancellor glanced nervously to the side as if to make a break to follow.

"I wouldn't," I told him, and only seconds later, the Viceregent reappeared, stepping backward, a sword at his chest. Andrés held it and emerged with more soldiers behind him. His expression was as shattered as Kaden's.

"You killed my comrades," Andrés said. "You should have let me die with them." He lowered the sword and swung his fist, sending his father stumbling toward me.

A line of blood ran from the corner of the Viceregent's mouth. I kicked the back of his legs, bringing him to his knees, and yanked on his hair so his eyes jerked up to meet mine.

"*You killed my brother,*" I said, my face drawing close to his. "He and every good man with him were massacred. They had *no* chance." There was no mistaking the dangerous strain in my voice and I saw fear flash through his eyes. "They were outnumbered five to one because *you* sent word ahead. I buried them all, Viceregent. I dug graves until my hands bled while you were here sipping wine and conspiring to kill more."

I whipped back to face the lords. "*This* is the man who sent my brother and thirty-two soldiers to their deaths! He is the one who poisoned my father! He is the one who led his rat's nest of conspirators to plot against us all!" I looked back at him, my knife pressing against his neck. "You're going to die, Lord Viceregent, for your crimes against Morrighan, and if we don't get to my brothers and their squads in time, you will die slowly. That is my promise to you."

He looked at me, his eyes defiant again. He whispered low so no one else would hear, "I have an agreement with the Komizar. I may spare whichever lives I choose."

I smiled. "An agreement? The Komizar chose his fools well."

"It's too late," he said, still denying the reversal of our fortunes. "You can't stop us. But I could—"

"You're right about only one thing, Lord Viceregent. It is too late. For you. I have done exactly what you always feared. I have exposed the wicked."

I stared at him, my breath seething, and I let go of his head. My blood-soaked bandage left a bright red stain against his white-blond hair. "Lock him up," I said, and Rafe's soldiers dragged him away. The room grew hot, my head light.

"Lock them all up," I ordered, waving at the rest of the cabinet. "And the Citadelle Guard. I'll parse out later which of them is innocent and fit to serve."

A lord stood. "You have no authority to order high-level—"

Rafe cut him short. "Princess Lia is ruling Morrighan for the time being. She can order anything she wants."

A flurry of objections erupted, Lord Gowan's rising above them all. "With all due respect, Your Majesty, this is not your kingdom, nor is it your decision to make. You are suggesting anarchy. Protocol and Morrighese law dictate that—"

"Until my husband recovers, my daughter assumes the position of king's regent and will appoint her own cabinet."

The room snapped silent, every head turning toward the queen on the balcony. She looked at me and nodded, guilt shimmering in her eyes. "Jezelia is now carrying out the king's judgments. She is a soldier in his army and will be true to his wishes." She looked pointedly at Lord Gowan. "Does anyone object to this?"

Before he could answer, Andrés called out "Jezelia" and fell to one knee. One by one, the soldiers with him did the same—a vote, a public count and long-ago tradition I had heard of but never witnessed. The soldiers in the north hall did the same, and the rumble of my name rolled through the room. *Jezelia.* The sister of their fallen comrade. My mother, and those on the balcony around her did the same, repeating the name I had never heard publicly on their lips. Half a dozen lords followed suit.

"It's decided, then," my mother said, rising again, and Lord Gowan and the rest of the lords reluctantly nodded. In a matter of minutes, their world had been turned upside down. The upheaval was only beginning.

I stepped forward, their faces blurring in and out of focus, the floor shifting unevenly. "Exposing the traitors is only the beginning of the work ahead of us," I said. I heard my words, echoing in a strange, remote way, and then the sound of my knife clattering to the floor. "The conclave is not adjourned. You need to know exactly what we're facing—and what we need to do to survive. We'll reconvene again tomorrow, but for now, I—"

I wasn't sure if I finished my last sentence. The last thing I remembered was Rafe's arm slipping around my waist and my feet lifting from the floor.

CHAPTER SIXTY-SIX

I HEARD WEEPING.

Felt the sweep of soft hands across my forehead.

The scent of roses.

Weeping.

The trickle of water.

The whisper of doors opening.

Hushed voices.

A cool wet cloth on my brow.

Numb tugging on my arm.

Will she lose it?

Something sweet on my tongue. Warmth.

I'll keep the next watch. Go.

A heavy throb in my chest.

Guarded footsteps.

Weeping. Husky and strained.

The slithering of a beast, the flick of its tail.

I'm coming for you. It is not over.

I opened my eyes. The room was dark. *My room.* A log glowed in the hearth. Heavy drapes were drawn across windows, and I wasn't sure what time it was or how long I'd been out.

I turned my head. Kaden was slumped in a chair next to me, his feet propped on a stool, his head leaning back like he'd been asleep, but his eyes focused on me now as if the mere opening of my lids had wakened him. My hand was elevated on a pillow, heavy, a numb throb pulsing beneath the fresh bandages. I wore a soft nightgown.

"Dear gods," I groaned, remembering my last moments in the hall, "please don't tell me I fainted in front of everyone."

A hint of a smile tugged at the corner of his mouth. "Passed out. There's a difference. It happens when you lose enough blood to fill a bucket. You're not immortal, you know? I don't know how you stayed on your feet as long as you did. If it's any comfort, I think a few of the lords fainted just watching you carried out of the room."

Carried. Rafe carried me. I wondered where he was now. I glanced toward the outer chamber.

"He's taking care of a few things with his soldiers," Kaden offered, reading my mind.

"Oh," I said simply. For someone who had traveled thousands of miles with a highly trained squad to help me, he seemed to be keeping his distance from me. Even back at the armory, he had sent someone else to break down our door.

"Who did this?" I asked, lifting my bandaged hand.

"Your mother and aunts and a physician—one called from the village. The court physician is locked up. So are the others."

I heard the catch in his tone.

Others. And one in particular.

I reached out with my good hand and held his. "How are you doing?" I asked gingerly.

He looked at me, hesitating, the pained expression in his eyes returning. "I don't know." He shook his head. "Just before I walked into that hall, I thought I was going to be sick. Sick like a little schoolboy."

I heard the disgust in his voice. "There is no shame in that, Kaden."

"I'm not ashamed. Just angry that he could still do that to me. I couldn't even recognize myself. I didn't realize what seeing him after all this time would do to me." He shook his head. "I don't know how one person can be so afraid and so full of rage at the same time."

I understood completely. I was still afraid, still angry, but mostly right now I was aching for everything I saw in Kaden's face.

He paused, a deep breath filling his chest, his nostrils flaring. "He hadn't changed. Even then, when he looked at me, all he saw was a liability. In that moment, if he could have sold me off for another coin, he would have. I felt like an eight-year-old boy again."

I squeezed his hand. "You're not a boy, Kaden. You're a man. He can't harm you anymore."

"I know." His brows pulled together. "But look at how many others he's hurt. Andrés . . . he's worse off than me. Maybe I was lucky to be tossed out when I was. He can't get his mind to grasp what happened, that men in his company that he trusted with his life were betrayed by his own father." He looked up at me. "He was half crazed when he rode out with scouts to find your brothers and their squads."

"Did you—"

"Yes, Rafe and Sven interrogated the prisoners. They got nothing. And we sent four different units riding the fastest Ravians. You were still issuing orders when Rafe laid you on the bed, and those were just two of them."

"I don't remember."

"Most of your words were mumbled, and Rafe finally told you to shut up and listen to the physician."

"Did I?"

"You passed out again. I guess that's listening."

"What time is it?" I asked.

He shrugged. "Past midnight."

He told me what had transpired after I passed out, most of which he had learned from my aunt Bernette. The entire citadelle had been bustling awake through most of the night. After leaving me, my mother had seen to my father. She had him moved back to their marriage chamber and threw out all medicines the court physician had ordered for him. He was bathed and given herbal drinks to flush his system. Kaden didn't know enough about the poisoning effects of golden thannis to know if it would help. Vendans knew not to touch it. Just a nibble could bring down a horse. Andrés had recovered, but he was young and healthy and hadn't been poisoned over a long period of time the way my father had. I worried that it might be too late to reverse the effects of the poison and my father would be trapped in a foggy stupor for the rest of his life. I worried that it might be too late for everything.

"Will all this be enough, Kaden?"

"To stop the Komizar? I don't know. I think the rule Rafe threw your way is shaky—even with your mother's nod of support."

I saw it too. Parading a First Daughter out for ceremony was one thing, having her rule the kingdom was another. The troops Andrés marched into the hall with had supported me, but the majority of the lords weren't convinced.

"I think your lords are still dubious about the threat," he added.

I didn't expect anything else. They had a lifetime of believing that Morrighan was the chosen Remnant and nothing could bring it down. "I'll convince them," I said, "and prepare them to oppose Venda."

"Then what? As much as we both want to stop the Komizar, I can't forget I'm still Vendan."

His eyes searched mine, worried. "I know, Kaden." His fears renewed my own. "But we both need to remember that there are two Vendas. The Komizar's Venda that's on its way here to destroy us, and the one that we both love. Somehow, together, we have to make this work."

But I wasn't sure how. We both knew the Komizar and

Council would never back down. The prize was in their sight, and they intended to have it. *It's my turn now to dine on sweet grapes in winter.* I lay there, Kaden's hand still in mine, the coals of the hearth dimming, my lids growing heavy, the future swirling behind them, and I heard the soft moans again. This time, I knew it wasn't my mother or my aunts I heard weeping. These cries came from far away, past a savanna, beyond a great river, past rocky hills and barren glens. These cries came from the clans of Venda. He had slaughtered more for whispering the name *Jezelia*.

CHAPTER SIXTY-SEVEN

PAULINE

YOU NEED TO NAME HIM.

But I had no name. My mind was too swollen with other thoughts to make such a decision.

I eased the child from the wet nurse's arms and rocked him, fingering his locks. They were the color of a bright high sun. Like Mikael's.

But after what Mikael had done, I didn't want to think that he was any part of this child.

You have kin, Pauline. You are not alone.

But my aunt's cold stare surfaced again and again.

After Lia's hand had been treated and bandaged, we had cut away her clothes and washed her. She lay unconscious, limp, and they stared at her battered body lying across the white bedding. A diary of these past months was written across her skin. They saw the jagged scar on her thigh. The nick on her throat. The fresh cut on her lip where the Chancellor had struck her, the bruises on her face where the guards had hit her. And when we turned her to wash her back, they saw the raised scar on her ribs from where an arrow had been cut away, and then there were the remnants of the kavah trailing over her shoulder.

As every new mark was discovered, the queen or Lia's aunts choked back a sob at her broken body, and the queen's attendant—my own aunt—cast me an angry glare.

"*This* is what you led her into!" she finally snapped accusingly.

I turned my attention back to rinsing a cloth in the basin, unable to meet her gaze. Guilt rushed through me. It was true. I was Lia's accomplice. If I hadn't helped her, she might never have left. But if she hadn't—

I looked up, staring into my aunt's face that was rigid with anger and disappointment. "It was her choice to make."

She pulled in a startled breath. "It was *your* duty to stop her! Not—"

"I don't regret my decision," I said, "and I would do it again!"

My aunt's mouth fell open, appalled, but Lady Bernette reached out to her, putting a hand on her shoulder. "Pauline is right," she said softly. "It was Lia's choice and beyond any of us to stop her."

My aunt remained silent, but condemnation still shone in her eyes. The queen sobbed quietly at Lia's bedside, Lia's hand clutched to her cheek.

I blinked back tears. "I have something else I need to attend to." I spun and left the room, stepping out into the dark hallway. When I had closed the door behind me, I leaned against it, trying to swallow away the painful throb in my throat. Doubt flooded through me. I hadn't even told her about the baby yet.

"What is it?" Kaden had rushed out of the shadows toward me. I'd forgotten he'd been waiting for word on Lia.

"She's fine," I said. "We don't know about her hand yet, but the bleeding is stopped and her heart is strong."

"Then what is—" He lifted his hand toward my cheek, then pulled back as if afraid to touch me. Even in the darkest shadows, he had seen my tears, but there was still a wall between us, distrust I couldn't set aside, even now, and he knew it.

I shook my head, unable to speak.

"Tell me," he said quietly.

My chest shuddered with uneven breaths. I forced a smile that I felt nowhere inside, but the tears flowed down my cheeks unchecked. "I have only one living kin in this entire world, and she thinks this is all my fault."

A frown pulled at the corner of his mouth. "Your fault? We've all made mistakes, Pauline, and yours—" He reached up and his thumb grazed my cheek, wiping away a tear. "Your mistakes are the very least among them."

I saw the regret in his eyes, my hurled accusations still swimming behind them. He swallowed. "There is not only blood kin, Pauline. Some family you are born with, other family you choose. You have Lia. You have Gwyneth and Berdi. You are not alone in this world."

A long quietness hung between us, and I wondered if the

mention of family had reopened his own wounds. I saw the same pained expression on his face that I had seen hours ago when he confronted his father. I wanted to say something, offer him some sort of kind words like he had just given me, but something fearful still paced behind my ribs. He drew in a deep breath and filled the silence for me.

"And you have the baby too. You need to give him a name."

A name. It shouldn't be so hard.

"I will," I had whispered, and brushed past him, telling him he'd be able to see Lia soon.

I placed the baby back in the wet nurse's arms. "I need to leave him here a little longer," I told her. "The citadelle is still in turmoil. It is no place for a baby. I'll be back."

She nodded understanding, promising to take good care of him, but I saw the doubt in her eyes. She rubbed a gentle knuckle over his cheek, and my still unnamed baby nestled happily into her arms.

CHAPTER SIXTY-EIGHT

A SOFT RED HUE SEEPED BEHIND THE EDGES OF THE DRAPES. For seventeen years it had been my familiar signal of dawn. It was odd to move about my room again. *Home.* But it didn't feel the same. It was tight, confining, like trying to pull on a jacket that no longer fit. Too much had changed.

My mother hadn't been by. Aunt Bernette and Aunt Cloris had come three times during the night to check on me, both of them weary, with red-rimmed eyes. They gave me doses of the thick, syrupy medicine the physician had prescribed.

"It will help restore your blood," Aunt Bernette whispered and kissed my cheek.

When I asked her how my father was, her face dimpled with worry, and she struggled with a hopeful reply, saying it would take time.

Aunt Cloris cast wary glances at Kaden, who dozed in the chair beside me. She didn't like it, but clucked only mildly at the breach of protocol. Finally, late in the night, she shooed him off, having prepared a room elsewhere in the citadelle for him. I had slept fitfully after that, one dream dissolving into another, and I finally shook awake when I dreamed of Regan and Bryn riding together in a wide valley. I didn't want to see what came next.

Per Aunt Bernette's orders, I took another dose of the sickly sweet syrup. I didn't know if it was the sleep or the elixir, but I was feeling steadier on my feet.

I tied back the drapes, and light flooded into the room. I looked at the bay, a rare clear day where the rocky island of lost souls was visible in the distance, its white crumbling ruins catching the morning sun. Ancients who were once imprisoned there were said to still rail against walls that no longer existed, caught in a timeless prison of another kind, memories caging them as strongly as iron bars. My attention traveled west to the last standing spire of Golgata, still leaning, facing its imminent demise with stoic grace. Some things last . . . and some things were never meant to.

I heard a tap at my door. Finally. There were clothes in my dressing chamber—all still locked in trunks—the ones Dalbreck had dutifully returned. They had never been opened. But if I was to address the conclave this afternoon, or for that matter, any of the many tasks before me, I couldn't do it in a thin borrowed nightgown. Aunt Bernette had gone to fetch someone with keys. I was about to search for a hairpin so I could pick them open myself. It was going to be a long and full day.

"Come in," I called as I pulled back a drape from a window in the dressing chamber. "In here."

I heard footsteps. Heavy ones. Boots. My heart thumped against my breastbone, and I stepped back into my room.

"Good morning," Rafe said. He was back in his own clothes, no longer needing to hide who he was.

My chest beat harder. Every emotion I had tamped down bubbled up at once and I heard the eagerness in my voice. "I was wondering when you'd come by."

There. I saw it in his eyes again. Saw it in his swallow.

"You're looking better than you did last night," he said.

"Thank you for coming to help."

"I'm sorry I didn't come sooner. I guess I was waiting for a note."

"I recall you telling me not to send any."

"Since when have you listened to me?"

"Since when have you paid attention to my notes?"

His worried expression was replaced with a grin, and that was all it took. I ran toward him, reaching for him, his arms folding around me, both of us holding each other like we'd never let go, his fingers sliding through my hair, his faint whisper of *Lia* in my ear, but when I tried to turn my lips to his, he pulled away, stepped back, grasping my arms and deliberately returning them to my sides.

I looked at him, confused. "Rafe?"

"There's something I need to tell you."

"What is it?" I asked, the panic rising in my voice. "Are you all right? Did something happen to—"

"Lia. Listen to me." His eyes burned into mine.

"You're scaring me, Rafe. Just say it."

He blinked, something shifting in his expression. He shook his head as if his thoughts were racing ahead of him.

"I need to tell you about the circumstance of—The truth is— What I need to tell you is, I'm betrothed."

My mouth went dry. I waited for him to laugh. To declare it a poor joke.

He didn't.

I stared at him, still not believing it. My mouth opened to say something, but I couldn't think what. He loved me. I knew he did. I had just seen it in his eyes.

At least I thought I had. Yes, we had parted ways weeks ago, but was that all it took to forget? Less than a season of days? I searched for something to say. "You found someone so soon? Which kingdom?" I asked, the words numb on my tongue.

He nodded. "She's from Dalbreck. The assembly wanted me to marry right away. They thought it would add the stability that was needed."

I turned away, blinking, trying to focus, trying to make sense of this. "Your kingdom is in such terrible straits?"

"Both of my parents were dead for weeks. I was missing. The kingdom was without a ruler. It created problems. More than we expected."

"The general who challenged you?"

"He's been one of them. I had to—"

I spun around to face him.

"Do you love her?"

He looked at me, stunned. "I don't even know her."

"You didn't know me before our wedding either."

"You mean our wedding that didn't happen."

I stared at him. He meant this. He was going to marry some-one else. On the assembly's advice. He was meeting his duty, just as he had when he came to Morrighan once to marry me. Was that all marriage was to him? Duty? In the same breath, I hated myself for disparaging his motives. What had I done but leave him behind because of my duty?

I heard Jeb's words again: *His word is true.* I didn't want it to be, but I said things to fill the painful silence. Things I didn't mean or even hope for. "Perhaps it will work out better for you two."

He nodded. "Maybe so."

We stood there looking at each other. My insides were jum-bled, as though everything had been kicked loose and shaken. Strangely, he looked exactly how I felt.

"So where does this leave us?" I asked.

He paused as if trying to figure it out himself, but his gaze still remained locked on mine. "It leaves us as two people—*three*—who need to stop the Komizar."

"Three?"

"You told me I had to make my peace with Kaden. I have." His tone was wooden.

Aunt Bernette rushed in, jingling the keys. "I have them!" She stopped when she saw Rafe, as if she knew she had inter-rupted something. I heard myself speaking, sounding like my mother rising to the occasion, trying to gracefully smooth

out an awkward moment. "Aunt Bernette, I'd like to introduce the king of Dalbreck. King Jaxon, this is my aunt, Lady
Bernette."

"We met last night. Briefly. Your Majesty," she said, and curtsied deeply, giving Rafe the full honor of his position.

"Lady Bernette," Rafe answered and took her hand, lifting
it to his lips, uttering polite niceties, and then excused himself,
turning to leave without another word to me. He walked toward
the door.

How many times did I have to let him go?

No more.

This was the last time.

He hadn't even made it through the door when footsteps
sounded in the outer chamber. Gwyneth rushed in followed by
a cluster of Rafe's soldiers—with the Field Marshal in their grip.

"This couldn't wait," she said apologetically, seeing me still
in my nightgown. "It's about your brothers."

I PACED MY ROOM. I HAD SENSED LAST NIGHT THAT THE
Field Marshal was innocent, but I had felt myself fading. It was
safer just to order them all locked up where they would be
secure until I could question them.

"Why didn't you tell us this last night?" I demanded.

"In front of everyone? After what you revealed? I didn't think
it wise, considering I'd just found out about the snakes infesting
the ranks. It's not something we want everyone to know, in case
it affords the princes any advantage. I demanded to speak directly

to you from the moment I was whisked away, but *he* wouldn't listen." He nodded toward Rafe.

"Everyone wanted to speak with her. Lia was indisposed. I told you to talk to me," Rafe answered.

"The king of a foreign nation who stormed in during a conclave? I'm supposed to immediately trust you with every kingdom secret?" The Field Marshal looked at Gwyneth. "This kind lady finally listened to me."

Gwyneth admitted she had gone down to the cellar where the prisoners were held in separate rooms to gloat at the Chancellor—and to reassure herself that he was still there. She'd been woken by a nightmare, dreaming he'd broken loose and was headed for Terravin. When the Field Marshal saw her pass by the small opening of his cell door, he begged for a moment to speak to her. All he would say was that he had news about my brothers that I needed to hear.

He told me about a conversation he'd had with my brothers before they left. He hadn't been happy about the diplomatic mission proposed by the cabinet, and he was surprised my brothers had agreed to it so easily. He suspected they were up to something.

He privately confronted the eldest prince, asking him what they were plotting. Regan hadn't tried to deny it. "You know what we're doing. The same thing you'd do if your sister was wrongly accused."

"I'm going to pretend I didn't hear that."

"I thought you would," Regan had answered.

And then the Field Marshal wished them luck.

I sat on the bench at the end of my bed, resting my face in my palms. My breath swelled in my chest. He said my brothers had never planned to go on to Gitos or Cortenai after they set the memorial stone in the City of Sacraments—only on to a few cities to recruit more help, and then they were heading to Venda to get me back and prove I wasn't a traitor—which meant the trackers we had sent were headed in the wrong direction. By the time they figured out the princes had planned a new route, they would likely be too far behind to catch up. But this also meant those lying in wait to ambush them had to regroup too. It might give my brothers an advantage, but even if they evaded those sent to kill them, going all the way to Venda was a sure death sentence. Even a dozen regiments at their sides wouldn't be enough to defend themselves against the Vendan army they would meet.

"The Aberdeen garrison," I said. "After what happened to Walther's company, that's where they'll go next, to recruit more and double their numbers. We'll send riders there."

Rafe shook his head. "No. Your brothers would be past there by the time riders arrived. We have an outpost northeast of the City of Dark Magic. Fontaine. We can try to intercept them near there."

"That's even farther away," the Field Marshal scoffed. "How would you get a message to them in time?"

I looked at Rafe, my heart gripped in a fist. "You have Valsprey with you?"

He nodded.

We sat down at my desk immediately to write messages. One

from me to my brothers so they would know the interception wasn't an attack by Dalbretch soldiers. The other from Rafe to the commanding colonel at Fontaine to set patrols combing the landscape for Morrighese squads. It was still a long shot. There were miles of wilderness, and those lying in wait to ambush my brothers could still reach them before they were warned. But it was something. Rafe looked over my message and rolled it up with his. No one else saw what he wrote, because it was written with ciphers known only to his officers. "I told the colonel I wanted a well-armed battalion to escort your brother's squads home if he finds them."

Alive. It was unsaid, but I saw the word looming behind his eyes.

He left to get the message into the hands of the Valsprey handler. If all went well, he said, it would be there by tomorrow, but he warned me there would be no return message. It took months to train a bird to fly to a distant location. They weren't trained to return to Civica.

I looked at the Field Marshal, nodding thanks and apologies in the same gesture. "And from this point forward, you must trust the king of Dalbreck as one of our own. His word is true."

I told the soldiers to release him, and ordered the Huntmaster, the Timekeeper, and Trademaster freed as well. The rest of the cabinet would remain in their cells to face trial and execution—if I didn't kill them first. My threat to the Viceregent had been real. If any harm came to my brothers or their comrades, his death would not be an easy one.

Devastation looked down on us,
But a green valley lay ahead.
The end of the journey was in sight at last,
And I did what I knew I would do all along;
I buried my knife deep in my betrothed's throat,
And as he gasped for his last breath,
As his blood soaked into the earth,
There were no tears
Among any of us,
Especially none from me.

—The Lost Words of Morrighan

CHAPTER SIXTY-NINE

RAFE

IT WAS A WARM DARK HOLE I CLIMBED INTO AS I HAD IN-
terrogated the prisoners that morning. It had no bottom, a
free fall that invited me to let go. All I could see in the darkness
as I asked questions were barrows full of bounty taken from
Dalbreck's dead soldiers. With every swing of my fist, I saw Lia
sitting in a dank Vendan holding cell, grieving for her dead
brother. And when I drew my knife on the Viceregent, I saw
only Lia, bleeding and limp in my arms. Sven had finally pulled
me back.

The Viceregent dabbed his lip with his sleeve, then smirked.
"I had planned on killing you both, you know? An ambush staged
to look like a common robbery by Dalbretch bandits on your way
back home after the wedding."

His eyes glowed with smugness. "You think I don't have my

reasons, just as you think you have yours? Don't we all get tired of waiting for what we want? The only difference between you and me is I stopped waiting."

The man is insane, Sven had muttered as he stopped my fist mid-swing. *Enough*, he said and pushed me away. He locked the cell door behind us and then turned my attention elsewhere, reminding me that I still needed to tell Lia.

I ENTERED THE QUARTERS THAT LIA'S AUNT CLORIS HAD USH-ered me into earlier, still feeling like an intruder. It seemed wrong to be staying in the room that Lia's brother had once shared with his bride, Greta. Most of their belongings had been removed, but in the corner of the wardrobe I found a pair of soft kid gloves sized for a woman's hand, and on the bedside table, two delicate pearl-tipped hairpins. I took one look at the large four-poster bed and chose to catch an hour of sleep on the settee instead. I would have preferred staying on a bedroll in Aldrid Hall, where many of my men were, but Lady Cloris insisted I take the room, and I didn't want to begrudge her hospitality.

When I walked in, Orrin was lying sideways across my bed, asleep with his mouth hanging open and his legs dangling over the side. Jeb was spread out on the settee, his eyes closed and his hands neatly woven across his stomach. They'd both been up all night securing the citadelle and assigning posts. Only Dalbreck's soldiers were to guard the prisoners until we were certain there were no more Vendan soldiers among the ranks. Sven was seated at a table, eating a game pie and reviewing files seized from the

Viceregent's apartments. Tavish sat at the other end, his feet propped up on the table, sifting through papers in his lap.

"Anything?" I asked.

Sven shook his head. "Nothing of import that might help us. He's a clever devil."

I grabbed a boiled egg from a tray of food and washed it down with milk.

"Did you tell her?" Tavish asked.

Both Jeb and Orrin opened their eyes, waiting for an answer too.

I nodded.

"She needed to know, boy," Sven said. "Better to hear it from you than have it spill out at an inopportune time."

I looked at him, incredulous. "She's going to address the assembly today. Now is a bad time."

"So there was no good time. It still had to be done. It's behind you now."

It would never be behind me. Her dazed expression when I told her cut a hole through me.

I shook my head trying to blot the memory out. "It's not an easy thing to tell the girl that you love more than life itself that you're going to marry someone else."

Sven sighed. "Easy things are for men like me. The difficult choices are left to kings."

"The general's a conniving bastard," Orrin said, yawning, "who needs an arrow in his tight ass."

Jeb sat up and grinned. "Or I could take care of him quietly.

Just say the word." He made a clicking sound—the snap of a neck—as if showing how quickly it could be done.

It was only a show of solidarity. I knew neither would ever assassinate a legitimate officer of Dalbreck, nor would I let them—though it was tempting.

"And what would you do about the general's daughter? Kill her too?"

Orrin snorted. "All she needs is one look at my pretty face, and she'd call it off with you. Besides, I'm an archer. I bring home dinner. What do you have to offer?"

"Besides a kingdom?" Sven mumbled.

"You could call it off and try to weather it out," Tavish offered.

Sven sucked in a breath, knowing the consequence. My position in Dalbreck was precarious. Weathering it out was a risky option. I had everything to lose and nothing to gain. The betrothal was the general's victory and my own private hell—the cost of saving Lia's life. And while the general played his games, his daughter was caught in the middle of it. I remembered the fear in her eyes, and her trembling hand as she signed the documents. The girl was afraid and wanted no part of me, but I had ignored it because I was desperate and angry.

"Let's move on," I said. "What happens between me and Lia isn't something that needs to be on the table. We have an unbeatable army marching this way."

"You don't believe that," Sven said, finishing off his pie, "or you wouldn't be here."

"I got a look at the troops this morning, and it's worse than we thought. Azia called it pathetic."

Sven grunted. "*Pathetic* is a strong word. The few I saw seemed astute and able."

"The *few* you saw is exactly the problem. It's not that they lack skill or loyalty, but their ranks are depleted. This is their biggest training post, but they've been dispersed all over Morrighan in small units. Only a thousand are stationed here right now. Gathering them all back here will take weeks. Even then, it won't be enough."

"The Vendan army may not all be headed this way. Dalbreck is a closer target. We'll sort it out. First things first. The assembly this afternoon. Strategizing a plan after that."

A plan. I had decided not to tell Sven what I had done. It would either work out or it wouldn't, and telling him would only incur a blistering lecture about being impulsive. But it hadn't felt impulsive when I rode to the camp outside the city gates where the handler was ensconced with the Valsprey. After I gave him the messages, I looked back at Civica, and the weight of its history settled over me. I felt the centuries of survival. This was the beginning, the first kingdom to rise after the devastation, the one all the other kingdoms were born from, including Dalbreck. Morrighan was a jewel the Komizar hungered for, a validation of his own greatness, and once he had it, along with its abundant resources, no kingdom would be spared. My doubts vanished. He was coming here first.

Sven eyed me suspiciously, as if he could see the inner workings of my mind. He set his papers aside. "What did you do?"

We had been together for too many years. I sat down in an

overstuffed chair and threw my feet up on the table. "I added a request in my message to the colonel at Fontaine."

"A request?"

"An order. I told him to send his troops to Civica."

Sven sighed and rubbed his eyes. "How many?"

"All of them."

"All of them as in *all of them*?"

I nodded.

Sven jumped to his feet, jarring the table and spilling his cider. "Have you lost your mind? Fontaine's our largest outpost! Six thousand soldiers! It's our first line of defense for our western borders!"

"I sent the same message to Bodeen."

By now Orrin and Jeb were both sitting up.

Sven sat back at the table and rested his head in his hands.

Orrin whistled at the staggering news.

I figured this was a good time to leave. Any more revelations, and Sven might burst a blood vessel. My decisions were made and there was no changing them now.

"Not a word to anyone," I said. "This isn't an answer to all their problems. They need to remain earnest in their efforts." I walked toward the door.

"Now where are you going?" Sven asked.

"First things first," I said. As much as I hated to admit it, Kaden would be a critical part of the plan to save Morrighan. "I promised to make some peace."

I CHECKED HIS ROOM. WHEN HE WASN'T THERE, I FOLLOWED my next best guess, and I was right. I spotted him, one hand pressed to the wall, poised at the top of the stairs that led to the lowest level of the citadelle—where the prisoners were kept.

He stared down the dark stairwell so consumed by his thoughts he didn't notice me at the end of the passageway.

He is Morrighese, I thought, just as Lia had claimed.

He was born from a line of nobility that went all the way back to Piers, one of the fiercest warriors of Morrighan lore. A Holy Guardian, Sven had called him. He had given me a brief history lesson the night before, when I noted my surprise at Kaden's parentage. A statue of a muscled powerful Piers dominated the entrance to Piers Camp.

Kaden didn't look powerful now. He looked beaten.

But last night—I swallowed, remembering how they looked together when I went to check on Lia during the night. I had seen his hand resting on her bed and her hand curled over his. Both of them were asleep, peaceful. I backed out of the room quietly so they wouldn't see me. Maybe that was what had given me the courage to tell her the truth. I knew she didn't love him in the same the way she did me. I had seen her eyes when she first saw me in the armory, and then the hurt when I told her about my betrothal, but she cared about Kaden too. They shared something that she and I didn't—the roots of one kingdom and their love for another.

He still hadn't noticed me. Instead he stared into the darkness and his hand absently fingered the sheathed dagger at his side, as if a scene was playing out in his head. I could imagine what it was.

I swallowed my pride and approached him. I had told Lia I had already made my peace with him. Now I actually had to do it.

CHAPTER SEVENTY

KADEN

I DIDN'T HEAR HIM COMING UNTIL HE WAS UPON ME. I startled and turned. "What do you want?" I asked.

"I'm here to talk about—"

I swung, catching him in the jaw, and he flew backward and fell, the sword buckled at his side clattering on the stone floor.

He slowly got to his feet, his expression livid, and he wiped the corner of his mouth, blood staining his fingertips. "What the hell is the matter with you?"

"Just preempting a shot from you. I seem to recall that the last time you snuck up on me wanting to talk, you punched me, then slammed me up against the barracks wall, accusing me of all kinds of delusional things."

"Is this a preemptive strike or a payback?"

I shrugged. "Maybe both. What are you sneaking around for this time?"

He studied me, his chest heaving, rage sparking in his eyes. I knew he wanted to take a swing, but somehow he managed to keep his hands at his sides. "One, I wasn't sneaking," he finally said, "And two, the reason I came was to thank you for staying by Lia's side."

Thank me? "So you can take her back to Dalbreck now?"

The anger drained from his face. "Lia is never going back to Dalbreck with me."

I was suspicious of the sudden turnaround in his demeanor almost as much as his declaration.

"I'm betrothed to another," he explained.

I huffed out a disbelieving breath.

"It's true," he said. "The news has been heralded all over Dalbreck. Lia will never be going there."

It was the last news I expected to hear. He was moving on? "Then why are you here?"

His lips quirked in an odd way. He didn't look like the arrogant farmer or emissary, or even the prince I had known.

"I'm here for the same reasons you are. The same reason Lia is. Because we want to save the kingdoms that matter to us."

"They all matter to Lia."

His expression darkened. "I know."

"And that pains you."

"We've all had to make hard choices—and sacrifices. I recognize the one you made helping us escape from Venda. I'm sorry I didn't say it before."

The words came out stiff and practiced, but were still an apology I never expected to hear. I nodded, wondering if he was still going to take a crack at me. There hadn't been time when we met up at the cottage. Finding Lia, Pauline, and Gwyneth had been all that mattered.

I reached out cautiously, offering my hand. "Congratulations on your betrothal."

He took it with the same caution. "Thank you," he answered.

Our hands returned to our sides in the same measured moves. He continued to eye me as if there was more he wanted to say. I had heard him come in last night and saw him when he quietly left the room. For someone betrothed to another, he didn't hide his feelings well.

"I'll see you out in the plaza," he finally said. "What she faces there today will be harder for her than the traitors she confronted last night. She won't be facing those she needs to throw in prison, but those she needs to rally. She'll need us both there."

He started to leave, then glanced down the dark stairwell and back at me. "Don't do it," he said, his gaze meeting mine. "The time will come, but not now. Not this way. You're better than him."

And then he walked away.

I LEFT MY WEAPONS WITH THE GUARD BEFORE I ENTERED the cell. My father's eyes locked onto mine, and immediately all I saw in them was calculation again. It never ended.

"Son," he said.

I smiled. "You really think that will work?"

"I made a terrible mistake. But a man can change. Of my sons, I loved you the most, because I loved your mother. Cataryn—"

"Stop!" I ordered. "You don't throw people you love out like garbage. You don't bury them in unmarked graves! I don't want to hear her name on your lips. You've never loved anything in your life."

"And what do you love, Kaden? Lia? How far will that get you?"

"You don't know anything."

"I know that blood is thicker and more lasting than a fleeting affair—"

"Is that all it was with my mother? The one you claim to have loved so much? A fleeting affair?"

His brows pulled together, plaintive, sympathetic. "Kaden, you are my *son*. Together we can—"

"I'll make you a deal, *Father*."

His eyes brightened.

"You sold my life for a single copper. I'll let you buy yours back right now for the same. Give me a copper. It's little enough to ask."

He looked at me, bewildered. "Give you a copper? Now?"

I extended my palm, waiting.

"I don't have a copper!"

I withdrew my hand and shrugged. "Then you'll lose your life, just like I lost mine."

I turned to leave but stopped to tell him one last thing. "Since you plotted with the Komizar, you'll die by his justice too. And just so you know, he likes those facing execution to suffer first. You will."

I left and heard him calling after me, liberally using *son* in his appeals, and I knew if I hadn't left my knives behind, he would have been dead already, and that would have been too easy an end for him.

CHAPTER SEVENTY-ONE

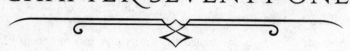

"SIT," I ORDERED.

"Where?"

"The floor. And don't move. I want to speak with her alone first."

I looked at the soldiers who had accompanied me. "If he moves so much as a toe, you are to cut it off."

They smiled and nodded.

I WALKED THROUGH MY PARENTS' LIVING QUARTERS AND opened the door to their bedroom chamber.

My mother lay in a disheveled heap at the foot of the bed, looking like a child's rag doll that had been emptied of its stuffing. My father lay in the center, pale and immobile. Her hand rested on the bedcovers that swallowed him up, as if she lashed him to this earth. No one, not even death, would sneak past her. She had already lost her eldest son, her other sons were missing and in grave danger, and her husband had been poisoned. How she had managed to gather the strength to stand with me yesterday I wasn't sure. She had drawn from a well that looked empty now. *There is not always more to take*, I thought. Sometimes so much can be taken that what is left doesn't matter.

She sat up when she heard my footsteps and her long black hair fell in disarray over her shoulders. Her face was gaunt, her eyes veined from tears and fatigue.

"It was you who ripped the last page from the book," I said. "I thought it was someone who hated me very much, and then I realized it was just the opposite. It was someone who loved me very much."

"I didn't want this for you," she said. "I did everything I could to stop it."

I walked across the room, and when I sat beside her, she pulled me into her arms. She held me fiercely, a quiet sob lifting her chest. I had no tears left, but my arms locked around her, holding her in all the ways I had needed to in these past months. She said my name over and over again. *Jezelia. My Jezelia.*

I finally pulled back. "You tried to keep the gift from me," I said, still feeling the hurt. "You did everything you could to guide me away from it."

She nodded.

"I need to understand," I whispered. "Tell me."

And she did.

She was weak. She was broken. But her voice grew stronger as she spoke, as if she had told this story in her own mind a hundred times. Maybe she had. She told me about a young mother and her child, a story I had only seen from my vantage point.

Her tale had seams I hadn't seen; it was colored with fabric in shades I'd never worn; it had hidden pockets heavy with worry; it was a story that didn't hold just my fears, but hers too, the threads of it pulling tighter each day.

When she had arrived in Morrighan, she was eighteen, and everything about this new land was foreign to her—the clothing, the food, the people—including the man who was to be her husband. She was so filled with fright she couldn't even meet his gaze the first time she met him. He had dismissed everyone from the room, and once they were alone, he reached out and lifted her chin and told her she had the most beautiful eyes he had ever seen. Then he smiled and promised her it would be all right, that they could take their time getting to know each other, and then he delayed the wedding for as long as he could, and he courted her.

It was only for a few months, but day by day, he won her over—and she won him over too. It wasn't exactly love yet, but they were infatuated. By the time they married, she was no longer looking at the floor but happily meeting the eyes of everyone—including the stern gazes of the cabinet.

Though the seat of First Daughter on the cabinet had been ceremonial for centuries, when she told her new husband she wanted to be more active in her role at court, he heartily welcomed her. She was known to be strong in the gift, sensing dangers and folly. At first the king considered everything she said. He sought her advice, but she sensed a growing resentment among the cabinet at the king's attentions toward his young bride, and she was slowly, but diplomatically, pushed aside.

And then the babies came. First Walther, who was the delight of the court, then Regan and Bryn, who added to their happiness. They were allowed every freedom, which was new to her. She came from a household of girls, where choices were limited. Here she watched her young boys nurtured and encouraged to find their own strengths, not just by her and the king, but by the whole court.

Then she became pregnant again. There were enough heirs and spares, and now everyone waited with expectation for a girl, a new generation to carry on the tradition of First Daughter. She knew I was going to be a girl before I was ever born. It filled her with immeasurable joy—until she heard a rumble, a growl, the hunger of a beast, pacing in the corners of her mind. Her misery grew each day, as did the thump of the beast's footsteps. She feared that it stalked me, that it somehow knew I was a threat, and she felt strongly that this was because of the gift. She saw me being torn away from my family, from everything that I knew and dragged across an unimaginable landscape. She chased after me, but her steps were not as swift as the beast that had ripped me from her arms.

"I vowed I wouldn't let that happen. I spoke to you as you grew in my belly and made a daily promise that I would somehow keep you safe. And then on the day you were born, in the midst of my fears and promises to you, I heard a whisper, a soft, gentle voice as clear as my own. *The promise is great, for the one named Jezelia.* I thought that was my answer, and when I looked into your sweet face, the name Jezelia fit you best above all the others the kingdom had placed on your tiny shoulders. I thought the name was an omen, the answer I was hoping for. Your father protested at the breach of protocol, but I wouldn't back down.

"Afterward, it seemed I had made the right decision. From the time you were an infant, you were strong. You had a lusty cry that could wake all of Civica. Everything about you was vibrant. You squalled louder, played harder, hungered more, and thrived. I gave you the same freedoms as your brothers, and you ran freely with them. I was happier than I had ever been. When your formal schooling began, the Royal Scholar tried to tailor your lessons to nurture the gift. I forbade it, despite his protests. When he finally confronted me, asking for a reason, I told him the circumstances of your birth and my fear that the gift would bring you harm. I insisted he focus on your other strengths. He reluctantly agreed. Then, when you were twelve—"

"That's when everything changed."

"I was afraid and had to enlist the help of the Royal Scholar to—"

"But the Royal Scholar is exactly who you needed to be afraid of! He tried to kill me. He sent a bounty hunter to slit my throat, and he's secretly sent countless scholars to Venda to devise ways to kill us all. He conspired with them. However you may have trusted him once, he turned on you. And me."

"No, Lia," she said, shaking her head. "Of this much I'm certain. He never betrayed you. He was one of the twelve priests who lifted you before the gods in the abbey and promised his protection."

"People change, Mother—"

"Not him. He never broke his promise. I understand your mistrust. I've lived with it ever since you were twelve years old. It made me conspire with him all the more."

"What happened when I was twelve?"

She told me the Royal Scholar had called her into his office. He had something he thought she should see. He said it was a very old book that had been taken off a dead Vendan soldier. Like all artifacts, it had been turned over to the royal archive and the Royal Scholar had set about translating it. What he read disturbed him, and he consulted with the Chancellor about it. The Chancellor had initially seemed disturbed too. He read it over several times, but then declared it barbarian jibberish, threw it into the fire, and left. It wasn't unusual for the Chancellor to order barbarian texts destroyed. Most made no sense, even when translated, and this one was no different, except for one key thing that had caught the Royal Scholar's attention. He retrieved it from the fire. It was damaged but not destroyed.

"I knew when he handed me the book along with the translation that something was very wrong. I felt queasy as I began to read. I heard the heavy steps of a beast once again, but by the time I got to the last verses, I was trembling with rage."

"When you read that my life would be sacrificed."

She nodded. "I ripped out the last page and threw the book at the Royal Scholar. I told him to destroy it just as the Chancellor had ordered, and I ran from the room feeling like I'd been betrayed in the most wicked of ways—tricked by the very gift I had trusted."

"Venda didn't trick you, Mother. The universe sang the name to her. She simply sang it back, and you listened. You yourself said the name seemed right. It had to be someone. Why not me?"

"Because you're my daughter. I would sacrifice my own life, but never yours."

I reached down and squeezed her hand. "Mother, I chose to make the words true. You had to have felt it in your heart too. You gave me a special blessing on the day I left. You asked the gods to gird me with strength."

She looked down at my bandaged hand in my lap and shook her head. "But this—" I saw all the fears she had harbored for years crystallized in her eyes.

"Why didn't you ever share this with Father?"

Her eyes shone with tears again.

"You didn't trust him?"

"I couldn't trust him not to speak to anyone else. A wedge had grown between us as far as the cabinet was concerned. It had become a contentious subject between us. He seemed as married to them as he was to me. Maybe more so. The Scholar and I both agreed it was too risky to tell him because it seemed *betrayed by her own* could mean someone in a position of power."

"And that's when you conspired with the Royal Scholar to send me away."

She sighed, shaking her head. "We were so close. On your wedding day, I thought you'd soon be gone from Morrighan, and if there actually was anyone here who sought to harm you, you'd be away from them too. Dalbreck was a powerful kingdom that could keep you safe. But then as I admired your kavah along with everyone else, I remembered the verse, *the one marked with claw and vine.* I had always thought it meant a different kind of mark— the scars made by an animal or whip—but there among all the heraldry and intricate designs on your back, in one small part, on your shoulder, there it was, a Dalbreck claw and a Morrighese vine. It was only an innocent kavah, I tried to tell myself, only a coincidence. It would wash away in a matter of days. I wanted to believe it meant nothing."

"But you had the priest offer the prayer in your native tongue. Just in case."

She nodded, exhaustion lining her face. "I wanted to believe my plan would still work, but really, I didn't know what would happen next. I could only pray for the gods to gird you with strength, but when King Jaxon laid you on your bed, and I saw what they had done to you—"

Her eyes squeezed shut.

I held her, comforting her as she had comforted me so many times. "I'm still here, Mother," I whispered. "A few marks are nothing. I have many regrets, but being named Jezelia is not one of them. Neither should it be yours."

My father stirred, and both of our attentions shot to him. She moved to his side, her arm cradling his head. "Branson?" I heard the hope in her voice.

Incoherent rambles were all he offered back. There was still no change. I watched her shoulders slump.

"We'll talk more later," I said.

She shook her head absently. "I wanted to be with him. The physician forbade it, saying my presence only agitated him." She looked up at me, her eyes sharp, fierce as she had once been. "I will see the physican executed for this, Jezelia. I will see all of them dead."

I nodded, and she turned back to him, her lips grazing his forehead as she whispered to a man who couldn't hear her, who might never hear her again. I was ashamed I had ever called him a toad.

I lingered, staring at them together, feeling dazed, watching the desperate worry in her eyes, and remembering how my father had called for her, *my Regheena*, the tenderness in his voice, even as he lay delirious. They loved each other, and I wondered how I hadn't seen it before.

I LOOKED DOWN AT THE ROYAL SCHOLAR STILL SEATED ON the stone floor. He'd been there waiting for an hour.

"I see you still have all your toes," I said.

He stretched out a leg and winced, rubbing his thigh. "You and your henchmen were convincing. I assume I can move now?"

"I've always loathed you," I said, glaring down at him. "I still do."

"Understandable. I'm not such a likable fellow."

"And you hate me as well."

He shook his head, his black eyes looking unapologetically into mine. "Never. You exasperated, annoyed, and defied me, but it was nothing less than I expected. I pushed you—perhaps too hard at times. Your mother wouldn't let me discuss the gift with you, so I did as she ordered. I tried to make you strong in other ways."

I held on to my hatred, nursing it like a treasured habit, like a nail I had chewed down to the quick. I wasn't done. I wanted more, but I already sensed a truth beneath his deceptions.

"Get up," I ordered, trying to make every one of my words sting. "We'll speak in your *former* office. My mother is resting."

He struggled to his feet, his legs stiff, and I motioned to a guard to help him.

He adjusted his robes, smoothing out the wrinkles, trying to regain his dignity, and faced me. Waiting.

"My mother seems to think you can explain everything. I doubt that." I put my hand on my dagger as threat. "Your lies will have to be very good to convince me."

"Then maybe my truths would be better."

I SAW, ONCE AGAIN, THE ROYAL SCHOLAR I HAD ALWAYS known, the one who could snarl and spit at the slightest provocation. His ears flamed red when I accused him of sending scholars to Venda. "Never!" he shouted. When I told him about their dirty work in the caverns there, he jumped to his feet and paced his office, calling out the names of the scholars. I confirmed with a nod after each one. He whipped around to face me. Now it wasn't just anger I saw in his face but stabbing betrayal, as if each scholar had personally gutted him with a knife.

"Not Argyris too?"

"Yes," I said. "Him too."

His rage caved inward, and he faltered, his chin briefly trembling. I heard my mother's words again. *Of this much I'm certain. He never betrayed you.* If this was an act, it was a very convincing one. Apparently Argyris was the lowest blow. He sat down in his chair, his knuckles tapping his desk. "Argyris was one of my star pupils. We had been together for years. *Years.*" He leaned back in his chair, his lips pulled tight across his teeth. "The Chancellor claimed I kept losing my lead scholars because I was difficult. They all left with little notice for remote Sacristas in Morrighan. So they said. I went to see Argyris a month after he left, but the Sacrista said he'd stayed only a few days and then moved on. They didn't know where he had gone."

If he was angry when I told him about the scholars, he was incensed when I questioned him about the bounty hunter sent to slit my throat. He pinched the bridge of his nose and shook his head, mumbling *stupidity* under his breath.

"I was careless," he finally said. "When I found the books missing and your note in their place, I went about looking for them." A single brow rose and he shot me a pointed stare. "You did say you reshelved them in their proper place. I thought they would be in the archives." He said the Chancellor found him and his assistants tearing the shelves apart and asked what they were searching for. An assistant jumped in with an answer before the Royal Scholar could say anything. "The Chancellor was furious and searched through a few shelves himself before he stormed out of the room yelling for me to burn the book if I found it as I'd been ordered to do in the first place. After five years, I found it odd that he even remembered the text, since he had declared it barbarian jibberish. "I began wondering about him at that point. I even searched his office, but turned up nothing."

That didn't surprise me. My results had been the same. The Royal Scholar leaned forward, the anger draining from his face. "I was required by law to sign the single warrant for your arrest and offer a bounty for your return. It was posted in the village square, but that warrant didn't include murder. I never sent a bounty hunter to kill you, nor did your father. He only sent trackers to find and retrieve you."

I stood, walking around the room. I didn't want to believe him. I spun to face him again. "Why did you ever hide the Song of Venda away in the first place? My mother told you to destroy it too."

"I'm a scholar, Jezelia. I don't destroy books, no matter what they contain. Such old texts are a rarity, and this appeared to be one of the oldest I had ever come across. I'd only recently placed the Testaments of Gaudrel in the drawer beside the Vendan text in what I thought was a secure hiding place. I was eager to translate it."

I saw the energy in his eyes when he spoke of the old texts.

"I translated most of the Gaudrel text," I said.

His attention was riveted, and I told him about the history it contained, cautiously gauging his reaction.

"So Gaudrel and Venda were sisters," he repeated as if trying to eat a tough piece of meat, chewing on words that he couldn't quite swallow. "And Morrighan the grandchild of Gaudrel? All one family." He rubbed his throat as if trying to coax the words down. "And Jafir de Aldrid a scavenger."

"You don't believe me?"

His forehead furrowed. "Unfortunately, I think I do."

He went to the bureau I had taken the text from, and I watched with surprise as he opened a drawer with a false bottom.

You have secrets. I had known it that day, but once I had found one secret, I hadn't searched for more.

"Just how many secrets do you have, Royal Scholar?"

"I'm afraid this is the last of my surprises." He laid a thick sheaf on his desk.

"What is it?" I asked.

He opened it and spread out multiple documents. "Letters," he said. "They were found decades ago by the last Royal Scholar, but they contradicted certain facets of the Morrighese Holy Text. Like me, he did not destroy rare texts, but they were an anomaly we didn't understand."

"So they were hidden away because they told a different history."

He nodded. "These support what you just told me. It seems the revered father of our people, Jafir de Aldrid, was a scavenger who could neither read nor write when Morrighan met him. After they arrived here, he practiced his reading and writing skills by writing letters. I've translated about half of them." He shoved the stack toward me. "These are his love letters to her."

Love letters? "I think you've made a mistake. They couldn't be love letters. According to Gaudrel, Morrighan was stolen by the thief Harik and sold for a sack of grain to Aldrid."

"Yes. The letters confirm that. But somehow . . ." He shuf-fled through the pages and read from one that had been trans-lated. "*I am yours, Morrighan, forever yours . . . and when the last star of the universe blinks silent, I will still be yours.*" He looked back at me. "That sounds like a love letter to me."

The Royal Scholar had been wrong. He did have another sur-prise for me, and it seemed the real history of Morrighan would always hold some secrets.

CHAPTER SEVENTY-TWO

THE PLAZA WAS FULL. THEY HAD COME TO SEE PRINCESS Arabella hanged. Instead I had to tell them I would be leading them in the fight of their lives. I stood on the portico balcony, my mother standing on one side of me, the Royal Scholar on the other, Rafe and Kaden on either side of them. What was left of the cabinet stood behind us.

Down below, a row of fidgeting lords, discomfited that the conclave was convening with the citizenry, was afforded seats at the front of the plaza. Just behind the lords, Berdi, Gwyneth, and Pauline stood shoulder to shoulder, looking up at me, their assured gazes giving me strength. Sven, Jeb, Tavish, and Orrin, along with squads of soldiers, were poised on the perimeter, watching the crowd.

There was confusion, a murmur rippling through the plaza when my mother stepped forward to speak. She told them the king was ill after having been poisoned by traitors, the same traitors who had sent her son and his company into an ambush, and then she named the traitors. At the mention of the Viceregent, a shocked hush fell, as if he stood at the gallows and his neck had just snapped at the end of a rope. Of the cabinet, he was a favorite among the people, making it harder for them to fathom. She told them the plot had been uncovered because of Princess Arabella's loyalty to Morrighan—not betrayal—and that now it was time for them to listen to me.

I stepped forward and told them of the threat coming our way, one I had witnessed with my own eyes, a terrible greatness not unlike the devastation described in the Holy Text. "The Komizar of Venda has amassed an army and weapons that could wipe all memory of Morrighan from this world."

Lord Gowan rose, his hands tight balls at his sides. "Beaten by a barbarian nation? Morrighan is a strong kingdom. We've stood for centuries—the oldest and most lasting realm on the continent. We are too great to fall!" Several lords rumbled agreement, rolling their eyes at the naïve princess. The crowd shifted on their feet.

"Are we greater than the Ancients, Lord Gowan?" I asked. "Did they not fall? Is the evidence not all around us? Look at the fallen temples that form our foundations, the magnificent tumbled bridges, the wondrous cities. The Ancients flew among the stars! They whispered, and their voices boomed over mountaintops! They were angry, and the ground shook with fear! Their greatness was unmatched." I eyed the other lords. "And yet they and their world is gone. No one is too great to fall."

Lord Gowan stood firm. "You forget that we are the chosen Remnant."

Another lord called out. "Yes! The children of Morrighan! The Holy Text says we have special favor."

I stared, uncertain if I should tell them, remembering Pauline's disbelief, afraid I would push them too far. The air stirred warm, circling. They waited, breaths held, heads turning, as if they felt it too.

Dihara whispered in my ear. *The truths of the world wish to be known.*

I looked at Pauline, the struggle in her eyes, the truest daughter of Morrighan. She lifted two fingers to her lips and nodded.

The Royal Scholar added his nod to hers.

Tell them. Venda's voice reached out to me across centuries, still stepping forward, unable to rest. She was blood kin to this kingdom as much as the kingdom named after her.

Only one thing was certain in my heart. Long, long ago, three women who loved each other had been torn apart. Three women who had once been family.

Tell them a story, Jezelia.

And I did.

"GATHER CLOSE, SISTERS OF MY HEART,
    Brothers of my soul,
    Family of my flesh,

And I will tell you the story of sisters, a family, and a tribe, blood kin of another kind, sewn together by devastation, and loyalty."

I told them of Gaudrel, one of the original Ancients, a woman who led a small band of survivors through a desolate world, trusting a knowing within her. She fed her grandchild stories when there was nothing else to offer, stories to help a child understand a harsh world, and to keep her silent when predators drew too close.

I told them of Gaudrel's siser, Venda, another survivor who kept her people alive with her wits, her words, and her trust. After being lured away from her family, she would not be silenced, not even by death, reaching through the centuries for hope for an oppressed people.

And I told them about Morrighan, Gaudrel's grandchild, a girl stolen by a thief named Harik, who sold her to a scavenger for a sack of grain. Morrighan was a girl brave and true, who led the scavengers to a place of safety. She trusted the strength within her that was passed down by Gaudrel and the surviving Ancients, a knowing they turned to when they had nothing else, a seeing without eyes, a hearing without ears. Morrighan was not chosen by the gods. She was one of many who were spared, a girl like any among us, which made her bravery all the greater.

"Morrighan called on an ancient strength within her to survive—and helped others do the same. That is what we must do now."

My gaze skimmed the plaza, the lords, and those standing on the balcony with me. My eyes paused on Rafe and my throat tightened. "Nothing lasts forever," I continued, "and I see our end in sight."

I leaned forward, focusing on the row of lords. "That's right, Lord Gowan. *Sight.* I have seen the destruction and ruin. I have seen the Dragon bearing down on us. I have heard the crunch of bone between his jaws. I have felt his breath on my neck. He is coming, this I promise you.

"If we do not prepare now, hope is gone, and you will feel the bite of his teeth as I have. Shall we cower and wait for the Komizar to destroy us, or do we prepare and survive as our kingdom's namesake did?"

A small voice.

Prepare.

Another, *prepare.*

A fist in the air, Gwyneth's. *Prepare.*

The plaza ignited in shared determination to survive.

I kissed two fingers, lifting them to the heavens, one for the lost, and one for those yet to come, and called back to them, "We prepare!"

CHAPTER SEVENTY-THREE

"YOUR HIGHNESS."

Rafe, Kaden, and I were just passing the plaza fountain when the general intercepted me. A dozen soldiers, including Gwyneth, Pauline, Berdi, and Jeb, came to a grinding halt behind us. The general reached out and took my hand, patting it. "Forgive me for my boldness, Princess Arabella, but I am relieved that the misunderstanding of your treason has been cleared up."

I looked at him uncertainly, already sensing this wasn't going to end well. I remembered him only vaguely, as one of the generals in longest service to the crown. "It wasn't a misunderstanding, General Howland. It was a well-orchestrated lie and plot."

He nodded, his lower lip curling in a pout. "Yes, of course it was, a plot by traitors of the worst kind, and we're all indebted to you for exposing them. Thank you."

"No thanks are necessary, General. Exposing treachery is the duty of every—"

"Yes," he said quickly, "duty! And that is what we wish to talk to you about." Generals Perry, Marques, and three other officers stood behind him. "With your father ill and your brothers away, so much has fallen on your tender shoulders. I want you to know there's no need for you to worry yourself about military matters. I can see you've already gotten yourself worked up over this barbarian army, which is understandable considering what you've been through at their hands."

I swallowed. *No, not going well at all.* Rafe and Kaden shifted dangerously on their feet beside me, but I put my hands out on either side. *Wait.* They got the message.

"*Worked up*, General?" I asked. "Have you ever met the Komizar?"

He laughed. "Barbarians! They change their rulers more often than their underclothes. Today's Komizar is tomorrow's forgotten gutter brat."

He glanced over his shoulder at the other officers, sharing a small chuckle with them, then turned back to me. He tucked his chin close to his chest and angled his head, and I suspected he was ready to confide a great truth that I had overlooked. "What I am telling you is this is not something for you to fret about. You are not trained in military tactics or even in assessing threats, nor are you a soldier. No one expects you to be. You're free to return to your other duties. We will handle this."

I smiled and in my sweetest voice said, "Well, that is a relief, General, because I did so want to get back to my needlework.

way?"

His smile faded.

I stepped closer, narrowing my eyes. "But before you do, would you please tell me how you'd address the fact that both of these soldiers at my side agree with me about the threat that you think I got *worked up* over?"

He gave Rafe and Kaden a cursory glance, then sighed. "They're both healthy young men, and how shall I say this delicately . . . easily influenced by a pretty face." His smile returned as if he had just educated me on the ways of the world.

I was so astonished at his shallow opinion of all of us that for a moment I couldn't speak. I eyed the fountain behind him, but Rafe and Kaden beat me to it, their rage bubbling ahead of mine. They stepped forward in unison, each scooping him under an arm, and dragged him backward. The other officers leapt out of their way as they hurled him into the fountain.

Rafe and Kaden turned, eyeing the other officers, daring them to step forward to help the general. I watched their rage turn to satisfaction when they heard the general coughing and sputtering behind them. My rage wasn't so easily cooled, and I marched to the fountain edge.

"And now, General, I hope I can say this *delicately* enough for your tender ears. In spite of my utter disgust, instead of calling you an ignorant, delusional, pompous, self-absorbed buffoon, I am going to extend my hand and strongly suggest that you take it, because I will not let your patronizing insults nor my pride get in the way of saving Morrighan. As much as I may loathe the idea, I need whatever miserable expertise you will bring to the table, and so when we convene to plan our strategies at a time and place *I* shall designate, you will be there ready to serve your kingdom. Because, make no mistake about it, I am ruling Morrighan now as my father's regent, and I will get worked up over silly little things like traitors and armies that seek to destroy us. Do you understand?"

His chest was a barrel heaving with anger and water dripped from his nose. I extended my hand, and he stared at it, looking at the other officers, who dared not rush to his aid. He reached out and took my hand and stepped from the fountain. He nodded as if complying with the order and walked away, the sucking sound of water sloshing in his boots. I didn't think the word *pretty* was swimming in his thoughts anymore.

Gwyneth heaved out a generous *whuf* of air. "Well! I'm glad you didn't call him a buffoon."

"Or pompous," Pauline added.

"Or ignorant," Jeb chimed in.

"Or an ass," Kaden said.

"I didn't call him an ass."

Rafe grunted. "You may as well have."

Now it was settled. I may have had the confidence of the troops, but at least a few of the officers were still entrenched in a system that had no place for me. Some things last, even after a decisive uprising, and I knew they'd be counting the days until my father recovered or my brothers returned.

CHAPTER SEVENTY-FOUR

RAFE

WE STOOD ON A LONG STONE DAIS THAT LOOKED OUT ON THE camp. I imagined Piers setting the first stone when it was only a fledgling kingdom. The dais was now eight stones high, with centuries of battles and victories behind it. Anyone who stood here commanded the attention of the entire camp. Lia spoke to the troops first, and then she introduced me. It was the third group we had addressed. It was necessary to keep the numbers small, especially in this last group. It held all the newest recruits according to the Field Marshal—a hundred in all. I told this group of soldiers what I had told the others. My presence and that of my soldiers did not mean an invasion, only an effort to help stabilize and prepare their kingdom. I assured them I had no other motives, because with the looming threat, what benefited Morrighan also benefited Dalbreck.

When I finished, Lia spoke again, emphasizing the joint effort of our venture and evoking the nods of the generals who stood on the dais with us, including the water-soaked ass whose tongue had dried up considerably since his dunking yesterday.

I watched Lia. Watched every movement. Watched her pace the dais as her voice rose, reaching the last row. Watched the soldiers watching her, their attention fixed on every word. Whatever goodwill she had sown before she had left I didn't know, but the respect the lords had halfheartedly yielded was given freely here. The soldiers listened, and I saw what I had already known, what I hadn't wanted to accept back in Venda. She was a natural leader.

This was where she needed to be. Letting her go had been the right choice, even if the decision still burned in my gut.

She spoke again, this time getting ready to introduce Kaden, and we were all prepared for what was to come. She began her speech as she had the others, but then there was a noticeable departure—at least for some of us.

"Vendan drazhones, le bravena enar kadravé, te Azione."

Jeb, Natiya, and Sven stood behind us, whispering a translation for those of us on the dais who didn't know the language. *Vendan brothers, I give you your comrade, the Assassin.* Lia lifted Kaden's hand with her last words, the two of them standing together as a strong unified front, then she stepped back so he could speak to the troops.

It was both trap and opportunity. We knew Vendans had infiltrated the citadelle guard, but we needed assurance they weren't also among the ranks. The Field Marshal and other officers could vouch for the majority, but newer recruits who claimed to be from the farther reaches of Morrighan were more of an uncertainty. Lia had addressed them in Morrighese at first, but then switched tongues as effortlessly as a breath. A dozen of us stood on either side of her. It appeared we were there for support, but we had been carefully watching the soldiers, their eyes, movements, and twitches, the clues that would reveal understanding or confusion.

Kaden continued the address, not just to root out, but to appeal to Vendans like himself, who might be swayed. He and Lia had arrived at this strategy together, because Vendans working with us could be useful.

"Trust the Siarrah, my brothers," Jeb interpreted quietly. "The Meurasi have welcomed her, as have the clans of the plains and valleys. *They* trust her. The Komizar is the one the Siarrah fights, not our brothers and sisters who are still in Venda. Now is your chance to step forward and fight with us. Remain silent, and you will die."

Most of the soldiers turned to each other in confusion, not understanding the sudden change of tongue. But a few remained focused, their attention locked on Kaden.

Second row, a frozen gaze. The soldier's pupils were pinpoints. Worried. Understanding. But he didn't come forward.

Another on the far right.

"Third row, second from end," Pauline whispered.

And then in the first row, a hesitant step forward.

This prompted another in the middle.

Only four.

"Back row, left end," Lia whispered to Kaden. "Keep speaking."

Five Vendan soldiers were found among the ranks, and with the eight citadelle guards, that totaled thirteen imposters—which in itself was a feat. Learning to speak flawless Morrighese could take years. The troops were dismissed while other soldiers moved in to detain the suspected Vendans.

With Lia's first break in three hours, her aunt Bernette swooped in with medicine. Lia took a chug from the bottle, circles still under her eyes. I watched her wipe the corner of her mouth, the tired blink of her eyes, the leveling of her shoulders as she faced her next task—interrogating the prisoners again, hoping one would slip with information or turn on the others as the court physician had. Suddenly, Terravin was selfishly fierce within me, the air, the tastes, every moment, every word between us, and I wished we could have it again, if only for a few hours, wished I really was the farmer that she had wanted me to be, a farmer who knew how to grow melons, and she was a tavern maid who had never heard of Venda.

I watched her walk away with Kaden to speak with the Vendans, and then I left in another direction. We weren't in Terravin and never would be again. Wishes were for farmers, not kings.

CHAPTER SEVENTY-FIVE

PAULINE

THE TIMEKEEPER WAS BESIDE HIMSELF. HE STOOD OFF TO THE side of the dais, fidgeting, waiting for Lia to finish. He had been exonerated, but now he had to follow Lia instead of dictate to her. His pocket watch and ledger had become useless. Tradition and protocol had always been the wheels and grease of Morrighan. Now Lia was.

Her aunt Bernette was standing beside him, waiting too. I saw pride in her expression but also worry. No one was quite sure how to navigate this new Lia. She moved about Civica with force and purpose and no apology. No words were bit back. She didn't have the time. As far as I could see, no one doubted her—she had saved the king's life and exposed traitors who had been plotting right beneath their noses—but I knew they wondered what she had seen and endured these past months. She was a curiosity.

As was I.

I saw the glances and heard the whispers about Pauline, the quiet, meek attendant who had always followed the rules. What had become of that girl? I wondered myself. Some parts of her were still here, other parts gone forever, and maybe others, I was still trying to find. It wasn't just tradition and protocol that had been shattered, but also trust.

When the last address was finished, we made our way down the steps at the end of the dais.

"Hold up," Gwyneth called to Natiya, then sidled up to me. "When are you coming back to the citadelle? I don't like you off by yourself at the abbey."

"Natiya's there too."

Gwyneth grunted. "And that's supposed to comfort me? She's a kettle ready to explode."

We both watched Natiya, who still scanned the dispersing troops, her hand resting on the hilt of the sword that dangled from her hip. Ours weren't the only stares she drew. A young girl armed with three weapons—and happy to flaunt them—was not a common sight for anyone in Civica.

"She's finding her way," I said.

Gwyneth's eyes narrowed. We both knew Natiya's history. "I suppose she is," she sighed, and turned back to me, saying she was taking Natiya back to the citadelle. "She needs a break from her murderous ways." She shot one last pointed look at me. "I'll see you there too—with all your *belongings*. Right?"

"We'll see," I answered.

A frown pulled at the corner of her mouth, but she didn't push the matter further. She strolled over to Natiya and slung her arm over her shoulder. "Come on, you bloodthirsty imp. Gwyneth's going to teach you a few new things about subtlety today."

I left in the opposite direction. I was just past the statue of Piers at the gate entrance when I heard someone call my name.

"Pauline! Wait up."

I turned to see Mikael, and I came to a dead stop, stunned that he had the nerve to approach me.

"I know what you're thinking, Pauline," he said, "but I was only following orders. I'm a soldier and—"

"And you've already spent all the reward money? Or are you afraid now because I'm part of the new cabinet and I could do all manner of things to you if I choose to?" His eyelids twitched, and I knew I had hit the mark. "Get out of my sight, you groveling parasite!"

I pushed past him, but he grabbed my arm and whirled me around. "What about our baby? Where is—"

"*Our baby?* You're mistaken, Mikael," I growled. "I already told you the father is no one you know."

I tried to yank away again, but his fingers dug into my wrist. "We both know that I'm—"

And then there was the crack of a fist on flesh and he was flying through the air. He landed with a thud, flat on his back, a cloud of dust erupting around him. Kaden was upon him, grabbing him by his collar and hauling him to his feet. Molten rage twisted Kaden's face. "You have a question about the father, soldier, I'm the one to ask! And if you ever lay a hand on Pauline again, it will be more than a split lip I give you."

Kaden pushed him away, and Mikael stumbled back, then froze. He knew who Kaden was, the Assassin of Venda who could have easily gutted him without making a sound. But more than that, I saw another assumption settling over Mikael's face. Maybe it was true, maybe he hadn't been the only one in my life. His inroad to me was gone. He wiped his lip and turned away, disappearing into the milling soldiers.

I saw Kaden's shoulders heaving as if he was trying to dispel the last of his anger. He told other soldiers who had stopped at the commotion to go back about their business before he finally turned to face me. He brushed the hair from his eyes. "I'm sorry, Pauline. I saw you trying to pull away, and I—" He shook his head. "I know I had no right to intervene or imply that—"

"You already knew who he was?"

He nodded. "Lia told me he was still alive, and I put it together. The same shade of blond as the baby. Your reaction."

The color on his neck suddenly deepened, as if just realizing his admission—he had been watching me. His eyes bore into mine, and I saw a hundred questions behind them I hadn't seen before. *Would I ever forgive him? Had he gone too far? Was I all right?* But mostly I saw the kindness in them I had seen the first time I met him. Silence and dust motes hung in the air between us.

"I'm sorry," he finally said again, and glanced at his knuckles that were red from the blow to Mikael's face. "I know you wouldn't want it to appear that a barbarian Assassin—"

"Will you walk me back to the abbey, Kaden?" I asked.

"If you have the time? Just for appearances, in case he's still watching?"

He looked at me, surprised, perhaps even fearful, but he nodded, and we left for the abbey. Both of us knew that Mikael wasn't watching.

CHAPTER SEVENTY-SIX

AFTER MY AUNTS AND GWYNETH HELPED ME BATHE AND dress, I shooed everyone from my room. For almost a week now, I had been consumed in meetings with generals, officers, and lords, and today I had addressed more regiments who had arrived after being called back to Civica. I needed one quiet moment. I remembered what Dihara had told me about the gift. *The walled in, they starve it just as the Ancients did. . . . You're surrounded by the noise of your own making.* And there had been a continuous stream of noise, most of it passionate and loud.

Rafe, Kaden, and I led private talks with Generals Howland, Marques, and Perry, Captain Reunaud, the Field Marshal, and Sven and Tavish. I personally greeted General Howland, trying to put our rocky start behind us. Our team of ten gathered maps, made lists, and devised our strategies. Kaden and I told them in vivid detail about the weapons and numbers we faced, a hundred and twenty thousand. When the Field Marshal suggested that the Komizar might divide his forces to attack on many fronts, Kaden assured him he wouldn't. The Komizar would hit with his full force on Morrighan, ruthlessly plowing his way to Civica to make it a quick decisive victory. I agreed. The Komizar's blood pulsed with the power this army gave him. He wouldn't divide it. I remembered his face as he beheld his creation—its immense, crushing impact was a thing of beauty to him.

During our meetings, arguments erupted over everything from timing to routes the Komizar would take to the best ways to arm our soldiers. One thing was clear—we needed more—so that call was sent out too. More weapons, more soldiers. The lords were sent back to their counties with the same orders for recruits and supplies.

All of Morrighan was enlisted in the effort. Metal of all kinds was brought to the forges to repurpose into weapons. Gates, doors, teapots, no item was too small or too important that it couldn't be used to save the kingdom. The mill was tapped to work around the clock. More wood was needed to build stockades, polearms, and defenses yet to be imagined. Training began as well, the sharing of skills, because it was undeniable that Dalbreck's soldiers had a refined discipline that would be helpful. Initially this rankled the officers, the prospect of Rafe's regiment of one hundred soldiers training Morrighese troops, but I snuffed that argument cold, making it clear that pride was not to be an obstacle to our survival, and Rafe smoothed it over, genuinely reaching out for advice from them as well.

I was caught off guard several times when I saw Rafe and Kaden explaining—or arguing—strategies. I saw them both in ways I never had before, in ways that had nothing to do with me. Ways that were all about their own histories and hopes, obligations and goals. I watched Kaden, skillfully skirting questions about the future of Venda even as he plotted to strengthen Morrighan. Some of our battles had to be waged later. They still called him the Assassin, not in a disparaging way but almost as a badge of honor that a Morrighese citizen had infiltrated enemy ranks and now returned to his own with Vendan secrets.

As the days passed, meetings ran long, and tensions ran high, I realized most of the outbursts were not about pride as much as dawning realization of the monumental fight ahead of us—they fully grasped it, including General Howland—and everyone searched for answers that were not easy to find. How does an army of thirty thousand, still scattered across the kingdom, take on one that is a hundred and twenty thousand strong and armed with far deadlier weapons? But we kept trying to find an answer.

When we pulled out maps and unrolled them across the table, I tried to read the Komizar's mind. I looked at the roads, the hills, the valleys, and walls surrounding Civica. The lines and landmarks blurred, and something faint tapped beneath my breastbone.

The details of our meetings whirled constantly in my mind. It was hard to block out the noise, but I knew I needed to use other strengths as well, a knowing that would help guide us because my doubts about all our strategies were growing, and each day wrung tighter with worry about my brothers and their squads.

I threw open my window, the cool night air shivering over my face, and I prayed, to one god or four, I wasn't sure. There was so much I didn't know, but I knew I couldn't bear losing two more brothers.

There had been no word, but Rafe had already told me there would be none. They would either come or they wouldn't. I had to hope and trust that the message had gotten there in time. *Bring them home*, I begged the gods. And then I called to my brothers, just as Walther's words had reached out to me. *Be careful, my brothers. Be careful.*

I stared out over Civica, the eventide remembrances quieting, a thin song still clinging to the air. *So shall it be for evermore. For evermore.* A city dark except for golden flickering windows watching over the night.

Peace settling in, meals being prepared, chimneys billowing.

But then the peace was disturbed.

Sounds crawled up my spine.

Sounds that weren't from the world outside my window.

The crunch of stone.

The hiss of steam.

A keening howl.

Fervor, Jezelia, fervor.

My heart sped. I felt the Komizar's breath on my neck, his finger tracing the kavah on my shoulder. I saw his onyx eyes in the darkness and the smile behind them.

"Shall I walk with you?"

I jumped and whirled.

Aunt Cloris poked her head into my chamber, her question a reminder not to be late.

I smiled, trying to mask my alarm. While my aunt had tolerated the complete lack of protocol on every level with surprising grace, I saw the signs of her impatience returning. She wanted things to go back to the way they were before. I couldn't promise that but I could give her tonight.

"I'll be along," I said. She left as quietly as she came, and I shut the window, returning to my dressing table. With only one hand, there would be no fancy braids tonight—not that I was ever particularly skilled at braids even with two hands. *But I had become skilled at using a sword and knife with either one.*

When the physician checked and rebandaged my hand today, I got a good look at it for the first time. The wound itself, except for the three small stitches on either side, was barely visible but my hand was still swollen. It looked like a blue-veined glove stuffed with fat sausages and felt just as foreign and numb. Something inside had cracked or torn—probably when I shoved the bolt loose to kill Malich. The physician was dismayed by the continued swelling and said it was essential that I keep it elevated on pillows at night and he crafted a sling for me to wear by day. When I asked about the numbness, he only said, "We'll see."

I set aside my brush and looked in my mirror. My hair trailed loosely over my shoulders. On the outside I mostly looked as I had before, perhaps a little gaunt, but on the inside, nothing was the same. It would never be the same again.

He's betrothed.

The thought came unexpectedly, like a sudden gust of wind. A mountain of demands had blocked it out, but now a single unhurried moment had let it back in.

I jumped up from my dressing table, adjusting my belt, my sling, sheathing my knife at my side, learning to do with one hand what I had always done with two.

THE FAMILY DINING CHAMBER WAS FOR SMALLER MORE intimate meals, but tonight there would be sixteen of us. I would have just sipped some broth in my room and fallen into bed, as I had previous nights, or eaten through our late-night meetings, but my mother had come to me herself and suggested it, and she hadn't left her room in days. I thought about my doubt in the days after Aster had died and how Rafe had told me I needed to regroup and move forward. It seemed like that was what she was trying to do now.

My aunts chimed in, saying that in the frenzy of activity over the last few days, they'd met everyone only in frantic passing moments. They said we had a long fight ahead of us and a shared meal would give us a chance to knit tighter together. I couldn't argue with that.

Berdi and I were the first to arrive in the dining room, and when she hugged me, I got a warm whiff of fresh bread and saw a dusting of flour on her cheek. "Have you been in the kitchen?"

She winked. "I may have stopped in. Your mother asked, and I was happy to oblige." I was about to ask her what she had been doing there when Gwyneth and Natiya walked in behind us.

Natiya's gaze immediately rose to the high ceiling and then she surveyed the tapestry-covered walls. I remembered the first time I had ever dined with Natiya. She'd met my gluttony with wide-eyed innocence and questions. Now she observed quietly with the eye of a cat in the bushes, ready to leap, not unlike the rest of us. We all wore weapons to the table, which in the past would have been forbidden by protocol. Tonight no one would object, not even Aunt Cloris.

We settled at one end of the table.

My mother and aunts, and Pauline's aunt, Lady Adele, came in next. My mother's hair was combed and braided, her dress neatly pressed, and the fire in her that had been buried these past days had surfaced again. I saw it in her eyes, her level shoulders, and high chin—the traitors would not win. I was surprised to see her chatting with Berdi like they were old friends.

Orrin, Tavish, Jeb, and Kaden strolled in together, all of them looking slightly uncomfortable, but my mother greeted them warmly and directed them to seats, and I realized how little all of them really knew everyone else, though we had been here for days. We did need to knit together. A shared meal was for more than nourishing bodies. Servants began filling goblets with ale and wine. Though my mother had promised to keep the fare simple, the sparkling cherry muscat was the exception.

"Where's Pauline?" I asked Gwyneth.

Lady Adele heard my question and perked up, waiting for an answer too. I knew that after their clash on our first night here, Pauline had avoided her. That was why she stayed at the abbey with the baby. Today she had moved back.

"She had to go to the abbey to pick something up," Gwyneth answered. Of course, we both knew what that something was. "She'll be here soon," she added, but when Lady Adele looked away, Gwyneth shrugged as if she too, was uncertain what was delaying Pauline, or if she would come at all.

Sven walked in with Captain Azia, and I was surprised to see them both dressed in officer's uniforms. Captain Azia blushed at the fawning of my aunts, and I realized how young he truly was. He and Sven quickly became engaged in conversation with them and Lady Adele. I wondered what had happened to Rafe. I sipped my muscat and then I heard his footsteps. I knew them as well as my own, the weight, the pace, the slight jingle of his scabbard. He hurried in and paused in the doorway, his hair slightly windblown, dressed in his Dalbretch blues too. My stomach squeezed against my will. He apologized for being late—he'd been stuck in talks with some of his men. He greeted my mother with additional apologies, then turned to me. He noticed my sling.

"The physician said it would help reduce the swelling," I explained.

He looked at the sling, back at me, at the sling again, and I knew he was searching for words while others swirled in his head. I knew his tics, his pauses, his breaths. Would his betrothed ever know him as well?

"I'm glad you're following his advice," he finally said.

It was only a few spare words, but everyone had paused from their own conversations to watch us. He turned and took his seat at the opposite end of the table.

Before the first course was brought in, my mother turned to

me. "Lia, would you like to offer a remembrance?" It was more than simple politeness. It was her recognition of the position I now held.

Memory tugged behind my sternum, and I stood. *An acknowledgment of sacrifice.* But there was no plate of bones to lift. I said some of the words only to myself, others for all to hear.

E cristav unter quiannad.

"A sacrifice ever remembered."

Meunter ijotande.

"Never forgotten."

Yaveen hal an ziadre.

"We live another day. And with it, may the heavens grant us wisdom. *Paviamma.*"

Only Kaden echoed back *paviamma* to me.

My mother looked at me uncertainly. It was not a traditional prayer. "Is that a Vendan prayer?" she asked.

"Yes," I answered. "And part Morrighese prayer."

"But that last word?" Lady Adele asked. "Paveem?"

"*Paviamma,*" I said. My throat tightened unexpectedly.

"It's a Vendan word," Rafe answered. "It can mean many things, depending on how it's said. Friendship, forgiveness, love."

"You know the language, Your Majesty?" my mother asked.

He kept his eyes averted from mine. "Not as well as the princess, and of course, Kaden, but I know enough to get by."

My mother's gaze shifted to Kaden and then to me. I saw the worry in her eyes. A Vendan language, a Vendan Assassin seated at our table, a Vendan prayer, and Kaden's lone response to it. He and I shared far more than just an escape from Venda.

Sven seemed to notice my mother's pause and jumped in, saying how he had learned Vendan after being a prisoner in a mine for two years with a fellow named Falgriz. "A beast of a man, but he helped keep me alive." He entertained everyone with a colorful story, and I was grateful to him for drawing the attention away from me. My aunts were spellbound by the daring account of his escape. Tavish rolled his eyes as if he'd heard the story before—many times over.

The first course was served—a cheese dumpling.

Comfort food. I looked up at my mother, and she smiled. It was what she served whenever I or my brothers weren't feeling well. I was grateful she hadn't gone to great lengths to impress King Jaxon. In light of everything that had transpired, a simple meal seemed the most appropriate.

When my mother inquired about the Valsprey, Sven told her the message had surely arrived at the outpost by now but we wouldn't hear anything back. He explained it was a one-way message only that we had to keep our hopes in.

"Then we shall keep that hope," Aunt Bernette said, "and be grateful to all of you for providing it."

My mother lifted her glass and offered a toast to Rafe, his soldiers, the Valsprey, and even for the colonel who would receive the message and help her sons. A rally of toasts followed, circling the table and offering gratitude to all those present who helped uncover the conspiracy.

My chest warmed with my many sips of muscat, and a server stepped in to refill my goblet.

"And to you, Kaden," my mother said. "I'm so very sorry for how you were betrayed by one of our own, and doubly thankful you are helping us now."

"A Morrighese son, returned home," Aunt Cloris said, lifting her glass.

I watched Kaden squirm at the assumption that he was no longer Vendan, but he nodded, trying to accept the acknowledgment with grace.

"And to—" I lifted my glass, trying to divert the attention from him. Heads turned my way as everyone waited to hear who or what I toasted. I looked at Rafe. It was as if he knew what I was going to say before I did. The blue ice of his eyes drilled into mine. We had to get past this. *Regroup, move forward. It's what a good soldier does.*

I swallowed. "I'd like to offer congratulations to King Jaxon on his upcoming marriage. To you and your bride—I wish you a long and very happy life together."

Rafe didn't move, didn't nod, didn't say anything. Sven lifted his glass and elbowed Tavish to do the same, and soon a flurry of good wishes rippled around the table. Rafe threw back the rest of his wine and said a quiet "thank you."

My throat was suddenly sand and I realized I didn't truly wish them well at all and I felt small and petty and an ache bloomed in my chest. I gulped down my drink, draining my goblet.

And then we heard more footsteps.

Small, hesitant, the soft tap of slippers on stone.

Pauline.

Heads turned toward the door expectantly. But then the soft sound mysteriously stopped. Lady Adele's brows pulled down. "Maybe I—"

Kaden pushed back his chair and stood. "Excuse me," he said, and with no further explanation, he left the room.

CHAPTER SEVENTY-SEVEN

KADEN

SHE WAS SITTING ON A BENCH IN THE SHADOWS OF AN arched passageway, the baby in her arms, her gaze lost in some distant world. Her long honey locks were neatly tucked into a netted cap, her dress reserved and buttoned, every stitch and line of it conveying propriety.

She didn't look up as I approached. I stopped, my knees almost grazing hers.

Her gaze remained fixed on her lap. "I was on my way," she said, "and then I realized, he doesn't have a name. I can't go in there without a name. You said it yourself, I need to give him a name."

I bent down on one knee, and lifted her chin to meet my gaze. "Pauline, it doesn't matter what I say or what anyone in there thinks. You choose a name when you're ready."

She studied me. Her eyes traveled over every inch of my face, her gaze restless and afraid. "I thought he loved me, Kaden. I thought I loved him. I'm afraid of making wrong choices again." She swallowed and her restless search stopped, her gaze settling into mine. "Even when a choice feels so completely right."

I couldn't look away. My breath was suddenly trapped in my chest, and I was afraid of making wrong choices too. All I could see were her lips, her eyes, everywhere, only Pauline.

"Kaden," she whispered.

My breath finally rattled free. "I guess if a choice feels right, maybe it's best to test it first," I said, "take it slowly, see if it can become something more . . . something you can be sure of."

She nodded. "That's what I want. Something more."

That was what I wanted too.

I stood. "I'll go in first. I'll tell them you'll be along."

I RETURNED TO THE DINING ROOM JUST AS THE NEXT COURSE was being served—Berdi's fish stew. Lia had risen and walked around the table to kiss her cheek and tell her how many times she had dreamed of every morsel, every scent, every taste that was Berdi's stew. I knew as soon as I caught the scent, that yes, it was better than Enzo's, but then I asked everyone to hold off for just a moment. "I think I saw Pauline coming down the hall-way. She should be here any moment."

And in only seconds, she walked in. She paused, standing in the arch of the doorway, her cap pulled loose, the blanket drawn back from the baby's head so his blond wisps showed and his little fist was free to stretch in the air.

"Hello, everyone. I'm sorry I'm late. The baby had to be fed."

Silverware clattered somewhere in the room.

"The baby?" Lady Adele said.

"Yes, Aunt," Pauline answered. She cleared her throat, then lifted her chin. "This is my son. Would you like to see him?"

Silence vibrated through the room. Lady Adele's mouth hung open. "How is it possible for you to have a son?" she finally asked.

Pauline shrugged. "Oh, I got him in much the usual way."

Her aunt looked at me and my white-blond hair and then back at the baby. I saw the assumption she was making, and I was about to correct her, but then I said nothing. I would leave that to Pauline.

The baby broke the silence with a loud wail.

"Bring him here," Berdi said holding her arms out. "I know how to rock that sweet potato so he—"

"No," Lady Adele said. "Let me see the child. Does he have a name?"

Pauline crossed the room. "Not yet," she said as she laid the baby in her aunt's arms. "I'm still trying to find the right one."

Lady Adele patted, jiggled, and shushed the baby, and he quieted. She looked up at Pauline, her eyes blinking, her hand still patting, and it seemed, her mind spinning. "Finding a name isn't so hard," she finally said. "We'll help you. Now go sit, your stew is getting cold. I'll hold him while you eat."

CHAPTER SEVENTY-EIGHT

EVEN THROUGH THE CLOSED BALCONY DOORS, I COULD HEAR the laughter in the dining room. It was a good thing. A rare thing. It was momentary, I knew. The worry would close in again, but for a few hours, it was a blessed saving grace from the cares that gripped us. Names for the baby had been bantered around the table. Orrin offered up his own name several times, but most of the names were drawn from revered historical lines in Morrighan. When Kaden suggested Rhys, saying that a name that had no Morrighese history to live up to might signify a fresh start, Pauline agreed and it was settled. The baby was named Rhys.

I had waited for at least five minutes after Rafe left to excuse myself. I didn't want anyone to think his departure hastened my own—but it had. The room suddenly grew hot, and I needed air. He had never spoken or looked at me again after my toast, which shouldn't have bothered me. There were so many at the table, so many conversations, and we were . . . nothing. At least nothing more than two leaders working together to find answers.

I heard the door open behind me, the conversations from the dining room growing briefly louder, then muffled again as the door clicked shut.

"Mind if I join you?" Sven asked.

I waved to the balcony rail beside me, though I really didn't want any company. "Please do."

This wing of the citadelle looked out on the forested hills—the same ones Pauline and I had disappeared into months ago. The tops of the trees were a black jagged edge against the starlit sky.

Sven stared out into what was mostly darkness. "You're not cold out here?" he finally asked.

"What's on your mind, Sven? It's not the goose bumps on my arms."

"I was surprised you offered a toast to the king's betrothal."

I sighed. "There's been awkwardness. You've probably seen it. I thought it might be best just to get it out in the open and behind us."

He nodded. "You're right. It's probably for the best."

Bitterness rose in my throat. I hated things being for the best. They never really were. It was a phrase that sugarcoated the leftover crumbs of our options. "But I was surprised at how swiftly the betrothal happened after we parted."

Sven looked at me oddly. "You do understand that he had no choice."

"Yes, I know, for the stability of his reign."

A furrow spread across his brow. "He turned down plenty of barons offering their daughters for the *stability of his reign*, but he couldn't turn down the general's offer."

"Then the general's daughter must be very special."

"Without a doubt, she is. She—"

Why was he doing this to me? I turned to leave. "Excuse me, Sven, but I—"

He reached out and lightly touched my arm to stop me. "I figured he didn't tell you everything. You need to hear this, Your Highness. It won't change anything. It *can't* change anything," he said more gravely, "but maybe it will give you a better understanding of what the king had to do. I don't want you to think him so shallow that as soon as you were out of his sight, he forgot you."

He told me that Rafe had returned to a kingdom in more turmoil than any of them expected. The assembly and cabinet were at one another's throats, commerce was in shambles, and the treasury greatly depleted. Dozens of decisions that had been put off were thrown at Rafe. He worked from sunup to late into the night. Everyone was looking for the young king to restore confidence and offered him a hundred opinions on how to do it, and all the while the general was breathing down his neck like a lion ready to pounce—the same general who had challenged him.

"But through it all, I know there wasn't a day he didn't wonder and worry about you, questioning whether he should have let you go or whether he should have gone with you. The first thing he did was have that book of yours translated."

"The one he stole."

He grinned. "Yes. He was hoping you'd made a mistake. That he could stop worrying."

"But he learned otherwise?"

He nodded, then looked at me pointedly. "He also discovered the two passages that you failed to mention."

"What does any of this have to do with his betrothal, Sven?"

"He didn't tear out of Dalbreck only to save your kingdom or his—those thoughts came later. He was only a young man racing against time, desperate to save someone he still loved, but he knew he had to be clever about it too. He ordered the general to outfit a special company of soldiers by the next day so he could slip undetected into your kingdom with the very best men at his side. The general agreed—on one condition."

My stomach slowly crawled into my throat. A condition. "He blackmailed Rafe?"

"I think the words *negotiation* and *compromise* were bandied about. He claimed he only wanted to ensure that Rafe returned home this time."

As stunned as I was, I also felt something lift in me. "Then it's not a real betrothal at all. When he gets back to Dalbreck, he can—"

"I'm afraid it is very real, Your Highness."

"But—"

"One thing you should know. A betrothal agreement is the same as law in Dalbreck. Why do you think our kingdom became so enraged when your betrothal to the prince was broken? In our kingdom, it doesn't matter if it's written on paper or offered with a handshake. The word of a man is a promise. And this time, Jaxon has given his word to his own people. He has already pushed the limits of their trust by his long absence. A king, in the eyes of his subjects, who cannot be trusted to honor his word is not a king to be trusted at all. If he broke this promise, he wouldn't have a kingdom to return to."

"He could lose his throne?" My mind spun with how much Rafe had risked.

"Yes, and he cares deeply about his kingdom. They need him," Sven answered. "It's the kingdom of his fathers and ancestors. It's in his blood to lead."

I understood the weight of promises, and Rafe's strength as a king mattered more to Morrighan now, than it ever had. It mattered to me.

I stared out at the jagged line of forest, feeling the stinging irony of Rafe's choice: To help me and the kingdom of Morrighan survive, he had been forced to cut out my heart.

"Is she kind?" I finally asked.

Sven cleared his throat and shrugged. "She seems agreeable enough."

"Good," I said. "He deserves that much."

And I meant it.

I left and went to the roof, where it was only me, a thousand blinking stars, and the beauty of darkness stretched to the ends of the universe, snuffing out the endless games of courts and kingdoms.

They passed through the long valley
and the sentinels of devastation,
looked down on Morrighan,
from the towering peaks,
whispering that the end of the journey was near.
But Darkness roared, striking out again,
and Morrighan fought for the Holy Remnant,
spilling the blood of darkness,
vanquishing it forever.

—Morrighan Book of Holy Text, Vol. IV

CHAPTER SEVENTY-NINE

I SIPPED HOT CHICORY OUT OF A TALL MUG, STUDYING THE maps spread across the table in the meeting chamber. I moved them around as if looking at them from a new angle would make me see something I hadn't before. *There.* It swirled inside me, a distant voice pushing me to look again and again, but I didn't know what I was searching for. *There.* An answer? A warning? I wasn't sure.

I'd arrived early because I couldn't sleep. It was still dark when I heard the cries of children. I threw back my quilt and looked out the window, but the cries weren't coming from outside. They hovered in my room and swam behind my eyes. I saw them huddled, afraid, the young Vendan soldiers who were on their way. And then I heard the brezalots, their breath hot and fierce, the steam from their nostrils filling the night air, and finally the whispers of the Komizar crawled beneath my skin like vermin raising my flesh. *Fervor, Jezelia, fervor. Are you understanding me at last?*

There was no going back to sleep after that. I dressed and crept down to the kitchen, where a kettle of hot water always steamed, and while my chicory steeped, I knelt beside the hearth, saying my morning remembrances, thinking of Morrighan crossing the wilderness with no map to guide her, and the courage she must have conjured. I prayed for that same courage.

There were at least a dozen maps laid out on the table. Ones just of Civica, others of the whole kingdom, and still more of the whole continent. The maps blurred and a scent streamed through me, fragrant, like crushed grass in a meadow. The tiny hairs raised on my neck. *There.* A voice as clear as my own.

I earnestly rearranged the maps again, this time examining the southern routes, but they had no more answers for me than before. There were dozens of possibilities. We had gone around and around about which route the Komizar would take, though once he spilled into Morrighan, it would make little difference. It wouldn't take a hundred and twenty thousand soldiers long to quash villages along the way and then engulf Civica. Another looming question was when they would get here. How long did we have? Much depended on the route, though the difference between southern and northern routes was still only a matter of days. Lookouts had been sent to provide early warning, but they could not scout every mile of a vast wilderness.

The last two weeks had taken much of our strategizing

outdoors, riding the surrounding countryside, trying to find strategic locations to mount and fortify our defenses. Civica was miserably vulnerable, and the blockades being built on the two main arteries seemed woefully inadequate. During this time, I began training again. As soon as the sling and bandage came off, I tried to regain the strength in my left hand, but the numbness persisted. It was good for holding a shield and little else. I couldn't hit a target from ten feet. My right hand had to work harder. I tried to hide my frustration as Natiya and I trained dozens of women who had come forward to serve in the effort, many of them already skilled with bows and swords.

When he saw women among the troops, General Howland's jaw clenched so tight I thought it might crumble into a hundred blustering splinters. "Every willing soldier is welcome and needed, General," I told him, stamping out his arguments before they could begin. "A woman will be leading you into battle. Why would you be surprised to see them among the ranks?" He had looked at me, stunned, and I realized it was the first time he had grasped that I would be going into the battle with him. Yes, he was counting the days until my father recovered or my brothers returned, but there were still no signs of either one.

The door opened, and I glanced up. Rafe stood there, a steaming mug in his hand too. I looked back at the maps. "You're early."

"So are you," he said.

I hadn't told him that I knew the circumstances of his betrothal. My toast hadn't entirely eliminated the awkwardness between us. There were times he caught me looking at him, and I would quickly look away. At other times, his gaze lingered on me even when our conversation was finished, and I wondered what he was thinking. But we eased into a rhythm. Friends. Comrades. Like Kaden and I were.

He walked over to my side of the table and looked at the sprawled papers with me. His arm brushed mine as he pushed a map aside. My skin burned with his touch. Burned in a way it shouldn't between friends. It wasn't right, I knew, but I couldn't help what I felt.

"See anything?" he asked.

I saw only that our efforts seemed futile. "No."

"We'll find a way," he said, reading my thoughts.

KADEN ARRIVED, AND WE CONFERRED, AS WE DID EACH morning before everyone else joined us, about what needed to be addressed that day. The discussion of evacuating towns along likely invasion routes needed to be broached, but we knew that could stir panic and disrupt supply chains that we desperately needed. We leaned back in our chairs, our boots resting on the table, and hours later, we were in much the same position as we listened to Tavish and Captain Reunaud wrestle over ways to bring down a brezalot. They were nasty charging creatures and perfect for the delivery of the Komizar's most destructive weapon. Both men had seen them killed with spears, but that would require too close a proximity to the exploding animals. They agreed a siege crossbow would work, but without knowing exactly where the enormous horses would charge from, we would need dozens of the weapons. Morrighan had four that hadn't been used in years. Heavy siege weapons weren't useful for most battles that occurred in remote field locations. Killing a man required only a sword or arrow. The order went out for more siege crossbows to be built.

There was a knock at the door, and a sentry announced that servers were here with the midday meal. Maps were moved to a side table, and platters were brought in. As we ate, talk turned back to the training of soldiers, and my thoughts returned to my brothers. I looked at Rafe across the table from me. I wasn't sure I had ever thanked him for requesting an escort home for my brothers' squads, and then I selfishly wondered how many soldiers were in a Dalbretch battalion. In Morrighan, a battalion consisted of four hundred soldiers. Once here, would his men stay and help us?

I knew the same thought had simmered in Kaden's mind, and then between bites of his brisket and bread, the Field Marshal suddenly spoke aloud the question that we all had on our minds—would Dalbreck send more troops to help Morrighan? The room fell silent.

The question had already been asked. Rafe had maintained since his arrival in Civica that he and his men were there only to help root out traitors, stabilize our kingdom, and help us prepare our forces for a possible invasion. The Field Marshal had put Rafe in an awkward position by asking again. Dalbreck was in jeopardy too. Rafe had his own borders to think about, not to mention his own troubled reign. He had already risked much just in coming here. I saw Sven's focus sharpen, waiting to see what he would say.

Rafe studied me, weighing his answer carefully, then looked back at the Field Marshal. "When I sent the message to Fontaine, I also made a request for troops."

Expressions around the table brightened.

"How many?" Marques asked.

"All of them."

Sven leaned back in his chair and sighed. "It's our largest outpost. That's six thousand soldiers."

A few hushed seconds passed.

"Well. That's—" The Field Marshal's brows were slivered moons above his wide eyes.

"Remarkable!" Howland finished.

"And very much welcomed," Marques added.

"I made a similar request to Marabella," Rafe added. "They'll pick up troops at two more outposts along the way. That's another two thousand. I'm certain they'll all come, as long as the Valsprey got there without incident. I can't make a promise about the rest."

I wasn't sure we had heard him right. "The rest?" I said, as stunned as everyone else.

Sven stood, his hands pressed against the table. *"The rest?"*

"The thirty-two thousand troops still in Dalbreck that I'm pulling from our borders. As I said, I can't promise they'll come. The transition of power has had some obtacles. The general I had to request the troops from is also the one who recently challenged me. He might use this request as a way to resume his campaign for the throne. It's unlikely, though—" Rafe looked at me, hesitating.

"Because you're betrothed to his daughter," I finished.

Rafe nodded.

"*Unlikely?*" Sven stared at Rafe in disbelief, his eyes blazing, then turned and walked out of the room, slamming the door behind him.

Rafe nodded at Tavish to go after him, and Tavish left too.

There was a quiet lull, officers staring at the door, Sven's anger still hovering in the air, and then the Field Marshal looked back at Rafe. I saw the doubt in his eyes. Helping a princess with a rebellion to expose traitors was one thing, but a king abandoning his own borders was an act of insanity. "Why in the gods names would you do that? It will leave your own borders vulnerable."

Rafe's composure didn't falter. "I have no doubt the Komizar will attack Dalbreck—but not before he attacks Morrighan. He's coming here first."

"So the princess has said, but how can you be certain that—"

"It's a calculated risk. Not bringing my troops here is the greater risk. It could spell our own destruction. From a strategic standpoint, you have the ports and resources to take over every other western kingdom. Once the Komizar has Morrighan, he's unstoppable."

He paused, his eyes briefly searching mine. "But it's far more that makes me certain. Someone once asked me if I ever felt something deep in my gut." He looked back at the Field Marshal, then skimmed the walls around us and the ancient mural that told the story of the girl Morrighan, his gaze rising to the ceiling, the stones, and it seemed, the mortar of the centuries that held it all together. "This is the jewel the Komizar hungers for. Morrighan is the oldest kingdom—the one that gave birth to all the others. It has never fallen. It's a symbol of greatness—but more than that, it's the kingdom the gods ordained from the beginning. To the Komizar, conquering Morrighan is the same as conquering the gods. I saw that desire in his eyes when I was in Venda, and he will settle for nothing less."

We sat there for long stunned seconds, and I knew Rafe had perceived the Komizar's ambitions with amazing clarity.

"Thank you, King Jaxon," I finally said. "However many may come, each soldier will make us stronger, and for each one we will be in your debt." But I was thanking him for more than his troops. He was in this as knee-deep as Kaden and I were now. It was all or nothing.

A renewed exuberance erupted in the room, the generals and officers adding their thanks to mine, but Kaden, Rafe, and I exchanged a knowing look. If all the troops Rafe requested came, our combined forces would number seventy thousand. We were still outnumbered almost two to one by an army that would descend upon us with more deadly weapons. Rafe tempered their response with a reminder that this was only a bandage on a gaping wound. What we needed was a needle and thread to stitch it shut.

"But it's a damn good bandage," the Field Marshal said.

Discussions resumed. With the added forces in mind, the generals began talking of more defensive blockades on key Morrighan arteries.

A needle and thread.

I stared at Kaden. His mouth was moving, but I couldn't hear the words. The room grew hazy. The deliberations became a distant rumble, even as other sounds rose to the forefront.

A creak.

A crunch.

A wheel on stone.

I remembered hearing the clang of the bridge. It came too soon. Before first thaw. The sounds in my head grew louder, the room dimmer.

The hiss of steam.

A keening howl.

Hurried footsteps.

Fright, thick as night.

Fervor, Jezelia, fervor, a hot whisper in my ear.

And then another voice, soft and quiet, as thin as a flutter of wind.

There.

"Lia?" Kaden said, touching my arm.

I jumped, the haze vanishing. Everyone stared at me, but all I could think was, *pachegos.* My chair squealed back behind me, and I raced to the side table where the piles of maps lay. "Move the food!" I yelled as I carried the armful of maps to the table and spread them out.

"What the devil?"

"Did you see something?"

"Someone tell me what she's doing."

I shuffled through the maps until I found the one I wanted. *There.*

"A northern route," I said. "This is the way he's coming."

A wave of arguments rose. "We already discounted a northern route. He could get caught in a late snowfall."

"Farther north," I said. "By way of Infernaterr. It's the perfect route. It's flat, and winter never reaches there."

By now both Kaden and Rafe were looking over my shoulder at the map too.

Kaden stepped back and shook his head. "No, Lia. Not there. He would never come that way. You know the clans. Even Griz and Finch. Too many in his army fear the superstitions of the wastelands."

I leveled my gaze at Kaden. "That's the point. He is using that fear."

He looked at me, still not understanding.

"*Fervor*, Kaden. He no longer has me. He'll create his own. A different kind of fervor to push them forward."

The dawning rolled through his eyes—and then the worry. How much sooner would they reach here than we thought?

"I've heard them," I said. "The cries of the young soldiers. The howls of the pachegos. The Komizar uses their fear to rally them. And what better way than the wastelands of Infernaterr to move his army swiftly across the continent?"

I looked back at the map, eyeing an expanse between Infernaterr and Morrighan. More words sounded in my head. Rafe's words, chiding me as my sword blocked his.

Attack! Don't wait for me to wear you down!

"What is this?" I asked, pointing to what looked like a V-shaped line of peaks at the end of Infernaterr.

Captain Reunaud stepped closer to see what I pointed at. "Sentinel Valley. Sometimes it's called Last Valley." He explained it was believed to be the last valley Morrighan led the Remnant through before they reached their new beginning. He had traveled through it a few times in convoys headed to Candora.

Keep on the move! Let surprise be your ally!

"Why is it called Sentinel Valley?" I asked.

"Ruins," he answered. "They sit atop the high hills that hem in the valley as if they're watching you. Light can play tricks there. It's an eerie trail, and when the wind whistles through the ruins, soldiers say it is the Ancients calling to one another."

I asked him specifics about the terrain, the height of the peaks, the length of the valley, and the multiple canyons that lay beyond the peaks.

Advance! The sword is a killing weapon, not a defensive one. If you're using it to defend, you're missing a chance to kill.

Reunaud said it was ten miles of valley that narrowed to a point less than fifty yards wide. I already envisioned the Komizar's front lines. They would be the youngest whom he would consider the most disposable of his army. *Venda has no children.* He would throw it in my face, expecting it to undo me as it had that day on the terrace. Undo every Morrighese soldier who was reluctant to lift their sword against a child.

"We're wasting our time trying to defend Civica. We need to advance."

"Advance? Where?" General Howland grumbled. "What are you—"

"This is our needle and thread. Containment. We funnel his army and then hit him with surprise attacks from the side. We take on the strongest while we are still strong. It might be our only chance."

I pointed to the small V on the map. "There. This is where we'll meet the Komizar's army. We move all our troops to Sentinel Valley."

The arguments exploded. Howland, Marques, and Perry came at me with everything they had, thinking I was crazy to move our entire forces to one very distant location on what they called a hunch. Rafe and Kaden studied the maps, quietly conferring, then both looked at me and nodded.

The Field Marshal and Reunaud seemed caught between it all.

"Do you know how long it would take to move thirty thousand troops that far?" Howland bellowed, shaking his finger at me.

"So you're saying that a barbarian leader can move a staggering army of a hundred and twenty thousand troops across the entire continent and we can't manage to move our smaller forces to a location just outside our borders? Perhaps we should just give up now, General?"

"But there's no proof he's coming from the north at all!" Marques shouted.

Perry threw his hands up in the air. "Leave Civica unprotected? You can't—"

"*This point*," I said sharply, "is *not* under advisement. We begin laying out new strategies in the morning. We head out by the end of the week. You're free to leave now to prepare our troops to move—"

Howland stepped toward me, his fists rigid at his sides. "This is not going to happen!" he yelled. "I'll take it up with the queen. You are not—"

Rafe and Kaden both tensed, looking as if they were ready to send him for another swim in the fountain—by way of the window—but then pounding shook the door to the chamber. It flew open and the Timekeeper burst into the room, pushing past the sentry, his eyes bulging and his face shining with sweat. Pauline and Gwyneth rushed in on his heels.

"What is it?" I asked, my heart jumping to my throat.

"It's the king," he said, between labored breaths. "He's awake. And he wants to see all of you in his chamber. Immediately."

CHAPTER EIGHTY

GENERAL HOWLAND WAS THE FIRST OUT THE DOOR, AS IF this were a gift delivered into his hands by the gods themselves.

My father is awake. It is a gift, I thought. *But maybe not a timely one.*

Rafe and Kaden both balked, wondering if their presence was actually requested. Pauline assured them it was. Neither seemed eager to meet my father.

We walked briskly through the hallways, the Timekeeper and General Howland leading the way. Pauline and Gwyneth told us the queen was at his side and the king had already been informed of everything that had transpired.

"You mean that little thing called a rebellion?" Rafe said, and rubbed his neck like it was headed for a noose.

"Not amusing," I said.

Our footsteps echoed in the hallway, sounding like a small stampede of nervous goats. It felt like we would never get there, but then, before I was ready, the door to his outer chamber opened and we were ushered in by my aunt Cloris. The rest of the cabinet members, including the Royal Scholar, were already there.

"Go on in," she said. "He's waiting."

My pulse pounded, and we filtered into his room.

He sat in his bed, propped up with pillows. His face was lined and gaunt and looking far older than his years, but his eyes were bright. My mother's chair was beside the bed, and their hands were laced together in uncharacteristic familiarity.

His eyes landed on me first, lingering for a long scrutinizing moment before he finally moved on, eyeing the others present.

"I understand you were having a meeting," he said, "and I wasn't invited?"

"Only because you were indisposed, Your Majesty," I answered.

His brows pulled together. "I guess a daily dose of poison didn't quite agree with me."

"Your Maj—"

My father scowled. "I'll get to you, Howland. Wait your turn."

The general nodded.

"Which of you is the king of Dalbreck?"

"That would be me, Your Majesty," Rafe answered.

My father lifted his hand with much effort and waved Rafe closer with a crooked finger. "You here to take over my kingdom?"

"No, sir, only to assist." It was clear my father was still very weak, and I knew Rafe measured his words carefully. I also detected a certain nervousness in his response, and Rafe was never nervous. It made my breath catch.

"Come closer. Let me get a better look at you."

Rafe stepped forward and fell to one knee at his bedside.

"What are you on your knee for?" my father growled. "One king doesn't bow to another. Your steward didn't teach you that?" His eyes danced, and he briefly glanced at me before turning back to Rafe. "Unless you're on bended knee for another reason? If that's the case, you're facing the wrong person."

Oh, dear gods. He was toying with Rafe. This was not my father. Had the poison addled his brain?

"No other reason," Rafe said, and quickly returned to his feet.

My father waved Rafe back.

"And you must be the Assassin," he said to Kaden. He waved Kaden forward in similar fashion. Kaden did not fall to a knee, but I knew he wouldn't. He would never have bowed to royalty, even if it cost him his life. My father didn't seem to notice the snub and studied Kaden. He swallowed, and I saw a glimmer of regret in his expression, as if he saw the resemblance between Kaden and the Vicergent. "I knew about you. Your father told me your mother took you away."

"Deception has always been his strength," Kaden answered.

My father's chest rose in a ragged breath. "And yours too, I understand."

I glanced at Pauline. She had been in on the briefing, but had she told him about Terravin?

"You here to kill anyone, boy?"

A faint grin lit Kaden's eyes. He was ready to play this game with my father. "Only on your daughter's orders."

"She order you to kill me?"

Kaden shrugged. "Not yet."

My father's eyes sparked, the game invigorating him, bringing him back to life. His gaze turned to me. He scowled again. "You disobeyed my orders, Arabella, and I understand you bartered off the wedding cloak jewels that have been in our family for generations. You must be punished."

Generals Howland and Perry shifted happily on their feet.

"Your Majesty," Rafe intervened, "if I may—"

"No you may not!" my father snapped. "This is still my kingdom, not yours. Step back, King Jaxon."

I nodded to Rafe, trying to assure him. *Wait.*

My father settled back against his pillows. "And your punishment is that you will continue to reign in my stead, enduring all the endless absurd peckings of the office until I am fully recovered. Do you accept your punishment, Arabella?"

My throat was thick, aching. I stepped forward. "Yes, Your Majesty, I do." I swallowed and then added, "On one condition."

Surprised mumbles erupted.

Even in his weak state, my father managed to roll his eyes.

"A condition on your punishment? You haven't changed, Arabella."

"Oh yes, Father, I most definitely have."

"The condition?"

"You will support me in whatever I decide, because there are many hard decsions that still lie ahead—and some of them will not be popular with everyone."

"Unpopular like the coup?"

"Yes, that unpopular."

"Then I approve your condition." He looked past me at every-one else. "I am confident that Arabella will meet her punish-ment to my full satisfaction. Does anyone object?"

No one spoke, though I knew words silently raged on some tongues.

"Good," my father said. "Now everyone out. I want to speak to my daughter. Alone."

AS SOON AS THE ROOM WAS EMPTIED AND I TURNED BACK to him, I saw that his performance had drained him. He sank deeper into the pillows, weaker than before.

His eyes glistened. "I am sorry, Arabella."

I curled up on the bed beside him, nestling my head on his chest, and he managed to put his arm around my shoulder and pat my arm. He apologized for many things, not the least of which was becoming so weary of his position that he allowed corruption to creep in right beneath his nose.

"I've failed as a father and as a king."

"We all make mistakes, Father. Hopefully, we learn from them and move forward."

"How did you end up with an assassin and newly crowned king as your confidantes?"

"The gods have a wicked sense of humor."

"And you trust them?"

I smiled, thinking of all the deceptions and betrayals that had passed between us. "With my life," I answered.

"Is there anything more to this union?"

Far more, I thought. Maybe more than any of us really understood.

Together they will attack,
Like blinding stars thrown from the heavens.

"Yes," I answered. "They not only give me hope, they are Venda's hope too."

"I meant—"

"I know what you meant, Father. There is nothing more between us."

"And what is this unpopular decision?"

I told him about the valley where I was moving our forces against the generals' wishes, and then I told him more of my plan that I hadn't told anyone else.

"Arabella, you can't—"

"You promised, Father. This decision is mine." I slid from the bed. "You should rest."

He sighed, his lids drooping. "The other kingdoms will never—"

"They will have no choice. On this I won't be swayed. Please trust me."

His brows pulled down with worry, but then another question faded on his lips, the last of his energy spent, and his eyes closed.

MY SPIRITS WERE BUOYED AS I RETURNED TO MY ROOM. THE image of my parents' hands laced together kept surfacing. It was a simple gesture that was as unexpected as a summer shower. Some things survived, even when—

Rafe's door swung open as I passed it, and he barreled out, plowing into me. We stumbled and caught ourselves, his hand landing on the wall behind me.

"Lia," he said, startled. We were both steady on our feet now, but he didn't move. The air crackled between us, alive in a way that made my skin tingle. Strain showed in his eyes, and he stepped away, creating space between us, the movement awkward and obvious.

I swallowed, trying to convince myself this was all part of letting go. "Where are you tearing out to?" I asked.

"I need to speak to Sven before dinner. I want to make sure he doesn't bring his temper to the table. Excuse me, I—"

"I know," I said flatly. "You need to go."

He raked back his hair, hesitating. I knew, with that small movement, he was struggling to let go too, a piece at a time.

Love didn't end all at once, no matter how much you needed it to or how inconvenient it was. You couldn't command love to stop any more than a marriage document could order it to appear. Maybe love had to bleed away a drop at a time until your heart was numb and cold and mostly dead. He shifted on his feet, his eyes not meeting mine.

"I'll see you at dinner," he said, and he left to find Sven.

SHADOWS DANCED ON THE WALLS FROM THE FIRE IN THE hearth. I removed my belts and weapons, hanging them on a hook, and crossed the room to my dressing chamber, feeling my way through the darkness as I let the rest of my clothes fall to the floor. I lit a candle on the bureau and grabbed a towel to wash up, but then something crept over me. A presence.

Jezelia.

I spun, my heart beating wildly, searching the corners of the chamber. His scent filled the air, his sweat, his confidence. My eyes frantically swept the room, combing the shadows, certain he was here.

"Komizar," I whispered. I heard his steps, saw the glint of his eyes in the darkness, the chill as his hand circled my neck, his thumb pressing the hollow of my throat, feeling for the beat of my heart. *There is always more to take.*

And then he was gone. The chamber was empty as it always had been, and my breaths skipped through my chest. *The lies, they will force themselves upon you.* His lies. He taunted and cursed me with every mile he traveled. I had done the unthinkable—

worse than stabbing him—I had stolen some of his power. I tried to force calm back into my heart.

I wouldn't let his lies steal the victories of this day.

I took a cleansing breath and poured water into the wash-basin, but then I froze, staring at the glistening surface. The pitcher slipped from my fingers, crashing to the floor. Blood swirled in the water, fingers of red spinning before my eyes, a tempest that carried the wails of battle, the slice of a sword across flesh, the dull thud of bodies falling to earth. And then, just as quickly, it was only water again, clear and tame.

I backed away, trying to breathe, stumbling blindly through the room.

My brothers' squads.

A painful gasp finally filled my lungs, and I searched for my clothes. My hands shook as I dressed, buckled belts, sheathed weapons, pulled on boots. My word was as true as Rafe's. I headed for the cell that held the Viceregent.

CHAPTER EIGHTY-ONE

RAFE

TAVISH TOLD ME SVEN HAD GONE TO SPEAK WITH CAPTAIN Azia about the rotation of soldiers guarding the prisoners. He hadn't been able to get a word out of Sven. He was still close-mouthed and steaming when he left. "But you know Sven. He always bellows about your half-assed decisions."

"You think I'm wrong too?"

Tavish shrugged on his vest, getting dressed for dinner. "I always think you're wrong. It usually works out. Don't worry, he'll come around." He pulled on his boots then paused when he had one half-way laced. "But I'd hold off telling him about your other decision. That might blow the top of his head off."

I nodded and poured myself some water.

Tavish grinned. "You know, if you die in this battle, you won't have to marry anyone."

I choked mid-sip, spilling water down my shirt. "Well, that's a bright thought. Thanks."

"I'm a tactician. Always thinking."

I dabbed a towel to my shirt. "Maybe you should look for another line of work."

His grin faded. "You'll be able to weather this out. We'll stand by you."

I had told Tavish of my decision not to marry the general's daughter. It wasn't for Lia's sake, or mine, but for the girl's. She didn't want to marry me anymore than I wanted to marry her. She was being forced into it the same way Lia had been. I had already made that fatal mistake once. I wasn't about to make it again, even if it cost me my throne. The girl deserved to choose her own future—not one contrived by the general to serve his needs.

"Did you tell Lia?" he asked.

"Why? So we can dredge up the same argument we had when we left Marabella? I can't go through that again. My decision won't change anything between us. If we survive all this, I will still return to Dalbreck and she will still—" I shook my head. "She won't go with me."

"How can you be certain?"

I thought about the fury in her eyes when she danced with me at the outpost, the bones she secretly slipped from the dining table into her pocket, the way she paced the dais at Piers Camp and then lifted her hand with Kaden's when she addressed the troops. "I know her. I'm certain."

"She's made other promises?"

"Yes."

He stood and clapped a hand on my shoulder. "I'm sorry, Jax. If I could change any of this for you, I would."

"I know."

He left to meet up with Jeb and Orrin. I changed my shirt, then headed out to find Sven, still chewing on his words. *He'll come around.* But this time felt different. Sven had exploded at me before, but never in front of outsiders. Maybe that was what rankled him. I'd made decisions that put my throne in jeopardy—the very position he'd spent a good portion of his life preparing me for—and I'd done it without consulting with him first.

I remembered back when I was saddling my horse and leaving on a blind quest to find a runaway princess. He hadn't been in favor of that either, but after hitting me with a barrage of questions, he stepped aside, letting me go. That was what Sven always did—he raised arguments until my resolve became steel. And when I was torn, he goaded me—*make your decision and live by it.* Even when I had been ready to tear the general's head from his shoulders, Sven made me reconsider. *Which do you want more, the satisfaction of ripping off his head, or to reach Lia as soon as possible? Because in this much he is right—no one can get a special team together for you as quickly as he can.* And it was true. Any delay, even by one day, and I wouldn't have reached Lia in time. It had been the right decision, and Sven had helped me reach it.

But with the decision to pull troops—there was no changing my mind. I hadn't needed his counsel. I knew what I had to do, not just for Lia, but for Dalbreck. I'd explain it to him. By now he had probably cooled off. He'd be sorry he had missed a meeting with the king.

Lia's father hadn't been what I expected. Now I knew where Lia had gotten her calculating straight face from. He'd made me squirm. I hadn't realized he'd been playing with me until he issued Lia's punishment. Somehow he knew there had been something between us. *There was still something between us.* Something I was trying to forget. It had been all I could do to tear my hand away from her arm when I'd stumbled into her. I had been careful in my movements when I was around her, conscious in a way that had become tiring. It was like I was standing on a log in a wrestling match again. One misstep, and I would be up to my waist in mud. When we were busy with tasks that needed to be addressed, it was easier—we simply worked together—but in those unplanned moments like when I stumbled into her, everything was unsettled, teetering, and I had to renavigate the space between us, remembering not to do what had been so natural before.

"Sentry," I called, when I reached the east wing, where the prisoners were held. "Colonel Haverstrom passed this way?"

"Yes. Some time ago, Your Majesty. He's still down there," he said, nodding toward the stairs at the end of the hall.

No doubt he was chewing off the captain's ear now, instead of mine. I would owe Azia.

I entered the passage, and the stairs were dark. Night had crept up quickly, and the guards had failed to light the lanterns. Only the flickering torches from the lowest level provided any light at all. Just a few steps down, I sensed a pervading quiet, a silence that seemed too deep. There were no murmurs, no clatter of metal trays or plates, though it was the dinner hour. My hand went to my sword, and when I turned at the landing, a body lay facedown, sprawled at the bottom of the stairs. It was Sven.

I drew my sword and ran.

I rolled him over, and that's when I saw another body, and another. A soldier. A servant with trays of food spilled around him. Their eyes were open, unseeing. The cell doors were all ajar. My blood raced, trying to attend to Sven and look for danger at the same time.

"Sven!" I whispered. His abdomen was soaked in blood.

"Guards!" I bellowed up the stairwell. "Sentry!"

I turned back to Sven. His breaths were shallow, his lips barely moving, as if he was trying to speak. I heard a noise and spun. Another body lay in the other direction. Azia. I crept down the hall toward him, my sword raised, and bent to feel his neck. Dead. It was the trickle of his blood into a drain that I'd heard.

I peered into the first cell. The court physician lay in the center of the room, his throat cut wide open. The next cell had another dead soldier. The rest were empty.

Guards trampled down the stairs, Lia right behind them. "They've escaped!" I yelled. "Call a physician! Sven is still alive!"

But barely. I pressed on the wound. "Come on, you old curd! Stay with us!"

"Close the city gates!" Lia shouted. "Alert the guard and camp!"

She dropped to my side and helped me press on the wound,

but it seemed there was no way to stop it. Blood oozed through our fingers. Kaden ran down the stairs, taking in the grisly scene. He pushed past us, his sword drawn.

"They're gone," I said. "I should have let you kill the bastard when you had the chance."

I pulled off my jacket and used it to help stop the bleeding. Lia's and my hands were both soaked with blood.

"Stay with him until the physician comes," I told her. "Don't let him go!"

And I ran up the stairs to hunt down the animals who had done this.

CHAPTER EIGHTY-TWO

EVERY CORNER, EVERY TUNNEL, EVERY PASSAGE, EVERY LEDGE and chamber in the citadelle was searched. Rafe, Kaden, and I—along with hundreds of soldiers—were up all night, scouring the city, door to door, sewer to sewer, rooftop to rooftop. Civica was locked down, even as it came alive with torches. The search went past city gates into the surrounding hamlets. Not a single clue or missing horse was found. They had vanished. Trackers were dispatched.

The prisoners' empty cells turned up piles of dirt and empty wooden boxes—weapons that had been buried long ago, a backup escape plan in the event they were ever found out. Now I understood why they had risked dragging me in the open all the way to the armory instead of imprisoning me here. They feared I would sense their secret stash. Even with the weapons stowed, they had bided their time, waiting for the right moment. For turning on the Viceregent, the court physician had paid the ultimate price.

Kaden, Pauline, and I waited outside Sven's chambers. Rafe was inside with the physician. The day had raced away from us and night was closing in again. None of us had slept more than a few hours this afternoon.

"I should have killed him," Kaden said, shaking his head. "I should have done it when I had the chance."

But the blame lay with me. I'd stayed the execution, thinking one of them might break, one might turn like the physician had and give us information that might be useful. And if the Viceregent feared a painful death, he might break himself and tell me something that would help my brothers. I had played the Komizar's game, trying to find the best use for prisoners under my thumb. But I had lost.

Now four men were dead, Sven was fighting for his life, and the traitors were free, probably on their way to join the Komizar and tell him I was ruling Morrighan now.

Berdi and Gwyneth had taken over arranging for a proper Dalbretch funeral for the dead soldiers, including Captain Azia. We had little experience with funeral pyres, but I wanted to make sure they received the proper tributes.

"If they're running to meet up with the Komizar, he'll make them fight," Kaden said. "No one riding with him gets a pass."

"The Watch Captain hasn't lifted a weapon in years," I said. "But the Viceregent and Chancellor . . ." A sigh hissed through my teeth. Sword practice was a daily part of their routines. They claimed it was only a simple way to remain fit. They were both skilled. But what were two more soldiers among thousands?

Pauline's lip lifted in disgust. "I'm betting the cowards will crawl into a hole and wait for the danger of battle to pass."

I rubbed my temple. My head ached. The blood, the bodies, Rafe's face; it all replayed through my mind over and over again. The broken catch in Rafe's throat as he worked to save Sven. *Come on, you old curd!*

The door to Sven's chamber opened, and Tavish stepped out. We all looked at him anxiously. "How is he?" I asked.

Tavish shrugged, his face drawn and weary. "Hanging on."

"And Rafe?"

"Hanging on too. You can go in."

RAFE SAT IN A CHAIR NEAR SVEN'S BED, STARING AT HIM, HIS empty gaze tearing at my heart. I knew their last conversation together had been contentious, with Sven storming out of the room. What if that was how it ended? What if, after all they had shared, that was their final moment together? I stared at Rafe, a shell of who he had been only hours earlier. He had already lost both of his parents in just a few short months. How much could one person lose?

I wanted him to weep, or be angry, or react in some way. He barely shook his head when I asked if I could get him something.

Gwyneth and Berdi joined us later. In those tired moments, I thought I could love neither one more. Gwyneth poured water, shoving it into Rafe's hand, and she joked with Sven, talking to him as if he was listening. Maybe he was. Jeb and Orrin trudged in later, their lids heavy with exhaustion, but none of us wanted to be in our own rooms tonight. It was a vigil, as if all of our heavy hearts were anchors that could pin Sven to this room. Kaden sat in the corner, silent, carrying guilt he didn't deserve. Gwyneth and Berdi brought in food, fluffed pillows, wiped Sven's brow. Gwyneth chided Sven, telling him he'd better perk up soon, because she couldn't take much more of these stony faces, then eyed all of us, trying to prod us out of our gloom. She kissed his cheek. "That one's on the house," she said. "The next one will cost you."

When I encouraged Rafe to eat something, he nodded, but still ate nothing. *Please*, I prayed to the gods, *please, let them have a few last words. Don't leave Rafe with only this.*

Gwyneth walked over and sat on the side of Rafe's chair, slinging her arm around his shoulder. "You may not be able to hear him, but he can hear you. That's the way these things work. You should talk to him. Say what you need to say. That's what he's waiting for." Tears filled her eyes. "You understand? We're all going to leave now, so you two can talk alone."

Rafe nodded.

We all left the room.

I went to check on him an hour later.

Rafe sat on the floor asleep, his head tilted back against the side of Sven's bed. Sven was still unconscious, but I noticed his hand lay limp on Rafe's shoulder as if it had slipped from the bedcovers. Or maybe Rafe had placed it there.

CHAPTER EIGHTY-THREE

I WATCHED FROM THE UPPER GALLERY, HIDDEN FROM VIEW because I couldn't bear for my mother to see me, to catch my eye. To know that I knew too. She and my aunts played their zitaraes, the haunting music plucking at my ribs, my mother's wordless song a mourning dirge drifting, skimming, seeping into every cold vein of the citadelle. It was a song as old as Venda's, as old as evening mist and faraway valleys soaked in blood, a refrain as old as the earth itself.

I hadn't forgotten my vision, the swirl of blood, the cry of battle, the whir of an arrow. More death lurked. I saw it in the deadness of my mother's eyes. She'd had the same vision as mine. *My brothers' squads.* I leaned against the pillar. The citadelle already overflowed with grief, the funeral pyres just behind us yesterday.

In two days we would leave for Sentinel Valley. *Nurse the rage.* I tried to with a blinding zeal, but the sorrow crept back in.

The Dragon will conspire,
Wielding might like a god, unstoppable.

Unstoppable.

How much more was there still to lose?

The truth sank in, the gluttony, the grip, the reach. The Komizar was winning.

Heavy footsteps sounded in the hall, and I turned to see Rafe finally returning from Piers Camp. Yesterday he'd gone straight there after the funeral pyres had burned out, his eyes fierce again, attending to preparations with vengeance. He'd been there all day today too. I'd only just gotten back myself. It was late. Dinner would be waiting in my room. But when I heard the zitaraes—

I looked back at my mother. This was another reason she hadn't nurtured my gift. Truth had sharp edges that could gut us whole.

The footsteps paused at the gallery. I was tucked in the shadow of the pillars but Rafe had spotted me anyway. He walked over, his stride slow, tired, and he stopped at my side, looking down into the hall below us. "What's wrong?"

I looked at him uncertainly, not sure what he meant.

"I haven't seen you idle since we got here," he explained. His voice held a weariness I had never heard.

I didn't want to explain my fears about my brothers. Not now, when Sven barely clung to life. The physician hadn't given much hope for his recovery. Whatever last words Rafe had whispered to Sven, he had to trust Gwyneth's claim that Sven had heard them.

"Just taking a moment," I said, trying to keep my voice even.

He nodded, then updated me on troops, weapons, wagons, all the things I had already checked on, but this was the language between us now. We had changed. The world was beating us down into something we had never been before, molding us day by day into two people who had no room for each other.

I watched him, the smoothness of his brow, the stubble of his cheek, watched his lips moving, and I pretended he wasn't talking about supplies. He was talking about Terravin. He was laughing about melons and promising to grow one for me. He was licking his thumb and smudging the dirt on my chin. He was telling me that some things last, the things that matter. And when he said *we'll find a way*, he wasn't talking about battles, he was talking about us.

He finished with his updates and rubbed his eyes, and we were back to our world as it really was. I saw the numbing grief that gripped him and felt the hollowness it left behind. *Regroup. Move forward.* And we did, because there was nothing else to do. He said he was going to bed. "You should do the same."

I nodded, and we walked down the hall to our rooms, the walls of the citadelle closing in, my chest squeezing with the pluck of the zitaraes and what I knew tomorrow could bring.

We reached my door, and the emptiness twisted tighter. I wanted only to bury my face in my bed and block the world out. I turned to him to say good night, but instead my eyes became locked on his and words I hadn't even allowed myself to think were suddenly there, despairing and raw.

"So much has been stolen. Have you ever wished we could steal some of it back? Just one night? Just for a few hours?"

He looked at me, a crease deepening between his brows.

"I know you don't plan to marry," I blurted out. "Tavish told me." My eyes stung. It was too late to hold the rest back. "I don't want to be alone tonight Rafe."

His lips parted, his eyes glassy. A storm raged behind them.

I knew I had made a terrible mistake. "I shouldn't have—"

He stepped closer, his hands slamming against the door behind me, caging me between his arms; his face, his lips inches from mine, and all I could see, all I could feel, was Rafe, his eyes broken, glistening, and the strain behind them.

He leaned closer, his breaths labored and hot against my cheek. "There isn't a day that goes by when I don't wish I could steal back a few hours," he whispered. "When I don't wish I could steal back the taste of your mouth on mine, the feel of your hair twisted between my fingers, the feel of your body pressed to mine. When I don't wish I could see you laughing and smiling like when we were back in Terravin."

His hand slid behind me and pulled my hips to his, his voice husky, his lips brushing my earlobe. "A day never passes when I don't wish I could steal back an hour in the watchtower again, when I was kissing you and holding you and"—his breath shuddered against my ear—"and I was wishing tomorrow would never come. When I still believed that kingdoms couldn't come between us." He swallowed. "When I wished you had never heard of Venda."

He leaned back, the misery in his eyes cutting through me. "But they're only wishes Lia, because you've made promises and so have I. Tomorrow will come, and tomorrow will matter, to your kingdom and to mine. So please, don't ask me again if I wish for something, because I don't want to be reminded that every day I wish for something I cannot have."

We stared at each other.

The air prickled hot between us.

I didn't breathe.

He didn't move.

We made promises to each other too, I wanted to say, but instead I only whispered, "I'm sorry, Rafe. We should say good night and forget—"

And then his lips were on mine, his mouth hungry, my back pressed to the door, his hand reaching behind me to open it, and we stumbled back into the room, the world disappearing behind us. He lifted me up in his arms, his gaze filling every empty space inside me, and then I slid through his hands, my mouth meeting his again. Our kisses were desperate, consuming, all that mattered and all there was.

My feet touched the ground, and then so did our belts, weapons, and vests falling in a trail across the floor. We stopped, faced each other, fear beating between us, fear that none of this was real, that even these precious few hours would be ripped away. The world flickered, pulling us into protective darkness, and I was in his arms again, our palms damp, searching, no lies, no kingdoms, nothing between us but our skin, his voice warm, fluid, like a golden sun unfolding every tight thing within me, *I love you, I will love you forever, no matter what happens.* Rafe needing me as much as I needed him, his lips silky, sliding down my neck, my chest, my skin shivering and burning at once. There were no questions, no pauses, no room left for anything more to be stolen. There was only us, and everything we had ever been to each other, the days and weeks when only we mattered, our fingers lacing together, holding, fierce, his gaze penetrating mine, and then fear and desperation faded, our movement slowed, and we memorized, lingered, touched, swallowing tears that still swelled in us, the reality setting in—we had only a few hours. He hovered over me, the flame of the fire lighting his eyes, the world stretching thin, disappearing, his tongue sweet and slow and gentle on mine, and then more urgent, pressing, hungry, the moment becoming the promise of a lifetime, a feverish need and rhythm pulsing between us, our skin moist and searing, and then the shudder of his breath in my ear, and finally, my name on his lips. *Lia.*

WE LAY IN THE DARKNESS, MY CHEEK ON HIS CHEST. I FELT his heartbeat, his breaths, his worries, his warmth. His fingers absently grazed lines down my arm. We talked like we used to, not about lists and supplies but what weighed on our hearts. He told me about the betrothal and why he couldn't go through with it. It wasn't just that he didn't love her. He already knew what I had been through. He promised himself he wouldn't do that to someone again. He remembered what I had said about choice, and he knew she deserved that too.

"Maybe she wants to marry you?"

"She's only fourteen and doesn't even know me," he said. "I saw her trembling and afraid, but I was desperate to get here to you so I signed the papers."

"Sven said breaking the betrothal could cost you your throne."

"It's a risk I'll have to take."

"But if you explain the circumstances, what the general did—"

"I'm not a child, Lia. I knew what I was signing. People sign contracts every day to get what they want. I got what I wanted. If I don't fulfill my end, I'll look like a liar to a kingdom that's already deeply troubled."

He was facing an impossible choice. If he did marry her, he could ruin the future of a girl who deserved one. If he didn't, he could lose the confidence of a kingdom he loved and push it into further turmoil.

I asked him about Dalbreck and what it had been like there when he returned. He told me about his father's funeral, the obstacles and problems, and I heard the concern in his tone, but as he described it, I also heard his strength, his deep love for his kingdom, his yearning to return. *Leading is in his blood.* It made the risks he had taken for me and Morrighan all the greater. The ache in my heart surged. A farmer, a prince, a king. I loved him. I loved all that he ever was, and all that he would be—even if it was to be without me.

I rolled over, hovering over him this time, and I lowered my lips to his.

WE SLEPT AND WOKE THROUGHOUT THE NIGHT, ANOTHER kiss, another whisper, but finally dawn and the world crept back in. Raspberry light glowed around the drapes signaling that our lifetime was up. I lay curled in the crook of his arms and his fingers strummed my back, lightly touching my kavah. *Our kavah,* I wanted to say, but I knew the last thing he wanted was to be drawn into Venda's prophecy, though it was already too late for that.

We dressed without speaking.

We were leaders of kingdoms again, the sound of boots and buckles and duty hanging in the air around us. Our few hours were gone, and there were no more to spare. He would begin his day by checking on Sven, and I would leave to inform the Timekeeper of my duties so he could find me as the need arose, because I'd forbidden him to follow on my heels.

When my last lace was tied, I broke our silence. "There's something I still have to tell you, Rafe, something I've already told my father. When we get to the valley and meet the Komizar's army, I'm going to offer a peace settlement."

His nostrils flared, and his jaw turned rigid. He bent to pick up his baldrick from the floor as if he didn't hear me. He slipped it over his head, adjusting the buckle, his movement punctuated with anger.

"I plan to offer the Vendans the right to settle in the Cam Lanteux, a chance for a better—"

He slammed his sword into his scabbard. "We are not going to offer the Komizar anything!" he lashed out. "Do you hear me, Lia? If he were on fire, I wouldn't so much as piss on him to douse the flames! He gets nothing!"

I reached out to touch his arm, but he pulled away. I knew he was still reeling from the loss of Captain Azia and his men. "Not an offer to the Komizar," I said. "I know he'll settle for nothing less than our slaughter. The offer is to the Vendan people, Rafe. Remember, they are not the Komizar."

His chest heaved. "Lia, you're fighting an army, the Council, the thousands who are behind him and want the same things he does. They're not going to listen to any peace settlement from you."

I thought about those who supported the Komizar. The *chievdars*. The governors who drooled over bounty and wanted far more. The quarterlords, who breathed power like it was air. The soldiers who massacred my brother and his company, then sneered at me as I buried them, and the hundreds more like them, those who reveled in destruction. Rafe was right. Like the Komizar, they would not listen.

But I had to believe there were others who would—the clans pressed into service, and others who cowered and followed the Komizar because they had no other options. The thousands who were desperate for any kind of hope. They were the ones I had to take a chance on.

"Before the battle begins, I am going to make the offer, Rafe."

"Did your father agree to this?"

"It doesn't matter. I am regent."

"The Lesser Kingdoms will never agree to it."

"They will if Dalbreck leads the way. If we lose, it's going to happen anyway. And if we win—it still has to happen. It's the only way for us to move forward. Everyone needs hope, Rafe. I have to give it to them. It's the right thing to do."

He argued that there was no time to offer a settlement and the battlefield was not a place to negotiate one. There were tens of thousands in an army that would stretch for miles—I couldn't speak to them all, and the Komizar wouldn't listen. The moments before battle were charged with uncertainty.

"I know. But I'll find a way. I'm just asking you to help me. Without Dalbeck in agreement, I will only be offering them false hope."

He sighed and raked his fingers through his hair. "I don't know if I can make that promise, Lia. You're asking me to break a treaty that's centuries old." He stepped closer, his anger receding. He brushed a wisp of hair from my cheek. "I know what else you plan on doing. I'm asking you one last time. Don't. Please. For your sake."

"We've already discussed this, Rafe. It has to be someone."

His eyes sparked again, resisting—it wasn't what he wanted to hear—but then our attention was drawn to an urgent knock at the door.

It was Aunt Bernette, breathless and holding her side. "Dalbreck troops!" she gasped. "They've been spotted! An hour out of Civica."

My heart caught in my throat. "And the squads?" I asked.

Her eyes glistened with worry. "We don't know."

RAFE, TAVISH, AND I, AND A DOZEN SOLDIERS RODE OUT TO where the troops were marching toward Civica. We saw a brigade of maybe five hundred. Not the six thousand Rafe had requested.

"The rest may be farther back," Tavish commented. Rafe said nothing.

When they spotted us riding toward them, the caravan halted. Rafe hailed the colonel and asked where the rest of the troops were. The colonel explained that General Draeger had already recalled them to Dalbreck before the colonel got Rafe's message. I saw the heat glowing in Rafe's eyes, but he moved on to the subject that at the moment, was more pressing—the princes and their squads.

"They're here, Your Majesty, riding in the middle," he said, nodding over his shoulder. "I'm afraid there were losses. We didn't—"

My heels dug in, and my horse and I flew toward the middle of the caravan. When the Dalbretch blue gave way to Morrighese red, I jumped from my horse, looking for Bryn and Regan and calling their names.

I spotted five horses with large bundles tied up in blankets draped over their saddles. Bodies. My throat closed.

A hand touched my shoulder.

I whirled and faced a man I didn't recognize, but who seemed to know me. "They're alive, Your Highness. This way."

He walked me back in the caravan. He identified himself as a surgeon and then described my brothers' injuries. The brunt of the attack had been directed at them. "Their men fought val-iantly, but as you can see, some lost their lives."

"The attackers?"

"Dead, but it would have been the other way around for the whole Morrighese squad if the king hadn't sent a message."

We reached the wagon, and the surgeon hung back, letting me meet with my brothers alone. My temples pounded. They both lay on bedrolls, their ashen pallor lit with a greasy sheen, but when Regan saw me, his eyes brightened.

"Sister," he said, and tried to sit up, then grimaced and fell back. I crawled up into the wagon beside them and held their hands to my cheeks. My tears ran through their fingers. *They're alive. Bryn, Regan.* I whispered their names aloud as if to convince myself they were really here. Regan's eyes were wet with tears too, but Bryn's remained closed, a sleeping elixir keeping him in a dream world.

"We knew it was a lie," Regan said. "We just didn't know how deep it ran."

"None of us did," I said.

"Before we left, Father whispered to me, *find her.* He wanted you back too. Is he still alive?"

"Yes," I answered. I'd already told them about the Vice-regent in the message I sent, but now I told him what had tran-spired these past weeks, and our plan to meet the Komizar in Sentinel Valley. And then, though it hurt to relive it, I told him the truth of Walther's death.

"Did he suffer?" he asked, his eyes sunken and expression grim.

I wasn't sure how to answer him and the memory of Walther raging forward into battle surfaced again. "He was mad with grief, Regan. He suffered from the moment Greta died in his arms. But on the field he died quickly—he was a warrior prince, brave and strong, but greatly outnumbered."

"As we are now."

"Yes," I admitted, "as we are now." I couldn't sugarcoat the truth for him, even with his weakened state.

"Hold off a few days before you leave," he said. "And then I can ride with you."

I heard the hunger in his voice, his desire to avenge his brothers and ride at his sister's side. It burned in him. I understood his need, but I sighed. "You have a gash in your side, Regan, that required twenty-seven stitches to close. If it were the other way around, would you take me along?"

His head rolled back. He knew he wouldn't be able to ride in a few days or even a few weeks. "Damn surgeons. They love to count."

"You need to stay here. Bryn will need you when he wakes."

I looked at Bryn, peaceful in his drugged dream world. My sweet young brother looked more like an angel than a soldier. "Does he know what happened?" I asked.

Regan shook his head. "I don't think so. He was screaming and delirious. He hasn't woken since."

I looked down at Bryn's leg, half of it gone.

"If I'm not here when he wakes, tell him I will make sure they pay. For every life and pound of flesh they have taken. They will pay twofold."

CHAPTER EIGHTY-FOUR

TAVISH, JEB, AND ORRIN WERE DIRECTING TROOPS TO THEIR places in the caravan. We were leaving in three waves. Gwyneth, Pauline, and Berdi walked with lists, checking supply wagons, making sure they were evenly dispersed among the contingents.

I was about to go speak with another regiment that had arrived the night before when Pauline called me over, ostensibly to check on a wagon. I knew something else was on her mind.

"The jacket you ordered is ready," she said. "I put it in your room." She kept her voice low, glancing over her shoulder. I had asked her to be discreet. "The dressmaker was not happy. She didn't understand why you wanted scraps when she had perfectly good fabric available."

"But she did as I asked?"

Pauline nodded. "Yes, and she incorporated the sewn red scraps you gave me."

"And the shoulder?"

"That too." Her expression turned worried. "But you know what everyone else will think."

"I can't worry about what others will think. I need to be recognized. What about the tether?"

She reached into her pocket and handed me a long slitted strip of leather. I already had the bones for it. I had been saving them.

"I also need to talk to you about Natiya," she said. "She thinks she's coming with us."

I rubbed my forehead, not wanting to get into another match of wills with Natiya, fearing she would follow behind anyway. "She can come," I said. "She speaks Vendan. I'll have a task for her." I saw the concern in Pauline's eyes. "I'll do my best to keep her safe," I said, though my best hadn't been good enough yet. I was telling her my plans for Natiya when a loud voice boomed behind us.

"Well, if it isn't the smart-mouthed tavern maid and her pretty friend! Looks like I got here at just the right time. They have you servicing the soldiers now?"

I whirled to see a soldier—a familiar one. It took me a few seconds to place him, but then I remembered. His swagger and arrogant smile hadn't changed. He was the soldier from the tavern I had soaked with ale and then had threatened with a knife at the festival. It was obvious he hadn't forgotten me.

"You claimed that you'd be the one surprising me next time

we met," he said, drawing closer. "I guess it didn't work out that way."

I stepped forward to meet him. "You just arrived last night, soldier?"

"That's right," he said.

"And you're not familiar with my role here?"

"Easy enough to see what you're good for. And you promised that when we met again that we'd settle things between us once and for all."

I smiled. "Yes, I did say that, didn't I? And I must admit, you did take me by surprise. Good for you, soldier. But I might have a surprise for you."

He reached out and grabbed my wrist. "You're not pulling any knives on me this time."

I looked at his fingers gripping my wrist and then back at his leering face. "Oh, I would never do that," I said sweetly. "Why pull a knife when I have a whole army at my disposal?"

And before he could blink, Natiya, Pauline, Gwyneth, and Berdi were pressing swords to his back.

Kaden and Rafe stood a few feet away, taking note of the sudden activity. Their arms folded across their chests.

"Think we should help them?" Kaden asked.

Rafe shook his head. "Nah. I think they have it covered."

The soldier froze, knowing the feel of steel on his spine.

I smiled at him again. "Well, look at that. I guess I managed to surprise you after all."

He released my wrist, not sure what had just happened.

My smile vanished. "Now, go join your ranks, soldier, and

wait for me to address your company. This will be my very last warning for you to behave as an honorable member of the king's army. The next time I will be cutting you from your position like a rotten dimple on an apple."

"You're the one who's addressing the—"

"Yes."

He seemed to notice Walther's baldrick across my chest for the first time—along with its royal crest.

"You're the—"

"Yes."

He paled, blustering with apologies and began to drop to one knee, "Your Highness—"

I stopped him, pushing him to his feet again by the tip of my sword. "It shouldn't matter if I am a tavern maid or a princess. When I see you treating others with respect without regard to their station—or anatomy—then your apology will mean something."

I turned and walked away as he still blustered, weary that this was a battle I had to fight over and over again.

<hr />

THE TREK TO SENTINEL VALLEY TOOK TWO WEEKS. TWO very long weeks with rain, hail, and wind dampening spirits and hampering every mile. We began with fifteen thousand soldiers and picked up additional troops along the way. By the time we camped just outside of the mouth of the valley, we numbered twenty-eight thousand. It was nearly every soldier we had in Morrighan. I'd never seen so many in one place. I couldn't see the end of our encampment. Our supplies were abundant. Food. Weapons. Raw supplies of lumber to build barricades and defenses. Tents to protect against the weather as our final plans were laid in place. A vast impressive city. But it was still dwarfed by what the Komizar had rolling our way.

All of these troops were here on my orders, based on something I felt in my gut. The generals had grumbled the entire way.

Rafe had sent Jeb and Orrin with a contingent of soldiers to intercept Dalbretch troops who might be coming and direct them to Sentinel Valley. *Might be coming.* The words weighed heavily on me. With Draeger recalling thousands of soldiers to Dalbreck, it seemed unlikely that we would get any assistance at all.

Tavish explained that the general had recalled the troops long before he got Rafe's message. "They may still come."

May. Might. My anxiety grew. Each day passed like a low beating drum vibrating through me, marking time. Rafe promised that the Marabella forces would show, but we'd had no sign of them either. It could be that Rafe had already lost his grip on his realm.

The weather at least had finally become agreeable. Rafe, Kaden, and I left alone to scout the valley. I didn't want to hear the grumbles of generals, the pounding of tent stakes, or the calls of soldiers. A quiet voice had drawn me here. I needed quiet as I explored it and listened for any more secrets it might hold for me.

The opening into the valley was narrow, just as Reunaud had described it.

We rode in and dismounted. I sensed it immediately. Even Rafe and Kaden felt it. I saw it in their faces, and in the reverence of their steps. The air held the presence of something timeless, something that could be either crushing or liberating. Something that didn't care about us, only what was coming. It knew. We looked at the tall green cliffs and the ruins that towered over us. The weight of the centuries pressed in.

We walked together for a time. Rafe looking up at the cliffs, first at one side, then the other, Kaden turning, imagining, studying.

The grass of the valley brushed the tops of our boots.

I looked around in wonder. So this was the last valley Morrighan had led the Remnant through before they reached their new beginning.

"I'm going up top to see what's there," Rafe said, pointing at the ruins that looked down on us.

"I'll check out the other side," Kaden said, and both left on their horses, searching for trails that led to the summits. I walked ahead, deeper into the valley, listening to the quiet, the breeze, and then a whisper shivered through the grass, rushing toward me, its cool fingers brushing my face, my hands.

It circled my throat, lifted my hair.

This world breathes you in . . . shares you.

The wind, time, it circles, repeats. . . .

I felt the breath that was held, and then the slow exhale. I kept walking. The valley grew wider, little by little, like welcoming arms opening up to whatever lay at the other end. I studied the low hills, the rocky crags, the outcrops of boulders, the soft grassy ridges, the face of a valley that studied me too, its eyes turning, its heart beating. *Why are you here?* My gaze traveled to the valley's crown—the ruins. I heard Gaudrel speak, as if she walked by my side.

> *In an age before monsters and demons roamed the earth . . .*
> *There were cities, large and beautiful, with sparkling towers that touched the sky . . .*
> *They were spun of magic and light and the dreams of gods . . .*

I felt those dreams now, hovering, waiting, hoping, as if their world could be wakened again. *The universe has a long memory.* I kept walking and as Captain Reunaud had said, the ruins watched me as I passed. Ten miles of immense valley. Ten miles of towering wreckage. Breathtaking. Powerful. Frightening.

Rafe's warning hummed in my ears.

Their army will stretch for miles. You can't speak to them all.

I kept walking.

I would find a way.

Some of the ruins had tumbled to the valley floor. I passed giant blocks of stone taller than a man, now covered with moss and vine, the earth still trying to erase the fury of a star. Or was it many stars? What had truly happened? Would we ever really know?

But I knew the power and greatness of the Ancients had been unlocked by the Komizar. He would use it against us in a matter of days. We had little chance even with Rafe's troops. Without them, we had none. My heart beat faster. Had I brought everyone here to die in a distant forgotten valley? The cries of the Ancients whistled past on the wind, and the Holy Text whispered back to me.

> *A terrible greatness*
> *Rolled across the land . . .*
> *Devouring man and beast,*
> *Field and flower.*

Time circles. Repeats. Ready to tell the story again. And again.

The drum beat louder. The days were slipping by, and the Komizar was getting closer. *Keep going,* I told myself. *Keep walking.*

The scent of the crushed grass beneath my boots wafted up to meet me. I thought of Dihara and another meadow. It was a lifetime ago, but I saw her again. She spun at her wheel. Her head angled to the side.

> *So you think you have the gift.*
> *Who told you that?*
> *The stories . . . they travel.*

Her wheel turned, *whirred.* The valley waited, watched, its heartbeat a murmur on the breeze.

The truth was here. Somewhere. I walked on.

The pluck of a string.

And another.

Music. I spun, looking back from where I had come. The valley was empty, but I heard the mournful strum of the zitaraes, my mother's song floating, and then when I looked back to where I'd been heading, I saw something else.

All ways belong to the world. What is magic but what we don't yet understand?

A girl knelt on the rim of a wide bluff above me.

There.

The word fluttered in my belly, familiar. A word that had pushed and prodded me toward the maps, and then this valley.

Her eyes met mine.

"It was you," I whispered.

She nodded but said nothing.

She kissed her fingers, and I heard the Holy Text braiding with the air.

And Morrighan raised her voice,
To the heavens,
Kissing two fingers,
One for the lost,
And one for those yet to come,
For the winnowing was not over.

The song that had filled the valley only seconds ago, was now hers, winding, lengthening, beckoning. I stumbled up the steep trail to the bluff, but by the time I got to where she had knelt, she was gone. The bluff jutted out, and the long valley was in my view in both directions, as still and silent as ever—except for her voice. I dropped to the ground, kneeling, feeling the warmth of where she had been, feeling her desperation from centuries ago. Feeling it now. *The winnowing was not over.*

Time circles. Repeats.

And the desperate prayers she had lifted to the gods so long ago became my own.

"LIA," RAFE CALLED, "WHAT ARE YOU DOING UP THERE?"

I turned to see Rafe and Kaden on their horses. They'd brought my horse along too. I got back to my feet and took one last look at the bluff, the hills, and the ruins that towered over me.

"Preparing," I answered, and I walked down the trail to meet them.

When we got back to camp, we sent scouts riding the swiftest horses to lookouts past the valley's eastern mouth to watch for the approaching army. The rest of us began our work in earnest. Rafe and Kaden had mapped out the terrain and trails that could support charging brigades of soldiers. There were seven on one side of the hills and four on the other. Ruins would hide them from view until we were ready. The entrance to the valley was three miles wide, but it quickly narrowed. The Field Marshal, Howland, Marques, and the other officers would lead the charges when signaled. Our timing had to be perfect.

One division—mine—would be held out as bait and decoy. Our drumbeats and our battle chants would draw them toward us.

The high grass of the valley would help hide some of our defenses. Deadly rows of pikes were constructed and hidden. Nets were positioned for launch. Seige crossbows were strategically placed, though that was the greatest unknown—where and when the brezalots would be used—but I was sure his Death Steeds and his child soldiers would be his first line of attack. The Komizar would see my few thousand troops blocking his path at the end of the valley and assume the rest of my army lay behind me. Sending in his charging animals would clear the path quickly.

We worked without stopping And waited. Waited for the Komizar. Waited for Rafe's troops. Neither came, and nerves grew raw. I said remembrances morning and night. I spoke to the troops, bolstered them, made promises to them and to myself.

Berdi, Pauline, and Gwyneth worked with the camp cooks to keep everyone fed and spirits up—at which they excelled. I pulled Natiya aside privately and walked with her into the valley. "Look there," I said, pointing into the valley. "What do you see?"

"I see a battleground."

I looked into the same valley but I saw a purple *carvachi* and ribbons twirling in the wind. I saw Dihara spinning at her wheel and Venda singing from a wall. I saw Morrighan praying from a bluff and Aster sitting wide-eyed in a tent listening to a story. A greater story. I saw a world past that didn't want us to give up. I looked back at Natiya. I didn't want her to give up on the world she had known either.

"One day you'll pass through here again, and you will see more," I promised. "Until then, I have a job for you. It's more important than anything else we will do, and for it, you will not need a sword."

CHAPTER EIGHTY-FIVE

KADEN

WE SAT IN THE TENT, TIRED, ACHING, BUT STILL PLANNING. Lia rubbed her eyes. Rafe rubbed his knuckles. The Field Marshal sat forward with his chin cradled in his hands. Tomorrow the brigades would be put into place. We had been holding off, hoping Dalbreck's troops would arrive, but we couldn't wait any longer. What little we had needed to be positioned. Our divisions would be outnumbered more than four to one.

With no sign of the Komizar or Dalbreck, Perry suggested we might want to consider retreating to Civica. To Howland's credit, as much as he grumbled and complained, he backed Lia up, saying this was no time for retreat. We had a miserable chance of victory here and none back in Civica.

I saw the weight of it in Lia's eyes. I felt the worry twist in my own gut, and I didn't like that Pauline was here. She had a baby back at the citadelle. *That is exactly why I am here*, she had told me.

Gwyneth breezed in with a frown and a frustrated hand on her hip. "There's a big ugly brute out there demanding to see Lia."

"A soldier?" I asked.

She shrugged. "He's outfitted to kill something. Something big."

"He'll have to wait," Lia said.

"That's what I told him, but he's not giving up. He keeps yammering for Queen Jezelia."

Howland's brows shot up. "Queen Jezelia?"

"That's right," she answered, "and he's got a frightening little ruffian with him. I wouldn't—"

I watched Lia's face brighten.

At the same time, Rafe's darkened.

"Queen?" Howland said again.

Lia jumped from her seat and flew from the tent.

I followed her.

She was already hugging and kissing them both. Neither Griz nor Eben resisted.

I walked over and greeted them. "About time," I said. "What took you so long?"

"Stubborn physician," Griz grumbled.

"He got lost," Eben explained.

Griz cuffed him on the back of the head, then grinned sheepishly. "He might be right."

"*Drazhones*," I said, and embraced them both too, clapping their backs.

I stepped back, and Lia pelted them with questions. They were only two more soldiers but to have them by her side meant everything to her.

A small crowd milled around, their curiosity piqued by the commotion—and probably the sight of a scarred giant like Griz and his well-armed sidekick.

Pauline walked over and stood beside me, eyeing them with interest. "Are they the soldiers I saw you with back in Terravin?" she asked.

"Yes, but they're more than just soldiers. They're family too," I said. "My family. Blood kin of another kind."

She brushed up close, her shoulder touching mine. "I want to meet them."

CHAPTER EIGHTY-SIX

RAFE

THE REST OF US FILED OUT OF THE TENT TOO.

They all watched Lia embracing Griz and then Eben. I saw the joy on her face. She spoke Vendan with them, reverting to it as naturally as if it were her own language.

I was glad to see them too, but not in the same way Lia was. Griz was a formidable foe. With every day that passed with no sign of my requested troops, I was reminded that we needed every soldier we could get.

"Why did he call her queen?" Howland asked.

I looked at Lia. She wore a jacket made in the Meurasi style, the red scraps of her wedding dress slashing over her shoulder and across the front. The kavah was exposed. Bones swung from her hip.

Everyone needs hope, Rafe. I have to give it to them.

"It's just a Vendan custom," Tavish told him. He looked at me and shrugged.

"Yes, only a custom," I agreed.

If Lia wanted to explain further, it was up to her.

I turned to go back in the tent, then stopped mid-step when I spotted Jeb walking toward me. Then Orrin. They both grinned and then I saw the general.

"Draeger," I said.

"That's right, Your Majesty. Your troops are here, as you ordered."

I studied him, still wary. "*All* of the troops?"

He nodded. "All. With a load of ballistas—and everything else you asked for."

THE CAMP WAS SILENT. DARK, EXCEPT FOR A FEW TORCHES lit between tents. Sleep would be difficult tonight. Tensions were high, but rest was ordered. Necessary. I walked to the valley entrance where the torchlight didn't reach. Only the moon weaving between fingers of clouds lit the meadow grass. Lia leaned against the rocky wall, staring into the valley.

"Company?" I asked.

She nodded.

We stood there, looking into the quiet. We had already said everything there was to say. Done everything we could do. Dalbreck's troops were in place. Our odds were better. Venda outnumbered us only two to one now. But they still had better weapons. Something deep inside me wanted to drag Lia away, keep her safe, but I knew I couldn't.

"We're as ready as we can be," I said.

She nodded again. "I know."

Her gaze traveled along the silhouette of ruins on the cliffs, their ghostly edges lined by silver moonlight.

"They were great once," she said. "They flew among the stars. Their voices boomed over the mountains. And this is all that's left. Will we ever truly know who they were, Rafe?" She turned toward me. "After tomorrow, will anyone know who we were?"

I looked at her, not caring who the Ancients were. All I could think was, *It doesn't matter how many universes come and go, I will always remember who we were together.*

I leaned down. Kissed her. Slowly. Gently. One last time.

She looked at me. She said nothing. She didn't need to.

THE MEADOW GRASS RIPPLED IN THE BREEZE. BY THE NEXT day, it would be trampled. Burned. Bloody. Our scouts had ridden in tonight. The Komizar's army would make it to the valley entrance by morning.

The crowned and beaten,
The tongue and sword,
Together they will attack,
Like blinding stars thrown from the heavens.

—Song of Venda

CHAPTER EIGHTY-SEVEN

⊰ LIA ⊱

NURSE THE RAGE.

My heart pounded wildly.

The army was a blur at the end of the valley. A solid rolling wave. Condensing. Rising. Solidifying as the valley narrowed.

Their pace was leisurely. Unworried.

They had no need for worry. I'd already seen them approaching from the cliffs at the entrance to the valley before I rode back to take my position. I had seen how far they stretched, how unstoppable they were. Even the trail they left behind them was staggering, like the dust of a star shooting across the sky. It reached back for miles. They marched in ten divisions, infantry at the lead, followed by what looked like supplies, artillery, and herds of brezalots. More infantry followed, and then a fifth divison of soldiers on horseback. There was a heaviness to this division, something thick and weighty and more foreboding than the rest. There was no doubt in my mind that was where he rode, in the middle, within quick reach of all divisions, keeping a close watch on his creation, sucking in its power and breathing it out again like fire.

The army's slow pace wore on nerves—just as he'd calculated.

A squad of their scouts had spotted us, then raced back to their front lines, probably reporting our pathetic numbers. Five thousand of us defended the exit of the valley—five thousand that they could see. More were ready to stream in behind us. The Vendan pace continued syrup slow, unflustered. We were merely a stone in the trail to be trampled underfoot. Even if the whole Morrighese army blocked the exit, the Komizar wasn't worried. If anything, we only whet his appetite. At last he was getting the first course of the feast he had anticipated for so long.

Morrighan.

I heard the name of the kingdom on his lips. Amused. Sticky and cloying like a jelly drop in his mouth. He swallowed it down like a treat.

If rage pulsed in my veins, it was masked by the fear that roared in my ears for the thousands who stood behind me. This might be the day they lost their lives.

Rafe and Kaden sat on horses on either side of me. While I was dressed to be recognized, their clothing served an opposite purpose. Both wore black cloaks with the hoods drawn—the uniform of Morrighese Guardians. Jeb, Tavish, Orrin, Andrés, and Griz were in a line behind us, wearing the same. We didn't want them recognized too soon.

"He's playing with us," Rafe said, his eyes locked on the slowly progressing cloud.

Kaden cursed under his breath. "At this pace, we'll be fighting by moonlight."

We couldn't rush forward. We needed them to come to us.

"It's just past midday," I said, trying to calm myself as much as him. "We have hours of daylight yet."

And then a horse broke free from their front lines. A distant speck at first, but then charging, fast. I heard the ratchet of the ballistas as it stormed toward us. But something about its coloring was wrong.

"Wait!" I said.

It wasn't a brezalot. And there was a rider.

As it drew near, I knew.

It was the Komizar.

He stopped a hundred yards off. He held his hands up to show he wasn't armed.

"What the hell is he doing?" Rafe asked.

"I request a parley with the princess," he called. "Alone!"

A parley? Had he gone mad?

But then I thought, *No. He is deadly sane.*

"And I bring a gift of goodwill," he called again. "All I ask for is a moment to talk—without weapons."

Both Rafe and Kaden balked, but then the Komizar reached behind his back and swung a child down to the ground.

It was Yvet.

My heart stopped. The grass swallowed her up to her waist.

I remembered the day I had seen her huddled in the market

with Aster and Zekiah, clutching a bloody cloth after her fingertip had been cut off. She looked even smaller and more terrified now.

The Komizar dismounted. "All yours," he called, "just for the price of a few minutes."

Rafe and Kaden railed against it, but I was already unbuckling and handing them my sword and knives.

"Our archers can take him down, and we can have the child too," Rafe argued.

"No," I answered. Nothing was ever that simple with the Komizar. We knew each other too well, and this was a very clear message to me.

"And when do I get Zekiah?" I called back to him.

He smiled. "When I've returned safely to my lines, I will send him. And if I don't make it back—" He shrugged.

He was enjoying this. It was a game, theater. He wanted to draw it out, squeeze all the game pieces a little tighter in his fist.

I knew Rafe and Kaden were both a heartbeat away from signaling the archers. The sacrifice of one child for the beast himself. A child who could die anyway. A child who would *likely* die anyway. And our prize was in our grasp. But it was a choice that came with a price, one the Komizar had already calculated. The air was taut with the decision. He stood there, unafraid, knowing, and I hated him more deeply. How much was I like him? Who was I willing to sacrifice to get what I wanted?

"The Komizar's fate will come later," I whispered. "Do not lay a hand on the beast yet."

I rode out to meet him, but when I was still ten yards away,

I dismounted and waved Yvet forward. Her wide frightened eyes turned to the Komizar. He nodded, and she walked toward me.

I knelt when she reached me and held her tiny hands. "Yvet, do you see those two horses far behind me with the cloaked soldiers?"

She looked past me at the thousands of troops, her lip trembling, but then spotted the two dark cloaked ones. She nodded.

"Good. They will take care of you. I want you to go to them now. I want you to run and not look back. No matter what you see or hear, you will keep going. Do you understand?"

Her eyes brimmed with tears.

"Go," I said. "Now!"

She ran, stumbling through the grass. The distance seemed like miles, and when she reached them, Kaden scooped her up and handed her off to another soldier. My stomach jumped to my throat. I swallowed, forcing the bile down. *She made it*, I told myself. I wrenched my breaths to a slow rhythm and turned back to face the Komizar.

"See?" he said. "I keep my word." He waved me forward. "Let's talk."

I walked to meet him, looking for lumps, bulges in his clothing, a knife waiting to pay me back. As I drew closer, I saw the lines in his face, the sharpness of his cheekbones, the toll my attack had taken on him. But I also saw the hunger burning in his eyes. I stopped in front of him. His gaze rolled leisurely over me.

"You wanted to talk?"

He smiled. "Has it come to this, Jezelia? No niceties?" His hand reached up as if to caress my face.

"Don't touch me," I warned. "Or I will kill you."

His hand returned to his side, but his smile remained chiseled on his lips.

"I admire you, Princess. You almost did what no one else was able to do in the eleven years of my rule. That is a record, did you know? No other Komizar has ever ruled that long."

"A pity it's about to come to an end."

He sighed dramatically. "How you still hang on to things. I care about you, Jezelia. Truly, I do. But this?" He waved his hand toward the troops behind me as if they were too pitiful to consider. "You don't have to die. Come over to my side. Look at all I have to offer."

"Servitude? Cruelty? Violence? You tempt me so, *sher* Komizar. We've talked. You can go back now."

He looked past me at the troops. "Is that the prince back there? With his *hundred* men who stormed the citadelle?" His tone was thick with mockery.

"So the Viceregent has come running to you with his tail tucked between his legs."

"I smiled when he told me what you'd done. I was impressed that you rooted out my moles. How is your father?"

"Dead." He deserved no truths from me, and the weaker he thought we were, the better.

"And your brothers?"

"Dead."

He sighed. "This is all too easy."

"You haven't asked me about Kaden," I said.

His smile disappeared, and his expression darkened. I knew

him well, too. Kaden was a blow he couldn't hide. There was something in this world he had loved, after all. Something he had saved, nurtured, but it had turned on him. Something that pointed to his own failure.

A small rush of pebbles suddenly streamed down from the cliffs above. He looked up surveying the empty ruins, turning to look at the other side. The silence of held breaths gripped the valley.

He looked back at me and grinned. "You thought I didn't know?"

Ice filled my belly.

He turned as if to leave but then stepped closer to me instead.

"It's the girl on the terrace that's bothering you, isn't it? I admit I went a bit too far. Caught up in the moment I suppose. Would an apology change your mind?"

Caught up in the moment? I stared at him. There were no words. No words.

He leaned down and kissed my cheek. "I suppose not."

He turned and walked back to his horse.

The rage came, blinding, bright, consuming.

"Send Zekiah!" I yelled.

"I will, Princess. I always keep my word."

⊰ KADEN ⊱

I HANDED YVET TO A SOLDIER. SHE CHOKED ON SOBS, BUT there was no time to comfort her. "Take her to Natiya," I said.

Lia had set up a camp outside the valley for whatever children we could capture. Gwyneth, Pauline, and more soldiers were there. Natiya spoke the language and would reassure them that they wouldn't be harmed—and hopefully help comfort them—assuming we were able to get any more of them out of the valley alive.

I got back on my horse, watching Lia step closer to the Komizar. It was madness. I surveyed the cliffs. Watched the wall of the army poised to attack. Watched and waited and knew this was not just a parley. It was tearing nerves loose. The slow draw of a knife over skin. A stalking howl in a forest. The horses stamped, knowing, nervous.

"Shhh," I whispered.

Make them suffer.

This was the Komizar, doing what he did best.

⊰ RAFE ⊱

I FINALLY BREATHED AS THE KOMIZAR RODE AWAY AND LIA got back on her horse.

Zekiah was delivered as promised, whole and alive. He was rushed out of the valley to wait with Yvet. I had been expecting the worst, pieces perhaps, as the Komizar liked to threaten, but he always knew how to turn the moment. To plant doubt.

Lia had warned me he knew there were troops up in the ruins, and I sent soldiers to alert them. He may have known they were there, but he didn't know exactly where they would charge from, or how many of them there were. It was a long valley, and when the Viceregent had escaped, he only knew of me and my hundred men—not about the whole Dalbreck army.

The cloud rolled toward us again, but this time with ravenous hunger. I felt the thunder of its feet, both human and animal, but united as one raging beast. I sensed our troops tensing, ready to spring. I stretched out my left arm, a signal to hold. *Hold.*

"You're sure he'll send them first?" I asked Lia. With the high hills around us, dusk was already closing in.

Lia's knuckles whitened. One hand clenched her reins, and the other, her hilt. "Yes. Him using Yvet and Zekiah is proof. He knows me. He knows what will unsettle our soldiers and make them hesitate. We are not like him."

We watched them get closer, and their features came into view at last, lines of soldiers, ten deep, a hundred across. None of them older than Eben or Natiya. Most much younger. They held halberds, swords, axes, and knives. As they advanced, I saw their faces, wild, barely recognizable as children anymore.

I signaled the shield guard to move forward into position. "Shields up!" I ordered. Their shields interlocked with practiced precision. "Archers forward!" Orrin called.

And then the first of the brezalots charged.

⊰ L I A ⊱

THE PRODDED ANIMAL STREAKED PAST THEIR FRONT LINES, heading toward the shield guard. The ballistas tucked above us moved to the ridges, ratcheted, cocked, and ready. I watched them turn, aiming. Tavish waited with distressing patience and finally signaled the two with the best angles. "Fire!" The iron spears flew. One missed, but the other was a perfect shot, spearing the animal in its shoulder. The brezalot stumbled, fell, and then the earth exploded a safe distance away, meadow, horse, and blood, raining down, the pieces still on fire. The smell of burnt flesh filled the air.

And then another brezalot came.

And another.

The second was downed, but the third was only grazed by the iron spear, and charged into the shield guard. There was a scramble to get away, but it was too late. It exploded, leaving a gaping hole surrounded by dead bodies and pieces of beast. Orrin and his archers were knocked to the ground by the blast. Rafe and infantry rushed forward to help them, and the Komizar used the resulting chaos to send his brigade of child soldiers forward to further demoralize us.

"Retreat!" I yelled, loud and frantic, so even the Komizar would hear. "Retreat!"

Our lines hobbled back, the guard holding their shields in disarray, but the infantry behind us moved into position. Ready.

I watched. Breathless. Waiting. Drawing on patience I didn't know I had. The shield guards staggered back. The child soldiers bore down on them, charging down the middle of the valley toward us.

"Retreat!" I shouted again. The Vendan troops behind the children stalled, waiting for their young soldiers to add to our chaos before they moved in with their heavy weapons. I watched, my heart hammering, and then when the last of the children crossed a designated line, I yelled, "Now!"

Dirt soared into the air. Chunks of meadow and grass flew as rows of sharp-angled pikes sprang from beneath the valley floor. Two impassable rows crossed the width of the valley, trapping the children on our side. The children turned, stunned by the noise, and then nets were launched, falling on them, ensnaring them further. The infantry rushed forward to subdue them and then guide them out of the valley to where Natiya, Pauline, and Gwyneth waited with more soldiers.

I raced forward, stopping at the wall of pikes. I knew I had only seconds before another brezalot was readied to break through our wall or another of their heinous weapons was launched.

⊣ KADEN ⊢

EIGHT VENDANS RODE WITH US—THE ONES WE TRUSTED, who had revealed themselves back at the citadelle. This was the part I knew Rafe objected to—or maybe feared—but he rode forward on one side of Lia, and I on the other, watching for archers or others in range to take Lia down.

There was calamity on the other side of the pikes, a ripple of disturbance behind their front lines, orders rolling back.

"Brothers! Sisters!" Lia called, drawing their attention back to her. More word rippled back. There were Vendans at her side, including Griz and myself. It triggered a strained silence. She made a plea for surrender, settlement, a promise for peace, but she hadn't even finished her proposal when the Komizar, Chievdar Tyrick, and Governor Yanos pushed through on their horses. The Komizar's eyes fell briefly on me, the fire of my betrayal still blazing in them, and then his attention turned to a soldier who had stepped forward and lowered his weapon, listening to Lia. The Komizar swung his sword, and the man was halved. The front line soldiers raised their weapons, gripped in fists hot with fervor again to avoid the same fate, and then a herd of brezalots charged toward us.

⊰ RAFE ⊱

I WAS THROWN FROM MY HORSE. SPLINTERS OF WOOD RAINED down on me. A horn sounded, reverberating through the valley. I rolled to my feet, my sword drawn and shield raised. The battalions were launched. On the cliffs in the distance, I saw forces led by Draeger charging down a trail. On the opposite side, Marques's men did the same in an effort to divide the Vendan forces in two. Tavish fought at my back, the loud ring of steel coiling around us, both of us swinging, lunging, and cutting down the wall of Vendans coming at us. We finally made it back to our horses, and killed Vendans who were about to claim them. From atop my horse, I searched through the bedlam of brown and gray and flashing metal for a glimpse of Lia. She was gone. We fought our way to band with other ranks, then plowed through enemy lines, and headed toward the fifth division.

⊰ LIA ⊱

I SCRAMBLED TO MY FEET, A KNOT OF SOLDIERS AT MY SIDE. Thick dust filled the air. I'd lost sight of both Rafe and Kaden.

Vendans swarmed in past the shattered pikes. I heard the burbling gasps of soldiers impaled with splintered wood. Darkness was creeping in, but the cliffs ignited with a line of fire, and stones were catapulted to scatter Vendan forces as Dalbreck's battalions swarmed to the valley floor. Jeb made it to my side.

"This way," he said, and with a Dalbretch platoon, we pounded our way through Vendan lines. The screams of battle filled the air, echoing mercilessly between the valley walls. I heard the wheeze, the coughs, the thud of death sounding over and over again. The Komizar had been quick to silence my voice before it reached even a small number of Vendans, but now, with the youngest Vendan soldiers safely out of his reach, I knew where I had to go, where more would hear me. Faces became a blur as we advanced, my shield raised, my sword swinging, Jeb watching my back, and I his. My shield took a powerful blow, and I was knocked to the ground. I rolled before an ax hit the ground where my head had been, then thrust my sword into a soft gut as the soldier came at me again.

I jumped to my feet, spinning, my shield lifting to deflect another attack and then, in the swirl of metal and shadow, my eye caught something, something baubled and blue.

⊰ KADEN ⊱

THE VENDAN TROOPS SCRAMBLED UNDER THE ASSAULT OF stones raining down on them. The attack launched from the cliffs was only a distraction until the battalions could reach the valley floor. My leg ran with blood, a piece of wood piercing my thigh like a bayonet. I couldn't pull it out, so I broke it off, even as I stabbed my sword into a charging Vendan—one I had known. And then I killed another. And another. Griz fought his way toward me. Lia had been only feet from us, and now she was gone. We charged deeper into the Vendan ranks. Minutes seemed like hours, our progress slow, a stream of Dalbreck and Morrighese soldiers fighting at our sides, and then an explosion rocked the valley.

⊰ RAFE ⊱

A FIERY PLUME SHOT INTO THE SKY, LIGHTING THE VALLEY with sparks and flames. Fire rained down, thousands of glowing embers lighting on men and animals alike, horses rearing back in fear, soldiers screaming as they were lit on fire. I ran to one soldier, pushing him to the ground and rolling him to douse the flame, and then I saw Tavish. He beat at flames that streamed up his arm, lighting his hair. I tackled him, using my gloved hands to smother the flames. He screamed in agony even after the fire was out. I leaned close trying to calm him.

"You'll be all right, brother," I said. "I promise you'll be all right." He moaned with pain, and I ordered another soldier to take him back behind our lines, then helped lift him onto a horse.

The soldier left with Tavish, and that was when I felt my palms burning, already blistering from dousing the flames. I ripped off my gloves. They were saturated with the fiery substance that had rained down. I knelt, pressing my hands against the cool grass, and then I saw another soldier lying on the ground beside me. It was the Viceregent's son—Andrés. Kaden's brother was dead. I had time only to close his blank, staring eyes.

I rode toward Draeger's battalion, watching Vendans fall by the tens and hundreds, but no matter how many we felled, there were always more to replace them.

When I got to our battalions, Draeger and Marques had successfully fragmented the fifth division, but were already losing ground.

I saw Kaden making his way to me. Lia wasn't with him, and my heart stopped. *Where was she?* "I lost her," he said when he reached me. "She's not with you?"

A Vendan as big as Griz came at us, swinging a mace in one hand and an ax in the other. He pummeled our shields, pushing us farther and farther back, until Kaden and I sidestepped at the same time and came from behind, both of our swords piercing his ribs. He fell like a tree, shaking the ground, and then behind him in the distance, we both spotted the Viceregent.

⊰ LIA ⊱

THE TERROR, THE BLOOD, IT WAS A WAVE CRASHING OVER us again and again coming at us from all sides. Every time a battalion gained ground, more brezalots were prodded forward, more arrows launched, more iron bolts whirred through the air piercing shields and flesh, more burning disks were hurled that clung to skin and seared lungs. The noise was deafening, roaring through the valley like a relentless storm. Fire and smoke rose, stinging ash fell. I lost my bearings, the bluff no longer in sight. Only moment by moment survival mattered. Swinging, stabbing, refusing to let him win. *It is not over.*

Jeb was vicious in his attacks, as determined as I was to break through their next wave of lines, but we made no headway, our forces thinning with every new barrage of weapons. I saw glimpses of a heavily armed battalion ahead, horsemen battling above the heads of the infantry. There was no time to search for Rafe or Kaden among them, but I knew that was where they had been headed. The familiar pained squeal of a brezalot screamed through the air. I knew what that meant. Another one had been loaded with explosives and prodded forward. I heard the fearsome thud of its hooves, the hiss of its raging breaths growing louder as it thundered toward us. The sounds echoed, multiplied, surrounded us. I turned, unsure where it would appear, and then a rough hand shoved me, throwing me back.

It was Rafe.

We tumbled to the ground, even as the world exploded.

⇥ KADEN ⇤

"YOU CAN'T DO IT."

His breathing was labored, his words short, still trying to convince me.

I saw the terror in his eyes. I was stronger. I was quicker. I was driven by eleven years of anger.

Metal met metal. Our strikes vibrated between us. *You can't do it. I'm your father.*

He thrust, his blade grazing my arm.

Blood trickled through my shirt, and his eyes lit with hunger. He glanced down at my leg, still impaled with the wood spike. I saw the calculation in his eyes. *How much strength did I have left?*

I wasn't sure myself. The pain was getting harder to ignore. The stream of blood was sticky in my boot. I drove him back, the clang of steel chattering in the air.

"I'm your father," he said again.

"When?" I asked. "When were you ever my father?"

His pupils were pinpoints, his nostrils flared. There was no scent of jasmine on him now. Only the scent of fear.

My blade pressed against his, holding, pushing, a lifetime of lies pulsing between us.

He pushed off and retreated back several paces. "I've tried to make amends with you," he hissed. "You can't do it. Son. Let's start over. There's still time for us."

I relaxed my grip on my sword. Lowered my guard. Stared at him. "Time? Now?"

His eyes glimmered, and he advanced, as I'd known he would, his swing fierce, knocking the sword from my hand. He smiled, ready to plunge his blade into me, but as he stepped forward, I stepped faster and, standing chest to chest, I thrust my knife upward into his gut.

His eyes widened.

"Your time is up," I whispered. *"Father."*

And I let him fall to my feet.

⊰ RAFE ⊱

I LAY OVER HER, PROTECTING HER AS METAL, WOOD, AND fire streamed down around us.

"Rafe," she whispered. A split second of relief raced between us before the battle closed in again. We got to our feet, grabbing our shields and weapons from the ground. A cloud of smoke filled the air, and dazed Vendans staggered toward us, the blast disorienting them as much as the enemy.

"I have to get to the bluff, Rafe. I have to speak to them before we're all dead."

We ran in the shadows of the cliffs. I spotted the bluff ahead, but then Governor Yanos closed in. The Watch Captain, Chancellor, and a squad of five soldiers stood behind him.

Yanos stepped forward. "Give her over."

"So you can put her head on a spike?" I answered.

"That's up to the Komizar."

My fist tightened on my shield. I felt the blisters on my palms bursting, liquid oozing between my fingers. "The bluff is right behind us, Lia. Go!" I desperately prayed that for once she wouldn't argue with me. I heard her run.

The Chancellor smiled. "The bluff's a dead end. There's nowhere for her to go. You just cornered our rabbit for us."

"Only if you can get past me." I raised my sword.

"Past us," Draeger said, and stepped up beside me. Jeb was with him.

⊰ L I A ⊱

I RAN TOWARD THE BLUFF, MY LUNGS BURNING WITH SMOKE. I heard the desperation in Rafe's command. *Go!* Too many were dying. Everyone was losing, except the Komizar. The valley still roared with battle. How would they hear me?

Sweat poured down my forehead, my eyes stinging, and I struggled to see the path ahead, but then the blue flashed again, a bauble, an unseeing eye. I choked on the acrid air, trying to see through the smoke, and then Calantha stepped out of the murky haze and blocked my path.

She was dressed as I'd never seen her before. She was no longer the mistress of the Sanctum. She was a fierce warrior with sabers and knives sheathed at her sides. One of the knives was mine. The glittering jewels reflected the burning fires.

Her knuckles were tight knots, gripped on sabers she was ready to use.

I slowly drew my sword. "Move aside, Calantha," I said, waiting for her to spring. "I don't want to hurt you."

"I'm not here to stop you, Princess. I'm here to tell you to hurry. Speak to them before none are left to know the truth of this day. They are not hungry for this. They hunger for another kind of hope."

A quarterlord charged through a veil of smoke, an ax in his

hand, poised to bury it in me, but Calantha lunged, slicing his belly wide, and his body tumbled, thudding into the base of the cliff. She looked at me, repeating Rafe's plea, "Go!" and then turned to take down another of her own.

⊰ RAFE ⊱

I HAD FOUGHT BY JEB'S SIDE BEFORE, BUT NOT BY DRAEGER'S. He knew instinctively which were the strongest fighters. We fought back to back. I kept the Chancellor in view as I smashed one soldier's face with my shield and sliced the calf of another to the bone. The Watch Captain hung back behind them all. Draeger's blows drove Yanos back, and the governor fell. Draeger ran him through, then spun to block the blows of another soldier. The Chancellor bore down. The jolt of his sword hitting my shield cracked the air, but I deflected the force and it glanced into the skull of a soldier at his side. He fell as Jeb thrust his sword into a soldier beside him. Now it was one on one, except for the Watch Captain who still cowered behind the others. My hands burned on my sword, slipped with the wet blisters, but I gripped harder, meeting the Chancellor blow for blow. Our swords crossed, pressing, our chests heaving.

"It was you," I said. He pushed away, and swung. Our swords chattered.

"I only killed the old one," he said, not even knowing Sven's name. His face glistened with sweat. "The Watch Captain and Viceregent got the rest."

"Sven's not dead," I told him.

Steel rang, and sparks flew between us.

"Do you think I care?" he said between heavy breaths.

My sword rammed his shield, the metal crumpling under the blows.

"Not any more than you care about impaling a princess or betraying your kingdom."

I pressed forward, not giving him a chance to attack, his arm weakening under the barrage, and finally his shield fell.

I thrust my sword forward. The blade slid through his ribs, my hand meeting his gut, my face inches from his.

"I don't expect you to care, Lord Chancellor. I just expect you to die."

⊰ LIA ⊱

I RAN, COUGHING AND STUMBLING THROUGH DARK RUTS. Night had closed in, but the valley glowed with pockets of light, the fires burning ridges, meadow, and bodies. Smoke hung in clouds, bitter and sharp, woven with the smell of burnt flesh. The clang of metal still reverberated from the valley walls. The cries of the fallen stabbed the air, and the animals caught up in the devastation keened with misery.

I wiped my stinging eyes, searching, falling embers burning my skin as I tried to find the trail to the bluff, hopelessness sweeping over me.

Don't tarry, Miz, or they will all die.

I choked and stumbed forward.

A finger of clear air opened, and I saw the trail. I ran,

tumbling and clawing my way to the top. I made it to the bluff's rim, and my soul tore in two. In both directions, the valley burned, the weapons boomed, the glint of metal flashed, the bodies writhed en masse, like a nest of dying snakes.

"Brothers! Sisters!" I called, but my words were lost in the roar of a valley that stretched too far and thundered too loud. They couldn't hear me. *Trust.* It was impossible.

I was desperate and cried out again, but the battle raged on. *Trust the strength within you.*

I lifted my hands and raised my voice to the heavens, reaching not just for the strength within me but the strength of generations. I felt something reaching back to me, and then what I heard wasn't my voice alone, but a thousand voices. They wove through me, around me, the world breathing us in, remembering, time circling. Morrighan stood at my side, Venda and Gaudrel on the other. Pauline, Gwyneth, and Berdi stood behind me and a hundred more. Our voices braided together, a steel reaching to the ends of the valley, swirling, sharing. Heads turned, listening, knowing, some swaths cutting deeper than others. The smoke coiled, thinned.

And then the battle stilled.

"Brothers! Sisters! Lay down your arms! I am your queen! Daughter of your blood and sister of your heart! I will stand by you. I will return to Venda." I told them there was another kind of hope—the one Venda had promised. I begged them to listen to their hearts, to trust a knowing as old as the universe. "The strength is within us. We will settle the Cam Lanteux. Build new lives. With my last dying breath, I promise you, we will make it happen together, but this is not the way. We can prevail against the Dragon who steals our dreams! Lay down your arms, and we will create a hope that lasts."

A universe stilled. The heavens watched. The breath of the centuries held.

The pause of battle stretched.

And then a sword was thrown down.

And another.

And while the *chievdars*, governors, and quarterlords still raged, not open to the hearing, the clans laid down their weapons in waves.

"I couldn't have asked for a better place to find you, my pet. Where they all can watch."

I whirled. It was the Komizar.

"Now they'll all know with certainty who the Komizar of Venda really is," he said.

I drew my sword and stepped back. "They're listening to me, Komizar. This is what they want. It is too late for you."

He lifted his heavy sword with both hands. I knew that stance. I knew what would come next.

"They want whatever I want," he said. "And I want you dead. It's as simple as that, Princess. That is what real power is."

He looked at the sword in my hand and smiled, its reach far shorter than his. He stepped closer, his face gleaming with lust for the power at his fingertips. I stepped back and felt the bluff's rim crumbling beneath my feet, heard the loose stones tumbling to the valley floor. My heart seized in a fist, and I saw the hunger in his eyes. *More.* The battle and my fear fed him. But then I saw something else, a flash of color. A jeweled blue eye.

"Reginaus!"

The Komizar's expression went cold, hearing his birth name said aloud, and then rage engulfed him. He spun and faced Calantha.

Grief shimmered in her lone pale eye, and maybe loyalty, love, and a thousand other things I couldn't name. *We have a long history*, she had once told me. Maybe that was what I saw in her gaze, the memories of all he had been to her and all that he was now.

"You gave me hope once," she said. "But I cannot let you do this. It is time for another kind of hope."

A dismissive huff of air had barely passed his lips when she charged toward him. He lifted his sword in a sharp move, and it impaled her long before she ever reached him, but her momentum had unexpected power, the sword running her through, and her body slammed into his. He stumbled back, one step, then another, then panic flashed across his face as he scrambled for footing, but it was too late. I leapt to the side as both of their bodies flew past me and tumbled over the edge, his scream echoing as they fell to the valley floor, but as I lunged, I felt myself sliding too, the ground giving way beneath me. I frantically grasped for anything, grass, branches, but it was all out of my reach, earth sliding around me and I was falling with them, and then I felt a hand lock onto mine.

CHAPTER EIGHTY-EIGHT

⊰ PAULINE ⊱

THE BATTLE MAY HAVE ENDED, BUT IT STILL RAGED ON IN dreams. It took a regiment of soldiers, along with Gwyneth, Berdi, Eben, Natiya, and me, to contain the child soldiers who were ushered out of the valley, and to comfort them in the following days. Even from the camp, we heard the explosions, the terror, the screams reverberating through the valley. Just before it ended, I fell to my knees in desperation, reaching out to Lia, praying for her safety and strength, praying her voice would be heard by the Vendans.

Natiya, who was only a child herself, spoke to the children with words that were familiar to them, and it seemed at times that was all that quieted them and got us through the night. The next day the children still trembled with fright, struck out, recoiled at our touch. It was hard to gain their trust. I understood too well that trust couldn't be forced or gained overnight, but I also knew it could come with patience, slowly, day by day, and I was ready to give them that time, however long it took.

When I went into the valley and saw the dead, and then helped care for the hundreds who were injured, I thought about the devastation described in the Holy Text and the handful of the Remnant who had survived. We had almost been them. I kissed two fingers, one for the lost and one for those to come, and prayed the winnowing was over.

We could spare no more lives to the heavens.

"I'm done with this one," the surgeon said. She wiped the blood from her hands, and I followed the sentries as they carried Kaden to the far end of the tent.

⊰ KADEN ⊱

I REACHED DOWN, FEELING FOR MY LEG.

"Don't worry. It's still there."

Pauline wiped my forehead with a damp cloth.

My head still swam with the elixir the surgeon had given me. The tent was full of the injured. There were a dozen more tents like this one. I'd had to live with the wood in my leg for three days. There were too many wounded for the few surgeons here to take care of at once. I'd almost taken Orrin up on his offer to cut it out for me. Tavish lay on a bedroll opposite mine, his arm and neck swathed in bandages. Half of his long ropes of hair were gone. He lifted his good arm as a welcome, but even that small effort left him grimacing with pain.

Rafe sat on a crate in the opposite corner while Berdi brushed a healing balm on his hands. Someone else dressed a gash on his shoulder, then put his arm in a sling. I could hear Gwyneth through the tent walls, giving orders to Griz for more pails of water, and Orrin tearing fabric for bandages. The aftermath was as loud as the battle but with a different kind of noise.

"The Watch Captain?" I asked.

Pauline shook her head. "No sign," she answered.

The coward had slithered away, and he and a half dozen of the Council were unaccounted for. It could be they were among the mass of dead bodies—not all were recognizable anymore.

"If they're alive, they've crawled into deep dark holes," Pauline added. "We'll never see them again."

I nodded and hoped she was right.

⊰ RAFE ⊱

"How are your hands?"

"Berdi just changed the dresssings," I answered. "I should be able to ride in a few days."

"Good."

"And how is your shoulder?" I asked.

"Sore—but more than worth it. You may pull it out of joint anytime you wish."

I had barely reached Lia before she went over the bluff with the Komizar and Calantha. My hands had still been wet with raw burned flesh, but I caught her wrist and pulled her back up. Even with our injuries, she and I were among the lucky ones. I'd told Kaden about Andrés, but his body had never been found, perhaps trampled beyond recognition by a brezalot.

Dalbreck's toll was high. By General Draeger's count, we had lost four thousand soldiers. Without Lia's plea and her promise to the Vendans, there would have been no end to it. There was no doubt in Draeger's mind now that the Komizar would have wiped Morrighan, and then us, from the face of the earth.

Dalbretch, Vendan, and Morrighese forces worked together during the aftermath, and Lia spoke to the Vendans daily, helping them prepare for their journey back home.

"We should be ready to leave in a few days too," she said. "The last of the bodies have been burned. There were too many to bury them all."

"Jeb?"

She nodded and walked away.

⊰ LIA ⊱

IT HAD BEEN ALMOST TWO WEEKS. THE LAST OF THE DEAD were buried or burned—including the Komizar. It was strange, looking at his lifeless body, the fingers that had clutched my throat, the mouth that had always held threat, the man who had looked out on an army city and imagined the gods under his thumb. Everything about him now was so ordinary.

"We can leave the dog for the animals," a sentry had told me. I imagined my expression must have suggested such a thought. I looked at Calantha lying beside him.

"No," I said. "The Komizar is gone. He is only a boy named Reginaus now. Burn his body alongside hers."

Jeb received his own funeral pyre. I had found him alive the morning after the battle as we searched among the piles of bodies. I had pulled his head into my lap, and his eyes had opened.

"Your Highness," he said, his face dirty and bloody but his eyes still shining with life.

"I'm here, Jeb," I said, wiping the blood from his brow. "You'll be all right."

He nodded, but we both knew it was a lie.

His expression pinched with pain as he forced a smile to his face. "Look at this." His gaze turned downward toward his bleeding chest. "I've ruined another shirt."

"It's only a small tear, Jeb. I can fix that. Or I'll get you a new one."

"Cruvas linen," he said, his breaths choppy.

"Yes, I know. I remember. I will always remember."

His eyes glistened, lingering with a last knowing look, and then he was gone.

I smoothed his hair. I whispered his name. I wiped his face. I rocked him. I held Jeb like he was everyone I'd watched die this past year, all those I hadn't had time to hold. I didn't want to let go of any more. And then I buried my face in his neck and sobbed. My fingers wove with his, and I remembered the first time I'd met him, a patty clapper kneeling in my room saying he was there to take me home. A sentry brushed my arm, trying to convince me to let him go, but I pushed him away. For once, I wouldn't be rushed to say good-bye.

It was the last time I'd cried, no matter how many more bodies we piled to burn or bury. The immensity of the death was numbing. But I knew at some point tears would come again. The pain would take hold of me unexpectedly and throw me to my knees. There were no rules to grief, but there were rules to life, and in those first few days, the requirements of the living demanded I keep going.

There were others—Perry, Marques, the Field Marshal—who hadn't made it either, others of the officers gravely injured, and still others who had fought just as valiantly and were unscathed. Governors Umbrose and Carzwil were the lone members of the Council who had laid down their arms along with the clans. They had another kind of hope too.

General Draeger was one of the unscathed, and he helped me in the aftermath of battle, sometimes doing the hardest and most heart-wrenching of tasks. We both held down a young Vendan as his mangled arm was cut free from the gears of one of the Komizar's ill-conceived weapons.

"I owe you an apology," he said one day as we walked back to camp. "You're not what I expected."

"No apology necessary," I said. "You're not what I expected either. I thought you'd be a power-mongering, insufferable ass."

He sucked in a surprised breath. "And now?"

"Instead, I find a man who is passionate and deeply loyal to his kingdom. I admire that greatly, General, but it can be a narrow line to navigate. Sometimes it might lead us to cross boundaries. I know what it feels like to have my choices taken away. I pray no daughter of your kingdom will ever have to fight for her voice to be heard as I have had to."

He cleared his throat. Apparently my subtlety was lacking. "That's why you ran from the marriage?" he asked.

"Everyone deserves to be loved, General, and not because a piece of paper commands it. Choice is powerful and can lead to great things if not held in the tight fists of a few."

THE FOOD SUPPLIES THE KOMIZAR HAD STOCKPILED HAD mostly survived. They would be enough to get us back to Venda. I met with the clans and wept on their shoulders, and they on mine. Day by day, I felt our resolve growing, knitting together like a broken bone, our shared scar making us stronger. I rejected the title of Komizar, but accepted the one of queen.

And even though my strength and hope grew daily, when we met at the end of the valley to say good-bye to Morrighese and Dalbretch troops, I felt some small part of that hope wither.

I hugged Tavish and Orrin, then Kaden and I shook hands with Generals Howland and Draeger. General Draeger hesitated as if he wanted to say something else to me, but then he only squeezed my hand and wished me well again.

Rafe stepped forward and clasped Kaden's hand. They said nothing, instead studying each other, and then they exchanged nods as if some words had passed between them.

I stared at Rafe and filled my mind with a hundred memories of what *was*, so I wouldn't have to think about what was to come. I thought about the first time he had scowled at me in Berdi's tavern, the sun slashing across his cheekbones when he came to Devil's Canyon, his fumbling over words when I asked where he was from, the small heart of sweat on his shirt as he swept webs from the eaves, the curious touch of his finger tracing the kavah on my shoulder, the rage in our voices as we argued right before our first kiss, the tears in his eyes as he lifted me from an icy bank.

But mostly I remembered our few stolen hours when kingdoms didn't exist for us.

"Lia."

My memories tumbled away, and the sun was suddenly hot and blinding.

Rafe walked over to me. Kaden and the officers looked on. There was no privacy in this moment, and maybe it was for the best.

"You need to return to your duties in Dalbreck now," I said. It was a statement, but I know he heard my question laced through it.

He nodded. "And you also have your duties in Venda."

The same question was hidden in his words.

I nodded. "I've made promises, just as you have."

"Yes. Promises. I know." He shifted on his feet glancing down for a moment. "We'll be drawing up the new treaties soon. We'll send them to you and the other kingdoms."

"Thank you. Without Dalbreck's lead, we couldn't make this happen. I wish you well, King Jaxon."

He didn't call me Queen Jezelia, as if he still couldn't accept either the title or the choice I had made. He had never loved Venda the way I did.

He stared at me for the longest time, saying nothing, then finally answered, "I wish you well too, Lia."

We parted, he going his way and I going mine, both of us committed to help the kingdoms we loved build a future. There were many ways a life could be sacrificed, and it wasn't always through dying.

I looked back over my shoulder, watching him ride away, and then I thought about Gwyneth's long-ago remark. *Love . . . It's a nice little trick if you can find it.*

We had found it.

But now I knew finding love and holding on to it were not the same thing.

I RODE BACK TO THE MULTITUDES OF VENDANS WHO waited for my signal, their faces filled with hope, ready to begin the future I had promised them, and I waved our caravan forward, in the direction of home.

With the dawn comes a better glimpse of our shelter.

It is safe to build a fire now.

The scavengers won't spot us.

We are cold and hungry, and Pata has killed a rabbit.

We gather what little fuel we see—a broken chair and a few books. The pages are precious dry tinder that will help the wood catch.

The others walk around in wonderment, looking at the walls that enclose us.

I watch the pages of the books curl, hear the sizzle of the rabbit and the rumble of our stomachs.

The child brings me a colorful sphere, most of it blue.

> *What is this?* she asks, and spins it, entranced with its beauty.

I am uncertain myself what to call it, but the words written across it are familiar. I search my memories, my own grandmother telling me how the world used to be.

> *It is a map of our world.*

> *Our world is round?*

It was.

Now it is flat and small and brown. But the child already knows that.

> *From the stars, Morrighan. If you fly among the stars, you will see the world far differently.*

> *What will I see?*

She is hungry, not just for food, but for understanding, and I have little to give her.

Come, child, sit in my lap as the rabbit cooks, and I will tell you what you can see from the stars.

Once upon a time, long long ago, there were not just the Remnant and the scavengers. There were nations of every kind, hundreds of kingdoms that circled this world.

Hundreds?

She smiles, believing it to be another of my tales. Maybe it is. The lines of truth and sustenance blurred long ago.

What happened to them, Ama? Where are they now?

They are us, child. We are what's left.

But there was a princess?

Yes, child, a princess. Just like you. A princess strong and brave who visited the stars, and from there she saw a different world and imagined new ones yet to be.

—*The Last Testaments of Gaudrel*

CHAPTER EIGHTY-NINE

RAFE

"YOUR MAJESTY, WHERE IS YOUR HEAD?" SVEN WHISPERED
between clenched teeth.

He knew where it was. The same place it had drifted to
countless times these last months, but she had her duties and
I had mine.

"Yes, go on, Lord Gandry," I said, sitting a little straighter in
my chair.

I returned my attention to the Barons of the Assembly, where
it belonged.

Sven had taken to heart my last words to him back in Morrighan. Words I thought he couldn't hear, and probably not the
last words Gwyneth had in mind. *Wake up, you old coot! You're not
dismissed from your duties yet. Wake up, or I'm going to go dump you
in a water trough. Do you hear me, Sven? I still need you.*

Whenever we argued over some matter now, he reminded me of my confession—that I needed him. It was true. I did. And not just as an adviser.

The Morrighese had kindly deposited him back on our doorstep as soon as he was able to travel. I kept his days short. He still tired easily, but it was a miracle he was alive at all.

After the battle in Sentinel Valley, the long ride back to Dalbreck had given General Draeger and me plenty of opportunities to talk. He told me he was having second thoughts about the betrothal. His daughter was young and bright and creative, and the weight of such a contract might hamper her growth and dampen her spirit. She was only fourteen, after all. With the defeat of the Komizar and my return to Dalbreck assured, the betrothal would prove a distraction to the work ahead of us, and the good of the kingdom was all that mattered, and would I find it mutually agreeable to dissolve the contract?

I had mulled it over, for about five seconds, and agreed.

When the assembly adjourned at last, I returned to my office. Commerce was brisk once again, and the coffers were healthy, in part due to an arrangement with Morrighan, no doubt strongly suggested to them by the queen of Venda. The port of Piadro was granted to Dalbreck in return for ten percent of our profits. It was a beneficial arrangement for both of us.

"Another message has arrived from the Keep of Venda."

Lia's right-hand man. Kaden. No doubt he was asking for another escort, more supplies, more of something. But I knew they needed it and wouldn't ask if it wasn't necessary. Lending a helping hand to their resettlement benefited all the kingdoms.

"Give him whatever he wants."

"She wants, you mean."

Yes, she. I knew the requests ultimately came from Lia. But she called equally on the other kingdoms for help too, and we knew the Lesser Kingdoms followed the leads of Morrighan and Dalbreck. We spoke only in messages through our emissaries. It made it easier for both of us. But I heard the reports. Venda was thriving under her reign. I wasn't surprised. One of their farming settlements was being established just beyond our borders. It made some citizens nervous, but I worked to reassure them. Venda was not the Venda it used to be.

"The Keep has included something with this message. You might want to take a look at it."

"Whatever it is—"

"Take a look."

He laid a small package on my desk that was wrapped in cloth and tied up with string, then shoved the message into my hand.

Wagons.
Grain.
Escorts.

The list went on and on. The usual requests.

But at the end, a note from the Keep:

I found this stuffed behind a manger in Berdi's loft.
I think it belongs to you.

"Shall I open it?" Sven asked.

I stared at the package for a long while.

I am yours, and you are mine, and no kingdom will ever come between us.

A very long while.

I knew what was in it.

Something white.

Something beautiful.

Something that had been tossed out long ago.

"Jaxon?"

"No," I said. "You can throw it away."

Journey's end. The promise. The hope.

Gather close my brothers and sisters.

Today is the day a thousand dreams will be born.

We have touched the stars and the dust of possibility is ours.

For once upon a time, three women were family

As we are now, and they changed the world

With the same strength we have within us.

We are part of their story,

And a greater one that still lies ahead.

But the work is never over.

Time circles. Repeats.

And we must not only be ready,

For the enemy without,

But also the enemy within.

Though the Dragon rests for now,

He will wake again,
And roam the earth,
His belly ripe with hunger.
Lest we repeat our history,
Let the stories be passed
From father to son, from mother to daughter,
For with but one generation,
History and truth are lost forever.
And so shall it be,
Sisters of my heart,
Brothers of my soul,
Family of my flesh,
For evermore.

—*The Song of Jezelia*

CHAPTER NINETY

I TIDIED UP THE PAPERS ON MY DESK AND LOOKED OUT THE windows of the gallery. A spring shower had left puddles on the veranda. They reflected the towers of a city that didn't look so dark anymore.

It was my first time alone in months, and I didn't quite know what to do with the freedom. I had said good-bye to my mother and father this morning. They were returning to Morrighan. Regan had ruled during my father's absence. Bryn was there too. Mother said he had wrestled with the loss of his leg, but was getting stronger and riding his horse again. This had opened up a new world to him, and now he hoped to come see mine—maybe the following spring.

My father was a changed man, not just by the events of these past months, but also by his journey here, seeing a world he hadn't had time for before. I didn't want to become that person who was so caught up in the details of my duty that I didn't live in the world that I governed.

I walked the streets of Venda every day. I shared cups of thannis on street corners. I shopped at the *jehendra*, listened to stories at the washbasins, and conferred with the new quarter-lords chosen by the clans. I attended their weddings. Danced at their celebrations. I fell into the rhythms of a world and people who were coming to life again.

In the past months, I had traveled to every province in Venda, meeting with the people and appointing new governors. At least half were women and elders of the clans. From this point forward, they would lose their positions by the will of the people, not by a sword in their back, and that was how I would maintain my position as well.

The work and the decisions never ended. With Dalbreck and Morrighan leading by example, the Lesser Kingdoms agreed to new treaties and contributed to the settlements in the Cam Lanteux. It didn't come without some resistance, but Morrighan and Dalbreck provided escorts to contingents of Vendan settlers. The first crops had been planted, and hope was blooming. The fruit of the work kept me going.

I couldn't have done any of it without Kaden. He worked tirelessly. All the compassion and tenderness he had gotten from his mother was finally able to shine, but the scars inside him were still there, just like the ones on his back. I saw it when he held Rhys, protective, his reflexes quick, as if no hand would ever scar the skin or soul of this child. I hoped he was right.

I knocked on the door of his meeting chamber, and when there was no answer, I went inside. All traces of the Komizar were gone—except for the table with the gash in it that had marked the Komizar's rise to power. Kaden's desk was piled as high with papers as mine was. I added more to his pile—a proposed trade agreement with Eislandia.

To help the settlements, we had refitted the Komizar's army city for other purposes. The smelteries, the forges, and the cooperages were now busy supplying tools for farming and trade. The testing fields—those we had left to the seasons to erase—the scars and rubble of destruction slowly being swallowed up by wind, rain, grass, and time.

The giant golden brezalots that had survived were freed. Now they grazed in herds on distant hilltops, and I saw them in a new way, as the beautiful and majestic creatures they were meant to be. If I ventured too close, if I saw the steam of their hot breaths or heard the pounding of their great hooves, terror would still flash through me, along with the memory of mangled bodies and the smell of burning flesh. Some scars took longer to heal than others, and some scars, I knew, were necessary. Some things you should never forget.

"Looking for me?"

I turned. Kaden stood in the doorway with Rhys on his hip.

"That baby's almost a year old," I said. "He's never going to learn to walk if his feet never touch the ground."

Kaden smiled. "He'll learn soon enough."

I told him about the additional paperwork I had left for him, and he took it in stride. He was everything I could ask for in a Keep—calm and steady, devoted. Loyal.

"Where's Pauline?" I asked.

His eyes lit up. "Hunting down Eben and Natiya."

I knew Pauline would prevail and find them. She was determined that everyone would learn how to read and write the language, which she herself was studying. She had begun morning lessons for them and anyone else she could wrangle. I didn't tell Kaden I had seen them in the work yard, battling with practice swords. The competition between them was fierce, but there was a playfulness too, and when I heard them chide and laugh at each other, my heart lifted, seeing that small glimpse of the children in them return. I prayed more would come with time.

"I was just saying good-bye to Griz," he said.

"I said my good-byes last night."

Griz was leading another group of settlers into the Cam Lanteux. Gwyneth would ride with the caravan too, and then she would continue on to Terravin. She had been helping me here in Venda but finally had to return home—and to Simone. It didn't matter if she had to love her daughter from a distance. That was where her heart was. She'd promised Berdi she would send news of how the tavern was faring. But with all the caravans that had departed, it wasn't lost on me that she left with the one led by the big ugly brute, as she still called him. Her wicked banter had frustrated Griz these past months, but he always seemed to come back for more, and I knew Gwyneth loved watching him struggle to maintain a scowl when a smile lurked in his eyes. They were a strange pair, but I wouldn't be surprised if Griz took a side trip to Terravin.

"Jia!" Rhys squealed and reached out. His swift little fingers yanked a strand of hair from my cap, and he beamed, delighted with his prize. Kaden gently pried his fingers free.

A dawning rushed over me, and I smiled. "Look at us, Kaden. You, me, here in Venda, and you with a baby on your hip."

He grinned. "Yes, I know. It occurred to me."

"Strange how we can glimpse our future, but can never know all of it," I said. "I suppose greater stories will have their way."

His grin faded. "Are you all right?"

He caught me now and then. Looking into the distance, wondering, my thoughts thousands of miles from here. Remembering.

"I'm fine," I answered. "Just headed to Sanctum Hall. I haven't eaten yet."

"I'll be down in a bit," he said.

I passed the Royal Scholar in the hall. He'd just come from the caverns. Argyris and the other scholars had been returned to Morrighan to face trial—and a rope. No books were burned in the kitchen ovens anymore, no matter how great or small their importance seemed to be.

"I'm working on that translation you wanted," he said. "It appears to be a book of poetry." I had given him the small ancient book that Aster had proudly stolen for me from the piles in the cavern. "The first poem is something about hope and feathers. I'll bring it to you later."

I smiled. A poem with wings?

How fitting that Aster had taken that one. I still imagined her every day, no longer as the forlorn angel with clipped wings, but as I had seen her when I walked that thin line between life and death. Aster, free and twirling in a meadow with long flowing hair.

Sanctum Hall, like everything in Venda, had changed too. Berdi had seen to that. It no longer stank of spilled ale, and now fresh rushes brightened the floor. The much-abused table still bore the marks of its past, but at least now it gleamed with a daily scrubbing and polish.

I crossed the room to a sideboard and fixed a plate from a buffet of hot parritch, boiled eggs, flatbreads, and fish caught from the river. At the end of the sideboard there was a plattter of bones. My fingers sifted through it, thinking of all the sacrifice.

Meunter ijotande. Never forgotten.

I slipped another bone onto my tether.

I ate alone at the table, looking at its length, the empty chairs, listening to the rare quiet, feeling full in ways I'd never thought possible. But in other ways . . . some things had taken hold of me that I couldn't quite shake. Things like Terravin—a new beginning that had led to so much more.

I took my dishes to the sideboard and grabbed a rag, squeezing it out in the soapy water. A servant walked in, but I turned her away. "I'll do it," I told her, and she left.

I wiped the crumbs I had left on the table, but then continued to scrub, working my way to the other end.

Pauline walked in, her arms full of books, and dropped them on the table. "What are you doing?" she asked.

"Just cleaning up a bit."

She grinned. "You look more like a kitchen helper than a busy ruler."

"There's little difference," I said, and dropped the rag back in the soap pan. I surveyed the floor and reached for the broom propped against the wall.

"The floor doesn't need sweeping," she said.

"The queen says it does."

Her lips pursed in mocking offense. "Then I guess you must sweep."

She left, I assumed to get another load of books.

The sweet scent of Berdi's stew hung in the air. There were still few luxuries in Venda, but her bottomless pots of stew were one, and as I swept, I saw a jeweled bay, heard the cry of gulls, remembered a gentle knock on my cottage door and a garland of flowers placed in my hands.

A happy squeal broke the silence, and I looked up to see Kaden and Pauline at the entrance to the hall quietly conferring. He handed Rhys to her, but they remained a tight knot, his lips brushing hers with ease. They grew closer every day. *Yes*, I thought, *there are a hundred ways to fall in love*.

I walked over and replaced the broom in its spot near the sideboard. I had no more time for daydreaming. Piles of paper waited for me and I—

"Lia?" Kaden called.

I turned. He and Pauline walked closer. "Yes?"

"There's another emissary here to see you."

I rolled my eyes. I was weary of the endless meetings with

the Lesser Kingdoms. It seemed nothing was ever settled once and for all. There were always more assurances I had to offer them. "He or she can wait until—"

"It's an emissary from the king of Dalbreck," Pauline said.

When I didn't budge, Kaden added a reminder. "Dalbreck has been very generous with their supplies."

I grunted and conceded. "Show him in."

Kaden looked over my drab attire. "Aren't you going to change into something more . . . presentable?"

I looked down at my work dress, then shot him a disapproving stare, saying more firmly, "Show him in."

Pauline began to protest too, but I stopped her.

"If this is good enough for the people of Venda, it's good enough for an emissary."

They both frowned.

I pulled my cap from my head and brushed my hair with my fingers. "There! That better?"

They both sighed and left. Minutes later, they returned, Pauline rushing in ahead, standing stiffly near the hearth. Kaden stood at the end of the hall, mostly cast in shadows. I could hear the shuffling of a contingent somewhere behind him. Kaden stepped forward and announced, "The emissary of Dalbreck, here to speak with the queen of Venda."

I waved my fingers forward impatiently, and Kaden stepped aside.

The emissary stepped forward.

I blinked.

I swallowed.

He walked across the hall toward me. The only sound was his heavy boots tapping on the stone.

He stopped in front of me, his eyes looking into mine, and then slowly, he dropped to one knee. "Your Majesty."

I couldn't find my voice. My tongue was sand and my throat like a stiff dried bone. Somehow I made my fingertips move, and I motioned for him to stand.

He rose to his feet, and I swallowed again, finally conjuring some moisture to my tongue. I surveyed his rumpled clothes, dusty from a long journey. "You look more like a farmer than a grand emissary of Dalbreck," I said.

His eyes gleamed. "And you look more like a tavern maid than the queen of Venda."

He stepped closer.

"And what brings you so far?" I asked.

"I brought you something."

This time it was he who motioned with his hand.

There was more shuffling in the dark hall behind him, then Orrin and Tavish walked in with wide grins plastered across their faces. Each of them held a crate filled with melons.

"I grew them myself," Rafe said. "Mostly."

My mind tumbled. *Melons?* "You are a man of many talents, King Jaxon."

Creases deepened around his eyes. "And you, Queen Jezelia, are a woman of surprising strengths."

I didn't move.

I wasn't sure I was breathing.

He reached up and caressed my cheek.

"I know hundreds of miles separate us. I know you have your endless duties here and I have mine in Dalbreck. But we've done the impossible, Lia. If we can find a way to end centuries of animosity between the kingdoms . . . surely . . . we can find a way for us."

He bent over, and his lips met mine, gentle, tender, and I trembled against their touch. I tasted the wind, sweet melons, a thousand dreams, and hope.

We parted and looked at each other, a better ending at our fingertips.

A way for us.

Impossible.

But that hadn't stopped us before.

And I reached up and brought his mouth back to mine.

THE END

ACKNOWLEDGMENTS

THE JOURNEY'S END.

What began as a loose idea about the things that last bloomed into a world I never could have imagined with my first step. It became a journey as far-reaching as the Cam Lanteux, and so many have gone down this crazy road with me. Just as Lia had an army behind her, so did I, and without them, these books wouldn't exist. I am indebted.

Let me begin with the unstoppable force that is my publisher, Macmillan/Henry Holt. You are, simply put, brilliant and infinitely creative. Thank you to Jean Feiwel, Laura Godwin, Elizabeth Fithian, Angus Killick, Jon Yaged, Brielle Benton, Morgan Dubin, Allison Verost, Caitlin Sweeney, Kallam McKay, Claire Taylor, Kathryn Little, Mariel Dawson, Emily Petrick, Lucy Del Priore, Katie Halata, Jennifer Healey, John Nora, Ana Deboo,

Rachel Murray, and the army of you who work behind the scenes. Thank you for believing in this series and getting it into readers' hands.

Let's just say it right here and now. Rich Deas is a cover god. I may have stopped breathing when I saw this last book cover. And the inside is just as beautiful. Anna Booth did absolutely wondrous things with the design, making me want to hug every page. I am stunned with gratitude to both of them.

My editor, Kate Farrell, as always provided sharp-eyed insights, questions that made me think, unflagging support, and friendship. Over the course of these three books plus a novella, we have wrestled, brainstormed, conspired, laughed, and *created* together. She is one in a million. I am, and will always be, so very grateful to her.

I am incredibly thankful to the librarians, booksellers, tweeters, booktubers, bloggers, and every reader who spread the word to one or many. I loved hearing your thoughts, theories, and hopes for these characters. Your awesome enthusiasm fueled me. (Yes, Stacee, I know. More kissing.) I truly felt we were on this journey together.

Thank you to Deb Shapiro, Peter Ryan, and the Stimola Literary Studio team for your creativity and keeping all that extra "author stuff" on a straight course.

From the very first page of the Remnant Chronicles we see a world where story sustains its inhabitants, and so I salute my fellow writers. It is not true there is no new story under the sun. You prove there is every day, with the new worlds and the new perspectives you create. Thank you for taking me on your journeys too. Story, like a hungry dragon, is one of those things that lasts, and maybe all that protects us from being eaten.

Special thanks to YA writers Marlene Perez, Melissa Wyatt, Alyson Noël, Marie Rutkoski, Robin LaFevers, and Jodi Meadows for support and advice. From manuscript critiques to virtual hugs and cookies, craft chats, cheerleading, and commiserations about the trials of writing a trilogy, you gave me much needed perspective. Many thanks to Stephanie Bodeen for fantasizing about goat cheese and other foods with me and challenging me to include an unlikely food—bacon-wrapped wienies—in the midst of a medieval world. The outpost foodie, Colonel Bodeen, was happy to oblige. Thank you to Jessica Butler and Karen Beiswenger for on-the-spot brainstorming, beta reads, and your wild musings about the Remnant world. You kept my brain spinning. I also want to thank Jill Rubalcaba, who offered advice on my first book and many thereafter. Her words of long ago when I was beginning the Jenna Fox book—*you can do this*—became my daily mantra to chase away doubt and push me to the finish line.

My family is the best, always my foundation: Karen, Ben, Jess, Dan, Ava, Emily, and sweet baby Leah, you're the balance, the smiles, the true joys of my life.

My husband, Dennis, was nothing short of heroic in helping me finish this last book. He was truly a warrior who shielded me, carried me, fed me, massaged my shoulders, encouraged me, and protected me from falling into an exhausted coma. I could not love him more.

Finally, I lift a glass (a fine Morrighese vintage) to Rosemary

Stimola, who has been my agent and friend for fifteen years. She is my Gandalf, my Yoda, my Dihara, a woman of uncommon strengths and wisdom. Without her, there would be no Remnant Chronicles. Thank you, Rosemary. You're the real deal.

To all, *paviamma*.

AN OUTLAW
&
A REFORMED THIEF

lock wits in a battle that may cost them
their lives—and their hearts.

DANCE *of*
THIEVES

Don't miss this stunning fantasy
set in the world of
THE REMNANT CHRONICLES.